# LILY CHU

sourcebooks
casablanca

For Elliott

Published by Sourcebooks Casablanca, an imprint of Sourcebooks
P.O. Box 4410, Naperville, Illinois 60567-4410
(630) 961-3900
sourcebooks.com

Cataloging-in-Publication Data is on file with the Library of Congress.

Printed and bound in Canada.
MBP 10 9 8 7 6 5 4 3 2 1

# ALSO BY LILY CHU

# ONE

N adine Barbault eyed the Cemeteries of New Orleans calendar as she rolled a small toy hearse around the miniature tombstones, coffins, and scythes littering her desk. The calendar was stuck to her cubicle wall with a thumbtack shaped like a skeletal hand, June 21 circled in red.

When she became the *Herald*'s obituary editor, Nadine had decided to leave everything as it was for one month. After all, Tom, her predecessor, had been in the role for over twenty years before it was time for his own story to appear on the section's back page. People were used to how he'd run things. It was better for Nadine to hold off before making changes—out of respect for the dead if nothing else.

Now the waiting period was over, and although she hadn't yet decided what to do with the section, a woman who had outgrown her goth years could only deal with so many ankhs. She put the hearse down and picked up a miniature of Dante's death mask from a long-ago *Herald* reporter's trip to Italy. *Palazzo Vecchio—La Commedia* was written on the bottom in thin Gothic script. She couldn't believe a man as dedicated to the dignity of the obituary had enjoyed all this funeral tat. Then again, Tom had also worn bow ties, so all bets were off.

"Hey, Lady Death." One of her colleagues tossed out the casual greeting as he passed, and she gave him the frosty stare she'd worked hard to perfect. He shifted his shoulders and winced. "I mean Nadine."

That was better. She returned to her scheduled decontamination.

Into the trash went the death mask, where it landed with a satisfying thud. Next was a dusty, never-lit vulture candle in a garish purple. She brought it to her nose and cautiously sniffed to find it emitted the faint smell of lilies, far preferable to a more realistic carrion. Still, into the bin it went.

She was about to tear down the calendar when a stern voice came from over her shoulder. "What are you doing?"

Nadine's hand stopped. The disturbance in the force had summoned Irina Skoll, keeper of the Crypt, the *Herald*'s in-house research library, and its first defense against change of any kind.

Irina moved to the side of the desk—located at the back of the newsroom and near the window, as if to separate the frenetic pace of the living from the slower gait of the dead—and pushed up her glasses to give Nadine her full and unwelcome attention. Under Irina's gaze, the invulnerable persona Nadine had cultivated for work crumpled like an old discarded draft. Irina's soft, drapey clothes and puffy hair covered an uncompromising terror of a woman. The entire newsroom had fond memories of the day Daniel Starr, the editor in chief, had suggested that perhaps, in the interests of saving half a floor of space, Irina digitize the *Herald*'s library. The two had gone literally toe-to-toe, Irina's head tilted almost horizontally to meet the gaze of their six-foot-tall boss. Daniel had been the one to back down that day, an act never repeated at the *Herald*, and it had cemented Irina's reputation as a woman not to be messed with.

"Hello, Irina. It's time for me to clear out this space." Nadine tried to channel cool unflappability and gestured to the desk with what she hoped was authority and ownership. "Make it my own."

Irina bent down with surprising grace, the deep scent of iris wafting from her pink shawl, and plucked the vulture candle out of the trash. "This was a gift from Maxwell Levins in 2008," she said. "A piece of newsroom history from one of Canada's preeminent columnists. He said it represented the establishment's perspective on his work." Irina's glasses magnified her pale blue eyes, mesmerizing Nadine like a mouse in a snake's sights.

"I thought it might be nice to organize the desk." Oh, pathetic. She *thought*. It *might*. She straightened her shoulders and firmed her voice and language. "None of this is good for my focus."

"A professional can concentrate in any environment. Are you not a professional?"

"Um, yes?" Dammit, her voice rose at the end. Farewell, intimidating poise.

"Good. Then it's best if the mementoes of lost friends stay, don't you think?" Irina put the candle on the table and glanced meaningfully in the trash before leaving. Chastened, Nadine reinstated Dante to his place of honor near her monitor.

It would only take minutes before news of her ignoble defeat made the newsroom rounds. Inmates of the *Herald* affectionately called it the *Crier* for the speed at which gossip traveled.

Keeping a stony expression on her face as she rammed down her irritation at Irina's interference and her own spinelessness, Nadine pulled up an editing task she'd been avoiding all morning. It was an obituary Daniel had strongly recommended she run because the deceased was a good friend of the *Herald*'s owner. The assigned writer had struggled mightily to find meaning and impact in a life that apparently revolved around cruises, galas, and being obliviously rich. His email noted that the woman's nickname had been Pandora, because she couldn't keep a secret and had ended several marriages thanks to her reckless gossip. **This provided some much needed color, but I decided not to include it,** he wrote.

Nadine tapped the toy hearse against the desk. Surely the woman must have done something else of interest—like have sex with Mick Jagger. Didn't everyone do that back in the day? She sent a note to the writer before moving on to her other duties.

After a quick scan of the *Herald*'s death notices that thankfully didn't list any young parents or children—those were guaranteed to make her choke up, and she couldn't have that at work—she opened her bookmarked tabs to search for stories that might be worth a full obit.

**Would you read about a woman who ran away to join the circus and later became an animal rights activist?** she texted Lisanne, her best work friend.

**Probably,** replied Lisanne.

**She legally changed her name from Katherine Brown to Lady Lionheart. She also tried to adopt her pet iguanas and named them in her will.**

**How many iguanas?**

Nadine checked. **Six.**

**Then unequivocally yes,** wrote Lisanne.

It would be a change to run an obit on someone like Lady Lionheart, or the world's only talking mime, who she'd read about yesterday. Too bad the *Herald*'s reputation as a capital-S serious newspaper meant Nadine's obituary subjects had to meet certain parameters and tended to be people who wore gray suits and white shirts rather than matching outfits with lizards.

Not that it mattered. She would do her best, but this was only a temporary stop to lick her wounds. Soon, she would be back to her old job on the politics team, covering real stories, ones that mattered.

Nadine pushed away a skull-shaped plastic chalice from the Paris catacombs and forced herself back to her work. It was time to call the widow of a self-proclaimed philanthropist who was always happy to support a hospital as long as they named a wing after him.

---

There were many things Nadine loved about her apartment. The controlled rent was a big plus, as were the long windows where she used to luxuriate in the perfect sunbeam on weekend afternoons and the rare days she was home before sunset.

What she didn't like was her familiarity with the shadows that crossed her laminate floor at three in the morning. Lately, she'd been up so often in the early hours that she could map out their patterns in her sleep.

If she could sleep.

Which she couldn't, too consumed with worries about strange sounds outside her window and the what-ifs her body repressed during the day to release in a slow, steady whisper at night.

Nadine lay in bed, eyes squeezed shut, trying desperately not to pick up her phone. It would distract her from the fact that she wasn't sleeping but keep her scrolling mindlessly for hours. She didn't have hobbies anymore. She had social media.

Not for the first time, she wondered if she'd made the right choice to take the obits job. The role was a metaphorical career graveyard in the eyes of most of her colleagues, although she'd done her best to save face by emphasizing that she took it to get experience as an editor. It was better to lie than have them suspect the real reason she needed a change. No one could know she was having trouble handling the pressure of her reporting job, so the ice queen of the political team had to become Lady Death. There was a grim cyclicality to it.

When the sun was up, it was easier to pretend her new obits job was something she chose. At night, it was hard to deny the knowledge that if she hadn't moved roles, she would have self-destructed from the stress of dealing with how her life had changed after the death threat. A forced choice was no choice at all.

She buried her face in her pillow. She could count sheep. Do a body scan. Think of beaches and waves and playful dolphins.

Or give up and get a cup of mint tea, which was relaxing despite tasting like garden scraps.

She hauled herself out of bed and stumbled to the kitchen. As her hand hovered over the box of tea bags, she caught sight of her liquor shelf. A whiskey would do more good than tea. No, a hot toddy. Her English grandmother had sworn by them, as well as a rye and ginger at five in the afternoon on the dot, a glass of wine filled to the brim when cooking and another with dinner, and then a nightcap.

Huh. Maybe Grandma had a problem. Or she was onto something.

Nadine added whiskey, honey, and lemon to some microwaved hot water, then checked her phone as a message came in from Raj, the night web editor. **Hey, on the off chance you're awake, did you hear about Dot Voline? Dead.**

She read the message twice before she absorbed the words. Dot Voline was dead?

Dot Voline, the literary icon.

Dot Voline, the recluse.

Dot Voline, whose classic book *River's Edge* Nadine read in her twelfth grade English class. It had been late October, and the school had turned on the furnace to get ready for winter when a surprise heat wave swept over the region. The warmth pressed down on teenage Nadine until she'd propped her head in her hand to strategically shield her drooping eyelids. Her gaze had fallen on Dot Voline's lines about love and self-knowledge, jolting her fully awake.

Then Angelika knew, with all of her thirsty heart, that there would always be doors in her life. Logan was one of them, a portal to a place she had yearned for. Yet he was not the destination. That distant landscape lay within herself and would stretch as far as she needed

For the first time, Nadine had understood words had the power to suggest thoughts she had never contemplated on her own. It wasn't an exaggeration to say Dot Voline was part of the reason Nadine became a journalist.

And now, according to Raj, she was dead.

Corroboration was the blood of life, so Nadine took a sip of the hot toddy, squished the bear for more honey, and settled down with her laptop for some old-fashioned internet sleuthing.

The first discovery was the most convincing, a short statement from Owens and McPhail, Voline's longtime publisher, linked from their social media. **We are saddened to announce that after a long battle with cancer, world-renowned author Dot Voline has died peacefully at her home in Toronto. We mourn the loss of Canada's first lady of letters.** Tributes poured into the social media post, the likes growing as she watched. Wasn't anyone sleeping these days?

Nadine leaned back. The publisher said she was dead. A quick search showed Dot Voline had eschewed her own personal social media, so there would be nothing there. She chewed her lip, tasting lemon and whiskey fumes. Voline was *probably* dead, but that wasn't *for sure* dead. She found the number for her contact at Owens and McPhail and called. No answer, so that wasn't helpful. It was the same for the *Herald*'s arts editor. Ideally, she could get this confirmed from another party, but she was willing to bet Owens and McPhail wouldn't make a mistake about their top author, and Voline had been ailing for years.

If Nadine had gleaned one thing from staff meetings, it was that Daniel was serious about making sure the *Herald* was first with breaking news. To be second to announce the death of a star like Dot Voline would be unforgivable, and she had already shown her belly by requesting the transfer off the politics team. She couldn't risk any other doubts about her capabilities.

Stress mounting, she checked again. Some night owl at the exceedingly trustworthy *Canadian Literary Review* had posted condolences. She glanced at the *Spear* website as well as a few other competitors. There was nothing yet, but it was only a matter of time.

Thanks to the modern office's lack of boundaries between work and home life under the guise of flexibility, Nadine could access the *Herald*'s content platform from anywhere in the world, including her kitchen counter. She was sure she'd seen Voline's file when she'd scanned the advance obituaries with a mix of professional and morbid curiosity, wanting to know whose lives Tom had found necessary to write up before the big event.

There it was, Dot Voline's life compacted into 2,178 words, with a photo of her receiving her first Governor General's Award. The obit was fine. All she had to do was add the date and cause of death, currently held with *TKTKTK*.

*To come. To come. To come.* Like death comes for us all.

Nadine paced around the counter. Back on social media, comments and condolences continued on the Owens and McPhail post, complete with replies acknowledging the more important commentators. It was only midnight on the West Coast, meaning the British Columbia media might scoop her. Breathing in slowly through her nose and out through her mouth, Nadine checked the *Herald*'s own social media pages, then stopped breathing altogether as she read the comments. Why hadn't the *Herald* posted the story? Was the *Herald* against Dot Voline? Against literature? Were women writers less worthy of respect? This was unacceptable. Were they against *Canada*?

She considered calling Daniel but wavered. Her gut said she should, but if she came running to him for guidance on every little thing, she would erode any faith he had left in her. She looked at his contact on her phone, and her chest tightened. The story was good, and it was important to be first. She had to trust herself to make the right choice and show him she was confident in her judgment.

Her phone dinged. Raj again. **Well?**

Nadine took a deep breath and ignored the little worm of doubt because she was running out of time. It was her call. **I'm going to run her obit.**

**You need any help from me? My shift ended five minutes ago, and I don't want to look at another screen until tomorrow. I say tomorrow but technically it's today. I should never have asked for my hours to be moved back.**

Nadine was editing the story to include the cause of death. **You go home. I have it covered.**

It took less than a minute to get the *Herald* on record as the first media organization to tell the world the brilliant Dot Voline had passed away. She clicked to the *Herald's* website to ensure it loaded properly, sipping the cooled toddy with the sleepy satisfaction that came from a job well done.

Then she went to bed and fell blissfully asleep.

# TWO

Whenever possible, Wesley Chen walked the forty-five minutes to the *Spear* office. It set him up for the day and provided a much needed separation between home and work. Unfortunately, this Wednesday morning offered none of the little pleasures he looked forward to. His favorite place to grab coffee had shut down for emergency maintenance. His second favorite had a line out the door of all the people who couldn't get into the first place. The third had apparently gone out of business last week.

He was deciding whether to get a watery cup from a chain store—he wouldn't enjoy it, but it would at least be coffee—when his phone rang. His spirits immediately soared when he saw it was his little sister, Ella.

"Hellooo." He drew out the greeting, but instead of the laughter he expected, all he heard was sniffling. Wes went on immediate alert. He should have known Ella wasn't calling to say hi. It wasn't even six in the morning where she was in Vancouver. "El? What's going on? Are you hurt?"

"No." More sniffles. "Ma just called."

Of course it was Ma. "What did she say?" He left out the *this time*.

There was a reason Ella went to university on the other side of the country, and it was their mother.

"Nothing. More of the usual. That I'm selfish for staying here. If I cared about her, I would come home. She's lonely since Amy moved out, and it's my fault."

Wes leaned against the brick wall of a design store and settled himself to calm his sister. "Ella, Ma is fine. I'm at home, and Amy's apartment is close."

"Are you sure?" Ella's voice had a little waver that made Wes's heart clench.

"Absolutely," he assured her. "What did I say when you left for Vancouver?"

"To get the yakiniku rice hot dog from Japadog, work hard, and not take open drinks from strangers," Ella repeated in a singsong voice.

"Correct. What wasn't on the list?"

"Worrying about Ma."

"That's my job."

"Things really are okay at home?"

"They really are," he said, almost believing it himself.

After they disconnected, Wes sat on a bench and watched people hurry by on their way to work. He stared at his phone. Then he called his mother.

"Hi, Ma."

She didn't return his greeting. "I want Ella home. I keep telling her she needs to be here, and she doesn't listen."

Wes knew the tone in her voice meant he had about thirty seconds to prevent a follow-up call to Ella. Luckily—or not—years of experience meant Wes had become the family's expert Ma whisperer, and he reached for his gold-standard tactic: redirection. "Oh? By the way, Ma, I called to tell you I won't be home for dinner."

His mother immediately turned her attention away from Ella and onto him. "Not coming home? Where are you going?"

Wes hadn't thought that far ahead in his lie, so went with the basic, "Out with a friend."

"What friend? You don't have friends. You don't need them. You have your family. I work to the bone to come home to an empty house? What kind of gratitude is that? Selfish. I've always known it. Only thinking about yourself after all I do for you. Useless."

He listened for another five minutes, not speaking, just gazing at the pigeons, until his mother wound herself down and abruptly hung up. He slid his phone into his pocket—there was no point calling back, as she wouldn't answer—and continued walking, shoulders tighter than usual with tension.

It was a glum and uncaffeinated Wes who arrived late at the office to some critical glances that he seriously did not need. The *Spear* expected early-morning starts from their staff, reflecting the rise-and-grind hustle attitude of their distant tech owner.

When they moved last year, the *Spear* implemented a first-come-first-served desk booking system to promote collaboration by forcing staff from different departments to mix. It had been an abject failure, and a week of cutthroat intrigue and backroom deals had resulted in each department staking out its own unofficial territory. Luckily, his editor, Rebecca, had survived the mechanisms of a socialist arts collective in university, thus ensuring her Lifestyle team eventually reigned supreme over the floor's most coveted area, a small quiet alcove in the corner away from copy machine socializing and kitchen smells.

The only downside was its location next to the investigative team, which daily forced Wes to face the fact that his career had stagnated. He passed Tyler Dawlish, who was stroking his beard and laughing at his own jokes while sitting at the desk Wes desperately wanted to be his again.

"What a cock-up." Tyler's voice drifted over like burned popcorn. "I told JJ it was incredibly poor journalism. Who doesn't confirm news of that caliber? That guy should be fired. The *Herald* is a joke."

JJ, who was Jason Jackson to people like Wes, was the *Spear's* investigative editor. A few months ago, Jason had rejected Wes's application for the latest spot on the I-team, all the more galling since Wes had already been there as part of a six-month secondment. They gave the permanent role to Tyler, moving him from Opinions and returning Wes to Lifestyle. Rebecca had welcomed him back with open relief and a pile of assignments she'd been saving for what she called his magic touch. Her appreciation had cooled the burn of rejection, at least a bit.

Wes tuned out Tyler's blustering as Rebecca appeared in front of his desk, blocking the sun coming through the floor-to-ceiling windows.

"Can you believe it?" Rebecca pulled back her long sandy-brown hair.

"Believe what?"

"Didn't you hear what the *Herald* did?"

"No." Wes hated feeling caught unawares, having internalized the idea that because he could know everything thanks to his phone and the internet, he should. It wasn't healthy, but omniscience—or the appearance of it—was a big advantage at the *Spear*. He couldn't afford to look like he was slacking if he wanted another chance at the I-team.

"The *Herald* screwed up. Like the mother of all screwups." She almost vibrated with excitement. "They ran Dot Voline's obituary last night."

"The author? I thought she was already dead."

"Me too, but she is very much *not* dead as of today. Which, you will note, is after her obit ran." She sipped her huge bubble tea with gusto.

"Whoa." That must have been what Tyler had been talking about. Since the *Herald's* owner considered the digital-only *Spear* a trashy upstart compared to the hundred-year-old *Herald*, it was pleasant to see them humbled.

"I've never worked obits, but you'd think the first rule is to make sure your subject's fully passed beyond this mortal coil," Rebecca agreed.

"Their editor's run that section for ages," Wes said. "My mother reads it religiously." All the while commenting on how she could have achieved more than the deceased, be they politician, entrepreneur, or athlete, had she not dedicated her life to her family.

"No, he died, and a woman took over a month or so ago." Her forehead scrunched. "Natasha Barbell? Something like that."

Wes looked up in surprise. "Nadine Barbault?"

"You know her?"

"We went to journalism school together, but she's on the politics team." He turned to his laptop. No, there she was on the *Herald*'s staff directory page: Nadine Barbault, Obituary Editor. An unexpected change, given how well she'd been doing, but probably the result of some long-game career plan. She was devious like that.

The sounds of the office drifted away as Wes basked in the keen enjoyment of his schadenfreude. A mortification of this magnitude could not have happened to a more deserving person. Nadine's blunder was a devastating defeat in their ongoing, never-declared battle for supremacy that had started the tenth day of JORN 102, Introduction to Journalism, when they'd tied for the highest mark in the class on their first assignment.

Her latest crime had been last year, when she scooped his story on unregistered lobbyists during his I-team secondment. Getting scooped was a risk for any journalist, but Jason had not been impressed to see the story Wes had been working on emblazoned on the *Herald*'s front page under Nadine's byline. It wasn't the reason he'd been sent back to Lifestyle but Jason might have fought harder for his transfer if Wes had been the first to break that huge story.

"It's a big drop from politics to the dead beat," Rebecca said. "Then to mess that up?"

Wes shook his head and shut his laptop. It hurt him to admit, but in fairness, Nadine was undeniably fantastic at her job. "It must have been a glitch in the system. Remember when Radio France Internationale posted a bunch of obits because of a web upgrade?"

"My baser self prefers to believe she blew it. Trust but verify." Rebecca made a motion as if reading the phrase from a marquee, causing her cup to slip alarmingly in her hand. "You know, we should do a story on Dot Voline to capitalize on this. Maybe get a comment from her about the experience."

"I'm on it," said Wes immediately, happy for any chance to one-up Nadine.

"Great. I also want to talk to you about some things before the morning meeting."

Wes had been waiting for this moment, so he put thoughts of Nadine aside. "Good, because I have a story for you."

She looked suspicious. "You know I'm always open to that."

He didn't bother to correct her. "New research says skin-lightening products are more carcinogenic than formerly believed."

"Sorry, Wes. It's not for us." Rebecca held up a hand to halt his objection. "I have my marching orders," she continued. "The vision for Lifestyle is to bring delight to a reader's inbox. Our readers engage most with joyful content."

"Cancer might not be delightful, but it's important."

Rebecca gave him a sympathetic look. She'd been a friend before she became his editor, and he didn't know if he would have lasted so long at the *Spear* without her support. That, and Rebecca letting him ransack her emergency jelly bean stash on bad days. He reciprocated by leaving bags of shrimp chips on her desk.

Rebecca lowered her voice. "I know you want back on the I-team."

"It's not that I don't like Lifestyle," he said.

"It's just not the kind of work you want to do," she finished for him.

"I give you my best," he protested.

"That's why I want you on my team. Your Lifestyle stories have the highest engagement scores across the company, and you know why that's important."

Wes did know. "Money."

"Muh-*nee*. Traffic for those sweet ad dollars that keep us employed." She cocked an eyebrow at him as if to ask, *Do you want to be employed?* They'd heard the rumors around the *Spear's* lack of profit, which neither of them had been able to confirm, so the question was relevant.

"I get it," he said.

"You're right though. It is important," Rebecca said. "Let's think about how we can sneak in that research without making it the whole story."

Wes was ready. "How about a skin care myths and facts feature?"

"That works. I can always count on you." Her phone rang. "Oh, give me a second. I was expecting this call."

Rebecca left for the phone room, and Jason came up as Wes logged into his email. "Wes, buddy, do me a favor."

"Yeah, of course." Wes sat straighter. Helping Jason wouldn't directly impact his chances to get back on the I-team, but it couldn't hurt.

Jason sat on the desk and put his foot on his chair, scratching at his reddish beard. His boot pressed into Wes's leg. "I need your perspective. What do the Chinese think about the International Monetary Fund?"

Wes had become used to these kinds of questions during his career and fell back on his usual line. "Why would I know?"

Jason gave him a come-on look. "You must have a sense."

It was on the tip of his tongue to tell Jason as the spokesperson for all Chinese people on earth the IMF sucked balls, but Wes restrained himself. "Sorry, man, couldn't tell you."

"Too bad." Jason shifted as if to leave, and Wes panicked, wanting to redeem himself. There was that pitch he'd been thinking about...

"Hey, Jason, you know I'm very interested in rejoining the I-team."

"I know that." Jason looked around as if checking for eavesdroppers. "Look, I'll be honest. You have solid ideas, but I barely heard you speak up in meetings. I need my team to be assertive, capable of fighting for a story."

Since that was what Wes was doing at the moment, it was a win-win. "It's connected to the lobbying piece I was working on," he said.

"The one the *Herald* ran? What about it?"

"I heard several Chinese cultural centers had their funding cut after work by unregistered lobbyists," he said. "A direct result of the changes."

Jason looked intrigued. "Yeah, I like it. There might be something there if we can broaden it out to other organizations."

"What do you think of me taking a look?" Wes tried to keep the golden hope from filling his every cell. "Rebecca would probably be open to me doing this on the side." She knew it was important to him and that he wouldn't let it interfere with his work for her.

Jason pressed his lips together. "No offense, Wes, but there might be concerns you'd be too close to the story."

"Too close?" Wes echoed.

"Yeah, we need to make sure our reporters can emotionally distance themselves from their reporting. Optics, you know. Journalistic integrity." Jason shrugged his thick shoulders. "Plus, you'd probably get scooped again." Jason took his foot off Wes's chair, the force causing him to spin slightly. "Hey, Becky. How's it hanging?"

Rebecca ignored him. "Wes, as I was going to say earlier, I want you to do a how-to on packing the perfect summer picnic."

Jason snorted as he left, and Wes reopened his laptop so violently that the screen almost hit the desk, then shrugged in apology when Rebecca raised her eyebrow. "Picnic ideas," he said to make up for showing his temper. "Let's do three versions and base it around different tablecloths people can use to sit on. Gingham for vegetarian, French Provençal for meat, and chintz for dessert."

She beamed at him. "Love it. Add matching nonalcoholic wines too."

"Bien sûr." He turned to his computer and caught sight of Nadine's profile from the *Herald* website. She had a slight smile and was looking at the camera with her body angled to the left and arms crossed over her chest. He cheered slightly as he shut the page down. At least his day wasn't as bad as Nadine's.

Two hours later, he'd finished interviewing a local decorator who had launched a new website to help people choose wall paint based on their pets' personalities and decided it was time for coffee.

In the office kitchen, waiting for the water to boil for the instant coffee he kept for emergencies, he pulled out his phone and found Dot Voline's obituary, which someone had copied and posted on the *Spear*'s internal message board so they could collectively gloat over it. Within two lines, he knew it wasn't Nadine's work. Over the years, he'd become familiar with the cadence of her writing and the turns of phrase that were wholly hers. Sometimes he thought he'd be able to recognize her hand faster than his own. This had a dry, academic tone and none of Nadine's usual flow.

Although the comments section was usually something he avoided, this time, he scrolled through to see if there was anything useful. Most were about Voline's contribution to the literary landscape or all-caps exhortations to hold politicians accountable for issues that had nothing to do with the story. Then he found one that made him pause.

**Wasn't there some scandal about 30 pieces? They never teach the good stuff in school.**

A scandal. Wes stirred the brown powder into his hot water. Scandal was good. That it was probably from forty years ago was bad. But it could be interesting. He did a quick search, but Voline's profiles all told the same story about a small-town teacher who made it big in the literary world with her razor-sharp insights into human nature and an acid perspective on social mores. Nothing about a scandal. Who could he ask? Wes was about to take a tour of the office to see who might know something when his colleague Eliza came in to grab a yogurt from the fridge. He liked Eliza, who was from the breaking news desk and won the pumpkin-decorating contest each year. Last October, she had carved out small divots and inserted radishes formed into eyes, then put the whole thing on top of a mannequin with tentacle limbs. It still popped up in Wes's nightmares.

More importantly, Eliza had been in the business for a long time and knew where a lot of bodies were buried.

"Hey, Eliza, did you see the Voline obit?" he asked.

She looked at his cup and quietly handed him a few creamers that he accepted with gratitude. "I did. What a mess."

"There was a comment about a scandal, but I can't find anything online. Do you know what it is?"

"I thought the only scandalous thing about Dot Voline was her fashion sense."

"No, it was about one of her books." He handed over his phone so she could read it.

Eliza looked thoughtful. "You know, there was something from early in my first job. One of the many stories that never get covered, and it was barely a scandal. More of a scandalette."

This was a good start. "Do you remember the details?"

"God, it was decades ago." Eliza paused. "Maybe *Thirty Pieces of Silver* was based on someone? I'm not sure, although that's the most likely story."

He thought. "Could it have been plagiarized?"

Eliza laughed. "Then I don't think it would be on the school curriculum. Sorry, Wes. That's all I have."

She left. Wes took his terrible coffee back to his desk to generate a listicle on the best plant-based ways to get rid of ants for the picnic piece, then did some more research on Voline. Nothing. This frustrated him beyond belief. Growing up in the internet age meant he refused to believe a fact existed that would not be available for him to find online. This Voline scandal, however, might be the exception.

He messaged Rebecca. **There might be a scandal about one of Voline's books. Thirty Pieces of Silver.**

Rebecca's reply was fast. **I had to do that in school. Forget the scandal. I want a nice puff story about Voline and her non-brush with death. Do it that way or the jelly beans get it.**

She was joking, but Wes knew there was no point fighting. **Fine, just leave the jelly beans alone.** The way his day was going, he was going to need them.

He stared at his laptop. He'd give Rebecca her story, but it wouldn't hurt to do some checking on that scandal. He knew it would bother him until he figured it out. Since he needed a quote from Voline anyway, he could ask her about the rumor at the same time. It might also further screw over Nadine, which would be a bonus. If it was truly juicy, it might be worth pitching to Rebecca or Jason. Double bonus.

He smiled. It felt good to investigate something that wasn't about whether crochet walls were the next big trend.

Which of course they weren't. Crochet banisters, however, had a chance.

# THREE

S erious journalists don't pout, especially when they work for one of the country's top media organizations, so Nadine kept her lower lip firmly against her teeth. Then she typed *sulk* into the thesaurus and checked over her options. *Funk. Fret. Mope.* None of them worked. *Aggrieved.* Yeah, that tied together her dual feelings of unfairness and WTF at being transferred—really, demoted—to night web editor after the Dot Voline travesty. She supposed she should be grateful she hadn't been fired. Good journalism jobs were few and far between, thanks to deep cuts in the industry over the last few years.

"How're you doing?" Lisanne came up with a bag of peach rings and poured a hefty amount into Nadine's waiting palm.

"I am aggrieved," announced Nadine, trying it on for size. "How's the feature on people creating a sea change in the business world?"

"As expected. Half of them used the term *accelerate innovation* like they invented it."

"Are they eating their own dog food?"

"No, but they've bootstrapped thought leadership to enhance dynamic connectivity."

"No one said that," said Nadine, feeling better.

"Truly, the guy building the menstrual app did. Want to get a coffee before starting your punishment night shift?" That did make Nadine pout, and Lisanne rolled her eyes. "Come on, you big baby. Look how happy you've made Raj. The bags under his eyes have disappeared for the first time since I've known him."

"I heard that," called Raj, who had been moved into Nadine's old obituary role. "Since I've only been on a normal sleep schedule for a day, you can thank the vitamin C eye patches Myriam bought me last week. She said I looked like a raccoon."

Lisanne stuffed her mouth with peach rings and glanced at Nadine. "Come on," she said in a lower voice. "I have news."

This was tempting. Nadine grabbed her wallet. She deserved a little treat.

The *Herald* was on Adelaide Street, close to what Daniel referred to as the *locus of power* in an ironic tone, but with slightly less exorbitant leasing rates. Although the most efficient coffee hit was the Tim Hortons in the PATH, the underground mall/tunnel/maze below Toronto's downtown, on nice days, they frequented a tiny café on Queen Street infamous for its sullen baristas.

"You never answered me about the night shift," Lisanne said, putting a hat on over her blond hair. She was so pale she burned instead of tanned and was permanently at war with the sun. "Although I know you just started."

"It'll be fine." Nadine wasn't fully comfortable sharing how much it bothered her to have been moved, the same way she'd downplayed other things that truly mattered, such as her fear of the death threats and their impact on her reporting. She liked Lisanne, but the *work* part of work friends too often got in the way of full trust.

"Will it?"

"Sure. No one will call me Lady Death." Unfortunately there would be few other benefits. The long hours of quiet last night gave Nadine plenty of time to relive the if-onlys that refused to die since she ran Dot Voline's obituary.

If only she had trusted the tiny part of her that said it was better to be sure than first.

If only she had called Daniel.

If only she hadn't looked at her phone in the first place. By morning, the hoax had been revealed, and she would have known it wasn't Owens and McPhail that had put out the notice but a troll with a fake Owens&McPhail account.

The shame of trying to explain to Daniel why she'd run the obit without confirming Voline's death had been intense. "I wouldn't expect this kind of carelessness from someone right out of school," he'd said. "Let alone an experienced journalist."

"You said to focus on being first." She'd instantly regretted her defense.

"In a way that maintains our integrity," he'd said with a disbelief so great it was like she'd announced an obit for the tooth fairy. "Obviously. The second paragraph of every *New York Times* obituary is the confirmation of death from a reliable source. Do you think they do that for fun?"

"No." What made it so much worse was that he was right, and she had talked herself out of her own initial doubt. She hadn't trusted herself.

"Nadine. We are doing our best to accommodate your..." Daniel hesitated as if trying to square what he truly thought with the potential liability that might come from saying it out loud. "Your inability to cope with the pressure of the political beat. I thought this would at least be within your capacity."

"I had death threats from a man who showed up at my apartment and was also going to dox me," she reminded him. "It was the risk to my *safety*, not the work."

"Which we dealt with in accordance with our policy," Daniel said with the displeasure of a man who had been over the same ground a multitude of times. "You didn't suffer any physical harm, and you agreed it was handled to your satisfaction."

That didn't change how she felt the day she opened her email to find a photo of herself in her pajamas taken through the window of her apartment with the eyes X'd out and **YOUR NEXT** written on it.

In her shock, the misspelling of *you're* had been almost as disturbing as the message. How could you trust a person—realistically, almost certainly a man—who couldn't be bothered to spell-check his threats? That kind of person was capable of anything, especially when he was arrogant enough to send it from his own personal and easily traced email.

The message had come after a story she'd run about changes to an immigration policy, which had resulted in a record number of hateful comments and emails from people who thought reporting on something meant endorsing it. Nadine was no stranger to shitty messages from shitty people. She and her colleague Kenzie had created a bingo card where they'd crossed off insults as they came. It took less than a week to fill the card, some squares showing four or five crosses. When Frank Paxton, the politics editor, had noticed, he'd shrugged.

"Need a thick skin for this job," he said. "I like to think the more comments we get, the better the story."

"Great," Kenzie had muttered. She took a buyout package in the semiregular round of layoffs that had come the next month, and Nadine continued to hide how much the constant barrage of insults bothered her. Frank didn't have much patience for feelings at work, and she'd learned early there were enough people looking for a gap in her armor that she needed to appear impervious.

However, the one thing Nadine never received—and one of two things she and Kenzie hadn't the stomach to put on the bingo card— was a death threat from a man who subsequently knocked on her door. She'd recognized him instantly from the online search she'd done after receiving the email.

Nadine had done everything by the book. Took photos of him lingering outside her apartment and a blurrier one of him in her hall through her peephole that she forwarded to her manager and HR. Waited for them to agree that, boy howdy, it sure didn't look great. They'd contacted the man, who admitted everything and insisted the email was a joke and he was only visiting a friend who lived in Nadine's building. They'd extracted a promise not to contact Nadine again and told her the problem was solved. Nadine heard it had been presented at a conference as a textbook method of dealing with such issues.

They hadn't even canceled his subscription, for God's sake, telling her there was no point as he'd probably get a new one under another name.

And fair enough, the man had left Nadine alone after that. It didn't stop her from having nightmares about opening that message or having to grip her keys between her fingers every time she left the elevator. Her apartment, which had once been so cozy, shifted between feeling like a prison, a fortress, and a target. She couldn't afford to move but added more locks on the door and windows, which she covered with thicker curtains and no longer opened for fresh air.

When she began to censor herself over anything a reader might disagree with, she knew things had to change. The fear impacted her reporting, and that was unacceptable.

"Next," drawled the barista. His name tag read "Gary."

They stepped up to the counter and ordered a plain black decaf for Nadine and a monstrosity of whipped cream and flavored raspberry syrup for Lisanne. The barista stared at Lisanne without expression as he rang in the order, the charms on his septum ring jingling merrily.

"Did you see that?" Lisanne whispered as they left. "He almost smiled. I'm sure he gave me extra maple sugar dust."

There were three grains topping Lisanne's cup.

"Are you going to tell me your news?" Anything to get Nadine's mind off replaying the discussion with Daniel.

"It's huge." Lisanne glanced behind her like a spy, then led Nadine down an empty side street. "A few weeks ago, I saw a discrepancy in the earnings report of one of the big pharmaceuticals that didn't make sense. Daniel gave me the go-ahead to look into it."

Lisanne took a quick sip, so Nadine had time to compose her face to that of a supportive friend. She took an extra second to struggle with, then hide the envy bubbling up inside her. It was good for Lisanne, but Nadine wanted to be breaking stories too.

"That's amazing," she said.

"This could make my career," said Lisanne intently over her whipped cream. "If I'm right, hundreds of thousands of people have been affected."

Nadine tried to react with enthusiasm, because Lisanne was right to be excited and to expect her to be keen as well. "How are you approaching it?"

Lisanne launched into a discussion of her next steps, which included asking Ying from the data science team for help. "It's the first time the *Herald* will be working on something with datasets this big," said Lisanne. "Daniel was so encouraging. He said it'll be groundbreaking."

Nadine gave the appropriate responses, her entire body overheating. She never thought she would feel stuck in place—worse, like she'd taken a huge step back—as Lisanne was about to launch herself up to the next level. Nadine wanted that. She deserved that. She'd worked as hard as Lisanne, and she hated that a man had succeeded in silencing her. She hated feeling like a failure and fragile.

Lisanne tossed her cup as they approached the office. "Are you sure you can handle this new job? You look tired, and I hear nights are rough."

Lisanne meant it out of concern, but Nadine's id and ego took it as a challenge as her superego told her to chill out. The situation didn't improve when Lisanne kept talking.

"Hopefully a break from more intense reporting means you can go back to your real work soon."

She gave a little wave and left Nadine seething at the door. Lisanne was only parroting what Nadine herself had said, but it was *different* when Nadine said it.

Too riled for her desk, Nadine decided to go to the *Herald*'s research library for five minutes to recalibrate. It was usually empty apart from Irina, who tended to ignore everyone who came in. Except for today.

"Ah, it's you." Irina smoothed down the front of her dress when Nadine appeared in the doorway. "I was disappointed in your Dot Voline obituary."

There went any hope of peace. Nadine accepted she was cursed before she said, "I bet Dot Voline wasn't too happy either."

Irina waved her hand. "Foolishness. We all die, and that's not the first time an obituary has run early. Daniel did it at the *Telegram*."

"Really?" Nadine perked up. It might be poor-spirited to take consolation in the mistakes of others, but she was at rock bottom with few comforts. The universe owed her a brief gloat over Daniel's fallibility.

"Yes, but his was at least well researched. Yours was not."

Nadine tried to lower her professional hackles. "I didn't write it. It was in Tom's approved files."

Irina gave her a withering glance. "You are the editor. It is your responsibility."

"Not anymore," Nadine muttered.

However, Irina was not a woman to bend to anything as weak as commiseration. Not when there was an error to be corrected. "You didn't mention the controversy."

Nadine stopped backing away. "Controversy?" There had been a cryptic comment under the obit before it had been expunged from the site, but Nadine hadn't given it much thought. The comments section was so often a garbage fire. "That note about *Thirty Pieces of Silver* was true?"

Irina gave a surprisingly insouciant shrug with her narrow shoulder, like a French actress before swinging her kitten-heeled leg over a Vespa driven by a man named Alessandro. "Someone believes it is. It seems like something to look into."

With that, Irina picked up the phone and held it to her ear without dialing or speaking, an indication the conversation was over.

Frustrated, Nadine stomped back up the stairs to her own desk, cursing herself for thinking she'd be allowed sanctuary anywhere in this office. Did Irina go home at night depressed if she hadn't ruined someone's day? Did she have a little dartboard with people's faces on it to choose her victims, and why was it always Nadine?

Back at her desk, she tapped dully at her keyboard as her colleagues began to leave for the evening. Words appeared and disappeared, leaving ghostly reflections on the screen. Written and rewritten, combined and recombined.

Irina was right. That comment was intriguing, and the old Nadine would have been curious enough to look into it. She used to be keen and eager to get to the bottom of things that piqued her interest. She used to be *interested*.

It was bad enough that she prematurely ran Dot Voline's obituary. But if Irina was right and it was inaccurate? That was unforgivable, as was Nadine's own lack of initiative. Was she losing her drive? She couldn't let that happen.

She gave up typing and grabbed the hearse, spinning the toy's wheels thoughtfully with her finger. Raj, who had been moved to her obit role, hadn't cared when she asked to take it, too busy looking askance at a memento mori from some long-gone Heraldian's trip along the Nile.

"Are these necessary?" he'd asked, picking up the mummy-shaped vase.

"Not at all. Feel free to tell Irina you dumped them because you have no respect for the *Herald*'s history," Nadine said casually, rearranging the figurines to bring the coffin pencil holder front and center. An animated corpse handed over a pen when the lid lifted.

"Irina?" He'd grimaced. "They can stay."

Nadine spun the wheels again. She had a lot to do. So why was she putting down the Hot Wheels hearse and typing "dot voline controversy" into her search engine?

Because she was curious, and she welcomed the feeling. After all, knowing things made her feel safe, as if knowledge was a protectant against life's ups and downs, an emotional pepper spray. She would redeem herself by finding out what she'd missed in that obit.

She clicked on a photo of Dot Voline wearing a zebra-striped caftan and so many necklaces they formed a scarf. Nadine studied it carefully. Voline's hair was carrot red, and huge square glasses covered her eyes. She looked like she would be a nightmare on an airplane and a delight on a cruise.

It took an hour for Nadine to decide that either Irina was wrong—doubtful—or there was more to this Voline scandal than met the eye. The physical evidence for a controversy was sadly lacking. There was only one reference in a profile to "whispers about the inspiration for her breakout book, Thirty Pieces of Silver, which might have reached Canada's upper power echelons." That was vague enough to mean nothing.

Out came her fidget hearse again, with the soothing *clickety-click* of its little wheels. She could ask her old politics editor, Frank, who was walking around the deserted office checking the empty desks to see what people were working on. Rumor said he could read upside down. Usually his expression was jovial. Unobserved, his eyes were cold and his mouth thin. No, it wouldn't be wise to remind people of her error with the obit.

Luckily, there was one person outside the *Herald* who knew the truth.

Tomorrow, she'd pay a visit to Dot Voline.

# FOUR

Wes drank in the sight from his car. The house facing him was a testament to what happened when someone with questionable yet extravagant taste could afford precisely the home they wanted. According to her inopportune obituary, Dot Voline had married a childless industrialist twenty years her senior, a patron of the arts and a fervent supporter of his wife's literary career until his death a decade later. Cattier profiles added that Allan Portson's fortune had dwarfed Voline's ample royalty money.

The grandiose wedding cake of a house was small compared to the properties on either side, but what it lacked in size, it made up for in visual impact. If Versailles had vomited up a bijou mansion that a Versace would consider excessive, it was Dot Voline's home. Gleaming gold-painted gates were topped with panes of stained glass lilies. They blocked him from seeing much apart from a fountain sitting in the center of the circular driveway where Botticelli's *Venus* spewed water out of her mouth. The entire place hurt his eyes, and he could tell Voline was a decorative lamp person rather than a functional overhead light person.

Climbing out of the car, Wes reviewed his plan of attack. He'd decided against calling for an interview since Voline was famously averse to granting them. He hadn't wanted to blow his chance to talk by putting her on alert by contacting her publisher.

That left the old-fashioned way—knocking on the door or, in this case, the gate. He pressed his face against the bars to confirm the swans floating in the fountain were fake and to note a very real hot-pink Bentley gleaming in the driveway.

"Wes? Wes Chen?"

A woman's sharp voice cut through the sound-dampening layers of old leafy trees and thick grassy lawn. Wes instantly knew who it was. Steeling himself, he turned around to greet his foe.

"Hello, Nadine."

---

This was unbelievable. Nadine couldn't speak. Wait, yes, she could. "What the hell are you doing here?" she asked.

Wes Chen. She'd known him for a decade, the weasel. He'd been a sliver under her skin since he'd stolen her dream internship right out of university. Then she'd snagged the job he'd applied to at an online news agency, and that had set them off. It seemed every time she had wind of a good story, Wes was already on it. At least she'd managed to scoop him on the lobbyist thing last year. After accepting her Canadian Journalism award, she'd been filled with satisfaction at the sight of his sour face. It made up for the year before, when the opposite had happened. She knew he kept track of the awards each of them won. She did too.

Wes didn't answer, instead turning to the intercom and pushing the button. No matter. She knew why he was in the Bridle Path: to show Nadine up in some unknown way.

"Get away from my source," she snapped.

"Your source?" He stared straight ahead, which meant Nadine was forced to address his very striking profile. She might dislike him, but there was no denying Wes had a nice nose. And cheekbones. Lips. Too bad when they were moving, it was usually to irritate her. "Sorry, I'm here because I wanted to meet the only woman to have been resurrected from the dead."

That was a low blow, but to be expected from him. "Doing a story about her interior decorating?" she asked sweetly. "Or a roundup of which of her books to pair with what snacks?"

Instead of answering, he pressed the button again, this time so hard his finger bent and turned white.

To Nadine's astonishment and apparently Wes's from the way he leapt back as if the intercom was electrified, a voice boomed out. "What do you want?"

Wes recovered himself first. "Dot Voline?"

"Who wants to know, handsome?" The voice dropped to a breathy but gravelly purr that might have emanated from a tiger trapped in a cement mixer.

"Uh." Wes stared wide-eyed at the intercom.

Nadine saw her chance and took a step forward, forcing Wes away from the speaker. "Ms. Voline, this is Nadine Barbault of the *Herald*."

"That old rag? I don't know what was worse, hearing I was dead or having to read through the stilted prose that made me wish I was. Three-quarters of it was a dismal summary of my own books that lacked insight or context and bored even me."

She supposed that confirmed the speaker. Wes's delighted smile lit up his face, and she glared at him before turning back to the intercom.

"About that." Nadine had barely started her apology—which she had written out and memorized—when Wes rudely interrupted, moving a half step in front of her.

"Wes Chen, of the *Spear*."

Nadine took a page from his playbook and tried to slide ahead of him. Wes anticipated the move and thwarted her, stepping around and forward with a snakelike motion. They ended up jostling each other like sunburned tourists at an all-inclusive resort competing for the last slice of bacon until Wes came out triumphant, getting so close to the intercom Nadine thought he could lick it.

"The *Spear*? Never heard of it," said Voline.

Nadine laughed. Wes shot her a look as she debated whether hip checking him out of the way would be considered assault or self-defense.

"It's a digital news—"

"I also don't care," said Voline. "What do you two lovebirds want?"

"Lovebirds?" gasped Wes. He reeled back as if he'd rather get into that cement mixer with the tiger than have anything to do with her. What a drama queen.

Nadine wedged herself in the space Wes had left to the intercom. "I'd like to ask—"

"No."

"No?" she repeated.

No answer.

Nadine refused to look at Wes, the monster who had ruined her chance to get an interview. He and Irina must be in a competition on who could wreck her day in the most annoying way possible. If so, Wes was the current standout champion.

"Ms. Voline?" he asked. "Ma'am?"

Silence.

Nadine looked through the gate as if Voline would be waiting at the steps ready to sweep down in a flurry of feathers and silk like a modern Gloria Swanson to berate them in person. "Dot?" she said loudly.

The intercom crackled back on. "That's Ms. Voline, you ambulance chaser."

"Doesn't that refer to lawyers?" Nadine whispered to Wes.

"Go ahead and correct her," he said. "She'll love that."

Dot Voline continued talking. "You've done enough damage. I've had vultures circling around me. My bank refused my allowance because they said I was dead. I had to go there in person and give the president what for."

Nadine felt Wes's eyes travel the same path as hers, to that pink car near the fountain. She indulged in a brief fantasy of Voline driving it—no, getting driven—downtown and leaving it idling on Bay Street while she waltzed past a sea of flustered executive assistants into a fiftieth-floor boardroom to harangue some poor CEO about her cash. "I'm very—"

"As for you, handsome, I don't need another bottom-feeding schmuck trying to get into my house or my pants. Too old for that kind of thing. Now, take a hike, the two of you."

Wes whispering, "Bottom-feeding schmuck," in a tone of utter disbelief was enough to send Nadine into gales of laughter.

He glared at her. "You didn't fare any better."

"Well, she didn't accuse me of wanting to sleep with her, so I consider that a win."

"I said scram!" The intercom made them jump, and Nadine heard the tail end of her muttering. "Didn't even bring a thing. Manners these days."

"Nice going," Wes muttered.

She shoved her face into the gate to get a better view of the property. "Like your Z-game charm offensive was getting us anywhere." She twisted her head to see more. "Are those real swans?"

"No."

Pity. "She seems more like a peacock person anyway," Nadine said, stepping away before Voline accused her of trespassing.

Wes laughed. "She does." Then, face blanched in horror that he'd had a positive reaction to her, he headed for his car.

It was the same one he'd been driving when they were in school, she noted as she trailed after him. As always, he was dressed to perfection, with a collared shirt under a thin black sweater with the sleeves rolled to the elbows and black jeans. Wes must not feel heat, because while she was sweating in her linen dress, he looked cool and unbothered. It was aggravating, and she couldn't help but feel this gave him an obscure advantage.

Wes pointed his frowning face back at her. "What are you doing?"

"My car is parked behind yours. I thought I would drive home if that's okay with you. Also, you didn't answer my question," she said. "Why are you here?"

He opened his car door with a god-awful screech of metal on metal. "Wes, don't you *think* of leaving without telling me what you're up to." He slammed the door shut.

"You can't do this," she yelled at the closed door, instantly cursing herself for losing her cool. It was excusable though. Wes Chen would try the patience of a King's Guard.

He started the car, ignoring her as he waited for the engine to catch in a fitful cough. Nadine bent down to stare at him, fists balled up on her hips so she didn't slam her hands through the window to grab him by the neck. Wes Chen brought out the worst in her and always had. She wanted to mess up that perfect hair. Snag those tidy sweaters. Scuff those polished leather shoes.

Should she stand in front of the car? Nadine debated before deciding not to risk it. Wes would have no qualms about running her over and leaving her bleeding in the middle of the street. They probably wouldn't bother to get an ambulance in this neighborhood. They'd call a street cleaner to dump her body in whatever pit they put dead squirrels in.

Wes put the car in drive without looking at her, as if he was the one with a right to be here and she was the interloper. His utter disregard of her presence was vastly more infuriating than if he'd done something obnoxious like waving at her with his familiar suck-it grin.

"Ahughah." The sound she made was inelegant but liberating. After all, it wasn't like anyone was around to hear it. Wes's car had driven out of sight—not out of her life, but a woman could hope—and Voline had made it clear there would be no more intercom-mediated conversations today.

She leaned against the side of her car. This trip was a failure, made worse because Wes had been there to witness it. She couldn't say she was surprised. After what Nadine had done, it was a big ask for Voline to be gracious and invite her in for tea or gin. If only she'd been able to get out the exquisitely crafted apology that the author in Voline couldn't help but admire. She would have if Wes hadn't been there trying to horn in.

She kicked her car's wheel gently with her sandaled foot. She'd worn them specially because of the gold and beading, which she felt would appeal to Voline. Why was he here really? With Wes, anything was possible. Apart from a brief stint doing investigations, he'd been writing Lifestyle for the last couple of years. She wouldn't put it past him to try to get an interview with Voline about the singular experience of reading the summary of her life before she'd finished living it.

What if she was wrong though? What if he heard about the controversy as well? Nadine knew how good Wes was.

Well, she was better.

She thought back over the conversation. *No manners,* Voline had grumbled. *No gifts.* Then Nadine nodded.

She had a plan of attack. She would have felt bad for Wes if she wasn't looking forward to destroying his chances of getting to Dot Voline.

He never should have interfered with her at the gate. Wes was doomed.

# FIVE

Wes had certain beliefs in life. The first was that knowing where to find information was more important than knowing the fact itself. The second was good grooming could make up for any number of perceived physical flaws. The last and most relevant to this particular moment was that the key to success in any endeavor was persistence.

Naturally not to the point of harassment, he thought as he drove to Voline's house the next day. In the passenger seat was a huge bouquet of opulent red roses and birds of paradise for the larger-than-life woman whose photos he'd analyzed, looking for a clue to her personality that might help him snag an interview. A huge monstera leaf completed the magnificent arrangement and made the entire thing a struggle to carry. It would be worth it, though, if it got him in. Rebecca wanted her story.

He wasn't surprised when he pulled up to see Nadine's filthy white car already there. If anyone else shared his third tenet of life, it was Nadine, who was waving a gigantic box of chocolates as she spoke into the intercom.

Wes fixed his belt—a match to his polished chestnut oxfords, since he felt Voline would appreciate a well-dressed man—and extricated his flowers.

Nadine assessed the armful of blooms. "Was a funeral home having a sale on leftovers?" she said.

He ignored her and hit the button. "Ms. Voline? It's Wes Chen from the *Spear*."

The intercom came to life. "Chocolates and flowers? The two of you have the seduction game of a teenager asking his crush to prom."

Nadine stared at the gate with the set expression Wes had learned to mistrust. "These are my favorite brigadeiros." Nadine slowly untied the ribbon. "The raspberry is incredible. So is the Mexican spice if you prefer some heat."

"Never had them," said Voline.

"That's too bad." The rows of perfectly round chocolates glinted like jewels in the sun, and Nadine selected one, staring at the camera as she bit in. "Ohh," she said as if taken by surprise. "It's good. So *good*."

Wes felt his neck get hot as he watched Nadine eat. Then she made a noise. A noise that wasn't quite a moan but immediately had Wes on full alert. The last time he'd heard a woman sound that satisfied, he'd been in bed. Naked.

This was not what he should be thinking of in conjunction with Nadine.

Making it worse, Nadine made eye contact with Wes as she spoke into the intercom. "They're rich," she said, her voice husky. "The perfect amount of creamy sweetness."

"What are you doing?" He tried to whisper, but it came out as a croak.

Nadine's glance turned haughty. "I am eating a chocolate."

She was eating a chocolate in the same way Lewis Hamilton was a guy who drove a car. The intensity didn't match the action. "No, you're not. No one eats like that."

A snorting laugh came from the intercom. "Sounds like someone's never had the right kind of sweet," said Voline.

The heat on his neck blossomed over his face as Nadine turned back to the box. She swept her tongue along her lower lip before choosing a second one. His palms were so sweaty, his grip slipped on the flowers. This was verging on pornographic. She was evil.

Nadine saw him watching and snatched the box away. "Keep your hands to yourself," she hissed. "Do you know how much these cost? They're the best in the city."

Right, it was the chocolates that had his attention.

"I said go," snapped Voline. There was a pause. "I suppose you can leave the brigadeiros. No point wasting them. Although you might want to give a couple to handsome there."

"I would do that when hell freezes over," said Nadine in a chipper voice. She closed the box and slid it under the gate. "I hope you like them."

Wes ground his teeth as he tucked his rejected flowers between the bars. After all, it wasn't like he was going to keep them, and he refused to give them to Nadine, who gazed at him with the contented smile of a woman who had completely trounced her opponent.

"Have a good day, Ms. Voline," he said evenly. "By the way, I was wondering if I could get your comment on—"

"Chocolates aren't real food," she grumbled. "Been ages since I had a pizza. Egg rolls. Now get out of here before I call the cops."

Wes tried again. "Ms. Voline, it will only take—"

"The *cops*."

That was clear enough, and he avoided looking at Nadine's face as they obeyed, moving off the property in tandem since neither of them was willing to leave first.

"That couldn't have gone worse for you," she said happily.

"Thank you. I appreciate that." He'd kill her with kindness, but Nadine refused to die.

"Your flowers make her gate look like a roadside shrine, by the way."

"They do not." He couldn't help but glance back to see the bouquet slide down to lie at the bottom, needing only some pillar candles and a stuffed animal to complete the picture. "Shit."

She smiled, and Wes didn't want to explore how that made him feel. Before their antagonism had exploded, he'd liked when Nadine's smile was aimed at him and to see the pretty dimple in her cheek.

"Better luck next time, Chen," she called from her car, not missing a chance to rub it in.

He watched her leave. There was no point pressing the intercom, because despite being sent away, his gut told him Voline saw this as a bit of fun. He supposed it eventually got boring splashing around in swimming pools of money.

Then again, she told Nadine to leave the chocolates. It could be that Voline was simply curious about their aphrodisiac qualities, if the reaction they caused in Nadine was anything to go on, but it could be more than that. Perhaps Voline was an old and sick woman desperately seeking amusement and distraction after being confronted with death. She might not mind them coming by.

He got into his car and tapped his fingers on the wheel. He suspected Nadine wanted more than to give Voline an apology. She could have emailed that or left a voice message. She must have seen that comment too, and it piqued her interest.

He drove past Drake's house, which was twice the size of Voline's and about half as interesting. If talking to Voline for his story and finding out the details of the controversy—which since yesterday had been enhanced by the intense desire to frustrate and eventually best Nadine—meant being entertaining, he would do what it took.

That scandal story was going to be his.

"Pizza?" Nadine frowned at the greasy box as Wes walked up with the aplomb of a waiter at a Michelin-starred restaurant. She herself clutched a white plastic bag stacked with takeout containers from a place that had the menu written in chopstick font. It was the kind of Chinese restaurant her mother had always refused to set foot in despite Nadine's childhood pleading, insisting on going to Chinatown to meet Pohpoh for what she called real dim sum.

Today, she'd also grabbed a few chicken balls for herself because the thick fried batter was like a drug. She licked her lips and tried to ignore how Wes stared at her, the same way he had when she'd baited Voline with the chocolate yesterday. Had he never seen a woman eat?

"The cheesiest pizza I could find," he said. "Chinese?"

"Chicken balls with red sauce, egg rolls, and special fried rice."

To her surprise, Wes laughed. She'd forgotten they'd occasionally amused each other before Wes had shown his true colors. "Looks like we're closing in on her tastes."

"Oh, trust me." Nadine pulled out her pièce de résistance, a box of generic white wine. "I've got the winner here."

Her triumph lasted only seconds because Wes gave her a big smile. "Good try, but I have the advantage." From behind his back, he pulled out…Nadine squinted.

"Is that a milkshake? I love milkshakes." Sometimes she dreamed Shamrock Shakes were on the full-time menu.

"I know. You used to bring a Hudson's cookies and cream one to class every Wednesday. I don't know how you drank them. Milkshakes are disgusting."

"Yet you hold one in your hand."

"Because Voline will love it. This is a chocolate malt milkshake from a diner that makes them the same way they did in the 1960s." He turned it around as if admiring his own ingenuity. "I brought it in a cooler."

Damn, and she'd been so proud of her wine box.

The food proved to be no more of a key to unlocking Dot Voline than the chocolates or flowers. She sent them away after asking if they were trying to turn her obituary into a prognostication. "Death by acid reflux is such a mundane way to give up the ghost," said Voline's gruff voice through the intercom. "Take it with you. All of it."

Nadine sat in her car eating the special fried rice out of the container—no point letting it go to waste—and debated her next move as she tried not to cut her mouth on the sharp edges of the plastic spoon. Across the street, Wes sat in his own car, a triangle of pizza hanging from his hand. It looked tasty. She could trade him an egg roll for a slice or maybe that milkshake he hated. As she was about to lower the window, Wes turned and saw her. He lifted that lovely milkshake to take a long pull on the straw, looking her straight in the eyes as he grimaced at the taste.

Be that way. She'd keep the egg rolls.

---

"We haven't digitized those materials yet," said the librarian as he led Nadine into the elevator and down to a space with the ambiance of a wartime bunker. "I can show you the old articles we clipped from papers and the microfiche."

"Anything will be appreciated," she said, looking around. The low room was filled with floor-to-ceiling card catalogues and metal filing cabinets with scrawled notes taped to the front.

"Like I told the Asian fellow when he asked, there isn't much about that old rumor."

That old rumor. Confirmed, Wes was interested in the scandal.

The librarian paused at the end of a stack. "Oh, there he is."

"Hello, Wes." Nadine had no choice but to face the inevitable. The shirt you most want to wear will be in the bottom of the laundry, you'll only forget to set your alarm on days you have an early meeting, and Wes Chen will be right there, inserting himself in the middle of your off-the-books investigation.

Judging from his expression, Wes had come to the same conclusion.

*I hate you,* she mouthed at him, thrilled to be able to say the words to his face.

He glared at her. *Ditto,* he said silently.

*Get off my turf.*

*The frog sings at midnight.*

Her lipreading might not have been as good as she thought. She turned her gaze from his mouth, with the edges that tilted up, and stared at the arm curled protectively around his work like the resource-hoarding twat he was. This wasn't only about Voline anymore. It was about the two of them. Nadine was going to beat Wes to this story if it was the last thing she did.

"Can you tell me what you told my esteemed colleague here?" Nadine asked. "So we're all on the same page."

If looks could kill, she'd be smeared on the battered steel cabinet behind her, but she deflected it with a saccharine smile she'd never directed at Wes in her life and never would again. That was unless it continued to antagonize him as much as this one apparently did. Then she'd get it surgically attached to her face.

"You're familiar with *Thirty Pieces of Silver*?" the librarian asked.

Nadine was. "Her third book, and the one that first garnered Voline international fame."

The man looked pleased. "A tour de force of a woman's experience, baring raw her soul and the core of her feminine energy. An examination of the nature of gender and workplace power dynamics and a woman's cry of impotent rage in a society dedicated to bending her will to that of Man."

Nadine could hear the capital M. She didn't dare look at Wes.

"It was about a lying politician who took advantage of a naive woman in love to save his career, although it destroyed her life," she said, hoping she could take a shortcut through the literary criticism.

"Dot Voline never confirmed whether the book was based on

personal experience," said the librarian with relish. "Of course she was only a schoolteacher in a small Manitoba town with no access to Ottawa's hallowed halls of power, so it was obviously the result of her rich imagination."

"There isn't enough known about her early years to prove that, is there?" asked Wes in a bland voice.

The librarian waved off that point with a pale bony hand. "She refused to take part in any official biographies. Profiles tend to focus on her productive years, when she was unfettered from small-town life and could spread her creative wings to *fly.*"

Nadine, who had been raised in a small town, bristled at this. "Was the rumor you mentioned that people thought she based it on her own life?" She kept her phrasing careful, to not give away anything to Wes.

The librarian laughed. "No, no, like I said, no one believed it could be based on Voline's experiences. There was an idea it was about a specific politician though."

This was new, and although he tried to hide it, she could tell from Wes's expression it was the first time he'd heard it as well. "Do you remember anything else?" she asked.

The librarian sucked his teeth and looked at the ceiling before raising his tweedy shoulders in defeat. "As I said, it was only whispers. I assume she heard some little tidbit, perhaps from one of the men in town, and let her imagination work. The story is exaggerated for literary effect."

Wes's eyebrows went higher. "Exaggerated?"

The librarian stiffened. "One must believe in the morality of our country's leaders. A married politician having a work affair and allowing his mistress to cover his financial misdeeds? He would have been shunned by those responsible for maintaining our institutions."

"Right, right," Nadine rushed in as Wes opened his mouth to reply. "Thank you for your help. I'll look around, and if you remember anything else, I'd appreciate it."

The librarian cast a suspicious look at Wes before bestowing a coffee-stained smile on Nadine. "Happy to help. It was such a shame about the mistake with her obituary in the *Herald*. I wrote a very strong letter to the editor about their journalistic standards and threatened to cancel my subscription."

Nadine felt her smile grow thin. "I'm sure they appreciated your feedback."

He nodded complacently. "It's my duty as a citizen to ensure accuracy in the fourth estate. Who will watch the watchers?"

Finally the librarian was gone, waving through the doors of the elevator as they closed. Nadine dropped her head on the table. "So grateful to all our subscribers," she said. "And for the purity of our political leaders."

Wes was too busy laughing to do anything besides tap her hand in what she assumed was a momentary and misplaced sense of camaraderie. "He told me the *Spear* wasn't a proper news organization and he actively opposes the library's purchase of a subscription."

"Good to know we both suck. He makes me grateful for the incredible librarians of my youth." She looked up. "He also blew your cover."

"I don't know what you're talking about."

"The rumor? *Thirty Pieces of Silver*?"

"Again, I'm only doing background research for a story on Dot Voline. You might not understand what it means to be thorough."

"I'm thorough."

He pulled out his phone to read aloud. "'Literary icon Dot Voline has died after a lengthy battle with cancer at the age of seventy-two.' Yeah, very thorough."

She wanted to throw a book at him. All the books. "That was a single error in judgment, and you have no right to come here and horn in on my story."

"It's not yours, but noted." He flipped through his clips.

"I have asked the gods to curse you in many inconvenient ways."

She always felt as if she was tempting fate to wish truly bad things on people, even if they deserved it.

"Like what?" He pulled out a pair of reading glasses and perched them on his nose. She ignored how cute they looked. Wes was not cute.

"Your shoes will become constantly untied."

He stuck out his foot to show a polished loafer. "Do your worst."

"Your coffee will always be decaf."

"I should cut back anyway." He opened a new folder.

Nadine felt a bit desperate. "Your favorite brand of notebook will be discontinued."

"Oh." Wes looked up at her, bowed lips turning down. "That's mean."

"You deserve it. I know why you're here. It's to upset me. It's part of your ongoing need to steal my ideas."

"That is narcissistic as well as wrong. You know that you take up a very small amount of my day?"

"Then why do you care about Dot Voline? It has nothing to do with you. Admit you're here because of the scandal."

He only shrugged, leaving Nadine seething.

"Fine," she said. "May your every meal be ruined by a person talking in exquisite detail about their dreams."

Wes ignored her and got up to check a cabinet, leaving her staring at his back.

It was confirmed. She hated Wes. She stalked off to the stacks to find her own answers to Voline's story. And to ask the gods to put salt instead of sugar into Wes's desserts. That would show him.

# SIX

Two days later, Wes's luck changed. Not at work, where he'd pitched a story about the impact of digital face editing hooked to the release of a new app and had been told what the *Spear* needed was a profile of a woman making furniture from abandoned tires.

"Sustainability is one of the *Spear's* editorial pillars," said Rebecca, patting him on the shoulder as they looked at the monstrosities the designer called chairs. "Make sure you stress that part."

Wes put his head in his hands. "Why me? Why?"

"Because people will read your story out of interest and not for the lulz." Rebecca scrolled to a stool or possibly a table. "Better add in a user's guide while you're at it. Oh, and nice work on the Voline story. It was too bad you didn't get that quote, but I loved the sidebar of obituary misfires."

"Thanks." He'd emailed Nadine the link. She hadn't replied.

When the phone rang an hour later, he nearly let it go to voicemail so he could continue his research on the environmental impact of tire manufacturing. Habit forced him to answer.

"Wes Chen, *Spear*." He might be frustrated with his job at the moment, but there was no way he'd get tired of knowing he'd made it. Atrocious design profiles or not, he was working in journalism.

"Wes, this is Brent Tatterly."

The name was familiar. "Tatterly. Dot Voline's nephew?" Nephew by marriage, technically, as Tatterly had been Voline's husband's sister's son. Or something like that.

"That's me."

Was Brent about to tell Wes where he could stick his story? It wouldn't be the first time that had happened, so Wes was more curious than worried about the call. He hadn't been by the house since his fruitless library search. At least Nadine had come up short as well, obvious from her defeated expression as she left the basement research bunker.

"I hope Ms. Voline is okay?" he asked, heart lurching as he grasped another reason Brent might be contacting him.

"She's fine and why I'm calling. I'd prefer to talk about this in person. Do you have time later? Say three this afternoon?"

"I can move some things if it's urgent," Wes lied, calmer knowing Voline was alive. He didn't want to look too desperate.

"It will be worth your time." Brent gave him the location, which was nearby. "I'll see you soon."

The day dragged, but at 2:48, Wes was on his way to the café for Brent's meeting. His legs were stiff after hours of sitting, and lengthening his stride to get a stretch did nothing to work the tension out of his calves. His friend Caleb was always on his case to build in walking breaks, but Caleb was the kind of guy who did triathlons and polar dips for fun. His opinions on exercise could not be trusted.

A text came from his mother. **I can't get the kitchen tap to close all the way.**

He counted to ten before replying. **I'll fix it when I get home, okay, Ma? No, the dripping is terrible. It's ruining my day off. I don't know what to do.**

He waited for the light to turn so he could cross the street. **Use a towel to stop the noise.**

**All it does is drip.**

He tried to relax his jaw. **Take a towel, and put it under the tap to absorb the water.**

The phone rang and he ignored it, preferring to keep their conversation on text. **You're not picking up. I need to talk to you.**

**Sorry, I'm in a meeting.** A very pale white lie, as he was about to be in one soon.

**What kind of towel?**

**Any kind. Use a dish towel.** His fingers hurt from how hard he tapped the message.

**It's too much. You don't care. Go do your job since it's more important. Amy can help me since you're too lazy to do anything.**

**Don't call Amy at work.**

No answer. Amy told him he should take their mother's silences as the blessing they were, but all he felt was guilt. He could call a plumber for an emergency visit, but Ma hated being in the house with strangers. Either he or Amy had to be there for any repairs. She'd have to wait for once.

Stressed in the way only his mother could make him, Wes tried to focus on the upcoming meeting. The café was on a side street with chairs chained to the two iron tables in the front. A small window sold drinks and pastries to passersby too busy to open the door and walk four steps to the counter. He stepped in, breathing the comforting smell of roasted coffee and melted butter, and then stopped dead.

In the back corner sat Nadine, laughing with a man in a blue Henley shirt and jeans, her dark hair pulled back in a ponytail that showed off her ears. She had a new piercing, he noticed as he came closer, making it three in her left and one in her right. Why he noticed that about her, he couldn't say. Well, he'd been trained to observe details, so that was probably it.

She looked up, and her smile flashed out of sight.

"Ah, you must be Wes. I'm Brent." The man rose to a casually polite half crouch. He was tanned with brown hair, the kind of man who populated streetscape shots in movies because he faded so well into the background. He didn't offer his hand and instead gave a small wave, which was a relief. Wes never trusted men who acted as if a strong handshake was some sort of stand-in for masculinity. Tyler had an intentionally crushing shake.

Brent sat down and tilted his head at Nadine. "I believe you know Nadine Barbault?"

"We know each other." The grit in Nadine's voice said she hadn't expected Wes to be at the meeting either. Wes beamed at her, and she snapped her head away so fast her ponytail whipped around to hit her in the face. He took his chair as she pulled her hair out of her lip gloss.

"Good, good." Brent smiled at them. "I'm pleased to meet you. I always wanted to be a journalist."

Wes heard that a lot. "What happened?"

Brent lifted one shoulder, his face wry. "I'm a terrible writer, to be honest." He brightened. "You know what you should look into? Pylons."

"Pylons?" said Nadine blankly.

Brent waved his hand. "You know, traffic cones? How many times have you driven down the highway and seen kilometers of orange cones but no construction? I bet there's some kickback scheme there."

Had Wes wandered into a different reality? "You think organized crime is behind road pylons?" he asked.

Brent looked earnest. "You never know, do you?"

"I guess not," Nadine said.

Wes nodded in agreement, not sure what answer to give.

That was apparently enough for Brent. "That's what I'd look into if I owned a media company. Well, let's get down to it. I'm here on behalf of my aunt, Dot Voline." Brent folded his hands on the table and looked at them. "She says you've been coming by the house."

"Yes," said Nadine before Wes could answer.

"My aunt rarely gives interviews," Brent said.

"I know." Wes readied himself for the back-off warning.

"Her rule is that everything she needs to say finds its way into a book, and she can't be expected to explain it to every Tom, Dick, and Harry who refuse to use their own brains."

"Okay," said Wes. That definitely sounded like the woman who had been yelling at him over the intercom.

"That has changed. She's willing to speak to you."

Wes saw Nadine's surprise. "Both of us?" she asked. "We work for different organizations."

Brent smiled and sipped his drink, so milky it was the color of eggshells. "My aunt would say that's your problem. This is her offer. The obituary forced her to think about her mortality and legacy. She wants to talk to you 'so those deathmongers can get the damn story right.'" He gave them a cheerful smile. "Direct quote."

"Then there is a story." Wes slid his hands to his lap so Brent couldn't tell how eager he was. He glanced at Nadine, who looked as cool and collected as she always did when working. Wes's phone buzzed, and he silenced it. It would be his mother again, and although he'd pay later for ignoring her, he needed to concentrate.

"I'm not sure about a story," said Brent. "All I know is she said she had a promise to keep. She also gave me some rules."

"What are they?" Wes asked. "Obviously they have to work within our ethical standards." When did *my* become *our*? Were he and Nadine a team? No. It was simply a practical linguistic shortcut.

"They're reasonable." Brent took a long sip of his drink. "The first, as I said, is she'll only deal with the two of you together. Second, you can't tell anyone you're doing this. Finally, you may not publish, allude to, or speak about what you learn until she's dead."

"That might be years," Wes said. He felt Nadine's disgust at his tactlessness.

"It might be." Brent looked at his hands. "But probably not."

"I agree," said Nadine promptly.

Wes took a breath. "Sorry, can you give us a moment, Brent?"

"Sure." He drained his cup. "I'll be right back."

Wes waited until Brent was safely ensconced in the washroom, which was a closet off the main space. It irritated him that Nadine looked unperturbed about this offer. He wanted to break through that facade to the real Nadine, the one who had almost strangled him in front of Voline's gate.

"You can't be serious about working together," he said.

She flicked him a dismissive glance. "Sure I am. I know this will be a stretch for you, but quit being contradictory, and look at it reasonably."

"I'm not being contradictory," he said in full knowledge that the statement was itself contradictory.

"The reason we're having this meeting is because I left a note in the chocolates," she said. "You're only along for the ride."

"The flowers had a card with my name and number."

"Fine, whatever." Although her voice sounded the way an eye roll looked, he knew it was as close as he would get to Nadine giving in. "I don't know why you're digging into Dot Voline, but I assume there's a reason beyond pettiness."

He thought about Tyler and Jason, to that place on the I-team he wanted back so bad he could taste it. "I don't know why you're so focused on it either," he pointed out.

"Because I ran an obit to find not only was Dot Voline *alive*, but there were facts *missing*?" She sounded more outraged about the inaccuracy than the running of the obit.

"Then what, you owe it to her?" He meant it as a bit of a dig—he knew that was uncool—but Nadine put her hands on the table and looked him in the eyes.

"Yes. Or at least to the story."

"What was missing?" he asked.

"I know you know what was missing." Her voice was tight. "You said as much to the librarian."

"Maybe I do, maybe I don't. But I want you to tell me." He wanted to make sure there wasn't something else he didn't know.

"Why should I?"

Wes gave an exaggerated glance at Brent's empty seat. "Because it seems you need me to get access to Dot Voline. You depend on me in fact."

She puffed out her breath. "You are so annoying. You're the worst."

"What do you know, Nadine?"

Nadine's mouth was tight. "There was a comment under the obituary I ran about a scandal. I can't find any information about it, and I want to ask her."

"Was that so hard?"

She was trembling with infuriation. "You got what you want."

He smiled at her. "I knew it already. I saw the comment too."

Nadine breathed out slowly. "Of course you were being an ass as always. Are you going to wreck it for the both of us?"

He fixed his expression to look like he was considering all his options, just to make her sweat.

Brent sat down with the friendly expectation of a golden retriever waiting for the tennis ball to be thrown. "Well?" said Brent.

Nadine resembled a thundercloud as Wes pretended to consider his answer. "Let me get it straight. We have to work together, keep it secret, and withhold publication until after death?"

"Yes."

"How often would we meet Ms. Voline?" he asked, partly out of curiosity but mostly to see if he could make Nadine's brain explode.

Brent pursed his lips. "Those are details you need to sort out with my aunt. I was only sent to get an answer. What's it going to be? Yes or no?"

Wes waited another few seconds until the redness started to climb up Nadine's throat. The ice queen was turning into a fire demon. He smiled.

"Yes."

# SEVEN

Nadine barely had time to think about Brent's offer, because she went straight from the café to a chaotic newsroom dealing with reports of a potential police standoff with a domestic terrorist north of Saskatoon. Luckily, they'd been able to disarm the man, and the newsroom went off to write stories that weren't about mass murder.

Raj in particular looked vastly relieved. "They told me for large-scale tragedies, I'm part of the advance team," he whispered to her. "I wanted to be in the sports department, for God's sake. I thought they'd pay me to go to *games*. Did anyone in the world grow up wanting to do this? I want to meet the kid who told their parents their dream was to run the obituary section instead of being an astronaut." He paused. "Never mind. I don't want to meet that kid at all."

By hour six of her shift, everyone but the cleaning staff had left, and Nadine had worked through enough of her tasks to feel she deserved a break. Pulling up Dot Voline's obituary, she read it over again. The woman was right. It was dreary, and so far nothing she'd learned of Voline was dull. That was the *Herald*'s standard model, though, as set out by the previous editor, then continued by Nadine and Raj.

She closed the file, feeling as if she'd failed Dot Voline twice. First by running it when she was alive, second by allowing this memorial to carry none of her personality.

When Nadine had taken the obit job, she'd been too caught up in her own problems to do much research into what it would entail. Since she'd been tossed in with almost no training, she'd focused on reading the *Herald*'s archive to get a sense of what was expected. It had taken her time to figure out the hierarchy and processes of obituary options, from the death notices, usually paid for by families and run through the advertising department, to the editorial obituaries undertaken by Nadine and her freelancers if the deceased had enough public significance. Could she have done more while she was editor? Possibly, but it was too late now. Raj wouldn't be impressed if she stuck her nose back in.

With a faint feeling of regret, Nadine decided it was time for coffee. The motion-activated lights clicked on with a disturbing crackle as she strolled through the rows of empty desks.

She wished her career had started back in the days of typewriters and telex machines, when the office combined a lively mix of chatter and the noise of work. Even on busy days—and those were rare as so many people worked from home—the *Herald* retained the faint sense of a monastery, with soft typing and low-voiced conversations taking place through headsets. Most people wore gigantic headphones. Apparently the travel editor, who saved his expansive commentary for his stories and did his best to avoid conversation with his colleagues, had found mushrooms growing in his ears from wearing earbuds too often.

The place was one zombie away from being a horror movie, and she was almost grateful to arrive in the kitchen unbitten. She collected the various pods for a vanilla spice latte and devoted the necessary time cajoling the machine into making actual coffee instead of simply sputtering out coffee-adjacent hot water. Then she opened her texts. Her mother's daily check in was easily dealt with, and so was Lisanne's brief mention of a new lead for her super awesome huge project.

The next one was from Wes. How did he get her number? Scrolling up, she saw the last message was from almost a decade ago, organizing a location to meet for one of their school assignments. She hadn't known her phone kept texts for that long.

She slapped the coffee machine to get it brewing again and reread Wes's note. **We should set some ground rules before the weekend.**

Before they'd left Brent, the three had negotiated a time for their first meeting with Dot Voline and had settled on Sunday, since it was the only day Nadine and Wes had off in common. It had immediately become the thing Nadine was most looking forward to in the world.

Nadine considered Wes's text. She wasn't opposed to ground rules but felt a faint flare of irritation that she hadn't taken the initiative in setting them. Regardless of what Wes thought, this story was rightfully hers. She was the lead.

Like telling someone you were *just* about to call them, it was too transparent an attempt to save face if she replied with *I was going to talk to you about that*. Instead she wrote back, **What kind of rules?**

**Rules of engagement,** Wes typed.

**Like combatants in a war?**

**If that's how you see it. I prefer to think of it as starting together in harmony.**

She glared at the screen, feeling as if he'd bested her by being a better and less suspicious person, although he'd been the one to suggest limits in the first place. She didn't trust him either, but at least she had reason to. He was snaky, as he'd proven all the times he'd gotten the better of her. Intellectually, she understood it was part of the job, but that didn't make the impact of seeing his name on a story she'd considered hers any easier. Trusting Wes with Dot Voline would be like a frog trusting a scorpion. It was every reporter for themselves.

**I propose that neither of us is allowed to contact Voline or her nephew alone,** he continued.

She couldn't let him think he was ahead of her. **That was on my list** too, she lied. **I also want us to keep all information we find in a central location.**

Wes immediately sent a link to a shared document, and she took an aggressive sip of coffee that would have burned her mouth if the machine heated anything past lukewarm. He had a doc. *She* should have had a doc ready. Wes was winning. Unbearable. She usually worked harder to beat Wes when he was around, but they hadn't been intersecting as often with his job in Lifestyle. She had to get her edge back.

Another question came before she could retaliate by one-upping him. **Does the Herald know you're doing this?**

Nadine hesitated. The *Herald* wouldn't be pleased if they found out she'd been acting on her own. She could lie, but she had a feeling he knew the answer. It would be easier to be straight from the beginning as well as give the impression that she was confident in what she was doing.

**No. Does the Spear?**

Wes's answer came right away. **No.**

**Are you going to tell them?** That was the question, wasn't it? If Wes told his editor, Nadine would be under pressure to tell her own, just in case word got out she was involved.

Like before, the message was short. **No.** Another came through. **At least not if you don't. Will you?**

**Not planning to,** she wrote back.

**Then my next ground rule is that neither of us can go to our editors without a discussion on what we're doing with the story.**

This was reasonable but... **Do we need to agree with the other person? Like, if I want to run what we have and you say no, what happens?**

**We don't go ahead until we figure out how to do it fairly. Deal?**

It made sense. **Deal.**

She sent the text with a little thrill to know they were secretly working together. Then she shook her head. God, she needed to get out more if she considered working with Wes exciting.

———————

He was officially involved in a covert investigation with Nadine Barbault.

Sitting on his bed, Wes listened to the sound of his mother grumbling at the TV from the living room. Ma wanted to make it clear that although she wanted to talk, she was very specifically refusing to talk to him, although he came straight from the café to fix the dripping tap. He tried pinching his earlobes to reduce the headache that threatened. No go.

He waited.

Three, two, one.

There it was. The guilt. It was the last stage in the cycle of doing his best to please her, failing, and losing patience. If he tried harder to be a good son, perhaps she'd be less...he hesitated over the word, but his sister Amy's dry voice supplied it in his head. *Miserable?*

He winced away. His mother had told him countless times over the years that he was the man of the house since his father went back to Singapore when Ella was a baby. He barely remembered his father, except for the smell of his Irish Spring soap. He hated it, although he didn't hate his father. On bad days, he understood why his father had simply walked out the door and never looked back. He wished he could himself.

On other days, he thought about his sisters and pitied his father for what he was missing.

A new message came. **See you Sunday.** Then Nadine was gone. Wes stared at the phone for a few more seconds, wishing she was there to talk to about Dot before he came to his senses. Nadine was his competition and only temporarily his collaborator. The fact that they'd had a relatively civil interaction meant nothing. He pulled out his copy of *Thirty Pieces of Silver* and started taking notes.

*Politician James Walton wearing a sand-and-brown-spotted tie. Like a hyena? Opportunistic backstabber from the beginning or terrible 1970s fashion?*

He had reached the scene where Walton's mother says he'll never fill his famous father's shoes—Dot had written it with a pathos that made him feel for Walton even as he was disgusted at his arrogant entitlement—when he received a text from Caleb. **I'm in town for the weekend. You free Friday for drinks?**

It would be good to see Caleb, who was in Calgary for a long-term project for his management company. Wes alternated his Fridays with Amy so one of them was always available to keep their mother company as she watched TV, and this was his week off. Amy insisted an adult woman didn't need her grown children at her beck and call, but she was a good sister and watched three hours of a Turkish soap opera every second week to give Wes a break.

He set a place and time to meet Caleb, and got back to work on *Thirty Pieces of Silver*. Four hours later, when he pulled up their shared document, it was to find Nadine had entered tabs for the book as well as Voline's other works. He clicked on *Thirty Pieces of Silver*.

Her first note was *Hyena tie. Get list of disgraced politicians from 1950 to 1988 (publication date). One might be Walton.*

Goddamn Nadine, always one step ahead.

Then he pasted in the list he'd generated of every publicly embarrassed politician at the federal and provincial level from 1950 to 1988.

Check and mate.

# EIGHT

adine sat on the couch nursing a cup of tea and listening to her grandmother and mother chat as they finished preparing lunch. Or as Pohpoh finished, because she took over the cooking whenever she came to visit. Her father passed by with a stack of plates to set the kitchen table since the larger one in the dining room was covered with her brother's latest school project, which seemed to involve a lot of wires.

"Hey, sis." Noah poked his head into the room.

She checked out the contraption he was wearing. "Are those welding goggles for that bomb you're constructing?"

"Funny. It's a VR headset. Wanna try?"

She shuddered. "No thanks. Those make me nauseous."

Noah nodded, sandy hair bouncing over the top of the headset. "Motion sickness happens in about a quarter of users, and women are generally more susceptible."

"And why is that, brother dearest?"

He looked astonished. "Gender bias in engineering, of course. Like most things, VR tech is designed with a man's perspectives, experiences, and measurements in mind."

She toasted him with her mug. "Tell Preeti I love her." Noah's girl-friend of a decade—they met in eighth grade, and Nadine didn't know if it was weird or sweet that they'd been together for so long—was brilliant, ambitious, and kind. Nadine loved her.

Noah made a face. "I found that out for myself doing a project on accessible design, thanks."

Nadine raised her eyebrows. "Preeti had nothing to do with it?"

"Preeti suggested the topic," he admitted.

She went into the kitchen. Her grandmother gave Nadine a critical look. "Good thing you came for lunch," she said. "Too skinny. You need to eat more."

"I eat, Pohpoh." She leaned over to give her grandmother a hug, which was tolerated for less than a second. Pohpoh showed her love in only two ways: food provision and criticism. She accepted affection fleetingly and rarely. Her grandmother handed her a bowl of chopped green onions, and Nadine knew without asking that she was to add them to every dish.

She began to sprinkle as she watched her mother and grandmother argue about whether to mince more garlic. Having lost the garlic fight, her mother took away Nadine's green onion bowl and peered into her face. "Your cheeks are gaunt. It's that job, isn't it?" she said. "It's too much for you."

Her dad came in to join the party. "Listen to your mom, pumpkin. You know she's always right."

This had been the soundtrack of Nadine's life, along with its B-side, *You should ask your father for advice.* "I'm fine."

Her mother's face creased with concern. "There was that awful man threatening you at your own home. We were terrified. You should move back with us. Your apartment isn't safe."

Nadine sighed, regretting that she'd told her parents about the threats. She couldn't let them suspect this conversation upset her because it would devolve into having to reassure them. It also meant a frank discussion of the incident or how she felt about it was completely off the table, because they would take any of her concerns as more proof she wasn't okay and should move home. She grabbed her chair. "It was dealt with, and nothing happened. Are we ready to eat?"

They crowded around the table, passing the food and casually dipping into dishes with forks and chopsticks. A platter of French fries shared space with the steamed fish, noodles, and fried rice because Pohpoh required meals to have the selection of a buffet to be acceptable. She'd also made what they called Chinese lasagna, layers of rice, greens, and hoisin chicken thighs cooked to tender perfection, topped with Nadine's spring onions.

"At least you've changed that job of yours," said her father as he served himself some noodles. "Obituaries are too morbid for a young woman."

"Like a grim reaper," added her mother. "I read one about some poor man's business failures. What happened to not speaking ill of the dead?"

"Jerry Hill's mismanagement wiped out the savings of thousands of vulnerable people and made him a multimillionaire." Nadine traded her chopsticks for a spoon. "It's as much a part of his legacy as anything else he did. Obits aren't eulogies."

"I can't believe his family allowed it," said her mother. "You need to leave people with their dignity."

"We don't ask permission." Nadine spoke into her plate and tried to push aside her temper and her parents' disappointment. "Those kinds of obituaries are in the public interest, and they should be fair and truthful."

"It's mean-spirited," said her father stubbornly. "Not the kind of thing I thought you would want to be involved in. We raised you better. It's not surprising things like that man would happen."

She put down her spoon as Noah's head shot up. "What do you mean?"

"Nadine, be serious," said her mother, exchanging a look with her father. "I don't want to say *I told you so*, but naturally people are going to respond negatively to your stories. Some of them aren't very nice."

"My job is to report accurately and keep people accountable," said Nadine through gritted teeth. "Not to be nice."

"All I'm saying is not everyone is going to agree. You should be like Rachel from golf's daughter. She's a physiotherapist," said her mother hopefully. "That's a good steady job."

"You need to come home before something serious happens," added her father. "Waste of money to rent these days anyway."

"Complete waste," her mother echoed. "At least you would have company here."

Nadine thought about those late-night shadows. It might be nice to have people around. Maybe she *would* feel safer at home.

Her grandmother dropped a serving spoon and winced, rubbing a hand thick with arthritis.

That was enough for her mother to turn her attention from Nadine. "Mom, have you thought more about when you're going to move into a retirement home?" she asked.

Pohpoh picked up the spoon again. "Yes. Never."

Noah covered a laugh as their father glared at him. "Noah."

"Sorry, Dad, but if Pohpoh likes to live on her own, she should. Like Nad."

"Your grandmother needs someone to keep an eye on her," said their mother. "What if something happens?"

Pohpoh waved her hand. "What if, what if. I can take care of myself."

Nadine kicked Noah under the table before her mother could respond, and he coughed loudly. "Hey, did I tell you about the cool thing I'm working on?" He didn't wait for a reply and started talking about his new VR project at length and past the point where any of them were interested.

It left Nadine to stew about her parents' attitude. Although they swore they only wanted her to be happy, they neglected to add, *as long as it doesn't upset us.* Her parents needed the comfort and stability that came from the familiar. They'd lived in the same house since before Nadine was born and worked in the same companies as their first jobs. They'd had taco Tuesdays for over a decade straight. Her mother didn't even like making left-hand turns in the car.

It had been hard for Nadine to go against their wishes to become a journalist instead of an accountant, but telling stories to make a difference was something she'd craved, and it had been worth it. Despite all the problems, it was worth it.

Not to mention she hated math.

After lunch, she and Noah chased out the rest of the family while they cleaned up, Noah tackling the pots in the sink while she filled the dishwasher. He glanced over. "It works better if you put the bowls—"

"Shut it, Noah."

"—on the top. Otherwise, they stop the water from circulating," he muttered to himself.

She put in another bowl and lowered her voice. "Why do Mom and Dad want to move Pohpoh? Is her health worse?"

Noah finished washing the pot before answering. "It's not that. They're worried about what might happen to her outside."

"Like falling down?"

He shook his head. "A guy pushed Mrs. Lee coming out of the grocery store."

Nadine gasped, feeling ill. "Mrs. Lee is *eighty.*"

Her brother glared at the dish in his hand. "You think someone like that is going to attack a person who can fight back? She had to go to the hospital and get stitches."

"Why didn't anyone tell me?" she demanded.

"What are you going to do about it?" he asked. "It's life. It sucks, but Pohpoh says she'd like to see some runt try it on her. I got her some pepper spray. It's illegal, but if she needs to use it, that's on them." Her brother's face was granite.

"That's why Mom and Dad are upset."

"Yeah, but Pohpoh doesn't want to live in fear. Or to be monitored."

They worked in silence for a bit, and when she looked over, Noah was frowning as he scrubbed. Nadine knew that face, which was the same one he wore when he was stumped by an algebra problem. "Hey," she said. "Pohpoh's tough, you know that. Remember when that guy tried to steal her purse and she broke his leg when she tripped him?"

"That's not what I'm worried about." He dropped a pot into the sink with a clatter. "Not all of it anyway. Are Mom and Dad right?"

"About what?"

"I've been reading a lot about the shit journalists get online, and I know it's worse for women." A deep line split his forehead. "Especially women who aren't white. You should see what Preeti has to deal with in her engineering classes."

"We're white," she said.

"I am. But you're more whitish."

Nadine understood what he was saying. Very few of Evelyn Tan's features had filtered down to her grandchildren. Noah was a mini me of their father, with light hair and eyes that shifted from gray to blue to green depending on the color of his shirt and, more bizarrely, the weather. Nadine looked more like their mother, with her small nose and round eyes that narrowed at the corners, and like her, Nadine somehow didn't look part Chinese but also didn't *not* look it. It depended on her expression and how she wore her hair. However she looked, it was enough to get her voluntold into the *Herald*'s diversity committee by Frank after her editor had come back from a managerial meeting.

"It's like a twofer," he'd said, tone making clear his belief that this entire diversity thing was another corporate trend that would soon fade. "A woman and some Asian. Think of it as good for your visibility."

Nadine hadn't wanted to join, the same way she hadn't wanted to join the social committee or any of the other committees almost totally run by women to improve the quality of office life for everyone else. That was time she couldn't do her actual job and for no extra pay, acknowledgment, or appreciable benefit. After all, she didn't care if they had a holiday party, and the best way to build visibility was by breaking good stories. "I'm not Asian."

"But—" Frank waved his hand at her face. Maybe she shouldn't have done the cat's-eye eyeliner that morning.

Nadine prepared for her standard Giving of the Genealogy. "My grandmother is Chinese. I'm a quarter, and it doesn't really impact my life." Despite her father urging her to say she was Asian to take advantage of what he apparently thought were the boatloads of perks available to diversity candidates, Nadine felt uncomfortable claiming a heritage she didn't feel matched her or that she had a right to. If she looked like Pohpoh, it might be different, or if she'd been raised with more of a cultural consciousness than learning to eat with chopsticks. Also, her dad had no idea what he was talking about.

She turned back to her conversation with Noah. "I changed jobs anyway."

"You lived for the politics beat," he said. "Are you going back?"

"Of course I am," she said with more confidence than she had. She loved providing insight on events as they were happening. The scrums. The rush when she knew a politician was lying, and she had the indisputable proof. The immediacy and the adrenaline had made it all worthwhile, until that one day when she simply couldn't take it anymore.

She had known she was tense and burned out by the armchair critics who forgot they were aiming their insults at an actual person. Or perhaps that was what made them do it, as long as they could act without fear of retribution. Yet she couldn't bring herself to tell Frank it was getting to be too much and she needed a break. The death threat had at least pushed her into action, which was the thinnest possible silver lining. She bit her lip, hand lingering on the cabinet.

Noah poked her. "Hey, earth to Nad. You okay?"

She shook off her fugue. "I'm good. Don't worry about me."

"Preeti says we need to care about the people we love when they can't care for themselves."

"Preeti is right." She gave him an impulsive hug, and he tapped her awkwardly on the back with his fingertips. "Thanks, brobob."

"Don't call me that."

"Goober."

"Stretch."

It had been so long, neither of them remembered where the nicknames had come from or why they'd been annoying. Over the years, they'd transformed into almost endearments, a way to say *I love you* without the embarrassment of having to utter the words out loud.

Nadine put on a smile and said her goodbyes, then got in her car. Tapping Voline's address into her GPS, she saw she had thirty-one minutes to put aside her parents' concern and unease about her grandmother before she arrived.

In the end, it took twenty-four minutes for the anticipation to rise high enough to drown her other worries. Nothing, not her family or work or putting up with Wes, would ruin meeting Dot Voline for the first time.

# NINE

As per their agreement, Wes waited for Nadine to arrive at Voline's ornate gate so they could go in together. He'd been almost an hour early to escape his mother's commentary on how he was deserting the family by working on the weekend, despite spending the morning grocery shopping and completing a series of errands to placate her.

He was also early because he was eager to talk to Dot Voline. Brent's mention of his aunt keeping a promise meant he could be looking at a bigger story than he anticipated. It could also be a dud, but Wes didn't think so, and neither did Nadine. He might not like her, but he could admit she had excellent intuition.

Nadine. He wasn't thrilled about having to share this story. It helped that the *Herald* would look much more unkindly on Nadine coloring outside the lines than the *Spear*. If push came to shove, she had more to lose than he did, putting the balance of power squarely in his hands, which was satisfying. He'd still have to stay on his toes to make sure she played straight with him.

Five more minutes. He rubbed his hands together, letting his inner movie villain take over. Despite their agreement, if Nadine was a no-show, Wes would be within his rights to keep the meeting and have an uninterrupted hour, or longer, to earn Dot Voline's trust. He'd take full advantage of it and make sure Nadine knew that she'd lost this particular round.

An arrow of misgiving shot through him at the thought that Nadine would miss this. He dropped his hands. There must be something wrong. Images of Nadine hurt or trapped filled his mind. The jaws of life. Sirens. Before he could panic or remind himself that she was probably only stuck in the permanent urban nightmare others would simply call traffic, a dirty car arrived.

It was Nadine.

"Don't you ever wash your car?" he asked as she got out, a strange relief making him skip over a normal greeting. She wore a pale blue dress that swirled around her tanned legs and held the bouquet of flowers they'd agreed would be an appropriate gesture. He'd transferred her half the cost, to the penny.

"Whatever, Dad."

The bouquet was pretty, with little white clusters he thought might be hyacinths. Rebecca had been on a big flower kick thanks to her blooming container garden. He should pitch a story on bringing unisex nosegays back in fashion. *Fresh flowers provide an elegant touch that never goes out of style and can be an olfactory lifesaver in a sweaty summer crowd.*

Nadine shifted the bouquet to her other hand to keep it away from him when he leaned in for a sniff. That was spiteful, but if she thought he wouldn't sink to her level, she was mistaken. He stepped closer to breathe in loudly and obnoxiously. The scent was so strong he had to shove down a sneeze.

"I thought you weren't going to make it," he said once he got himself under control.

"You wish."

"Is that the biggest bouquet you could get for fifty bucks?"

She barely glanced at him. "This is why I insisted on getting them. Bigger doesn't equal better. You'd probably get a bunch of carnations from the grocery store and call it a day."

"I like carnations."

"Right, but, Wes?" Her voice was deceptively sweet. "I know it can be hard for you to understand, but it's not about you, is it?"

"What's that supposed to mean?"

"I didn't buy the flowers for you. I bought them for Dot Voline, who was quoted in an interview as loving flowers with scent. Like these." She spoke slowly as she lifted the flowers to his face. "Not like your carnations, and not like the funeral flowers you brought last week."

It stung that he'd missed that interview. "There were roses in that arrangement. You're not a better journalist because you bought the right flowers."

"No," she agreed. "I'm the better journalist because I thought about my subject and did the research."

Wes clamped his jaws shut to stop himself from muttering like a child that she *wasn't* the better journalist. Nadine was in a mood. It didn't matter. They were here to talk to Dot Voline, not make nice with each other. They weren't friends, and there was no need to act friendly.

This time when they pressed the intercom, the gates opened inward. "Come up," barked Voline's voice. "Don't need all the neighbors knowing my business."

They got back in their cars, and he followed Nadine around the fountain and under the portico that protected the entrance, driving as slowly as if they were in a cortege.

Nadine got out of her car. "Damn, I forgot my battering ram at home," she said, looking up at the front door. It was at least twelve feet high and appeared to be made of solid wood. Golden bolts lined the edge and outlined a carved rose in the center panel.

"Figures," Wes said. "At least my catapult's in the trunk. Who's the better journalist now?"

"Still me, because first, catapults were for throwing things over walls and not breaking down doors, and second, you don't actually have one."

"Then it looks like we'll have to go with our plan B." Two gigantic brass pulleys took the place of doorknobs, and Nadine grabbed him when he reached out.

"What are you doing?" she asked.

"Knocking? How do you usually announce your august presence at someone's home?"

"I ring the doorbell."

Wes examined the ornate carvings surrounding the door, none of which resembled anything like a doorbell. "Be my guest."

Before Nadine could reply, the door swung open, much faster and without any of the creaking Wes expected.

"Took you long enough."

Wes recognized the voice.

Dot Voline at last.

Nadine's first thought at meeting the country's most lauded literary star was that pictures had not done her justice. Her hair remained the same orange as her decades-old publicity photo and was piled high in fluffy curls that may or may not have been real. Huge amethyst glasses perched on a long nose and wide ears that could easily take the weight of the thick frames. A gigantic jeweled cross hung around her neck and dangled off a purple, orange, and yellow caftan that looked like the tail end of a bad acid trip and swirled when she stood still. On the fingers gripping the handle of the portable oxygen tank glittered a Cartier display case's worth of gold and diamonds.

After she took in the marvel that was Dot Voline, Nadine's second thought was, *This woman is about to keel over.*

Wes must have thought the same thing, because he sprang forward with a chivalrous hand and more charm than Nadine would have expected. To her utter shock, Voline giggled. Like a schoolgirl. Nadine half expected her to thump him with a folded fan and say, *Oh, you.*

Instead, she said, "I'm not dead yet, handsome. Get out of my way."

Wes winked. He *winked.* Nadine nearly passed out. Wes Chen wore sweaters over button-ups. He was prim. Neat. Not a man who winked.

Voline looked amused. "You. Death girl."

"Nadine Barbault," she corrected.

"Death girl," said Voline with enough emphasis that Nadine knew it was her name from now on. Well, she'd been called worse. "Those for me?"

She hadn't realized she'd been clutching the bouquet to her chest. "Sorry, yes."

"You can put them in a vase when you come in," said Voline. "Presents that cause more work for the recipient aren't gifts. They're chores."

Nadine looked down at the bouquet, suddenly realizing that was the reason she hated getting flowers. The trimming, finding a vase, and arranging the stalks were all unwelcome work—and *that* was before the cycle of cleaning up dropped pollen and decayed petals. "I'd be happy to," she said.

"Then get in. You're letting in the flies."

Voline turned with difficulty, shuffling each foot with a deliberate motion to keep her balance. Nadine walked slowly to give her the dignity of moving at her own pace. Also, she was busy trying to take in the sight beyond her host.

"Shut the door, girl," called Voline.

"Sure, Ms. Voline."

"Christ on a cracker, that's for an old woman. Call me Dot."

"Dot," repeated Nadine politely.

"I'm right here, girl. No need to chant my name like a Benedictine monk."

Nadine made the mistake of catching Wes's eye behind Dot's curved back and gave him a rude gesture when he smirked.

Once properly through the door, it was easier to see the house's interior. Nadine had once gone to a French chateau and joined the crush of gawking tourists as they'd obediently filed through gilded rooms tiled with mirrors and painted with cherubs and gods and animals. Dot's house was the Vegas version via an English country hunting lodge.

"Lamps," muttered Wes. "I knew it."

"What?" Nadine asked.

"Nothing."

A taxidermy cheetah skulked near the wall, an ancient beaver top hat angled jauntily over a crooked blue eye. On the other side of the corridor stood a suit of armor with a conference lanyard around its neck and a large gold coin nestled in the plastic name tag slot. As she passed, Nadine saw the coin's face had a bearded man gazing off into the distance.

She was looking at a Nobel Prize.

"Do you think if we're good she'll let us touch it?" whispered Wes.

"No." Dot's voice traveled back and echoed off the marble floor. "That's not what you get to touch if you're good."

Wes made a noise that sounded like *meep* as Nadine snickered.

"Good lord, handsome, don't sound so scared. And girl, don't think of putting your paws on that gold. Sir Latimer guards it with his life."

The house had a surprisingly straightforward layout. The main doors led down a wide corridor with two halls branching to the right and left, leading to what Nadine assumed were more rooms. Cats wandered the halls, moving noiselessly along the marble floor. Nadine counted at least three.

At the very end, the hall opened to the left into a huge space filled with a dining table and couches and chairs so tufted and tasseled they were more decor than furniture. The ceiling was a calming mural of a surprisingly realistic sky, complete with wispy cirrus clouds and the silhouettes of birds wheeling near the crown molding. A wall of windows at the rear of the room opened into a conservatory, green with plants and dotted with the occasional bloom. Nadine hoped they were orchids. If it was filled with something prosaic like daffodils, she would be disappointed.

"Is that...a Group of Seven wall?" asked Wes. He sounded faint, which Nadine understood once she looked over. A Tom Thomson pine hung in the center, the dark shadowy tree a contrast against the ivory lines of the snowdrifts. Landscapes and images of isolated barns surrounded it in ornate frames that looked like they cost as much as the paintings.

"My husband collected them," said Dot, inching her way past a side table shaped like an hourglass and covered with Hummel figurines. "I took my favorites out of the art warehouse when he died."

Nadine slid her eyes over to Wes to check his reaction. His eyebrows were high enough to turn his forehead into a gigantic wrinkle, and she was relieved to have confirmation that a personal art warehouse was a legitimately wild thing to have in one's life. She felt like the two of them, despite their hostility, were a reluctant team in this strange new world.

"The kitchen is through that door," said Dot as she lowered herself to the settee. She pointed at Nadine. "Handsome here will keep me company while you put those in water and get the tea. Vases are in the butler's. Oh, hello, beautiful." A brown tabby had jumped up to the chair beside her. "This is Octavia. That's Murasaki near the door." She indicated a calico who sat with her tail wrapped primly around her front paws.

Nadine would have made a fuss about Dot asking the woman to do the domestic work, but she was the one holding the flowers, plus her desire to see more of the house outweighed any feminist complaints. As she pushed open the door, she heard Wes say, "You have quite the collection of Chippendale. Is that a cherry tilt-top table?"

Who knew Wes was a furniture nerd?

Nadine took two steps into the kitchen before she faltered, feeling as if she'd stepped through to another dimension. The space in front of her was bright and spare, an austerely functional marble and steel chef's dream that was the antithesis to the room she'd left.

A rattle came from around the corner. "Who're you?" It was a woman dressed in coveralls, with a spray bottle in one hand and a roll of paper towels in the other. She looked like she was in her late fifties, but if she'd said she was forty or sixty-five, Nadine would have believed it.

"Nadine Barbault. We're here to visit Dot Voline."

"Huh." The woman eyed her doubtfully. "Dot doesn't have friends visit."

"We're not really friends," confessed Nadine. "I'm a reporter."

She might have said, *I'm a serial killer,* for the reaction the woman gave. She practically growled as she shook her finger in Nadine's face. "One of the ones who said Dot was dead? Nearly killed her, you people did."

"I'm sorry."

She must have looked contrite, because the woman softened. "Well, I guess it wasn't your fault."

This was worse. "It kind of was. I was the obituary editor for the *Herald.*"

"Was?"

"They moved me to a new job."

"Should have fired you for incompetence," said the woman serenely. Nadine figured she deserved that, although it bit deeper than anything Daniel had said when reaming her out about the obit. "Well, if Dot says you can come in, I guess you can."

"Are you Dot's...?" Nadine trailed off, realizing she had no idea how to finish the sentence.

"*Housekeeper* will do. Maria Silva. Been here twenty years. What are you doing with them flowers?"

"Dot told me to put them in a vase from something called the butler's?"

"Butler's pantry. Over here." She passed by Nadine, trailing the smell of bleach.

If Nadine thought Maria would take the flowers to arrange herself, she was mistaken. She was led to a long, dark, narrow room before Maria took off, grumbling about Dot's new organizing kick and the never-ending dusting.

Nadine simply stood. Part of her knew she needed to get this task done so she could get to the real work of learning Dot Voline's story in this once-in-a-lifetime opportunity. She couldn't because she was immobilized by the rows of shelves filled with vases, platters, and bowls. A few were so huge they fell into the basin category. A small stepladder sat in the corner to reach the high items since the shelves extended to the ceiling. Why would anyone need so many? What was the point of this?

"Nadine?" She started at Wes's voice from the kitchen. "Are you here?"

She poked her head out to see Wes doing a slow circle to take in the space. "Hey."

"Are you spying?" he demanded. "That's against the rules."

"Like being alone with Dot?" she countered.

Beaten by her logic, he went on the offensive. "Dot wants to know what's taking so long."

She gestured wordlessly, and he came over.

"Oh. Having some decision paralysis over the vase?" he asked. "When in doubt, go blue."

"Is that like picking C on a multiple-choice test?" she asked. His arm pressed against hers, and she jumped away, then halted when her back brushed the shelf.

"Better watch it," said Wes.

"Don't tell me what to do," she said automatically. "Do you think *collecting* is a rich person word for hoarding? Like, is it hoarding when everything looks like it costs a million dollars?"

Wes pointed to the shelf behind her. "If that's the celadon-glazed vase I think it is, more like a quarter million."

She looked at him suspiciously. "You're lying. That's two hundred and forty-nine thousand, nine hundred and ninety dollars more than any flower vessel should cost."

"I have an idea. Why don't you break it and find out?"

Nadine wasn't sure if she believed him, but it was better to be safe than sorry. She held her breath and eased herself slowly away.

Wes reached past her to pluck a blue vase from the shelf. He smelled nice, she noticed. Clean but like linen spray, not vinegar. "Here," he said. "A plain old vase that won't bankrupt you when you smash it."

With his errand done, Nadine thought he would leave to go back out to Dot. Instead, he walked over to a tea tray on one of the tables and checked the water, waiting until she was done with the flowers. Wes groaned as he lifted the tray. "If I drop this, kill me. I'll never make enough money to replace it."

"What, that?" The serviceable, simple white ceramic looked like it came from IKEA.

"It's a Stoneman Aufort set from 1950. Trust me."

"Seriously?" She eyed it.

"I did a story on their collectability, and while I am happy to discuss the comparative value of midcentury tea sets, can we do it later? My arms are going to fall off."

"I don't want to know about Amfort tea sets," she snapped.

"It's Aufort, and I'm not surprised. You probably microwave water for tea and leave the bag in while you drink. Now can you *please open the door*?"

Chafing at what she knew was an insult although she couldn't identify why—hot water was hot water, and sometimes she liked a strong brew—Nadine took her revenge by sauntering over to the door as Wes grappled with the tray behind her.

"Damn these cats," he muttered as a dark shape crossed in front of his feet.

She looked through to see Dot on the settee, head bent sideways and forward. "Wes?" she whispered.

"What?" He came up beside her and followed her gaze. "Jesus. Oh no."

A snore erupted, and they sagged with relief.

He glanced over. "By the way, do you know CPR?"

"Yes."

He passed into the room. "Good to know."

There was a low table in front of Dot, and she woke when Wes put down the tray. "Cream and sugar?" he asked, holding the tongs over the cubes.

"Of course. I'm no animal." Dot took a wafer-thin shortbread cookie and ate it with satisfaction before handing the plate to Wes. "You need to eat up," she said. "Doesn't your girlfriend feed you?"

"Thank you." Wes took one. "I don't have a girlfriend."

"Big shock," muttered Nadine.

"Boyfriend?" Dot frowned. "You tell him for me that just because he's a man, it doesn't mean he can't look after you. That's their job if they love you."

"I'm not dating anyone, but I agree with your philosophy," said Wes casually, as if discussing his love life with famous authors was an everyday occurrence.

Maybe it was. Nadine looked at him closely, realizing that although she'd known him for years, she never really got to *know* Wes Chen. He passed the plate back to Dot, holding it at a comfortable height for her arm as she selected another cookie. Well, not that it mattered. They wouldn't be working together for more than a couple of weeks.

He deliberately didn't offer Nadine a cookie but put the plate down and angled his chair to face Dot in a rookie power move designed to crowd Nadine out of the conversation. When she dragged her seat forward, he shifted his shoulders to block her. Nadine kept her expression neutral as she moved to a new chair closer to Dot. Take that.

Two weeks was more than enough time to spend with Wes.

# TEN

Wes ate through the plate of biscuits—they were too fancy to be mere cookies—with Dot's encouragement as they chatted about world politics and how Dot hated the baying dogs of the neighbor next door, who, Wes learned, was a manufacturing billionaire who drove around in an electric Hummer. She seemed in good spirits, occasionally adjusting the transparent oxygen tube under her nose as though it was second nature.

Dot was easy to talk to, and Wes wasn't surprised she was well-versed in topics from the Romantic poets to the latest municipal controversy. He didn't mind when she continued to call him handsome, especially when he saw how it exasperated Nadine. Dot didn't make him feel dirty or used or like a toy. It was more like the teasing of a socially awkward but affectionate great-aunt.

Finally, Nadine gave him an impatient look that was easy to interpret as *let's get this show on the road.* It was time to broach the subject they were there for with the predetermined question he and Nadine had agreed on. He'd won the digital coin toss to decide who would get to ask, although Nadine had insisted on taking it to best of three, then five when she kept losing.

"Ah," Dot said as two more cats chased in. "You're in luck. Erma doesn't often like visitors. She's the black cat. Sidonie-Gabrielle is the tuxedo. She rarely comes out as well."

"Hello, Erma, Sidonie-Gabrielle," said Nadine, bending down and putting out her hand, which the cats ignored.

Wes shuddered. Cats. His mother refused to have any pets in the house, and he was not an animal person.

"Dot," he said, ignoring the rampaging cats and getting to business. "Thank you for allowing us into your home. We're grateful for your time."

"I want to apologize again for running your obituary," added Nadine. "I take full responsibility, and I know how distressing it must have been."

"A horrible experience for anyone," said Wes. Seeing Nadine's lips tighten, he added, "Truly and unimaginably awful."

She glared at him before turning back to Dot. "As I said, I'm very sorry."

Dot checked the diamond and platinum watch that dug tightly into her freckled wrist. "Time's up," she said. "See you next week."

Wes, who was on the verge of transitioning the conversation to ask Dot about her past, paused. "What?"

"You had one hour."

Nadine scowled at the pretty bouquet she'd arranged in the blue vase as though calculating each second she'd spent fluffing out petals.

"Yes, but we spent it talking about waterfront development projects," he pointed out.

"Not my problem." Dot clapped her hands, since her voice caught at the end with her breath.

"But—" said Wes.

"Maria!"

Wes had to admit they were beat, but his annoyance evaporated after another look at Dot. Her eyes were closing, making it obvious the meeting had been physically taxing. It was their own fault for not optimizing their time.

"Thank you for seeing us," said Nadine politely. "We'll be back next week."

A woman materialized near the door, hair pulled back in a bun so slick it would make a synchronized swimmer proud. "I found the postage stamps in a kitchen drawer with the twine," she said.

"Leave them," said Dot. "I put them there so I'd remember where they were."

The woman shook her head. "Like a squirrel, you are."

"So don't touch the nuts. Can you show our visitors out?"

Nadine smiled. "Hi, Maria."

"How did you meet her?" muttered Wes. Who was she? This was unfair. He should have known Nadine would manage to gain an advantage in the four minutes they'd been apart.

Nadine gave him that Cheshire cat smile as Maria waved for them to follow her through the main hall. Wes tried to peek down the corridor that branched off to the right. All he could make out was what seemed like a row of cabinets lining the wall.

Then they were past Sir Latimer and the cheetah and back outside.

"So," said Nadine when the door closed behind them. "That's Dot Voline."

"Not what you expected?" asked Wes, curious about her perspective.

"I'm not sure," she said. "As she was talking, I could almost hear some of her characters?"

"Aunt Sara from *The Day After the Day Before*?"

"That's the one!" said Nadine, giving Wes a faint satisfaction they were on the same page.

"I said time was up!" Dot's voice seemed to come from the heavens, causing them to jump.

"Does she have those intercoms everywhere?" Nadine squinted as she searched the ceiling.

"I wouldn't be surprised if that George III card table had a false top that hid the house's mission control," said Wes.

"How do you know all that design stuff?" Nadine pulled on her car door, which, unlike his, opened smoothly.

There it was, the not unexpected dig at his job. "The *Spear* has an award-winning arts and design section under Lifestyle," he said. "I don't spend all my days writing about picnics."

"I never said you did."

"Well, if you had spent less time checking over her vases like you were casing the joint, we might have been able to get somewhere."

"If *you* had finished with the small talk while I was getting the vase, we could have started right away."

Nadine slammed the door after what she obviously viewed as a killing blow. He watched her drive away, filled with retorts that he wanted to yell down the driveway. Then the door to Dot's house opened to reveal Maria. Wes got the hint and dragged his car door open.

Let Nadine try next time if she thought she could do it better.

———

"We need to skip the tea," said Nadine, kicking at the ground and swearing as pebbles lodged in her shoe. They were outside Dot's gate after their second meeting, which hadn't gone any better than the first. Dot Voline was a stubborn woman who wouldn't talk until she wanted to. This was especially annoying, as she had been the one to summon them.

At least she was with Wes. Despite his many faults and how much she hated to say it, he was a dream interviewer. Nadine wasn't too proud to admit that Dot responded better to Wes. She still called him handsome, but something had shifted when Wes had noticed a small miniature dagger tucked in a cabinet of curiosities beside a brain coral.

After asking if it was a Yoshi Morimoto, they'd embarked on a discussion of this Morimoto guy's philosophy of miniaturization, which Wes had skillfully related to some of the themes in *Lamplight*, her first short story collection. Dot had allowed Wes to pour her a second cup.

When Dot finished the tea and called it an hour, she'd been smiling and had told them to take off kindly instead of hollering it. Wes had been the one to make the connection that would hopefully get Dot talking, a fact he had pointed out to her before getting in his car and shutting the door in her face with what seemed liked extra smugness, if a door could be shut smugly. Nadine had refused to give him the satisfaction of addressing his comment when they'd met up outside the house to debrief a minute later. Dot didn't like them lingering on her property, so they were standing on the edge of the street.

"The tea is necessary," said Wes. It took Nadine a minute to remember why he was talking about tea, because although she'd mentally taken a journey to trust and relationships, she'd left Wes thinking about their approach. "She's deflecting us."

"I'd noticed," said Nadine, miffed that he thought her so oblivious. "That has nothing to do with tea."

Wes faced her, and she was surprised to see that in the sun, his eyes remained so dark they were almost black. It was strange how she'd been noticing more things about Wes lately. Knowing each other for years meant she had a mental template of Wes in her head she hadn't bothered to update since J school. Perhaps it was time to do an edit.

"It's comforting for her. Brent said there was a promise to keep." He reached into his pocket and pulled out two of the strawberry candies Dot always had in a small crystal dish. She took the one he offered and unwrapped it.

"If she was eager to tell the story, she wouldn't be doing this because of a promise," she said slowly. "She'd tell us straight out or would have told it before. She's worried."

"I think so, yeah. We need to figure out why."

Building up protective walls was familiar to Nadine. She bit into the candy as she thought and saw Wes make a face.

"What?" she asked.

"Those are hard candies. Not for chewing."

"Are you gatekeeping candies?" she asked in astonishment.

"It's not gatekeeping. It's a matter of principle. Gummies are for chewing. Hard candies are not."

She looked him straight in the face and crunched again.

"Fine," he said. "But don't come to me when you want more."

"No worries." She pulled one of the candies she'd snuck from the dish herself out of her pocket and popped it in her mouth. "To get back to our discussion, Dot could be delaying for two reasons. One is whatever that scandal is. She doesn't want to drag it up because it's difficult to talk about. That hints at something personal."

"Or she feels vulnerable about the truth," Wes said.

Nadine thought. "There's more."

They paused as a black car drove by them, slowing threateningly as it passed. "Private security?" asked Wes.

"Screw them. This is public space."

Wes grinned. "Tell me your Dot Voline theory."

"It's a bit of a game for her." The idea had come to Nadine gradually over this last visit, when she'd been examining the room as Dot sparred with Wes.

"What makes you think so?" For once, his tone was curious rather than combative, so Nadine answered in kind.

"You know that table shaped like a pineapple? Last week, it had a music box with a silver tree. This week, it was a copy of *Thirty Pieces of Silver*."

"Your big revelation is that an author had one of her own books on display?"

Nadine kept her temper for the sake of making her point. "Have you seen any of her other books out?"

"Dot might have wanted to change up her decor."

"No." Nadine was confident. "Nothing else in the room had changed. Also, she said she regretted not writing a mystery." This had come out after Nadine had seen a beautifully bound Agatha Christie.

She waited for Wes to debate her more, but he looked thoughtful. "You're probably wrong, but let's see if it happens again next week," he said. "It could be we're both right. She's scared and she's also having some fun."

"The second seems like her," Nadine said.

The black car with the shaded windows came by again, slowing down to almost a crawl as it passed. By common but unspoken agreement, both Nadine and Wes stared at it, briefly united against a common enemy. Would they have the nerve to try to tell them to leave? Nope, it looked like silent intimidation was their plan.

"We're done talking, but I don't want to give them the satisfaction of thinking they ran us off," said Wes.

Nadine waved her phone. "I have something to read and nowhere to be for the next ten minutes."

"That's some petty stuff, Barbault." Wes looked through the open window of his car, then leaned over to grab a book from the seat. She did her best to not check out his ass, but it was right there in front of her, looking surprisingly juicy for such a lean guy. Wes stood back up, and she made sure to be looking at something innocent. "Exactly what I expect of you."

It didn't sound like an insult, Nadine thought as she began scrolling. He sounded almost fond. She probably misread him.

"By the way," he said, looking up from his book with an earnest expression. "Do you think a person's inability to avoid chewing candies is related to increased levels of overall impulsivity and lack of patience? Asking for a friend, purely as a hypothetical."

Yes. She had definitely misread him.

# ELEVEN

f Wes had to give a lecture on the differences between the rich and the poor, at least one of his slides would feature transportation. When you were rich, it didn't matter where you lived because you could drive wherever you wanted. No car? Pay other people to drive you around. You had the luxury of not caring about good transit to your house because you never needed it. And if you didn't need it, why would anyone else?

He was thinking these deep thoughts as he stared out the dirt-streaked bus window at a woman walking multiple Chihuahuas and a single Great Dane, their leashes tied around her waist like a maypole. He was late to meet Nadine after his car gave a pathetic little shudder and died when he turned the key, forcing him to run for the first of three buses.

When he arrived at Dot's gate, hot and sweaty from jogging the six blocks from the final stop, it was to find Nadine waiting for him. She looked as cool as always, with her dark hair falling straight to her shoulders, streaked red in the sun, and a white linen blouse with a black linen skirt. Her outfit was flowing and unstructured, but the sunlight highlighted the outline of her body through the fabric. His throat suddenly went dry. Must be from dehydration.

"I was about to text you." She looked him over. "Did you run here?"

"Yeah, I'm becoming an ultramarathoner, and this is part of my new training regime." He passed a hand over his face and tried to breathe without panting. He hated feeling disheveled. That only worked for guys like Tyler, who turned coffee stains and rumpled shirts into badges of honor that demonstrated how hard they were working. Wes, on the other hand, felt the eyes of judgment linger over every shirt wrinkle.

"In those clothes?" She motioned to his pants, which had lost their creases.

"They've got a new category for people who hate spandex."

"I knew a guy who did one," Nadine said thoughtfully. "He trained for a year straight and broke his ankle on the last kilometer. He crawled the rest of the way so he could finish."

Wes adjusted his bag. "Dedicated."

"His knees were bloody." Nadine looked at his knees as if wondering if they were strong enough to crawl through a thousand meters of forest or desert or whatever.

"Sounds interesting," Wes finally offered. "Should we go see Dot?"

"Right. Get in." Nadine pointed to the car.

He didn't protest, although the drive from the gate to the door was only about fifteen seconds. She trained the air-con on his side, then handed him a pack of tissues, all without saying a word. He patted his face and let the cold air blow directly on his sweaty skin. It felt a bit clammy but good.

"You waited for me," he said as she pulled under the portico. The *why* was implied.

Nadine put the car in park. "Wasn't sure Dot would let me in without you."

He checked her expression, but it was unreadable. Was she teasing him, or did she mean it? He supposed it didn't matter. They were only there to get the story.

This time, Maria greeted them, saying Dot was in the library. Wes looked over to see his own eagerness reflected on Nadine's face. They hadn't been in any other rooms beyond the salon, the kitchen, and the powder room, which was a violent shade of mauve and painted with lilacs. The toilet seat was oak and the bowl lavender porcelain. He hadn't known they came in colors besides white. He wished he could have talked about it with Nadine but ran into difficulties figuring out how to open a conversation on water closets.

Nadine gave Sir Latimer a little wave, which somehow came off as naturally cute rather than painfully twee, and they passed through the main room. At the far side, Maria pushed open the double doors like she was about to present this year's debutantes to the queen and left.

Wes didn't blame Nadine for stumbling because the room was a dream. Unlike the color wars battling it out in the other parts of the house, this was all brown and olive and tan, soothing nature tones complemented by wood and leather furniture. The muted glow of polished brass gleamed on the cabinets. The space was two stories high, and books lined the walls. A wrought iron staircase led to a wide landing that circled the room, and a small electric lift had been installed on the other side.

He itched to sit in the reading nook on the upstairs landing, with its club chairs and those ever-present lamps, including one of a bronze owl holding a lantern in its beak. "That corner calls for brandy and a book," he muttered to Nadine.

"It would have to be a leather-backed classic," she said. "This room would incinerate a mass-market paperback."

Dot sat in the conversation area in the center, ready to hold court. Behind her was a large table with green-shaded lamps and an onyx chessboard. Against the far wall was a small dilapidated desk with an ergonomic chair and a typewriter. A sleek laptop was pushed to the side.

"That's where she worked," whispered Nadine with an awe he'd never heard from her. "She brought it from Manitoba and never wrote at any other desk." Octavia lay near the laptop, her striped tummy glowing as she absorbed the sun.

Tea was set up, and Dot waved them over. "Lemon squares today," she said. "Maria felt extravagant. Handsome, you look overheated." She put aside the newspaper she was reading, folded open to the obituaries, one already cut out.

"Do you often cut things out of the paper?" he asked. It seemed like an old-fashioned thing to do but very Dot.

"I do." She tapped the clipping with her finger, the nail painted a rich pumpkin orange, then handed it to Nadine. "There are all sorts of interesting things in a newspaper."

"'Mary Linquist died at the age of eighty-two, leaving behind two daughters, five grandchildren, and a garage filled with useless inventions,'" Nadine read. "'Her plan to make chocolate chips with her Chip-o-Tronic 2000 will live in family history thanks to the resultant kitchen fire.'"

Dot laughed, then adjusted her oxygen. "Sounds like a real character, doesn't she? You can keep that."

Wes made the tea as usual, letting Nadine dangle a breaking news item as a way to get Dot talking. Because Dot was Dot, it didn't take long for her to skip from the delays on the construction of a new subway line to talking about fascism, then the ability of music to foment social change.

"Leonard Cohen's 'The Partisan' was anti-fascist," said Wes as he gave Nadine her cup. "He wrote it about the French Resistance."

Dot turned to him, chin up and hand stroking Erma's back. "He what?"

"Wrote it about the French Resistance?" Wes had a sudden feeling of doubt. "Didn't he?"

"He didn't write it," said Nadine. "Anna Marly composed and

performed it first. Cohen's cover is simply more popular, so people assume the song is his."

Wes prickled at Nadine showing him up, but it soon settled to curiosity. "How do you know this?" he asked.

"I read her obituary," said Nadine, turning to Dot. "Did I get that right?"

Dot nodded her head. "Like so many women, she had her accomplishments attributed to a man. Nothing against Leonard. A lovely fellow." She pointed to a small ink sketch on the wall. "He gave me that."

"It's common in your books," said Nadine, leaning forward. "I was reading *A Glass and a Half* last night. Eliza's journal was stolen by her husband and turned into books under his own name."

"I based it on Zelda and F. Scott Fitzgerald," Dot said.

Wes blinked at this accidental literary revelation. It had long been suspected by critics, but like so much in her life, Dot had refused to confirm it.

"I thought there was a bit of Colette and Monsieur Willy as well." Nadine spoke casually, but he saw her hand twitch, almost as if she wanted to reach out and grab the answers that were so close.

Wes waited for his chance to join in before he realized Nadine had it under control. Also, he knew nada about Colette and Monsieur Willy. It was better for him to listen.

"At least we now acknowledge Monsieur Willy forced her to write the Claudine novels to publish under his own name. Zelda has still to get her full justice."

"Like Eliza, who never got hers."

"That's right." Dot leaned back and closed her eyes while Wes cast Nadine a look to encourage her to keep going. He knew better than to interrupt. Nadine was finally getting them somewhere, and at the moment, it was more important to hear Dot than to give in to the urge to outdo Nadine.

The opportunity to do that would come up soon enough anyway.

# TWELVE

*lease don't let me screw this up.* She could feel Wes's exhilaration but knew he would respect her taking the lead. Wes could be good like that, not letting his ego interfere with something he wanted. If the way to get Dot talking was to let Nadine do it, he would.

He probably thought he could do it better though.

Dot was dressed more sedately than usual, in a deep copper pantsuit with a cape that wrapped around her shoulders. She wore no necklaces, but a series of ebony bangles climbed up her wrists until they wedged into the flesh of her arm. Her weathered face was serious, and Nadine hoped this was a sign she was ready to stop messing with them.

"Was that something you saw in your own life as well?" Nadine asked to move the conversation in the direction she needed.

Dot adjusted her rings. "What do you think?"

"It would be impossible to avoid," said Nadine. "I once did a school project with a guy who took my name off and handed it in as his own. He said the ideas were his so it was his project. Forget that he did none of the work."

Wes twitched beside her, but both of them knew she wasn't referring to him.

Dot's expression didn't change. "What happened?"

"I complained to the professor, and he said idea guy deserved the benefit of the doubt. The prof gave me the same mark and considered it fixed."

"It often happened when I was a teacher." Dot sat forward and nudged the plate of squares toward Nadine. "Boys were encouraged to ignore boundaries to get what they wanted. Not only those of the girls, although they got the brunt of it. It was easy to see the men some of them would become. Selfish people who became vicious when they met resistance. They lacked empathy because they never had to see from another person's point of view. The world catered to them from when they were children. The more money and respect the family had, the worse it was."

"Is that what made you start writing?"

"I started writing out of boredom." Dot smiled, her big teeth unnaturally white and shiny. "However, I continued writing out of spite."

Nadine sat up, as did Wes. "Spite?"

"Some might call it revenge." Dot yawned. "Enough for today."

Although Nadine wanted to scream into the smooth leather of the couch arm, she didn't bother to argue, knowing when she was beat. Seeing that Dot was waiting for her to beg for more, she also wanted to give her back a little of her own medicine.

So instead of protesting, she nodded solicitously. "We've stayed past our hour. Get some rest, and we'll see you next week."

Dot frowned as Octavia jumped on her lap, displacing Erma. This wasn't how Nadine was supposed to react, but she'd boxed herself in.

Nadine hid her smile. It was rare to get the edge on Dot. If they played this right, they might get the full story out of her today. Chills went over her body at how close they were. At this point, she didn't care if it was an exclusive. She wanted the mystery solved for her own peace of mind. What was Dot hiding? She had to know but had a feeling that to flat out ask would mean losing her chance completely.

"You didn't finish the squares Maria made," Dot griped. "She'll be disappointed."

Nadine cast Wes a glance, hoping he would get the hint that it was his turn to step up. He looked back as if understanding the situation called for the good cop. Dot had given them the hint that she wanted to be convinced into telling them what happened, the same way she'd let them know they should keep coming to the gate while telling them to take a hike. She was ready.

He opened his mouth. This was their big moment. All Wes had to do was say something like, *I know you're tired, but could we finish these delicious squares?* Some suck-up phrase—he'd excel at that—so Dot could feel good about letting them stay, and Nadine could continue this conversation. She could follow up on that most tantalizing of comments.

"Some might call it revenge."

Revenge on who? *Who?* All she needed was a name. A date. Any fact she could trace like a hound with a scent.

Then Wes said, "See you soon!" and stood up.

Nadine looked at him in disbelief. She almost wanted to see if Dot had the same moment of, *You jackass, do you not know how to play this game?* The back-and-forth, like two people fighting over the bill?

But Wes was smiling at them as he adjusted his sweater. Who wore sweaters in the summer? What was wrong with the man?

"Thank you, handsome." Dot's voice was gleefully malicious, as if she knew what Nadine had been aiming for and was gratified to have witnessed this own goal.

Nadine stared hard at Wes but made sure her smile was pleasant when she turned to Dot. "You know," she said, trying to salvage the situation. "I would hate for Maria to think we didn't enjoy her squares. Perhaps we could stay and finish them?"

"Oh no, I couldn't have that, not when your colleague is so eager to leave." Dot's eyes glinted with joy behind her glasses. "I'll ask Maria to pack you some to go."

Nadine could have cried in rage. They were so close, but Dot was struggling to her feet and calling for Maria. She made one more attempt. "Can I ask you about—"

"Of course." Dot didn't turn around. "Next Sunday."

Dammit. Wes held out his arm to escort Dot from the room, and Nadine stood to follow. On the way, she caught sight of *Thirty Pieces of Silver*, this time propped up with a newspaper clipping poking out from its pages. She reached out to see what it was marking.

"Come along, girl." Dot's voice drifted over.

Nadine snatched back her hand. She'd get to the bottom of this next week. *Great job, Wes.* That was what she got for counting on him.

---

*There is always next week,* Wes thought as Maria handed him two containers of lemon squares. It wasn't Nadine's fault she'd been blocked by Dot, a woman who had achieved grand master status in mind games.

Then again, Nadine seemed more pissed than was warranted. She'd gotten some good traction, and he thought she'd be pleased about that.

Once the front door closed behind them, he turned to Nadine. "You shouldn't feel too bad about blowing it," he said generously. "You were getting there."

"You absolute..." She sputtered as if trying to think of a term before settling on "Walnut!"

"What, me?" He was astounded.

"What were you thinking?" She groaned. "You were supposed to step in and play peacemaker!"

"Peacemaker? How was I supposed to know that?"

"I don't know, context clues? Reading the room?"

"I did read the room," said Wes, peeved. "She said it was time to go. Why did you think this time to go was different from other times to go?"

"She was only pretending. This is the *game*." Nadine blew out her breath. "She wants to make us work for it. We could have gotten the answers we need, but thanks to you, we have to wait another week."

"You don't know that." He pinched the bridge of his nose to keep the frustration from spilling out of his brain. "What we do know is that she told us to leave. I'm not going to pressure her."

"I can't believe you."

They weren't shouting, conscious of the intercom, but they were whispering loudly and emphatically.

Wes took a breath. "Look, Nadine. Dot is an old and sick woman who said she was tired and wanted us to leave. You were paying attention to the wrong things."

"Oh, for... You have the social awareness of Sir Latimer." Nadine squeezed her eyes shut as if feeling physical pain. "Whatever."

She got in the car and slammed the door as Wes stepped back. He'd been hoping to get a ride to a subway stop, but the way Nadine gunned it out of the circular driveway said he was on his own. He tucked down the disappointment.

Worse was that Nadine's reaction called out a concern he'd had over the years that had resurfaced after the conversation with Jason. He had never been like Tyler, who pressed and pushed until he got the answer he wanted. Wes was confident in his work but disliked riding roughshod over people. He never saw the need for Tyler's chest-thumping performances. The loudest voice wasn't always correct.

He crossed the driveway with the two boxes of lemon squares, since Nadine had taken off before he could hand hers over. He lifted the lid and ate one as he squinted at the sky. The afternoon sun had disappeared behind a low layer of cloud, and the wind was picking up. He hoped he could get home before the rain.

To his surprise, Nadine's dusty car sat outside Dot's gate, and the passenger side window rolled down when he came out.

"Wes."

Part of him wanted to keep walking. If they didn't have to work together, he might. He stopped. "What?"

"Uh, do you want a ride?" she asked, looking past him.

The first fat drop of rain landed on his nose. He wasn't a martyr, and they should talk. "Fine."

She unlocked the door, and he got in, putting the box with fewer squares in the back for her.

"Where do you live?" she asked.

"West End. Dovercourt and Dupont." He glanced out the window. "If you want to drop me off at a subway station, that would be convenient."

"I'm at Ossington and Dupont, so I can take you home."

He looked over. "I didn't realize we were so close."

"I moved in a few years ago," she said, changing lanes to turn on Lawrence Avenue.

"Oh."

"Yeah."

Then Wes gave up on what was, by any measure, a pathetic conversation and returned to brooding about what happened. He was certain he had read the situation with Dot correctly. The silence in the car seemed extra heavy, and it took Wes a moment to realize it was because Nadine didn't have music playing, like an absolute weirdo.

Nadine changed lanes with more aggression than required for a ten percent twist of the wheel, then sighed. "Look, I don't like working together any more than you do, but you can't deliberately try to hamstring me."

"I know you want to think the worst of me, but she wanted us to go."

"No. We were in a delicate dance of wits, and you bungled it."

Wes wanted to tell her she was wrong and leave it at that, but she was correct about one thing. They had to work together, which meant they had to communicate and not only so she could see that he was right. This felt like one of those conversations where it was important to at least try to understand each other's perspective. He would keep his mind open to her almost certainly wrong viewpoint. "You think Dot wanted to be forced into talking?"

She frowned. "You're trying to make it sound bad."

"Sorry, what euphemism would you find acceptable? Urged to communicate? Provided an opportunity for verbal collaboration?"

She jammed on the brakes harder than necessary at the red light. "Fine. I do think that. She said to go, and I said okay. Then she started talking about how we didn't finish the squares, the same way she complained about us not bringing food to her gate."

When Nadine put it like that, her (mis)reading of what happened made a little more sense. After all, it was how they got an interview with Dot in the first place. "I didn't see it the same way," he said. "When we were at her gate, she could have stopped answering. This time, we were in her space, and I saw an old woman who was a little scared of what she'd said and needed to come to grips with it. She's on the verge."

There was a long pause as Nadine negotiated traffic. "Why do you say she was scared?"

He thought about Dot. "She jerked a little after she said the revenge thing, and her eyes darted to the side. Then she pressed her lips, almost like she was biting the words back, you know?"

Nadine tapped the wheel. "We're interpreting the situation in very different ways. All those things you noticed could have meant nothing."

"Except she also told us to leave. I'm not going to force her into talking if she doesn't want to. It's her story."

Nadine's mouth was set in a line. "A story she offered us."

He looked over. "She can change her mind if she wants."

Silence. They passed the big storage warehouse on Dupont. "I'm getting near your place," she said. "Tell me where to go."

He provided the directions to his house. When she pulled up, he opened his mouth to suggest they finish the discussion, but she was steadily looking out the windshield, hands at ten and two on the wheel.

He got the hint and got out. Nadine didn't look his way as he closed the door, leaving him feeling empty.

It didn't matter. Good riddance. He looked at the box in his hand. At least he'd kept the one with more lemon squares. Those things were delicious.

---

The next few days weren't great for Wes. Work had slowed with the summer heat, and Rebecca had insisted on planning out content for the fall. Looking at photos of the autumn trends—the usual corduroy and plaid, although he'd made a pitch to feature a collection of socks made of spun oatmeal—made him feel prickly despite the *Spear's* overly air-conditioned offices. At home, his mother had been upset because Ella wasn't back from Vancouver, despite Wes reminding her Ella had never set a return date.

Yet it was the fight with Nadine that weighed heaviest. He struggled against the need to reach out and smooth things over but knew he would inevitably be the first to break. It was what he'd always done in his relationships, the same way he'd agree instead of speaking up on everything from where to go for a weekend to what to have for dinner, feeding his intense need to simply make sure things went well no matter what.

Which was why he was surprised when his phone beeped with a message from Nadine on Wednesday. **You were wrong but do you need a ride to Dot's this week?**

Wes laughed out loud, feeling immediately lighter. That was what he would expect from Nadine, and he was glad not to have to talk about this misunderstanding ad nauseam. **You were wrong and I do need a ride**, he wrote back. **Thanks.**

Sometimes two people saw things in different ways, and that was it. It was good enough to agree to move on.

Even if one of them was totally wrong.

# THIRTEEN

adine pulled up at Wes's house a few minutes early and tried to decide the best way to deal with him. They hadn't texted after their semi-apology exchange on Wednesday, which was fine by Nadine. She was satisfied with how they'd gotten over their spat. It wasn't like they were friends, despite their long history, and they didn't need to have heart-to-heart discussions when they disagreed. The best way to move forward was as if they were work acquaintances from different departments. That was the energy she'd go for. In the spirit of good working relationships, she would even refrain from mentioning that she knew he ate one of the lemon squares from her box.

Pulling out her phone to tell him she'd had to park half a block away, she saw a text from Lisanne. **I heard something.**

Gossip was always a good bonding mechanism, particularly helpful since Nadine knew she hadn't been the best friend to Lisanne after the news about her big story. At least Lisanne had been too busy to notice. **Tell me**, she wrote, grateful text made it possible to camouflage emotional nuance.

The response came fast. **The Herald is hiring a Bay Area correspondent. It's for a year.**

Nadine read the message twice and felt her heart sink to her knees
then jump to clog her throat. It was an unnerving sensation. **Really?** She
wrote. That was neutral.

**You'd be perfect for it. Think of all those times you talked about want-
ing a foreign corro position.**

**They've been hinting at this for two years,** Nadine typed, which was
true. **I'll believe it when I see it.**

She could worry about applying when it happened. She wasn't going
to have to push herself yet.

**True,** replied Lisanne. **I can put in a good word to Daniel if you want.**

Nadine glared at the screen. She might not be the editor in chief's
golden child, but she didn't need Lisanne's help to get ahead.

**I'm good, thanks.** That should put an end to that.

She saw Wes looking around, dressed in a natty polo instead of his
usual sweater, a rare admission of sartorial defeat under the intense
onslaught of the July sun. She gave a little beep of the horn, and he
turned like a model about to board his yacht.

"Thanks for picking me up," he said when he opened the door.

"No problem."

He got in, and her eyes snapped to the deep line of his triceps as he
reached for the seat belt. She hadn't known Wes worked out, but she
appreciated the results. In a work acquaintance kind of way.

"Here." He handed over a small paper bag.

She looked inside. "A brownie?"

"I ate one of your squares from Maria accidentally."

"Accidentally?"

"Accidentally on purpose," he admitted. "Then I felt a bit bad
because they were pretty delicious."

The brownie looked amazing, with sea salt on the top. "Is this a
bribe?"

"For what?"

"I don't know. You tell me."

"Just eat the brownie, Nadine."

She did. It was good.

Neither of them mentioned their earlier texts, and she could tell he was making an effort to be collegial, the same as she was. They kept the conversation to the news and benign media chatter in a surprisingly companionable way as they zipped through the light traffic. It helped get her mind off Lisanne's text.

At Dot's, they found Maria at the door, ready to walk them in. "The conservatory today," she said with a faint air of displeasure. "She got it into her head to do some gardening."

Nadine gave her habitual wave to Sir Latimer as Wes nodded to the cheetah, which Dot had named Janice. The secret outline of a cat, maybe the elusive Sidonie-Gabrielle, disappeared down a hall as they passed, uninterested in the visitors.

The conservatory was two steps down from the salon, and the doors opened with a whoosh when Maria pressed against them, letting out a humid breath.

"Tea will be out here when you're done," said Maria. "I don't go in there. It ruins my hair."

Nadine touched her own head, a lost cause as the heat had already given her a thin layer of frizzies.

"This could be my favorite room," Wes said in astonishment.

"Better than the library?"

"Even the library. I've never seen anything like this."

Neither had Nadine. The conservatory was all glass, but the windows were thinly scummed with a brownish fuzz that gave the space a hushed feel. A koi pond contained orange fish swimming lazily around rocks and half-sunken statuary, and the surrounding paths wound through lush tropical plants.

"I didn't take you for a plant guy," she said.

"Yeah, I know my way around a bromeliad."

"Do you?"

"No."

"You're late." Dot appeared from around the curved corner of a path, dressed in a pale gold caftan and dragging her oxygen tank. Her bronze sandals slapped against the soles of her feet, and her jewelry was all silver. She looked like a slightly tarnished Academy Award.

Nadine didn't protest this lie. "This is incredible," she said.

"I would live here," Wes agreed.

Dot snapped a pair of small scissors at him, red-lipsticked mouth opening wide as she laughed. "The wages of sin."

She motioned for them to follow her deeper into the conservatory. Huge palms brushed Nadine's bare arms, making her shiver, and soon they arrived at a potting station. Dot pointed to a gigantic canvas apron. "Keep that dress clean, girl."

Nadine pulled it on, struggling to do the ties at the back.

"Good Lord, this is painful to watch," said Dot. "Handsome, give her a hand."

"I'm fine." Nadine dropped the sash again, and Wes sighed.

"Please let me help. Otherwise, this will take all day."

He stood behind her, hands tracing along her waist as he reached for the ends of the sash. Defeated, Nadine lifted her arms slightly to give him more space as he pulled the sash tight around her body. It didn't take him long to tie the bow, but she felt each tug of the fabric as if it was Wes's hands touching her. It wasn't until he was done that Nadine realized she was breathing harder than usual. This was different. This was unexpected. She quickly stepped away to adjust a fern.

Dot's thinly curved, penciled eyebrows raised high, but she only said, "Time to work."

She directed them with short commands. Wes picked up the potting soil and a bag of pebbles, and Nadine washed and sanitized some simple terra-cotta pots. They looked like the same ones she bought at the garden center every May but were probably of some fancy clay that cost several hundred dollars.

"Nadine," said Dot, wheezing slightly. Was this humidity good for her? Nadine didn't want to presume she knew the woman's health better than she did, but Dot didn't look well. Wes dragged over a wooden stool carved with butterflies, and Dot used his arm to lower herself down.

"Yes?" Nadine asked when Dot was seated. Wes dabbed at his face. She wasn't surprised that apart from a bit of glowy perspiration, he was as tidy as when they arrived. Her dress, on the other hand, was damp with sweat and her arms dusted with soil.

"Did you read the rest of that obituary I gave you? Mary Linquist?" Dot must have read in her face that she hadn't, because she brandished an old newspaper from a pile on the potting table. "Do you read obituaries at all?"

Nadine ran her fingers through the damp, warm soil. "Not since they changed my job."

"Why not?"

She glanced at Wes, unsure if she was comfortable speaking freely in front of him, then decided she'd have to risk it. If she wanted Dot to be vulnerable and share her story, she would have to share herself. "They're obituaries. They're depressing, and it upsets me to read about people who are gone forever."

"You were the obituary editor," observed Dot.

"I did the crime beat for a while, and I didn't like that either. I don't have to like something to understand it plays an important role in the paper and for people." Nadine tried not to feel defensive, but it was hard when Dot was looking at her with what felt like disappointment. "I did my best to make sure we covered the impact of significant people."

"Yet mine was dull as dishwater."

"The *Herald* has a..." Nadine struggled for a better word before admitting what it was. "A formula for their obits. It doesn't leave a lot of room for creativity."

"I see." Dot reached down the front of her caftan and pulled out a newspaper clipping. Wes's face was a study in a man doing his best to keep his eyes up.

Nadine grinned at her. "That's quite the filing system."

"You don't know the half of it." Dot unfolded the sheet. "Obituaries are life-affirming."

"They are?" Wes sounded interested and not dismissive, and Nadine relaxed. It was a relief not to have to be on her guard against him, at least as tightly. It made having this conversation with Dot, which seemed to be centered on Nadine's flaws, easier. She wished she could leave this topic to segue into what Dot said last week about writing for revenge, but it looked like she'd have to be patient.

Dot ran her pen along the newsprint to underline it. "This woman ran a bakery with the best buns in town—that was her tagline—and it turned out she had also saved three hundred people during World War II before she immigrated to Canada. She lived her life like it was the only one she had." She looked at Nadine over her glasses. "What does this tell you?"

Nadine hazarded a guess. "There are good people in the world?"

Dot waved that away. "Of course, but what else?"

Nadine glanced at Wes to indicate it was his turn, but he shrugged as if to say she was on her own. She tried again. "That people are more than what we see on the surface?"

"Yes." Dot hid the clipping away. "An obituary is a story. You were in the unique position of determining how a person would be remembered by telling that story. You were the final conduit between a human being's only life and the wider world. That was your responsibility, and for me, you failed to tell the story well."

The words were blunt enough that Nadine would have felt crushed and humiliated, especially in front of Wes, had Dot not said them so gently, almost tenderly, if that was a word that could be applied to Dot Voline. The obits job had been a job, and one Nadine had taken out of desperation and not desire. Had she squandered an opportunity?

Wes stepped slightly forward. "Nadine's section was always good," he said to Dot. "It's unfair of you to act as if she did wrong when she was doing what she was supposed to do. Her work was always appropriate for the section and the audience."

She felt a sudden rush of gratitude toward Wes. His eyes moved from Dot to give Nadine a long look that made her feel a little tingly. She might have to reevaluate him. No. It was smart to be cautious. Wes could be charming her into letting her guard down so he could get the advantage when he needed.

"True enough, true enough. You're young," Dot said. "Here's a word of advice from an old woman. Once you start digging for a person's real story, you can learn much. Remember that." She coughed and pointed to the pots as if to tell them to get back to work. By the time they were done and Nadine was washing her arms under the refreshingly cold water from the tap, Dot was panting.

Wes offered her his arm, and Nadine took charge of pulling the oxygen. Maria met them at the door, shaking her head as Wes helped Dot up the two steps to the main room. The fresh air hit like a slap, and Nadine's damp skirt clung unpleasantly to her legs.

Wes made Dot her tea without asking and fixed her a small plate of finger sandwiches and tiny scones jeweled with pralines. Nadine bit into her own, surprisingly hungry after working in the conservatory.

"What do you think would happen if we didn't?" asked Dot finally, dusting her fingers on a pale pink linen napkin.

Wes shot Nadine a questioning look but she shrugged, not knowing where Dot was going with this either. "Didn't what?" he asked.

"What if we didn't live like this was our only life?" Dot asked as if continuing a conversation she'd been having with herself. Her red lipstick was smeared under her lip, making her mouth a bruised shadow. "If we lived like we would live forever."

"That would be existing and not living." Nadine answered, not waiting for Wes. "Knowing there's an eventual end to this life is what makes me want to actually do things." She pushed aside the little voice that whispered *liar* in her ear. Thanks to the threats and the Voline slip, she was anxious about work and making mistakes. Anxious about *doing*.

No, anxious wasn't right.

Scared. She was flat-out scared, although she would never admit it to a soul. It would be like saying her parents were right. It was shameful to be frightened about making a mistake. Worried was tolerable. *Vigilant*, that was an action word, thus acceptable. *Anxious* had become such a watered-down default term that it seemed stranger when someone said they weren't anxious than when they were. But to be scared? That was for children.

Then Dot said, "I'm dying." Nadine opened her mouth with an instinctive need to deny it, but Dot gave her an amused look. "Don't bother," she said. "You called it, though I have *some* time left."

"Sorry," Nadine muttered. No wonder she dreaded making mistakes when she had to relive them for eternity. Not for the first time did she wish she had one of those monumental egos that simply refused to acknowledge the existence of any error that originated with oneself.

"Dying gives you clarity," Dot said, flexing her worn hands with their silver rings. "Not a lot. Not for everyone. It's a privilege to have an opportunity to reflect on your life." She looked at Nadine. "And a very specific privilege to know how you'll be remembered."

"Is that what you're doing?" asked Wes. He sat on the edge of the turquoise settee, hands flat on the seat. "Reflecting?"

Dot laughed, a long breathy gasp. "I've been doing that my whole life. Every book I wrote was a mirror. Before, it was subconscious, disguised under the pleasure of expressing the perfect line at the perfect time. Now I look back consciously, asking myself all the whys I never had the time or courage to answer."

Nadine didn't know where to look. Dot's voice had turned somber, and it was this shift from her usual light mocking tone that told her it was no longer a game. They had been cast as witnesses to the final days of a woman who knew it.

The room was quiet. Then Dot sighed, a soft sound that barely carried past the cup in her trembling hand.

"What whys in particular are you considering?" asked Wes.

Nadine was filled with relief. While she was struggling with what to say and how to say it, Wes's response was as honestly seeking as Dot's was expressive. It was a moment of confession he had heard and honored.

"The whys of regrets. The whys of decisions and of unintended consequences." Dot put her cup down. "Do you know, in my life, I can't think of a single negative that hasn't had some positive result? Rarely in the moment but always later. When I looked back with quieter eyes, I could see the golden threads of possibility knitting into that moment, readying themselves to be unfurled like flags."

Nadine shivered. This was the Dot she'd known from her books, the brilliant woman who crafted masterpieces at the rickety desk in the other room. Her voice had the cadence of an orator.

Then Dot pulled back, laughing enough to trigger another coughing fit. "Hopefully I'll remember those mistakes for my next life," she said. "Or maybe I won't need to because we enter the void of nothingness and become worm food. I'll let you know."

"How?" asked Wes, shifting with the mood faster than Nadine, who remained under the spell of Dot's earlier thoughts.

Dot winked. "I'll find a way."

Maria came then, to see if they wanted more tea. She took one look at Dot and said, "You need to rest."

"Quit your nagging," said Dot, but her eyelids were fluttering.

Wes was the first to stand, and this time, he held his hand out to Dot. Not to shake but simply to hold. She took it and said, "Look at this, still getting the boys in my dotage. Take notes, girl."

"We'll see you next week," said Wes gently.

"Wear something you can get messy," she said, eyes closing as she slumped against the settee. "I have work to do in the grotto, and you always look so clean. Like you were outlined with a marker instead of painted with watercolors."

"You got it," said Wes with a jaunty salute.

Nadine lingered at the door, then turned to look at Dot, wanting to say something but not knowing what. To her surprise, Dot was staring at her with glittering eyes. She pulled the obituary out from her top and tucked it into a book as if to mark the page.

"Remember" was all she said before waving Nadine away.

# FOURTEEN

n the car, Wes stayed quiet until they passed through the gates, thinking over the last hour. "That was weird," he said. "Do you think that was weird?"

Nadine flipped on the turn signal. "Yes. You might be right about her being nervous. Each time, she's getting closer to letting it go."

"We didn't get to follow up on what she said last week about writing for revenge."

"I couldn't find a way to bring it up," Nadine said, lifting her shoulders as if in defeat. "Not the way the conversation was going."

"Me neither. Also." He paused to find the words. "What she said about your obituary section."

Nadine held up a hand. "She was right." The firmness in her voice surprised him. "I could have done more. Thanks for sticking up for me."

"You're welcome." He changed the topic, not sure how to react to her gratitude, brisk though it was, which made him feel confusingly good. "I'll be sad when she tells us her secret and we have to stop going over."

"Maybe she'll let us come by for visits." Nadine sounded hopeful.

Wes had an idea he knew was woo-woo, then decided to say it. "What if she thinks when she tells us, she'll have nothing left to live for?"

To his surprise and relief, Nadine nodded. "That makes sense. I wonder if we can find a way to reassure her."

"I don't know if it's something rational you can be reassured out of."

"You're probably right. She didn't look well." Nadine glanced at him. "Should we call Brent?"

"I suggested it to Maria when we were leaving," said Wes. "She said she'd take care of it."

"I'm worried," she said.

Wes weighed his options—to be honest or to be comforting—then defaulted to the latter. "She'll be fine. She's thinking about the past, and I'm sure it's bringing up feelings for her."

"You're lying," Nadine said. "You're concerned too. You're thinking about what she said about death and if her nails looked blue or if it was your imagination."

"How did you know?" He was astounded at her perceptiveness.

"We've known each other a long time, Wes."

"Yeah. We have." He found a strange comfort in that. There was distance between them, but Nadine had been there to witness his first awkward attempts at writing and his terrible bowl cut when he was twenty. Mocking him lightly, to be sure. Always with an eye to beat him, absolutely. But she'd been there, driving him to do better.

He tried not to think about what he had named The Night. That winter university party when he caught her as she stumbled over someone's foot in the hallway, her hair wavy with the heat of the house instead of blown straight and tied back the way it usually was. Her brown eyes had seemed bigger than usual, which was saying a lot because Nadine in her natural state had what he mentally thought of as doe eyes, although it would take torture for him to admit it out loud. Her lips had been wet and red, and when she smiled up at him, his heart thumped so hard he felt it in his throat, and he thought, *Oh my God*. For the too-brief moment she'd been in his arms, she'd been warm and so alive he nearly burst.

Then of course he'd ruined it, making some crack about an award she'd won over him, and she'd stepped away, lips thinning and eyes narrowing.

Wes cursed his excellent memory, which had him reliving those six seconds from a decade ago with disturbing regularity.

"I like her," said Wes, rubbing at a streak of dirt on his pant leg and bringing the conversation back to the safer territory of Dot.

Nadine hummed in agreement. "She makes me feel like her books do, that there's always another meaning behind what I understand but can never seem to grasp."

Wes nodded vigorously. "I feel the same. I have a good feeling about week five. Five is the charm for Dot."

"I hope so." Nadine waved as he got out of the car.

He watched her drive away, Daft Punk drifting out of her open window from the radio, and was glad they'd handled this shift in their relationship like professional adults. It was much better to work with someone he got along with.

After the intensity of the afternoon, he couldn't bring himself to go into the house where his mother was undoubtedly waiting, so he went to the park down the street. A woman was tightrope walking between two trees, and a group of kids screamed on the pitch as they played a chaotic version of softball. Lounging people were scattered across the grass, and he did a quick scan of their picnic blankets. Not a swatch of chintz or gingham in sight.

No wonder he wanted to get back onto the I-team. It wasn't that he didn't like working for Rebecca—she was great—or minded most of the stories he did. He knew it was important for people to occasionally read the news and not be depressed. Sun care tips were service journalism after all, and highlighting local designers brought attention to their work. These were good things, and he should be grateful he had a job instead of bitter that it wasn't exactly what he dreamed of doing.

Morose, he pulled out his phone to text Caleb, who was always good for a pick-me-up and usually free to talk on Sunday afternoons.

**Hey,** he wrote. **How's Calgary?**

Caleb wrote back immediately. **Same old. It was good to come home for a visit. Isabel isn't too happy this contract was extended.**

Wes decided to call.

"Hey, man. What's up?" When Caleb finally answered the phone, Wes knew something was wrong. Caleb never sounded low. He was permanently wired to look on the bright side.

"Contract extension?" Wes asked immediately.

"Yeah, you know what this job is, but it's good money."

"You said Isabel didn't want you to take any extensions."

"Sure, but she wants all this fancy shit for the wedding, and I want to make her happy."

Wes watched a kid drop a ball. "Did you talk to her?"

"What's the point? She says she wants me home, but then she pulls out these, like, branded tablecloths that cost an extra few hundred bucks."

"It's your wedding too. If you don't want the tablecloths, you don't need to get them."

Caleb laughed. "Yeah, right. This is her dream day."

Wes had worked on enough wedding features to know that was often the primary message fed to engaged couples. "Marriage isn't about a day, and if you can't talk about stuff like that now, do you think it's going to get better? You hate being out west."

"It's fine."

"You don't sound good," said Wes doubtfully.

"I've had this feeling in my chest lately," Caleb said, tapping what must have been his sternum loud enough that Wes could hear his voice vibrate. "I've never had it before."

Wes stood up as if he could summon help from two provinces away. "Jesus. Are you having a heart attack? Can you feel your arms? Is your face numb?"

"What? No. My arms are fine. My face is fine. I was lifting heavy this morning, bro. I'm not having a heart attack. Also, face numbness happens with a stroke. Know your blockages."

Wes relaxed. "It's probably heartburn from that gross hot sauce you love."

"No, it's like I've been running super hard but I haven't been. My heart is racing, and I feel sort of sick but also like I need to take a shit."

Wes watched the tightrope woman wobble and regain her balance. "That's dread. Anxiety. You're anxious."

"Anxious?" Caleb sounded astonished. "About what?"

"Are you serious? You're getting married. You're living away from home for months at a time. You miss Isabel. That's a lot of stress."

Caleb paused. "I suppose that makes sense. I've never felt this before. I don't like it."

Wes wasn't surprised. Caleb was without a doubt the most well-adjusted person he knew. They'd done an online quiz for fun when Caleb was thinking of changing to sales and wanted to know what his personality strengths were. His score was in the top ten percentile of agreeableness and extraversion and almost at zero for neuroticism.

Wes's score had not been similar.

Which, surprisingly, put him in a good position to coach Caleb through baby's first anxiety attack. "You want to talk about it?"

"Talk about what?"

He gritted his teeth, unable to tell if Caleb was being deliberately or unthinkingly obtuse. This was why he could never be a therapist. "About what's bothering you."

"Nothing, I told you."

"Except feeling stuck in a place you hate, away from home, to pay for a single party you're at best ambivalent about."

The long pause meant he'd hit the issues dead-on. "I can't tell her that."

Wes remembered one of his stories from last year. "Have you considered a wedding therapist?"

Caleb burst out laughing. "Damn, you know how to cheer a guy up. A wedding therapist. Like I need that."

Wes recognized the tone and knew there was no point arguing with Caleb. "Well, I'm here if you want to talk."

"Told you I'm fine, bro. What's going on with you and working with that girl you had a crush on?"

"I didn't have a crush on Nadine," Wes said quickly.

"Sure, that's why you made me go to the same coffee shop where she hung out to study our entire last year of university."

"It was a convenient location!"

"Right. So how is it?"

"We're getting along better."

"You going to ask her out?"

"No." He didn't have to think before he answered. "It's not like that. We barely started treating each other as people."

"That's how it starts." Caleb's voice was that of the wisest sage on the mountain.

"I also know she wouldn't think twice about screwing me over if it benefited her."

"Oh." Caleb paused. "Okay, that's not usually how it starts. I've got to go. Sunday work call, if you can believe it."

They hung up, and Wes hesitated before sending the wedding therapist link over. It couldn't hurt, and sometimes Caleb was too focused on how he thought he should act about things instead of how he wanted to. Reading about the other couples Wes had featured might convince him to talk to Isabel.

A woman with dark hair and huge sunglasses strolled by, chatting on her phone. His heart gave a little lurch. Was that Nadine? It wasn't impossible, as she lived in the neighborhood. No, the woman was too tall, and when she laughed, it was nothing like Nadine's gasping chuckle.

He watched her kick a soccer ball back to the game to a chorus of thanks. A crush on Nadine. Maybe he'd had a little one all those years back, but that was a lifetime ago. Ask her out? God, he could imagine the look on her face. He shook his head at the ridiculousness of it, then walked slowly back to his house. A text from Caleb came in reply to the wedding therapist link, and all it said was **LOL**.

So that was a bust. Wes would make sure to keep up a regular series of calls and check-ins to see how he was doing. Caleb wasn't a guy used to needing help, and he'd bristle at any offer. Christ. Why were people so difficult?

Speaking of. He fished out his keys and let himself into the house.

"Ma?" Wes called out as soon as he came in the door, then nearly jumped out of his skin when a pale ghost rose from the table. "Shit."

"Wesley. Watch your language." His mother's chiding voice came right before the lights flashed on. "Did you eat?"

"Why were you sitting at the table like that?" There was no book or anything in front of her. She was just waiting.

"You're late."

"Sorry, Ma." At least she was in a pleasant mood.

"Sit. You need to eat."

"I'm good."

His mother bustled to the stove as if only activated when one of her children came home. "Go wash your hands."

He apologized to his stomach but knew when he was beat. To refuse would mean several days of assuring his mother that he loved her and she was a good mother.

Twenty minutes later, he was back at the table, picking at a plate of rice and flavorless greens. His mother must be the only Chinese woman on earth to not season her food with garlic. Or soy sauce. He felt the chalky grit of the boiled spinach in his teeth and cursed his mother's stint in England during her formative cooking years, although he knew that was unfair. Even the British used salt.

His mother sat on the other side of the table, using him as a captive audience to pour out a litany of complaints that he barely heard anymore. He'd tried so hard over the years to fix her problems, but nothing ever worked because another issue simply rose to take its place. He made the appropriate noises so she felt heard though, because the moment she sensed him tuning out, she would turn on him.

First it was the people next door. Their baby cried too loud, and she thought the woman smoked. So dirty. Ella wasn't answering her calls. Wes wasn't married. Amy was working too hard and getting wrinkles. "Aiya," his mother said. "No one will marry her if she looks old. She'll end up like me. Alone."

He ignored the last part. "She hasn't hit thirty."

"I had you when I was twenty-three," his mother announced as if she didn't constantly remind him.

"Amy has plenty of time to meet someone if she wants." Wes picked up his plate, having nobly eaten as much as possible, and went to do the dishes. His fingers ached, and he looked down to see his knuckles had turned white from gripping the edge of the sink. It was always like this with his mother, who simply refused to see the world through anyone else's eyes or accept it in any way other than what she wanted.

"Amy made me a doctor's appointment for tomorrow for my check-up," said his mother from the table. She hadn't moved. "Come to my office to take me for two in the afternoon."

Wes took a long breath and turned off the water. "I have to work."

"Tell work you need to take your mother to the doctor."

"I can't do that." He turned to face her. "You know where the doctor is, Ma. All you do is take the subway to Bay station and walk south."

"I don't like going alone." His mother's mouth was a stubborn line. "I can ask Amy since you're so busy. Amy said it's a shame the way you treat your mother."

He had an instinctive resentment toward Amy that he immediately extinguished. Divide and conquer was one of his mother's standard devices for getting her own way, and his sister would never say that.

"Amy has work," said Wes firmly. As the oldest, it was his job to stand up for his sisters. "You are not going to ask her."

Surprisingly, his mother backed down. "Then how do I get there if my son is too busy for his mother?"

"I'll call a cab to pick you up."

She didn't answer but went into the living room and turned on her favorite reality TV show.

Wes stood over the sink, soapy pan in his hands, until he eventually turned the water back on so he could finish the dishes. This was as good a resolution as he was going to get, so he should be happy. At least he had next week's Dot meeting to look forward to. His car should be fixed by then, but Nadine might be open to carpooling. It was good for them to have a chance to debrief. Plus, it was environmentally friendly. He'd text her this week to check. Doing the dishes soothed him in the way that creating order always did. Blocking out the sound of the television and humming the chorus to "Get Lucky," he finished up and thought about next Sunday, when he'd get to see Dot—and Nadine—again.

# FIFTEEN

N adine leaned over the steering wheel as they approached the mansion. She'd been impatient to talk to Dot today, not only because of the story but to see her. She liked Dot. Dot Voline was one of a kind.

When she'd gone home last week, the first thing she did was look up the obit Dot had mentioned of the baker with the best buns in town. The story had whetted her curiosity, and she'd clicked through several major newspapers, reading through recent obituaries to analyze the differences between their obits and those of the *Herald*. She was halfway through the fourth one when she realized she'd stopped reading with a professional eye and was reading for pleasure. She wanted to know about the woman who had run a community theater with people who had recently been released from prison and then about the man who had only received a pittance for recording one of Motown's songs of the century. She hadn't felt the same about the *Herald*'s obits, which always gave her the sense of reading a history textbook in preparation for a test and generally featured affluent white men over the age of seventy.

It would be interesting to talk to Dot more about obits. And life. And, hopefully, the secret she wanted them to know.

Beside her, Wes laughed with anticipation. "This is it," he said. "This is the day she tells us."

She hoped so, because apart from her blossoming interest in obituaries, her week had been shit, with Lisanne talking nonstop about her new investigation. At least it was less tense with Wes, although other concerns had leaked in. When he'd come out this morning looking better than usual, that tiny, minuscule crush she'd harbored when they'd first met years ago had made an unwelcome reappearance. She'd be wise to remember they were still competitors, and hot though Wes was, they weren't compatible as people.

The gate opened as if they were expected—strange, since every visit so far had started by reintroducing themselves at the intercom—and Nadine felt Wes's eyes on her.

"Did you do that?" he asked.

"How? I was sitting right here in the car with you."

"I don't know. Maybe Dot sent you the code."

"Did you see me put in a code?"

Still bickering, they drove up to the house and parked.

"Feels different," Wes said in a low voice.

He was right, but she refused to believe anything could stop them so close to their goal. Nadine peered ahead to the black Porsche SUV parked behind Dot's hot-pink Bentley. "I don't recognize that car," she said.

Wes was watching the main door as it slowly opened. "That's Brent."

Nadine saw her knuckles go white on the steering wheel.

Wes reached over. "Let's go talk to him," he said, giving her hand a slight tug. "It might not be anything."

They got out of the car. Brent stood on the top step, hands in his pockets and leaning back on his heels as he waited.

"Is everything okay?" called Nadine as they approached, trying to keep her voice normal.

"Let's talk inside," said Brent. His eyes were red, and Nadine was horrified to find her first reaction was *Wow, if Dot is dead, this is really bad timing for this story.*

Shameful. She was an awful fucking human being. She could never tell Wes.

The house seemed hollow, without even the cats sliding out of their hiding places. When they came into the empty salon, Nadine knew for sure, and Wes's soft exhale said he'd come to the same conclusion.

It was still a shock when Brent said, "My aunt passed away Friday. I wanted to tell you in person."

"I'm sorry." She and Wes spoke in a chorus.

Brent gave them a brief smile. "Thank you for asking Maria to call me. She can be protective and sometimes didn't want to face the reality of my aunt's health. But it meant we were able to spend her last days together."

Everything Nadine thought of saying sounded like a platitude. She'd been an obituary editor, for crying out loud. Dealing with the aftermath of death was her wheelhouse.

But it was different if you knew the person.

As if hearing her mental plea for help, Wes rose to the occasion. "We're incredibly sorry for your loss. We were only able to know Dot briefly, but she was an extraordinary woman."

"Thank you." Brent ran his hand along the velvety chair arm. "You know, she loved your visits. She said your youth made her remember all the mistakes she made and the ones she wished she had."

Nadine remembered something Brent might enjoy hearing. "She told me she dressed in bright clothes to chase off the men who only wanted sparrows. Then she suggested I go shopping."

Brent laughed loud enough to cause one of the cats—Erma, Nadine thought—to race out from under the chair where she'd been hiding. "When I first moved to Toronto, we had dinner plans. She took one look at my sleek little suit and said if I insisted on dressing like an undertaker, I needed to look like one with pizzazz. She brought me to Hermès and bought me a dozen pocket squares. I still wear them."

This time, they all joined the laughter, the sound eventually trailing out into the silence of the room. "Will there be a funeral?" asked Wes, who then flinched as if he'd said the wrong thing.

"Only for family." Brent raised his eyebrows at Nadine. "As an aside, the *Herald* has declined to run another obituary for my aunt."

Nadine frowned. "What?"

"They very kindly said I was welcome to take out a paid death notice." He shot Wes a sly look. "However, her publisher said the *Spear* was eager to run one."

That couldn't be right. She pulled out her phone and texted Raj as the conversation continued. **Is it true you won't run an obit for Dot Voline?**

His reply came quick. **Daniel said once was our usual limit for obits.**

That asshole. She was angry on Dot's behalf, although the thought of running another version of what had been in the files didn't sit well with her. Dot was so much more than those dates and book titles. Then Brent cleared his throat, and she put away regrets of Dot's obit. "There's something I want to discuss with you. She didn't tell you her story, did she?"

"No. I suppose it dies with her," said Wes with what Nadine considered admirable restraint.

"Or not. She gave me a message for you. Come with me for a second?"

Nadine exchanged a confused glance with Wes, then followed Brent into the library, where he climbed up to the second level. After fumbling with the edge of one of the shelves, a loud click sounded, and an entire bookcase opened inward.

Wes's gasp of utter delight made Nadine smile despite the blue news of Dot's death. "A hidden room?" he said.

Brent groped around for what Nadine assumed was a light switch. "Not quite a hidden *room*," he said. "Ah, there it is. This place is a maze of secrets. My aunt's filing was incomprehensible to anyone but her. I once found her recipe box in a closet. Apparently she kept it there because it was a box and boxes belonged in closets. I have no idea."

Dim lights flickered on to reveal an attic space straight out of every creepy movie imaginable. Dust sat thick on boxes randomly distributed in piles. Windows along the back wall might let in light on sunny days but now added to the gloom. Large metal filing cabinets that looked like they originated in a Bletchley Park code-breaking hut loomed near the far wall, and Nadine wouldn't have been surprised to see a skeleton lurking in the corner.

"These are my aunt's," said Brent with an expansive wave. "She hated throwing things out, as you could probably tell."

Wes checked a nearby box. "These are foreign language editions of her books."

"I wouldn't be surprised. She only kept a single copy of each of her books in the library. I don't know what's up here, to be honest."

"Why are you showing us?" asked Nadine. Her nose tickled, and she sneezed three times in a row. "Sorry. Dust."

"My aunt wanted whatever she was hiding to be known, but she ran out of time." Brent looked at the disarray. "She asked me to tell you she was sorry to have missed your meeting due to an unavoidable appointment with her maker and to show you how to get in here."

"You want us to continue looking?" Wes asked slowly, as if trying to understand what Brent was getting at.

"No," Brent corrected. "Dot does. She said to get your hands dirty and keep your eyes open so you can finish the job."

"We weren't having much success without her," Nadine said. "I'm not sure that would change."

"You didn't have access to the house before," said Brent, nudging a box with his foot.

"There must be thousands of documents here." Nadine felt faint.

"You don't need to categorize them," Brent assured them. "My aunt's literary executor has everything of value, and this is all getting shredded in three weeks to prepare for the house sale."

"Three weeks?" asked Wes.

Nadine silently agreed. There was enough here to keep them busy for a year.

"I wish I could give you longer, but that's all I can spare," said Brent with regret. "The upkeep on this place is expensive, and I've got a buyer for the property that I can't risk losing, not in this market. If it helps, you can live in the house."

"You trust us to live here alone?" asked Nadine.

"Dot did and I need someone to feed the cats. Maria didn't want to stay with my aunt gone." Brent looked at them. "Also, I could be wrong, but you two don't strike me as the kind to turn this place into a party house."

His phone rang with a little ditty that sounded like MC Hammer, and he excused himself to take the call, moving into the library and leaving Wes and Nadine alone in the attic. She turned around one more time. She wanted to do this. She wanted to know what Dot was hiding. She wanted to explore the secrets of this attic, and she wanted to do right by Dot.

She turned to Wes, who had walked away as if looking at the attic from another angle would make it more manageable. "Hey, Wes?"

Wes came out from behind a cabinet. "I think you mean Detective Chen, Agent Barbault."

She opened her mouth to protest him getting to be the detective but decided Agent Barbault had a nice ring. "Looks like we're on the case."

He grinned at her and put on the voice of an old noir gumshoe. "We've got a dame with a past and an attic that's our future."

Nadine tried not to laugh. She really did.

She failed.

# SIXTEEN

atisfied to have made her laugh, Wes looked around the attic as Nadine sneezed again. "Are you sure you can handle the job?" he asked. "The dust might kill you."

Nadine rubbed her nose. "Don't worry about me. Worry about how you're going to deal with sharing the house with a herd of cats."

"I like cats," Wes said with growing enthusiasm.

"No, you don't."

"I will make myself like cats if needed," he amended. Dot's looked nice enough.

"What about work?"

Wes looked around at the boxes. "I have vacation time due." Rebecca had been sending him increasingly sharp emails reminding him of the *Spear's* use-it-or-lose-it policy as he hadn't taken any time this year.

Nadine frowned. "I can put in the request, but it's pretty last minute. If it's not granted, I'll have to come here after work."

"I'll email my manager right now." He took a minute to rapidly tap out a message to Rebecca, apologizing for the late request, then bent to pick through a box. "God knows what secrets are in here."

"We might not find anything," said Nadine repressively, as if trying to tamp down her own hopes.

"Not with that attitude." Wes pulled out a theater program from a 1989 performance of *The Phantom of the Opera*, which he brandished at Nadine. "See?"

"Mystery solved. Brent will be thrilled." She looked around. "Three weeks isn't a long time, even if we sleep here."

"That, I'm not sure I can manage," he said, thinking about his mother's reaction. He hadn't been away for that long since his internships after school, when his sisters had still been home. Would Amy be willing to move back home for three weeks? No, that was too much to ask. "I might have to come in every day."

"Then you'll be here in the day, and I'll be here at night?" Was it him or did she sound faintly disappointed? She gave him a sly grin. "Admit you're scared to stay here."

"I admit it," he lied easily. A past girlfriend had called him a momma's boy right before she dumped him, and he didn't want Nadine to think the same.

Nadine's smile faded. "It would have been easier if Dot told us outright what happened. Why couldn't she have told Brent?"

"I'm sure for the same reason she couldn't tell us when we visited." Wes pulled out an old *Cosmopolitan* magazine. "We have one last chance."

"You're right."

"What was that? I was right? Can you repeat that?"

As he hoped, this broke her pensive mood, and she laughed. "Don't get used to it." Her face clouded. "Only three weeks. It would be more productive if you could stay overnight, especially if I have to keep going to work, but I get it."

"You'll be okay alone?" he asked.

Nadine looked down. "I can handle it."

Wes's stomach dropped at the idea that he was disappointing her. He looked at the mass of documents and thought about the extra work he'd be able to do if he stayed. He thought about the little waver in Nadine's voice that might be nervousness at spending the nights here alone, although she was trying to put a brave face on it.

Could he be selfish for once? He wanted to stay. He wanted this. He wanted this story and this time in the attic. He could get to know Nadine better. She wasn't too bad after all.

His phone buzzed. It was Rebecca, approving his vacation. **Finally,** she wrote back. **I was about to unilaterally put you on PTO. Send me a summary of what you're working on before you head out.**

He looked up to find Nadine flipping through what looked like sewing patterns. "My vacation was approved."

"That was fast."

"I have a good manager." Sometimes he took Rebecca for granted.

Brent came back, full of apologies, and accidentally kicked a stack of newspapers, sending up a plume of dust. "About my proposal."

"We're willing," said Nadine.

"Good. I'm glad you agreed." Brent looked relieved. "I'm not a superstitious man, but I don't relish the idea of Dot's ghost haunting me because she had unfinished business."

"So there's no misunderstanding, the plan is we'll stay here and feed the cats while we go through the attic," said Wes. "We don't need to keep anything for posterity."

"Correct," said Brent. "Obviously don't steal the art or any of my aunt's hideous figurines. I have a complete inventory."

"Too bad," said Nadine. "I was hoping to expand my collection of painted chamber pots."

"Sorry." Brent pushed aside a box. "I'm keeping those for my personal use."

He led them downstairs, and Nadine nudged Wes. "You said we'll stay in the house," she said. "*We* as in *both of us*?"

Unease over his mother's reaction faded with the thrill of the project ahead. "I'm staying too."

"Okay." It was only a word, carelessly delivered, but Wes heard the relief and smiled. She'd never admit it out loud, but Nadine wanted his company, at least if the alternative was staying in a huge mansion by herself.

"Since you're scared to be alone," he added.

This time, she looked away, and he had an uncomfortable feeling that he'd gone too far. He turned to Brent to ask about logistics.

After a few minutes of working through the cats' feeding schedule and how to use an induction stove, Brent walked them out. "Thank you for doing this," he said as he opened the door. "My aunt was a good person under all that bluster."

"She was," Nadine said. "We're grateful to have met her."

Although the rain continued, they were protected by the portico once they were outside. Nadine started the car, the windshield wipers kicking in to squeal on the dry glass. She shut them off, and they sat looking out past the pink Bentley to the swan bobbing in the fountain. The water had been shut off from the Botticelli *Venus*. Wes's eyes went to the huge door as Nadine pulled out of the driveway, wishing it was last week and he could have said something else to Dot. Something meaningful.

What that could have been, he had no idea.

It wasn't until the golden gates closed behind them that Nadine gave a shuddering sigh.

"Pull over," said Wes.

She didn't argue but did as he said and turned off the ignition. Rain beat down on the car, sliding down the windows in twisting lines.

He heard the sniff as he was fighting back his own sorrow. "Hey," he said.

"I only knew her a few weeks." Nadine's voice broke. "How can I be this upset?"

She burst into tears, and Wes didn't think. He unbuckled his seat belt and gathered her in his arms, feeling her shoulders shake as she cried.

He'd never seen Nadine cry. Two hours ago, he would have doubted it was possible and doubted even more that she would cry near him. Strangely, he was grateful he could be here for her. Concern for Nadine helped him avoid his own grief.

Finally, she sniffled against him. "Sorry," she muttered, knuckling at her eyes like a child. Wes felt his heart crunch into the tiniest nugget.

He opened the glove compartment, and thank God, there were tissues. He handed her one and took one for himself. "Here."

"Are you crying too?" she asked.

Wes steeled himself for the anger. His mother hated it when anyone cried besides her.

Nadine's hand, warm and firm, came over to cover his. "That makes me feel less alone," she said.

Wes's eyes stayed on her hand, blurred with tears, wondering if he'd heard correctly. Then she shifted her grip to hold him tighter, and he knew that he had. He wiped his eyes with his free hand so hard he saw shapes and found himself unable to answer. Death's concave mirror was turning all his expectations of Nadine upside down.

She sniffled. "I keep thinking about that obit in the *Herald*, the one I ran."

He managed to find his words. "What about it?"

She moved into her seat and leaned her head back, leaving Wes with a hollow feeling where she'd been. "Dot was right. I didn't do her justice. I let her be reduced to the things she did, with nothing of who she was."

Wes sat to face her fully, thinking about what kind of an obit could reflect the Dot he'd come to know. "Would you put in her sweet tooth?"

Nadine smiled. "I'd write about her house and how she said each item had a story she'd been waiting to tell."

Wes remembered that conversation. "And that she'd only told a few."

"I would have interviewed people who found solace in Dot's books and connected with characters like Peg and Alice."

"Ilsa," interjected Wes. "I liked Ilsa."

Nadine's mouth dipped. "There's no way to go back and fix it. I wish—" She hesitated. "I wish I could have done better by Dot."

"It wasn't your fault. Dot really seemed to live," Wes said, struggling for the right words. "That sounds...ugh. I mean, we all live, but she had a..." He trailed to a stop, unable to finish his thought.

"In the obits biz, we call it joie de vivre." She reached past him and got another tissue. "You know what's terrible?"

"What?"

Nadine laid her forehead against the steering wheel, speaking to her knees. "My first thought when Brent told us was that it was bad timing. I'm so self-centered. Dot died, and all I could think about was my career. What a piece of work I am."

Wes looked over in awe. "I thought the same thing."

She twisted her head to face him. "You did?"

"I was never going to say a word, but yeah. I did."

"We're evil." She sounded impressed at the depths of their joint nastiness. Then she grinned. "Dot would have had a laugh out of that."

"She would have." He shook his head. "I wouldn't put that in her obit though."

"No," said Nadine. "At least not past the first draft."

This time, they started laughing and didn't stop until they were wheezing. Wes thought Dot might have liked that as well.

# SEVENTEEN

N adine read the email from Daniel one more time. **Take the vacation**, he'd written. **We can cover your role with absolutely no problem. Get the rest you need.**

Although it was reasonable to assume Daniel meant no more than he wrote, Nadine couldn't shake the suspicion that he thought she was expendable. Well, there was nothing stopping her from getting to the bottom of Dot's story now. She would get this exclusive, and she would show Daniel what she could do.

Although Nadine felt enormously insensitive, as if she'd barely waited for the body to cool, Brent told her the sooner they got to work, the better.

"You saw the boxes," he'd said in a defeated tone when she'd called to confirm details of their invasion of Dot's home. "I want to help my aunt, but you'll have to do what you can in three weeks."

So the next morning, a holiday Monday at nine o'clock, Nadine met Wes at Dot's front door, each clutching a coffee. They observed their matching sustainable mugs without comment.

"Four two six seven," repeated Nadine, looking between her phone and where Wes stood at the keypad near the door. "That's what Brent sent to me."

"I told you it's not working," said Wes in an overly calm tone that screamed frustration.

"Try it again."

"I've tried it three times."

"Did you press pound?"

He rubbed his hand over his eyes. "Why would I push pound? So I can get to the customer service agent? It's a door, not an automated complaint line."

She shoved her phone in his face. "Brent's email says four two six seven. *Four two six seven.*"

He grabbed the phone and scanned the message. Never had a man tapped in numbers more smugly than Wes at that moment. "Four. Two. *Five.* Seven." The lock whirred, and he turned to her with an expressively neutral face before taking a long sip of coffee.

"Oh." Nadine squinted. "Huh. I guess it is a five. How do you like that?"

Wes didn't dignify this with a response.

Stepping into the foyer with Sir Latimer and Janice the wonky-eyed cheetah, uncertainty engulfed Nadine, and she almost left, overcome with a sense that she didn't belong in this huge empty house.

Before she could act, cats materialized from all directions. Erma wove around Wes's legs, purring loudly between head butts, while Octavia meowed piteously from around the corner.

"Someone has a fan," said Nadine. She could have sworn Erma was the one who avoided people, but she seemed happy enough with Wes. The cat skittered away when Nadine reached down for pets. She didn't like that. She was a cat person. Cats loved her. She'd be damned if she'd put up with the cat liking Wes better.

Wes eyed the cats. "They want food," he said. "Not friendship." He headed toward the kitchen, and the parade of four cats followed him like the Pied Piper.

"The two aren't mutually exclusive," Nadine said after him. She lingered in the hall. There was a lot of work to be done in the attic, but if she was living here for three weeks (with Wes!), then she needed to check out the rest of the house to make sure some distant cousin wasn't camping out unnoticed in one of the wings. Well, no research was ever wasted, and Brent had given them free rein apart from Dot's bedroom.

She was also nosy as hell.

"Are you coming, or do I have to feed these beasts by myself?" called Wes.

Nadine walked to the kitchen—slowly, to aggravate him, because although they were friendlier, old habits die hard—and found Wes in the middle of a group of incensed felines.

"I can't find the food, but they're circling," he said. "It's only a matter of minutes until they start chewing on my ankles, the land sharks."

"Did you check the cabinets?"

"Of course I checked the cabinets. Do you think I've been standing here trying to locate the food through clairvoyance?"

Trying to avoid tripping over the cats, the two of them ransacked the kitchen, looking for a bag of kibble or cans of wet food. Nothing.

"What about the fridge?" Nadine finally asked, hands massaging her neck as she tried to think where in this warehouse of a mansion the cat food would be. For all she knew, Dot had an entire room filled with racks of imperishables, like a nuclear fallout shelter.

"Who would refrigerate cat food?" Wes sounded doubtful as he yanked open the door of the massive Sub-Zero fridge. "Oh."

She looked around him. "I guess people who get it fresh."

Wes pulled out a container and read the ingredients. "Organic farm-raised salmon. These cats eat better than me. Are you sure it's cat food?" He double-checked it. "It is. Wow."

Grumbling about the amount of money people spent on their pets, Wes opened the container and put it on the floor. The cats crowded around, finally silent as they ate, and Wes checked his intact ankles with relief.

"I have a plan," announced Nadine after Wes washed his hands.

Wes leaned against the counter, arms crossed. "Okay."

She'd been prepared for a fight, so she examined him warily. "Just okay?"

"Yeah, Barbault, just okay. We've got three weeks and a library's worth of information to analyze. I'd love a plan. Plus you'd have an aneurysm if I tried to stop you."

That was true enough not to bother arguing. "First, I want to get familiar with the house. All of it, the nooks and crannies. We don't know if the attic is the only place she stored documents."

"Reasonably, the most likely place is her bedroom, which Brent said is off-limits," Wes pointed out over the sounds of cats fighting over the last scraps of food. "It's not like she's going to hide things in the commode."

"Can you be sure of that?"

Wes looked at the door that led to the library, eyes glazing as he mentally reviewed the clutter. "Point taken, but Brent specifically pointed us to the attic, and we have more than enough to do there."

"True, but I still want to see the rest of the house. For science."

"Fine."

"No arguing?" said Nadine.

"It's a logical step." His expression turned shifty. "I suppose I wouldn't mind looking around either," he admitted. "This house is better than a museum. God knows what we'll find. What's the notebook for?"

"To take notes," she said. "Also, we can rip out the pages and leave them as a trail in case we get lost."

That made him laugh, and Nadine would be lying if she said it didn't make her a little proud. Wes was always hard to impress.

"Let's go, Gretel."

Nadine led them to the west wing and a corridor made dark by the closed doors, then turned on the lights. The ornate crystal chandeliers added more sparkle than illumination. "I feel like one of Bluebeard's wives." Her hand lingered on the porcelain handle of a paneled door decorated with painted cherubs.

Wes brought his hand down on hers and gave a decisive push, cracking the door open. "At least we have permission so we can avoid dismemberment."

They took their time working through each room, six in each wing. There was only one level, so sadly that meant no grand staircase. When Wes saw Nadine checking behind curtains and in cabinets, he began doing the same without comment, as if he understood the impact of the sheer amount of true crime content she had consumed over the years, intensified by her parents' paranoia about safety. Her mother had solemnly handed over a dog-eared copy of *The Gift of Fear* to Nadine when she was fifteen.

An hour later, they returned to the kitchen to make some tea and discuss their findings in a more modern, less visually bewildering setting. Nadine checked her notes as Wes filled the kettle.

"We have three bedrooms in the east wing. One gold, one blue, and one Marie Antoinette," she said. "The east wing also has the carnival room with the carousel horses leaning against the walls and the musical instruments, the St. James gentleman's club study with the paneled walls and Victorian hunting art, and the games room at the end with the crokinole board, billiard table, and darts."

"Don't forget the bathrooms," said Wes. "Also, that was Regency-era art. Not Victorian."

She ignored him. "That wing has the bathroom with the fancy marble tub and the unusually plain one that's all white and bamboo. Only the Marie Antoinette has an en suite."

Wes held out an Earl Grey tea canister and one of herbal lavender rose without speaking, and she pointed her pen at the latter. "Wasn't the gold bedroom on the west side?" he asked as he spooned out the strongly perfumed leaves.

"No, the west wing had the silver bedroom with the stained glass on the door panel."

"Oh, right."

"Plus the fashion history room with the mannequins, the chinoiserie room with all that embroidery, and the room with the porcelain. There was the yellow rose bedroom and Dot's room at the end. Each of those bedrooms had an en suite."

Wes poured the water into the teapot. "We should pick rooms, unless you want to camp in the salon," he said. "Which is possible. It's big enough to host a fun fair."

"I'd like to be in the east wing." Nadine instinctively wanted to give Dot some privacy in death, although they were here to rummage through the detritus of her life. "Also, I'd like us to be near each other." That might sound insecure, but the house was big and empty.

To her relief, he didn't mock her. "I agree," he said. "You liked the Marie Antoinette room. Why don't you take that, and I'll take the blue one?"

"That's surprisingly magnanimous of you." She loved that over-the-top room, really more of a chamber, which fulfilled her every childhood princess fantasy.

"Trust me, it's not."

They took their tea back through the house to check the rooms' habitability, which was perfect. Maria had kept them spotless and stocked with clean white sheets that smelled like thyme.

"Towels are fresh too," reported Wes, coming back from his own room reconnaissance. He looked around, shading his eyes against the sun reflecting off the metallic thread that covered the bed canopies before looking over to where Nadine lounged on one of the many low chairs in the room, which was larger than her apartment. "Are you sure you can sleep here?" he asked, shading his eyes as he moved through a dagger of sun reflected off a golden pitcher.

"Sleep?" Nadine ran her hand along the velvet of the seat, reveling in the softness. "I could *live* here. It's sad though."

"The fact that she's successfully incorporated eighteen different decorating styles like a magician?" asked Wes as he closed the top to a rolltop desk painted ivory with delicate red poppies. "That's more impressive than sad."

"No, the fact that she had all this space and she was alone."

Wes sat down on a tufted stool. Nadine carefully moved her eyes from where his thighs strained against the fabric of his chinos to what she assumed was the much safer visual landscape of the mural on the wall, which was a rather more explicit version of Apollo and Narcissus than she was used to seeing. She hadn't noticed because the murals had faded into the background against the overall vibe of the room. She swept her gaze around, noting with horror that every wall portrayed seminude figures cavorting with each other. Wes watched with amusement.

"Looks like Dot loved Greek myths," he said.

She hauled herself off the chaise, eyes down to avoid Leda and the swan. "Let's look at your room."

By the house's standards, the blue room was peaceful and almost sedate with a nautical theme that included ships in bottles, oars, and green blown glass. The bed was plainly made, the corners pulled hospital tight, and it lacked the dozen embroidered throw pillows that covered the top half of Nadine's bed. The chairs were brown leather, and in the corner stood an old coatrack covered with Panama hats. Wes sorted through them while Nadine opened the huge wardrobe, half expecting to see a snowy forest with a single lamppost in the distance.

"This is perfect," he said with satisfaction.

"Excited for some Horatio Hornblower cosplay?"

"I'd prefer walking the plank to death by ruffles." Wes joined her at the wardrobe. "How about lunch?"

Nadine grimaced when she thought back to the fridge. "She only had cat food."

"Organic and farm-raised."

"Still cat food."

He adjusted the ship in the bottle. "If you're too good for that, I brought us a picnic."

She was about to make a joke about which tablecloth he'd matched it to but then thought of Wes planning ahead for what they would eat together and shut her mouth. For some reason, it made her wildly and inappropriately happy. Well, it stood to reason. She didn't have to cook, which was a gift.

"Sounds perfect" was all she said, but there must have been something in her voice, because Wes looked suddenly shy. His mouth tilted in a little smile, and his eyes lowered. She hadn't noticed how long his eyelashes were. Then he ran his hands through his hair and met her gaze before looking away again, that smile lingering but a little wider.

She liked the way it looked on him. A lot. She closed the wardrobe doors as if to trap the feelings in there. She didn't have time for liking anything on Wes outside his ability to sort boxes. She had priorities, and admiring Wes was not one of them.

# EIGHTEEN

Wes took his time assembling lunch, setting up in the kitchen since the weather threatened rain. He liked cooking for people, even if his mother grumbled about his food. Unsure if Nadine was vegetarian, he hadn't bothered with meat in the muffuletta, depending on the olive tapenade to provide a depth of flavor along with the vegetables and cheese he'd layered in the ciabatta bread. With a pasta salad and fruit, it would be enough to get them through the afternoon.

White dust speckled Nadine's dark hair when she came in to wash up at the sink. "Wes, this looks incredible." She sounded astonished he could cook, and he tried to take it as a compliment and not an insult.

She sat down, and he poured them water. "You have dust on your face."

"Oh." She pawed at the smear, making it worse, until he handed her a napkin.

Wes let her serve herself first, trying to keep his pleasure at her rapt expression close to his chest until she tried the food. This was usually when the complaints came, and if he knew Nadine, she wouldn't miss a chance to rag on him. He was used to it from home. Not enough of one ingredient. Too much of another. He knew his mother hated mustard. Did he hate his mother? No? But he included mustard, so he must hate his mother, who sacrificed so much for him. This was why she had to do all the cooking. He was lucky he had a mother, not like her, orphaned at the age of twenty.

To his shock, Nadine simply ate. She didn't sniff at the plate and push it away, claiming she was no longer hungry. She didn't open the sandwich to check what was in it or poke through the salad to leave a small hill of things she didn't like on the side. "This is the best thing I've had in ages," she said.

"Thanks." Uncomfortable with her praise, since that was not the dynamic their relationship was based on, but somehow needing more, he said, "I wasn't sure if you ate meat, so I skipped it."

Nadine gave him a startled look. "That's thoughtful." She paused. "I prefer not to, but I won't make a fuss. My pohpoh makes a chicken dish I love, so I eat that. You?"

"I eat anything." His stomach was iron after decades of his mother's cooking. She was so bad her congee somehow contained bits of uncooked rice.

"Anything? The water left over from boiling hot dogs?"

"Anything," he said with emphasis. "Hot dog water, coffee-flavored yogurt, the leftover Halloween candy you find the next summer that's stuck to the wrapper. You name it."

"I stand corrected if slightly grossed out." Nadine took another bite of her sandwich. "God, this is amazing. Anyway, I went up to the attic to see if it was as bad as I remembered."

That was where she'd gotten dusty. "Is it?"

"Worse." Her face had a worried frown, and Wes had an appalling impulse to smooth out the creases lining her mouth that he immediately axed. They were colleagues, and ones who had barely started improving their relationship. "We need a game plan."

"I thought you had one."

"I did. The plan was to organize her stuff and find our answer." She speared some of the peach he'd sliced. "We need a better one."

Wes couldn't answer because Nadine was licking the peach juice from the corner of her mouth. He wanted to slap himself. Although she was getting easier to deal with, he wasn't sure how he felt about her. There was history between them, and endless mistrust. What was he doing?

*You don't have to like someone to find them attractive,* sang out a little voice in his mind.

Even that was too much. They were on a tight deadline. There was no time for finding anyone attractive. He was here to sort files in a dusty attic on his vacation, like all the cool kids did.

No wonder he was single.

Nadine insisted on tidying up after lunch to make it fair, so Wes went up to the attic with Murasaki trailing behind him on soft paws. Walking through the secret door, he immediately agreed with Nadine's assessment.

"We're screwed," he told the calico.

The cat didn't care, which was rude but expected.

Wes strolled around the attic to get a feel for the enormity of the task ahead. The lights weren't strong enough, so they'd need flashlights or lamps for darker days. At least it smelled dry and not damp or moldy. The windows overlooked the back of Dot's estate, which included the conservatory, some gardens, and a path leading to what he assumed was her personal forest. That was for later exploration, when he was so fed up with looking at documents he couldn't bear to touch another piece of paper.

His phone rang, and he pulled it out of his pocket. Ella.

"Hey, big brother," she greeted him.

His heart lifted to hear her sounding happy. In the year before she left, Ella was so withdrawn that he and Amy had become almost frantic with worry. Ella was one of those sunshine people, born to laugh and sing. It was worth the money to get her out of the house so she could blossom away from their mother's shadow, and her time at school had transformed her.

"Hi, little sister." He ran a finger across the seat of a green leather club chair, then wiped the filth off. He'd walk and talk. "How's Vancouver?"

"Great!"

He frowned. He knew that voice and realized this wasn't Ella's true happiness. She was hiding something. "Ella. Spill."

"How do you always know?" she complained.

"It's a gift. What's going on?"

"I have some good news and bad news."

"Always the good news first." He tried to keep his voice light.

"An opportunity came up. A graduate year abroad in Italy to study fashion design," she said. "I was accepted into a program."

"A prestigious program?"

"It's okay. Good enough." Ella routinely minimized her abilities and achievements, so he knew this meant world-class.

Wes couldn't contain his smile. "I'm proud of you."

"The bad news is I only won a scholarship. It doesn't cover the room and board."

Of course. Wes looked outside at the conservatory, not for the first time thinking about how unfair life was. "How much do you need?"

She told him, and Wes did some quick calculations. It was more than he would have expected, but he had enough.

"I want you to accept the offer," he said firmly. "We can afford it."

Ella paused. "Wes."

"What?"

She made a snuffling noise that sounded like she was trying not to cry. "I knew you would offer, and I'm going to take it, but I feel bad. No one did that for you."

"None of that," he said. "What would you do if I had an opportunity like this and you could help?"

"I would," she said instantly.

"See?" He leaned against the window. "Life's cyclical. One day when you're a famous designer, you'll give me a hand, or Amy."

"Thank you, Wes." The relief in her voice was enough for him to know he was doing the right thing.

"When do you have to give your acceptance?"

She gave a short laugh. "Tomorrow. I wanted to make sure I couldn't get the money anywhere else from the school or the program. Apparently I got the highest scholarship they offer, and student aid said it was out of their scope."

"That's my girl. You'll have the money tonight."

Ella paused. "What about Ma?"

Wes knew what she meant. "I'll take care of it, Ella. I love you."

They disconnected, and Wes saw Nadine watching him with an unreadable expression. "Ella?" she asked in a flat voice.

He put away his phone. It was ridiculous to think Nadine was jealous, and she'd be horrified to know she was coming off that way.

"My youngest sister," he said.

"Oh. Oh, well. It's none of my business."

"If I have sisters?"

She went red, as if he'd caught her out, and turned away to inspect the attic. "Anyway. We don't have much time. There are a couple ways to approach this."

He hid his smile. She was in her element. There was a good chance her ideas were the same as his, but he'd have to be a real ass to ruin her fun when she was looking around with such bright-eyed determination. "What's your option A?"

"Scattershot. We jump in and look at things as they catch our interest."

"Not my favorite," Wes said with a diplomacy that surprised him. "Too easy to lose track."

"I agree. Option two is we work from one direction and look over everything in our path."

"Like we're beating the bush to flush out snakes?"

Nadine looked concerned. "Why would you want to do that? The snakes are minding their own business."

"Hypothetically."

"Doesn't matter. Leave the snakes alone." She went to sit down on the same chair he'd checked for dirt, but Wes stopped her.

"It's filthy," he said. "The snakes are not our focus. Is that your last option?"

"Yes." She examined the chair he'd warned her off. "We need to do some cleaning so we don't need hazmat suits."

"Agreed, and also it's time for my idea. I call it the scan and pile."

Nadine tilted her head. "You want to do a lightning assessment of everything, put all the promising stuff in a pile, and then go through it in more detail."

"Yes." He was only a little surprised at how accurate her interpretation was.

"Normally, I'd say that's not the worst idea, but we don't have enough time."

Wes poked around a rack of clothes. She was probably right, and he wasn't too obstinate to admit it. "You win. I vote for the beating of the snakes."

She grimaced. "Please don't call it that." Nadine walked over to the windows, and he tried to ignore the way her hips caused her skirt to sway. "It's stifling in here. Do these open?"

"They're painted over."

Nadine, stubborn as always, had to check for herself, struggling valiantly with the lock before admitting he was right.

"We'll bring a fan so we don't die of heatstroke," said Wes. "It's early. Want to start now?"

"Hell yes." Nadine was already halfway across the room.

He watched her go. Of all the people to be stuck with on this job, being with Nadine had a load of downsides. But he'd never have to worry about her work ethic, and that was a bonus. Back in school, they'd worked well together. He hoped time hadn't changed that.

If those first hours of searching were an indication of how the next three weeks were going to go, Wes was in for a rough time. His skin felt gritty, and his pants had fingerprints from where he'd unthinkingly wiped his hands on his thighs. Nadine groaned and stretched, and he looked over to see her shirt riding up to show a thin line of pale stomach that he did his best not to stare at.

"You have a handprint on your shirt," Nadine informed him from her side of the room. Her dark hair was a mess of waves from the heat, and her face flushed so red it almost obscured her freckles. "Did you bring water?"

"Was that my job?" He felt defensive, as if she'd found him lacking. She didn't seem to notice the tone. "Nah, I didn't either."

Wes waited for the blame, but all she did was yawn and make her way to the entrance.

As they passed Octavia curled up on one of the chairs in the reading nook, she opened one golden eye and gave a half-hearted swipe at Wes's leg, which he dodged with expert timing. In the kitchen, they took turns washing, then drank a good liter of water before they were in any mood for conversation. Wes pulled his shirt away from his skin. A pro bodybuilder prepping for a competition couldn't have sweat more.

"I assume you didn't find anything good?" asked Nadine as she poured her fourth glass. She'd slicked her hair back with water, making her look like she was at the beach. Or fresh from the shower.

Wes focused on the conversation. "Old grocery bills from 1995. It's shocking how cheap everything was."

She put down her glass. "I found some clothes. Nothing in the pockets, but it looks like she went through a real camouflage phase before she became a devotee of the caftan."

"Like army camo?" He tried to picture Dot in fatigues and failed miserably. She had been more about the bedazzled life.

"No, like the clothes you wear when you want to blend in and not be noticed. Navy dresses and nude pumps and beige turtlenecks. Office stuff."

"I can't picture her in that. It must be from another woman."

"The styles were from the 1980s." She shrugged. "You could probably make a killing at a vintage store with them."

"Brent can add that to his list of things to sell. It'll add a few bucks to the millions he's going to make from whatever is in the art warehouse."

Nadine laughed, then rubbed her forehead. "There's so much. What if we never get an answer?"

"We will." He couldn't let her get discouraged before they started, so he steeled himself for a pep talk. "You're a...uh. Yeah. You're a good reporter, Nadine."

She smirked at him until he added, "Almost as good as me."

She pretended to throw some water at him, then checked the fridge. "We need some groceries. Are you going to stay here tonight?"

He shook his head. "I'm coming back tomorrow. I can go to the store if you tell me what you like. How about you?"

"I have plans for tonight, so it would be great if you could pick up a few things." Erma jumped on the counter to sit down in a loaf with her paws tucked under and regarded them with disdain. Nadine reached out, but the cat leaned away to look at Wes with her big eyes, and gave a little trill.

As he pet the cat—she was cute, he had to admit—Wes tried not to think about Nadine's plans. He assumed if she had a partner, he'd have heard about it, but life had taught him assumptions were often wrong. It also felt weird to ask, as if he wanted to know for a reason other than curiosity.

Nadine smiled and his heart skipped. "I'll be here at ten tomorrow morning," she said.

"I'll be here at nine." Not knowing why, he held out his hand like they were sealing a deal.

"Eight it is." She didn't hesitate before taking his hand in hers, that little secret smile still on her face.

# NINETEEN

Nadine stared out at the construction site—another condo going in where there used to be a school—and drank her raspberry beer. The late afternoon sun had dropped behind the buildings, making the heat bearable for the first time all day.

"Let me get this straight," Lisanne said. "You're going to be on a secret assignment that has nothing to do with work."

"It's more accurate to say it's not sanctioned by work," corrected Nadine. She and Wes had agreed to stick to Dot's original *don't-say-a-word* rules for now, but it was a good idea for someone to know who she was working with if she was going AWOL for three weeks. She'd known Wes a long time, but a woman could never be too safe.

"Are you assuming it's better to beg forgiveness than ask permission?"

"Yes."

"Good call." Lisanne swung her sunglassed gaze over, forcing Nadine to carry on a conversation with her own doubled reflection. "Are you telling me so I can do wellness checks on you? Should I be worried?"

"I'll be in touch," Nadine assured her. "I'm working with Wes. Wes Chen from the *Spear*."

"The competition?" Lisanne stopped as the server came by with a cheese plate containing tiny wedges better suited to a mouse and ramekins of chutneys and jams.

"The source insisted on working with both of us."

"Sure, sure." Lisanne waved that off to narrow in on what interested her. "Wes Chen, huh?"

"Yes."

"Interesting. I didn't know you were friends."

"We're absolutely not. I've known Wes since school, and we happen to be working on the same story. That's it." She poured more water into a glass dripping with condensation.

"I remember him from the stint I did at the *Belleville Recorder*," Lisanne said, looking at her phone. Then she squinted. "Oh. Wes got *hot*. Like, the signs were there, but he has fulfilled his full hotness potential."

Nadine choked. "Wes?"

Lisanne brandished his photo from the *Spear* website. "Look, I may be biased because pickings are slim in our field, but Wes is an indisputably attractive man."

"I guess so." Too bad his personality got in the way.

Lisanne lifted the shades to sit on her head. "Hold up. Did you have a thing with him?"

"Oh my God, *no*." Nadine made a warding sign over the bread.

Lisanne didn't shift her gaze. "Nothing happened?"

Nadine clamped her lips shut before she forced out an answer. "Nothing. We had some misunderstandings, and we were always going for the same things. That's it."

"Liar." Lisanne was gleeful. "Stop lying, liar."

The drinks had put Nadine into that liminal zone where oversharing seemed like more of a bonding exercise than a first step to humiliation. "It was nothing," she insisted. "I might have had a small crush at first. Then there was this one time..."

"I knew it."

"I thought there could have been a moment, but nothing happened, you know?"

Lisanne nodded. "Did you want something to?"

"Not after I sobered up. I just...I don't know. The feeling passed."

He'd caught her when she tripped at a party. That was it, but they'd never been physically close before, and Nadine had become abruptly conscious that Wes was a man. She'd always categorized him, along with the other men in her program, as simply a co. Co-students. Potential coworkers and future colleagues. Men she refused to consider as people she could be attracted to because she wanted her personal life completely separate from her work.

Which was why, on that winter night, she was shocked to find herself looking at Wes's mouth and wondering what it would be like to kiss him. Then someone had shoved their way down the hall, yelling, "*Beer pong in the kitchen,*" and pushing her closer to Wes.

His arms had come up to wrap protectively around her, and ridiculously, in that student house that reeked of weed and was one rager away from being condemned, she'd thought, *This is what safe feels like.*

Obviously that was the cheap wine talking, because then, like now, Wes Chen was anything but safe. He was double-plus unsafe, the guy who applied for all the same scholarships and would be going for the same limited number of jobs. But for those few seconds, Wes's breath ruffling her hair and his heart thumping against hers, she wanted to press in closer.

Then it was over.

"What if the moment comes up again?" Lisanne asked.

"It won't." Nadine took some of the grilled bread. "He was always my nemesis."

"Me on the other hand, I wouldn't hesitate if Ying made the smallest move." Lisanne held up her fingers so close they were almost touching to demonstrate the precious little Ying would have to do to send her into a tizzy.

"You don't know if Ying likes women," Nadine said.

"She had a rainbow pin on her bag once."

"I have a rainbow pin. You gave it to me."

"Yeah, but I'm getting a vibe." Lisanne sighed. "It would help if she talked about anything besides work. She's so smart."

Nadine was grateful Ying had replaced the more unwelcome topics of Wes and Lisanne's fantastic career-making assignment. Since she was also lacking the emotional capacity to work through why she found those so volatile, she kept talking. "What about the date you went on the other day?"

Lisanne made a face. "I had to pretend I hadn't done a deep dive on the poor guy before we met and fake surprise when he told me about doing a charity bike ride. I'd already seen the post on his company's blog along with a photo of him in his gear."

"Was he wearing the shorts?" Nadine shifted on the incredibly uncomfortable seat and waved her foot around until it found purchase on a stool rung.

"With a shirt that had pouches on the back." Lisanne drained her beer. "You need to get out there. All you do is work."

"It's not all I do." She saw Lisanne open her mouth to disagree. "Almost not all."

"Close enough. You need a hobby," said Lisanne.

"I've started reading obits." At least she'd read a few.

Lisanne looked taken aback. "Okay. I didn't expect that. Why?"

"They're interesting." Nadine was sure that was part of the reason, even if she wasn't certain it was the full one. "But that's too morbid to be a hobby."

"Like cleaning moss off gravestones," said Lisanne, waving to the server for a fresh round.

"Or doing the rubbings of the engraved text."

"People do that?"

"Genealogists do it to get information from tombstones."

"That makes sense." Lisanne made a face. "My parents bought their grave plots last week. They were excited to tell me about it."

"Planning ahead is smart," soothed Nadine. "I know you'd rather not think about it."

"They got a place overlooking a little creek and said it's shady if I go to visit in the summer."

What was appropriate to say? "It's nice they're looking out for your comfort." Something occurred to her. "Did they get a family plot?"

"What do you mean?"

"Like, with enough space for you as well." Nadine dabbed her face with a napkin.

Lisanne's outraged gasp was answer enough. "No! I didn't think of that, but it's only for the two of them. Unbelievable."

"To be fair, don't you hate your hometown?"

"That's not the point," Lisanne whined. "Where am I going to go? Some pauper's plot? Do they still have those?"

"Why would I know this?" asked Nadine, pulling out her phone for a quick fact-check.

A man leaned over from the table next to them. "Unclaimed bodies are usually buried by the local government in the municipality the person dies in," he said. When they looked at him in surprise, he went bright red. "Sorry. I overheard your conversation."

"Oh, interesting," said Lisanne, putting down her drink. "Is that…? Do you work with bodies? Unclaimed ones?"

The man pulled on a ball cap and laughed as he picked his credit card off the table. "You could say that." He left with a little wave, and they stared after him.

"I'm intrigued," said Nadine.

"He was cute and kind of charming, so odds are good he's a serial killer." Lisanne took an olive. "It's hard out there."

Nadine offered her glass in a commiserative cheers, which Lisanne tapped with her own.

"Also, I saw the West Coast correspondent position went up," said Lisanne.

"Everyone knows it was tailored for Marcus," said Nadine as she bent to the cheese plate. "There's no point in applying."

"Nadine."

"It's not what I want to do, okay?" The words came out before Nadine could think them through. A quick, hard panic suddenly rose up in her chest at the thought of what might happen once her name was over a story again. Was she never going to be able to publish a byline without freaking out? No, it wasn't her. It was the job. She just didn't want to go to the West Coast. If a spot came up on the politics team, she would feel different. She *wanted* that.

"You hate the night shift and hated doing obits."

"I didn't hate obits," said Nadine. Not anymore, and it hadn't been hate. She didn't appreciate them; that was it.

"Think about it." Lisanne made a face at the chutney. "Nasty. This is garlic, not orange peel. The job would be good for you. Get you out of your comfort zone."

"I will when I'm ready." Nadine's voice was sharper than she intended.

The server interrupted the subsequent silence with a new round of drinks. That was enough to relieve the tension.

"I'm sorry," said Nadine, trying to keep polite. "It's not the right job for me."

Lisanne pointed at her. "You know the *Herald*. If you take too long, you'll be pigeonholed as the night web editor. It'll be some hot new thing coming through getting the jobs."

"I know."

"You don't want to be stuck," said Lisanne as she sipped her beer.

"I know," Nadine repeated.

Lisanne looked at her. "Think about it?"

"I will."

The conversation moved on. Nadine did her best to focus, but her mind kept drifting to tomorrow and Wes, who was going to be living with her for three weeks. Less if they found what they needed, although that thought gave her no pleasure. Did she want more time with Wes? She gulped down the rest of her drink without coming to a conclusion and listened to Lisanne talk.

# TWENTY

W es finished the plain noodles that made up the bulk of his meal and tried to avoid the tasteless chewy fish his mother had served. Across from him, Amy moved her own food around her plate as their mother complained about her job and the people she worked with.

Wes picked up a dish to give him an excuse to duck into the kitchen and marshal his thoughts. He'd told Amy about Ella's Italian internship, and she agreed he did the right thing. "At least she's done with school now, so you don't have to worry about tuition next year," she had said. He knew most of Amy's money went to rent and hadn't ask her to chip in. However, she'd been against his suggestion they cover for their sister, insisting Ella should be the one to tell their mother her plans.

"You're not doing her any favors by letting her avoid Ma," Amy had said earlier on the phone when he'd asked her to come for dinner. "Ella needs to learn to stand up to her."

"That would work if Ella was more like you," he said. "She's not. You let it roll off your back, but she dwells on it. Remember that recorder recital when she was nine?"

"She quit band because Ma kept telling her she wasn't good enough," said Amy. "Point taken. Well, I'm sure you'll hand-hold Ma through this new catastrophe."

"That's not fair," Wes said. He loved Amy, but she had little patience for their mother and what she called Wes's enabling.

"It's very fair, and the fact that you're asking me to give up my peaceful night at home to provide moral support because you can't tell her to act like a human being proves it."

Wes sighed. "Amy."

There was a long silence. "Hold on," Amy said suspiciously. "What are you holding back?"

Then Wes told her he would be leaving for a three-week work assignment, and Amy laughed and laughed. "You're going to dump all the news on her at once so she doesn't know where to get upset first," she said. "Sneaky."

"Then you'll come to dinner?"

"Oh, I wouldn't miss this," his sister said. "I'll bring dessert so we'll have one thing that's edible."

Now Wes listened to Amy making conversation with their mother as he cleared the rest of the table. Unlike Ella and Wes, Amy had a natural ability to tune out their mother that had been refined by a year of therapy, which she had started the second she moved out. She simply ignored all their mother's interruptions and talked about nothing in the most boring way possible. "Then this guy makes a left-hand turn..."

"I have a pain in my foot. Wes won't bring me to the doctor."

"The guy didn't signal once."

"You didn't thank me for making you dinner."

"I was behind him for three lights. Can you believe it?"

Wes put the cupcakes on a plate and brought them out. Their mother eyed them with disapproval. "Waste of money," she said. "Amy could have made them at home if she wasn't so busy working."

"Too bad I inherited the Chen baking gene or lack thereof on the female side," said his sister.

Wes stepped in before his mother took this as an insult to her cooking. "Ma, do you want chocolate, pistachio, or red velvet?"

"You know I only like vanilla," she said.

"They were sold out." Amy took the red velvet.

"Don't use that tone with me, Amy. You know I don't like it."

"What tone? The tone of relaying factual information?"

It was time for him to intervene. "Ma, why don't you try the chocolate?" Wes held it out.

Her expression was mulish. "No. Amy made me lose my appetite."

They ate in silence until his mother started up again. "Has Ella told you when she's coming home? I need to clean her room. It's dusty. She's been gone too long."

Amy kicked Wes under the table, and he clenched his jaw and released it to get out the tension. It was time.

"Ella has an opportunity. A job." Technically not true, but good enough. He knew his mother wouldn't care enough about the details to ask. "She won't be moving back after this summer."

"What?" Their mother uncrossed her arms, and the deep downward grooves of her mouth twitched. "What did you say? You tell her she belongs at home. She's breaking up the family, like Amy."

Amy took a deep breath but kept quiet.

"This is a great chance for Ella," Wes said, keeping his tone neutral so his mother wouldn't get more upset.

"At least a son never leaves his mother," she said, reaching over and grasping his hands. "Girls only think about themselves. A boy will protect his mother."

"Of course, Ma." Wes caught Amy's raised eyebrows across the table.

"You'll be here for me," continued their mother. She cast a sidelong look at Amy, easy enough to interpret, but Amy didn't take her eyes off Wes. Out of all of them, she was the one who packed the lightest for their mother's guilt trips. Wes tried to channel some of Amy's energy.

"Actually, Ma, I need to tell you something."

His mother yanked back her hands. "What?"

When he waited too long, Amy kicked him under the table again, this time hard enough to make him flinch. "I have a work trip that came up suddenly. It starts tomorrow. For three weeks."

There, it was out. He tensed, waiting for the explosion or the tears. She shook her head as if denying what he'd told her. "No."

"I'm sorry, Ma."

"Tell them you can't go."

On the other side of the table, Amy picked at her cupcake before putting it down on the plate, her expression tight. He felt like an asshole forcing her to be here when she'd specifically told him to deal with his own shit.

"I'll do the groceries before I go, and you can order online if you don't want to go to the store. Mr. Prescott next door can help with the garbage bins."

"I don't understand."

"You understand just fine," muttered Amy in a voice only Wes could hear. "You only pretend you don't."

Wes, on the other hand, felt helpless to do anything but play her game, the way he had for years. "I have a work trip, and it starts tomorrow."

"Why do you have to go?"

"Ma. Because it's work."

His voice must have betrayed his growing frustration, because she changed tactics. "What if someone breaks in?" she demanded. "You're leaving me to die."

Ignoring Amy's whispered "Good luck to that burglar," Wes said, "That's not true, Ma. You know I love you."

"Work, work, work." She was upset, her voice rising. "Work doesn't need you. You're replaceable there. Writing silly pathetic stories that no one reads. Anyone could do that. I could do that if I hadn't wasted my life having children."

"It's only three weeks," said Wes, ignoring the familiar verbal hits. "I've been gone longer before."

"The girls were with me then. I'll be alone." Their mother stared at Amy, who merely looked back instead of making the offer to stay their mother expected. That was enough to put her in a rage that she turned, as usual, on Wes. "You're not a good son. You're ungrateful, like your sisters. As bad as them. Worse."

Something snapped in Wes. It was as though a cable laid across his shoulders had been cut away, leaving him bobbing aimlessly but free. After all he did, it was never enough. He was never enough. There would always be more ways he'd be asked to prove himself. More ways to fail. He stood up. "Fine."

"Wes?" asked Amy, uncertain for the first time.

Wes left the table as his mother burst into tears.

Amy followed him into his room. "Wes?"

"I'm sorry, Amy." He threw a few final things into the bags he'd packed earlier. "You were right. I'm a weakling."

"Whoa, hey, I never said that." She caught his look. "In those exact words."

That made him laugh, at least a bit, and she smiled tentatively at him. "I'm sorry I made you come over for this," he said.

"We stick together." She put on a Humphrey Bogart voice. "The problems of three people can amount to more than a hill of beans."

"That doesn't make sense." Amy always cheered him up.

"Cut me some slack. I'm trying to work with the source material here."

From the dining room, their mother's sobs got progressively louder and more theatrical. Wes tried to ignore them. "I left a sheet for Ma in the kitchen with emergency numbers and information about garbage and recycling."

Amy closed the door to block their mother out, then grabbed him by the shoulders. "Wes. Listen to me. You do not have to leave emergency numbers or preorder groceries. She is perfectly healthy, and if she's capable of handling herself in the office, she can do it at home. She is choosing to do this, and it's not your job to parent her. Or Ella for that matter."

Wes heard the words—Amy had delivered this speech in various forms over the years—and as usual, he ignored them. It was easy enough for Amy to say, but she didn't have that same feeling of responsibility Wes did. Wes had to fix things. Had to make sure the people in his life were happy. He gave his usual response. "I know."

"I wish you did."

Amy waited until he was packed, and they went out to where their mother sat in front of the television. She didn't look up as they entered, and Amy poked him in a sisterly gesture of solidarity.

"It's okay," Amy whispered.

She was right. Ma was able to care for herself, and he wasn't a bad person for going to stay at Dot Voline's house. He wasn't selfish or negligent. That being said, it was best not to draw this out, because it wouldn't take long for the self-reproach to surge high enough to break his spirit, causing him to unpack and tell Nadine that she needed to stay in the big house all alone.

Nadine would say fine, but he knew it would upset her. In the end, it was thinking about Nadine sitting up at three in the morning worrying about the strange sounds outside that confirmed his decision. At least his mother would be at home and within shouting distance of the neighbors.

"You can call if you need, Ma," he said as he bent to kiss her cheek. She leaned away, refusing to make eye contact. "Don't be like this." He hated when she ignored him, pretending he was invisible. When he was younger, he sometimes felt he was.

Behind her, Amy mimed stabbing herself in the brain.

"Grow up, Ma," she said.

Their mother simply turned up the volume on the reality show she was watching.

Amy followed him to the door. "Sorry to leave you with the dishes," he said.

"No problem, big brother." There was an expression on her face that Wes couldn't read. It wasn't anger or resentment. Perhaps...pride? Whatever it was disappeared in a flash. "Bye, Wes" was all she said.

He sat in the car for a few minutes. He had to get groceries for Dot's house. He had to text Mr. Prescott to check on Ma. He had to...

He slumped over and leaned his head on the steering wheel. This wasn't the first time he'd gone against his mother, and he already knew what would happen in twenty-two days. He'd come home to at least a week of tears and accusations before life would continue on its same way.

Wes sat up. He would deal with it then. Today, he would go to Dot's twelve hours early and get a jump start on Nadine. Seeing her face tomorrow morning when he met her at the door with coffee and a full breakfast to emphasize he'd had the run of Dot's mansion without her would help the heaviness weighing down his chest. Three weeks was a long time, and he had a lot to do before he came back to his mother's house.

# TWENTY-ONE

A s Nadine anticipated, things with Wes got off to a rough start:

"That's my box," said Nadine, grabbing it out of Wes's hands on the first day of searching.

"No, it's not. It's mine." He snatched it back. "Stop cherry-picking the best boxes."

"What best boxes? What the hell makes one box better than another?"

"I don't need to explain myself to you. I know it when I see it."

"It was my box. Give it over."

They fought until it exploded in a flurry of dust and papers.

Nadine gave it a look. "Okay," she said. "It's yours."

---

Later. Wes wondered how he thought working with Nadine was a good idea:

"Brent confirmed there's no air-con up here and says Dot only liked fans," Nadine said.

"What gave it away? The heat waves coming from the floor? The fact that we drink a thousand liters of water a day?"

She ignored him. He looked up when he felt a slight breeze and saw she'd managed to get the window open. "He also told me we could chip the paint off to open these," she said.

"Thank God. Give me air."

"Get your own window. This one's mine."

"You can't be serious. It's a window."

"And it's mine." She leaned out and sucked in a lungful, smiling at him.

———————

Still later. Yes, decided Nadine. Wes was in fact the worst:

Nadine ran her sweaty hand over her sweaty hair. "Who's turn is it to make lunch?"

"Check the chore chart."

"The chore chart is a ridiculous idea, and two adults should be able to figure out lunch plans on their own."

"Yet here you are asking me."

"Wow, look at you shutting down avenues of inquiry."

"Nadine."

"What?"

He pointed to the wall. "Chore chart."

———————

A new day. Wes wasn't surprised when their partnership didn't improve:

"Where did you get those?" Nadine demanded, looking at the heaping bowl in his hand.

Wes chose a particularly succulent blackberry and popped it in his mouth. "Picked them last night from the garden and left them in the fridge so they got nice and cold."

"They look incredible. Can I have one?"

"Remember when you didn't let me breathe from your window?"

"No."

"Like hell you don't. No berries for you."

"Wes?"

"Yeah?"

"Eat a worm."

———————

The next day. Nadine decided she couldn't be held accountable if she accidentally managed to throw Wes out of a window:

"I checked that box." Wes's voice broke in on Nadine's daydreaming.

"Why would you check a box in my sector?"

"Technically, that's my sector. We decided the demarcation line had to swing around the steamer chest we couldn't budge."

"The demarcation line is wrong."

"Take it up with the person who insisted on laying it out on the floor with masking tape. Jesus, are you pulling over one of my boxes to your side to be obnoxious? What's the matter with you?"

"I'd argue it was at least fifty-five percent over the line, making it mine."

"Nice. Class act. I bet there's nothing there but some old tablecloths."

"Wrong. It's old curtains."

"I stand corrected. Have fun."

———————

Nadine started on the sink of dishes as Wes went back to work. Away from the heat of the attic, their frayed tempers had knit together enough for the meal to pass with surprising civility. As Nadine filled the dishwasher, she thought about the last few days. Their lack of success in uncovering anything of interest combined with the constant barbs fired in each other's direction meant she was finding it difficult to deal with Wes. Not only that, but he was getting under her skin in unexpected and deeply unwelcome ways, with his amazing, almost photographic memory and great cooking and kind of shocking sexiness that she was distressed to have clocked on day two, when he'd appeared after a shower with his hair wet and shirt clinging to his body. That had jump-started Wes carving out more of her brain space than she liked, which made her a little angry with herself. It might be unfair to take it out on him, but she was only human.

She finished the dishes, returned to the attic, and then walked into a wall because Wes Chen was shirtless.

Baggy shorts hung off his hips, and sweat gleamed on his chest as if he'd been working out. And the biceps. When did Wes get arms like that? Or shoulders? In the entire time they'd been working together, he'd never shown so much as a sliver of improper flesh, and now there were abs on display?

Wes looked up when she staggered back from the wall. "Don't sneak up on me." He put down a book.

"Where are your clothes?" she blurted out. Then, "Is that a tattoo?" He wasn't even reaching for a shirt to put on, as if it was totally normal to be standing in front of her looking that good.

Wes regarded his side as if making sure the snake winding up his ribs was there. She itched to look at it closer and had a vivid and entirely unwelcome thought of running her hand along it. Maybe her tongue.

*No, oh my God.* She averted her eyes.

"I got it a couple years ago when my favorite artist was taking final appointments before he retired," he said like it was no big deal that he, Mr. Button-Downs-and-Tucked-In-Sweaters Wes Chen, had a tattoo or, almost more surreal, a preferred tattoo artist. "Is that for me?"

The sight of Wes had wiped out the fact that she'd brought him a freezie. She'd wanted one herself and wasn't so big a jerk that she'd leave him hanging.

"Here. You're hot." What was wrong with her? "I mean it's hot here, so you would be hot. Physically." Not any better. "Your body would be hot." *Stop talking, Nadine.*

"Thanks." Wes had the decency to drag his shirt on, although that didn't help Nadine, who was forced to witness how his skin slid over smooth muscle as he lifted his arms through the sleeves. "Red is my favorite."

"I figured it would be."

"How?" He quirked an eyebrow, and Nadine was embarrassed at how it affected her.

"Easy. Red's basic." She waved her own blue one.

"A cheap and inaccurate shot, Barbault."

Wes laid the freezie against his forehead, then his wrists, before he tilted his neck to place it on his jugular. Nadine watched avidly before she realized she was acting like a creep and pulled her gaze away from the long line of his throat. His hair was mussed and fell in his face instead of his usual smooth style.

"I didn't know your hair was wavy," she said.

Wes slid the freezie into his mouth. "It's the heat."

"Right." Was she getting turned on from watching Wes eat a goddamn freezie? No. She had pride and self-restraint, and also this was *Wes.* "Did you find anything yet?"

"Actually, I did." He answered calmly, but she could read him well enough to know he was excited. "I was about to call you in."

"Tell me."

"Ask nicely."

"Tell me or I'll hide the ice cream I bought yesterday."

Wes caved instantly. "Give me a sec to get it."

She did her best not to check him out as he walked away, and failed. Wes must focus on RDLs or something, because those thighs were transcendent, and when he came back, she saw how his quads…bunched? Flexed? Did *something* that made her fingers twitch.

He waved a paper at her. "It might not mean anything," he warned.

"We've found nothing for days," said Nadine, doing her best to focus on work and not his legs—a difficult task as the shorts had ridden up in a distracting way. "Not much is a huge step forward."

Wes handed it over. "Have a look."

It was part of a letter, and although the salutation and date were missing, the signature, written in a flourishing hand, remained.

"Allan," Nadine said. "Allan Portson? Dot's husband?"

Wes nodded, and she lifted the page to read.

*...the story of what he'd done. I didn't react well, and I apologize. I know you dislike speaking of this, and I don't blame you. But think about what I said. It's important. The world would be a better place if potato-faced clods like him faced the justice they deserve.*

*With love,*
*Allan*

"It was in a box with some magazines, odds and ends like paper clips, and a recipe for something called a cheese ball," Wes said. "Like the last box packed on moving day."

Nadine looked at the letter again. It was something, but only barely. "'Potato-faced clod' could refer to a lot of people."

"It could, but it's also the first thing we've found, so I'll take it."

"True." She felt her elation rise. A small triumph was still a triumph. "Better put it somewhere safe."

"Great idea," he said with mock enthusiasm. "Do you have any other very obvious tips for me?"

Nadine waved him away and surveyed her space. She'd missed a box on top of an old wardrobe filled with woolen coats. She reached up, then higher on her tiptoes.

"Out of the way, short stuff." Wes's voice came from behind her, and all of a sudden, he was boxing her in against the sleek oak of the wardrobe.

It was that drunken night in the hall all over again, with his body firm against hers. His breath by her ear made her knees weak. If she shifted her eyes to the right, she would see that gorgeously muscled arm right by her face. She did, for one second. Then she stared back at the smooth wood of the cabinet to stop from wondering what would happen if she moved her head so her lips brushed his skin. Or turned around so they were face-to-face and close enough that she could feel him better than see him.

He pulled the box down. "Here," he said as he handed it to her, looking totally unruffled.

That shook her out of her reverie. "Next time I want your help, I'll ask for it."

"As if you ever ask for help."

He rolled his eyes, and that was it. That one incredibly small but massively obnoxious gesture did her in. It was the last straw and the match in the powder barrel and the nail in the coffin. She was frustrated and hot and tired and had no patience with him or with herself after that mental fantasy of kissing Wes's arm. She'd had enough of his little digs, and she'd be damned if she was going to live through any more of it.

"That's it." She clapped her hands together.

"What's it?"

"I've had enough of this. I'm done. You, downstairs."

Wes heaved a sigh so heavy it was like he was dragging it up from the bottom of Lake Ontario, but he followed her down the stairs to the big table.

"All right, Barbault." He pulled the chair out and slouched back, arms crossed, the very picture of a put-upon man. That was until she looked in his eyes. They were wary. "What's this about?"

---

Wes was not thrilled to have what he could tell was going to be a major talk. He had documents to sort and feelings to repress. It had been a mistake to reach over her for that box. He'd known it the moment he'd touched her and found she'd made him feel the same as he had so many years ago. It made for a messy situation, given that they were constantly at each other's throats.

"We have to work on this project together, and I refuse to spend the time in a low-grade war," Nadine said. "That means a reckoning. Here and now. You and me. We're going to have it out."

He sat up straight, feelings forgotten. "What the hell are you talking about?"

"I'm talking about us. I'm talking about when you stole my CBC internship."

"When I *what*? I didn't steal anything."

"You deliberately applied for it after I told you how much I wanted it. It's not like we were friends, but that was low."

"That was years ago."

"It doesn't matter how long ago it was! You screwed me over."

"Yeah, like you've done so bad for yourself." He exhaled. "First, I didn't see your name on that internship. Second, I'd already applied by the time you told me because I'd heard about it from Professor Graham."

"A likely story," she said.

"Is that why you scooped me?" Wes couldn't help his accusing tone.

"Which scoop?"

"'Which scoop.'" Seriously, this woman. "The lobbyist story last year. You looked right at me to rub it in when you won at the journalism awards."

"I did not!"

"You did so." He could still see every detail. She was at the podium, with that black dress with the little bows and those red heels, wearing the thick silver bracelets she'd had forever. And she'd stared him down in total triumph, lovely and untouchable, while he was stuck in the audience, wanting nothing more than to be up there with her.

No. Up there instead of her. That was what he'd wanted. Right?

"The lights were in my eyes. I couldn't see a thing, let alone you." She glared at him. "You didn't even come up and congratulate me like a normal person. You sat at your table talking to the woman with the blond pixie."

"Maddy?" Had Maddy been there?

"Anyway, you're one to talk. I had the perfect source lined up for my first big policy story, and you took her."

"I can't *take* a source." Wes threw up his hands. "How about when we were assigned streeters in our City Reporting class? You stood twenty meters away and snatched all my interviews."

It went on. Getting the highest mark on a test. Stolen stories. Pinched job references. Butting into coffee lines. Ten years of measly differences that kept piling up until they ended up here, yelling at each other across Dot Voline's oak library table.

Nadine's color was high, making her brown eyes darker, and he felt a quick thrill to finally, after all these years, be able to dig past her cold layers to the impassioned woman he'd known was there.

"And you got the last ticket to the special showing of *All the President's Men*!" she said. Her voice was croaky.

Wes had to grin. "You were furious. That was your favorite movie."

"It still is." She sniffed. "It's better than *Spotlight*."

"They filmed part of that in Toronto."

"Jesus, they film part of everything in Toronto." She caught his gaze across the table as he tried not to laugh. "What?"

"I can't believe you're mad about the wording on a slide from a class we took years ago."

"Shut up. You're upset because I liked listening to surf rock when I studied." She hummed the first few bars of "Wipe Out."

That was enough for Wes, who burst out laughing so loud the cats, who had been monitoring the situation from afar, ran from the room. Nadine stopped humming, a small smile on her face. Then she was laughing with him. It took them a few moments to calm down.

"God," she said. "I knew I could hold a grudge but never thought I'd find someone to match me."

"It's probably not something to congratulate ourselves on," he said, feeling better than he had in ages. The fight had been a pinprick deflating his long-standing balloon of bitterness.

"Gotta take the wins where we can." She smoothed her hair back behind her ears as if to indicate it was time to get back to business.

Wes leaned back in his chair. "Now what? You got your reckoning. Do you feel better?"

"A little." She shrugged. "I liked yelling at you for a while, that's for sure. You?"

"Yeah." He nodded. "The yelling was nice."

"Good, so we can move on to next steps. I see two choices for where we go from here. We can keep on as we were. Or..." She looked at him as if waiting.

It was easy enough to finish her thought. "Or we can bury the hatchet and start fresh," he said.

"For the sake of the project, I'm willing to let bygones be bygones if you are."

"Noble." Wes traced a finger along the table. "You know, none of what happened was really directed at each other. It's the job."

"That's true. There was no deliberate malice." She looked at him to confirm. "Was there?"

He snorted. "Not on my side, but I feel your very aggressive playing of *The Best of the Sixties Surf Rock Compilation* volumes one through four was deliberately targeted at me."

"Playing the music wasn't." Her look was impish. "Playing it on repeat was."

Wes shook his head. "I knew it."

"Yeah." She grinned. "That's what made it awesome."

Wes couldn't be mad when he saw that smile. "Then we're agreed. Fresh start? No lingering grievances?"

"Fresh start." She held out her hand, and he shook on it.

It was good they'd had this talk, he decided, feeling the tension drain out. A smooth relationship would make the time go much easier. Then something occurred to him.

"As we move forward in the spirit of collaboration, I'd like to reconfirm we don't do anything with this story until we talk it over."

"Agreed." She stood up, and Wes followed her gaze to the attic.

"It's like a treasure hunt mixed with a gambling table," he said. "I keep thinking, one more cabinet and I'll have all the secrets."

"One last roll of the dice and we'd have it," she said.

"Here's hoping we get snake eyes." He headed toward the stairs, then turned back. "Also, I fixed your demarcation tape. It was crooked."

He was curious to see if her promise would hold. For a second, he thought her usual rage would take over. Then she shook her head and laughed.

They were good. Or at least getting there.

# TWENTY-TWO

Nadine put aside a box filled with prairie-style nightgowns wrapped in their original but yellowing cellophane. Searching the attic was both physically uncomfortable and emotionally demoralizing, because although each box could hold the secret they needed, too often she found herself sorting through something like empty plastic containers of L'eggs hosiery. After a week, they'd found nothing.

When her phone buzzed, she almost pounced on it. She badly needed a break.

**Raj quit,** Lisanne texted.

**What?**

**There was an opening in sports, and he applied. They gave the job to Kyle.**

It took Nadine a second to place him. **The intern?**

**Former intern and current sports reporter for the Herald.**

Nadine shook her head. **Raj lived sports. He was goalie for his university hockey team.**

**I know that,** wrote Lisanne. **You know that. They asked if he knew what an assist was.**

Oh, that hurt. **Good for him then. Where's he going?**

**TSN. He figured he'd give television a shot.**

**We'll take him out for drinks when I'm done here,** Nadine wrote.

**How's the secret assignment going?**

**It's going. Haven't found what we need.**

**And Wes?**

**Fine.** To stop the questions, Nadine picked part of Lisanne's big story she could talk about without envy. **How's Ying?**

**Brilliant. She mentioned an ex. It was a girl.**

**And?**

**I casually mentioned my ex, Becca,** replied Lisanne. **Making progress. Neither of us are fully out at work so I'm going slow.**

**Seems wise.**

**Got to go, Hetty called a meeting. Daniel changed his mind and told her she couldn't hire that writer she wanted.**

This would infuriate Hetty. Daniel had been promoted over her to become editor in chief last year, despite the general understanding among staff that Hetty was perfect for the job and Daniel was not.

Grateful the conversation with Lisanne had been limited to a straightforward bit of gossip, Nadine opened the next box to find a collection of obituaries in an unmarked folder. Curious, she sat down in the chair they'd covered with an old sheet. All of them had notes in Dot's hand or a line or two highlighted. On some, the ink had disintegrated the paper, as if Dot had held the highlighter on the page as she read.

Nadine went through the collection, reading each one to appreciate how they brought people to life for one last hurrah. She'd been reading more obits in her spare time since her talk with Dot and had slowly seen what could have been done with the lives that passed by her desk.

She'd seen what she could have done with Dot Voline.

These obits weren't limited to the editorial items written by reporters at major news sites. There were also death notices from the back of the paper, usually written by grieving family and focused on the basics: cause of death, family members, appreciation of health care professionals, and funeral arrangements. Touching details colored in the small black-and-white photos that headed most of the clippings, such as the woman who had the same pot stewing for thirty years to serve as the first course for every dinner. Dot's note read, *What happened to this perpetual stew?*

What did happen? Did the eldest son take it to continue the tradition? Did they eat it at the funeral before covering the pot one last time? The obit, like death, left more questions asked than answered.

Her phone rang. It was her mother. "Where are you?" she demanded.

"What?" Nadine closed the folder. "What's wrong?"

"Nadine, are you okay? Are you safe?" Her mother sounded upset.

"Yes? What are you talking about?"

"We're at your apartment. You're not here, and we were worried. There's mail piled up in front of the door."

"I'm out," she said, confused. "I'm sorry, Mom, did we have plans? I must have missed it in my calendar."

She could hear her father rumbling in the background, then fading as her mother moved away. "No, no, we wanted to see you because we knew you were on vacation."

Nadine felt the anger building. She'd answered all her mother's texts promptly, yet that wasn't enough. "Are you upset because you came by my apartment without checking to see if I'd be there and I wasn't?"

"I don't like that tone, Nadine. We're looking out for your safety. You're a young woman living alone, and I don't feel good about it, not these days. I'm glad you're coming home."

"I didn't say I was moving back, and also I'm not a young woman. I'm thirty."

"You know it's the best choice."

Wes came into the attic and looked at her quizzically. She turned away and lowered her voice. "Mom, I am fine. You don't need to worry about me."

"We always worry about you. Where are you?"

"Enjoying my vacation, and I have to go. Bye, Mom." She hung up the phone and held her hand palm out to Wes. "Before you ask, it was my mother, and I have zero desire to talk about it."

"Fine by me," said Wes. "I came up to tell you dinner was ready early."

Nadine wouldn't tell Wes for fear of inflating his ego, but she loved it when he cooked. The food was always stellar, and unlike her, Wes had mastered the complicated art of synchronizing cooking times to make sure the dishes made it to the table when they should. Tonight, he served gazpacho with tomatoes from the garden, followed by a vegetarian paella. Every bite was perfectly seasoned, and once Wes found out she hated green peppers, they'd never reappeared.

"Amazing as always," she said, seeing him cast her an anxious glance as she ate. He relaxed slightly and smiled when she took another spoonful.

When they were done, Nadine went to the fridge. Alerted by the click of the container top opening, cats swarmed into the kitchen.

She counted them up and frowned.

"Wes, have you seen Erma?"

"Not since lunch." He looked around the kitchen as if the cat could be hanging from the ceiling, then joined her for a recount. "Only three, and Erma loves eating."

Erma never missed a meal and had made a habit of slapping Wes in the face with her paw at six thirty in the morning if they hadn't yet been fed, which he complained about regularly. She'd also learned to open his door, but when Nadine offered to show him one of her mother's tricks for keeping hotel doors safe, he'd refused. "I don't want her to feel unwelcome in her own house," he'd said. "What if she's lonely and misses Dot?" Nadine had felt bad enough to start leaving her own door open a crack in case a cat needed company.

"Let's check around." Wes looked under the table as he spoke.

They did a complete scan, one of them watching a room for movement while shaking a bag of treats as the other checked behind curtains and under furniture.

"I feel Erma would like the porcelain room," said Wes.

"She's a destructive animal."

"She is not." Wes defended her. "She likes the colors."

To their relief, Erma was not in the porcelain room knocking over small side tables filled with Royal Doulton. Nor was she in the fashion room, where Nadine checked under the ornate skirts as a portrait of the cats in Elizabethan dress looked on. "The Diors are safe," she reported, panting slightly as she rose to her feet.

"I believe those are House of Worth," he said.

"Really?" She looked back in. "I didn't realize you were so into fashion and design, but you know a lot."

"I like it, but I also remember a lot from my stories," he said, crossing his arms. "They impact us on a daily basis, so it helps me when I'm putting things in context."

"It's impressive."

"Oh." He looked at her in surprise, then frowned slightly as if he didn't believe her.

Erma wasn't in the library or the attic or the conservatory. They went back to the kitchen and opened another container of food. Overfeeding the cats was worth it to flush her out.

Wes paced in alarm. "Do you think she got outside?" He stared out the window. "She'll be scared. She's too small. What if there are raccoons? Coyotes? Those billionaire's dogs we keep hearing?" Before she could answer, Wes held up his hand. "Wait. Do you hear that?"

Nadine tilted her head to hear better. "No."

Wes turned in a slow circle. "I heard a noise."

"From where?"

"I don't know." He walked to the left, then back to the right.

Nadine went to the door and listened. "Too bad we didn't teach the cats to play Marco Polo."

"I was great at that game," said Wes absently. "Hold on. There it is again."

They stood by the window and listened until a faint scratching came from the door.

"That must be her," Wes said.

They speed walked through the kitchen and took up positions in the salon, Wes near the library door and Nadine close to the conservatory. "Erma?" called Wes. "Ermikins kitty cat?"

"Ermikins kitty cat?" asked Nadine.

Wes looked faintly embarrassed. "It's what she likes to be called."

It seemed he was right, because another meow drifted in. "The library," said Wes, dashing through the door.

The sound was louder here. Nadine zeroed in on a section of panel to the left of the door. "Is Erma in the wall?" she asked.

They pressed their ears against the wall. "She is. Like some sort of Lovecraftian rat." He raised his voice. "It's okay, Erms. I'm here."

Another imperious meow.

"Wait a minute." Nadine stared at the wall, then up to the secret entrance to the attic as a distant memory of an old murder mystery came to her. Like Brent had done the first time he'd shown them the attic, she ran her fingers along the panel until she found what felt like a depression. She pressed it, and with a smooth slide, the door rose to reveal a dark hole.

A black streak leapt out and into Wes's arms, purring and headbutting him in the chin. "Erma!" He lifted the cat up to look in her face. "You bad cat. How did you get in there?"

When she jumped out of his arms to stalk away, they turned to stare into the wall.

"It's a dumbwaiter," Nadine said. "Look at the pulleys. They used it to move things from one floor to another."

"There's a basement we didn't know about?" Wes looked down in shock, as if he could see through the floor.

She took her phone and turned on the video. "Let's find out."

# TWENTY-THREE

Wes waited for Nadine to set her phone up to her liking, then pushed the button on the edge of the dumbwaiter at her nod. It gave a pleasant click, and the box began to drop. They pressed close to peer down as it descended, before Nadine pointed out this could get their heads chopped off if something came from above. They took a swift step back.

"This is going to be great," Nadine enthused. "Anything could be down there."

"Or nothing," said Wes. He liked the idea of a hidden space in theory, but if it was as full as the attic, he would simply curl up and die.

"It could house a crypt," said Nadine.

"Or be empty."

"A kiss of vampires in their undead sleep."

"I'd prefer that to more boxes."

It felt like a year until the dumbwaiter came back up. Nadine snatched her phone, and they sat on the couch to review the footage. At first, it was difficult to make out any details as the screen went from darkness to slightly grayer darkness, which was compounded by the distracting fact that Nadine was sitting near enough that her thigh was firmly against him. The house was hot, and he should hate the extra heat she generated. But he wanted to shift closer.

On the screen, the video gave a small jolt as the dumbwaiter reached the bottom. Luckily, there didn't seem to be a door blocking their view.

"It's empty," said Wes with satisfaction. "Thank God we don't have another warehouse worth of papers and old clothes to sift through."

"I still want to see it for myself."

He nodded. That was a given. Its mere existence was cool enough to merit further exploration.

"Hold on." Nadine turned the screen around as if that would adjust the camera angle to allow her to see more. She zoomed in and pointed to the center. "There's something along that wall."

Wes didn't want to agree, but he had no choice. "Damn. Boxes."

"Boxes." She checked the screen again. "We need to go through them."

"This is the beginning of a horror story," he warned.

"As long as we stay out of the forest, we'll be fine." Nadine was halfway out of the library. "There's a flashlight in the kitchen. Let's go."

At least the heavy-duty flashlight that was stuck to the side of the wall was big enough to be used as a weapon if there *were* basement vampires lying in wait.

Nadine grabbed it and handed it to him. "Lead the way," she said.

"What, so I get killed first?"

She gave him an exasperated look and pushed back the lock of hair that had fallen out of her high bun. "No, because I don't know where the stairs to the basement are."

"Me neither." He shrugged. "They can't be hard to find."

Wes was wrong. An hour later, they were back in the kitchen, having checked every room for a door. He leaned against the huge island counter and rubbed his neck in frustration. "This house is wild," he said. "How could we not find it? We looked everywhere. It's a *door*."

Nadine came out from checking the pantry for the second time and put the flashlight on the table. "Could it be outside?"

An outside basement entrance seemed unlikely, but it wasn't like they were having any success here. "Or the conservatory?" he said. "We didn't look there."

"I'll check the conservatory, and you check the exterior." Nadine made the decision for them in her usual confident way.

"What did we say about staying out of the forest?" he asked.

"Dot's herb garden is hardly a haunted realm," she said.

"If I get Freddy Krueger'd out there, let it be on your head."

"I'll take my chances."

Despite his teasing, Wes didn't mind stepping out for some fresh air. He took the flashlight, and they split up at the kitchen side door, a shortcut they'd found into the back garden. The backyard—no, the outdoor part of the estate—was a mix of vegetables for the kitchen, flowers in ornate beds with walkways, and a patio space with a firepit. Wes circled the house, looking for anything that could be an entrance. Nothing. No root cellars. No trapdoors.

There had to be one. Had to be something. He retraced his steps, mentally mapping out the interior of the house as he went. This would be Nadine's room at the end of the east wing, mirroring where Dot's was on the west. He lingered, comparing what he saw to what he recalled from inside. He could have sworn Nadine's Marie Antoinette room was smaller than what the exterior of the house indicated.

Wes rushed back in to pass Nadine.

"I didn't find anything," she said. "Did you? You did. You're running. Was it ghosts after all? Wes, wait for me."

He slowed for her to catch up and led the way to the Marie Antoinette room. The en suite was to the south of the room, and the canopied bed, with two sleeping cats nestled in the multitude of pillows, was set against the wall to the north.

That was where the extra space would be.

"You think the basement door is in my room?" Nadine looked around in confusion.

"Let's find out," he said. "Give me a hand."

To her credit, Nadine simply grabbed the end of the bed instead of peppering him with more questions. In seconds, they'd discovered the bed was on wheels, and once they pushed up the locks, it was easy to move away from the wall. The cats jumped off with offended trills.

Neither of them paid attention because they were looking at a door. A door in the wall behind the bed that had been hidden by the canopy.

"What the fuck." Nadine's voice was flat. "I *sleep* here."

"Whoa, creepy. Have you heard sounds at night? Rustling? Voices? Chanting?"

"*Wes.*"

"Sorry, I got carried away." He gave her an apologetic look. He wouldn't have been thrilled to find a secret door behind his bed either. "Let's look inside. I'm sure it's nothing too disturbing."

She grabbed the flashlight and lifted it as if to check the weight before settling into a boxing stance. "I'm ready."

He supposed it didn't hurt to be cautious. "Southpaw, huh?"

"With a wicked hook, so be ready to open that door on the count of three."

Wes gave her a thumbs-up, and she counted down.

"One, two, three."

He threw the door open and leapt out of the way of Nadine's swinging arm, ready to jump in as backup. Nothing happened. Peeking in, he saw a lamp near the door and flicked the switch.

Wes wasn't sure what he'd expected, but it wasn't this. There was no cinder-block tunnel leading to the depths of the house. No stale air and torches. Instead, a sturdy leather armchair sat in the far corner, and the bare walls of the small room were painted a pleasant coral. A record player, still plugged in, sat near the chair with a rack filled with old albums. It was both a letdown and unbelievably confusing.

"This is weird," he said.

"There must be something else here."

"Like what?" He looked up to see a regular ceiling. It was simply a room. A secret room carpeted with ivory shag behind Nadine's bed.

"I don't know, but I'm going to find out." Nadine began knocking on every wall, searching for another way in or out, and Wes went to sort through the records. A thick layer of dust lay on the surfaces.

"Oh my God." He snatched his hand away.

It only took Nadine three strides for her to cross the room, no doubt dying to see what he'd found so shocking. "Let me see."

"No." He put it behind his back and thanked God the lamplight was dim so she couldn't see how red his face was getting.

She peered around him to see what he was hiding, and he weaved back-and-forth to block her. "I am sleeping in a sex room with a secret door," she said. "Trust me, it can't be that bad."

"It's not a sex room," Wes said. "Those kinds of images were common in ancient Rome."

"But not in twenty-first-century Canada, so let me see." She held her hands out and waited, then rolled her eyes when he didn't move. "Wes. Hand. It. Over."

He bit his lip. "Don't say I didn't warn you."

Nadine grabbed the record out of his hands. "*Songs for Stripping*," she read. "'Turn your lover on with these classics of the stripping arts. Instruction manual included.'" Wes looked at the album cover, which had a woman with platinum bouffant hair posing with a naughty grin and hands over her breasts. There were a lot of feathers. And garters. Nadine shook the album and peered inside. "The instruction manual is missing."

"Too bad."

She checked the back cover. "What are songs for stripping anyway?"

He knew what she was planning before she moved to the record player. "Don't do it," he warned. "Some things are better left unknown, and that includes Dot's preferred nookie tunes."

"Sounds like a dare." She fiddled with the record player and put down the arm.

They stared at each other as the music started. "That's more flute than I thought there'd be for stripping," said Wes finally.

"And trumpet." She shook her head. "My grade school band didn't sound like this."

"Is that a cowbell?" he asked.

They listened closer. "It is," she said. "Sexy. I can see the tassel-covered pasties."

"It reminds me of the burlesque show at Dilly's," Wes said.

"You go to drag brunch?"

"Of course," he said, insulted. "They have bottomless mimosas, and Lady Kiki sings ABBA."

Nadine laughed. "I'm sure they love you, all neat and tidy." She cast him a wicked glance. "Ready to be unwrapped like a present."

Was she flirting with him? He ran his finger around his collar, wondering if the room had gotten warmer. The saxophone played from the corner, and Nadine walked over to turn it off before he could think of a good reply.

"I don't think there's anything else here," she said, stomping on the floor to check for trapdoors. They backed out and put the bed in place, clicking the locks firmly. Wes stared at the wall, and Nadine leaned against the canopy.

"You know," she said. "I could use a drink."

So could he. They headed to the kitchen as Murasaki and Octavia settled back on the bed.

Nadine bypassed the beer and wine they'd stocked in the kitchen to head straight to the drinks trolley in the salon. She took the crystal decanter and poured a hefty amount into an old-fashioned glass etched with an image of Balmoral Castle, then watched Wes do the same with Holyrood.

"Good bourbon," he said, refilling his glass.

Nadine didn't care what it was or about the quality, as long as it had the desired effect of soothing her fired-up nerves. Her initial shock of finding a hidden room behind her bed had transformed into a deep and unyielding curiosity about what other mysteries the house contained.

"You would think that would be something for Brent to mention in his handoff notes," she said.

"He might not know," said Wes as he paced the salon, drink in hand. "That room looked like it hadn't been opened in years. God, what else could we find? A house with a hidden stripping room could have anything." He sounded thrilled and began to look behind the paintings on the wall.

Nadine's eyes fell on the copy of Miss Marple's short stories. Dot had put the newspaper obit about the woman with the best buns in town between the pages, and she picked it up to read again. Wait. She recognized the story Dot had marked. "Wes. Wes."

Wes turned from looking under a chair. "What's up?"

"Dot's not done playing games with us." She handed him the book. "She bookmarked 'Strange Jest.' Do you know the story? Agatha Christie."

"I don't think so." He skimmed the pages to see the end. "No. Are you kidding?"

"I am not. Miss Marple helps a young couple find their uncle's hidden treasure in his mansion." A thought occurred to her. "Dot started planning for us to look for clues before she died. She marked this page on our last visit and told me to remember."

Wes tossed down his drink. "Normally I would say this is too incredible to believe, but after our recent discoveries, I'm feeling very open-minded."

"We should give Brent a call," said Nadine. "See what he says."

They were in luck, and Brent picked up the phone. Nadine put it on speaker and gave him a quick summary.

Brent laughed heartily. "That would be just like her," he said with an admiration Nadine shared. Dot was something else. "It makes sense. Maria had been complaining about my aunt reorganizing over the last month when she should have been resting."

"Then we're not imagining things?" asked Wes.

"No, you might be onto something," said Brent. "She'd always wanted to write a mystery."

"She mentioned that," said Nadine. "Did she say anything about what we should be looking for?"

"Sorry," he said. "Nothing that I remember. Too bad you can't talk to Maria, but she's visiting her parents in Portugal on some remote island without email or cell service for a month."

Figures. Wes leaned over Nadine, and she looked up to see that perfect bone structure softened in the lamplight. "By the way, Brent, do you know where the door to the basement is?" he asked.

Brent paused. "There's a *basement* in that house? I had no idea. God, the Realtor is going to have a fit."

"There is, but we can't find the door," said Wes.

Brent couldn't help but promised to try to find some floor plans and wished them luck.

Wes sprawled out on the couch, Erma perched on the back behind him. "I have to admit, this is a new situation for me," he said. "I'm more used to investigations that are a little less adventurous."

Nadine laughed. "Beats looking at court documents for hours."

Wes folded his arms and looked at the ceiling, gifting Nadine with a view of a jaw that could cut glass. "What do we do next?"

"Are you asking, or is that rhetorical? Because I'm going to play her game." Nadine might suck at mysteries, but she still loved them. "We assumed we only had to search the attic because that's what she told Brent to show us. We were wrong. I think she was planning to do this for us, but she died before she could finish setting it up."

Both of them instinctively looked around. It was a big house, and

Dot had not been a fan of minimalist design. "We have three weeks," said Wes.

"Two," corrected Nadine.

"Right, thank you." Wes sat up and fixed Nadine with a narrow look. "I have an idea."

Nadine wasn't sure why that made her heart hammer. His voice had gone low and challenging. "What?"

"I work better under pressure, don't you?"

"Maybe." She wasn't going to commit until she knew where this was going.

"I have a proposal."

"I'm open to listening."

"What if we make this into a competition? When one of us finds something, a clue, they get a point."

Nadine put a considering expression on her face so he didn't know how much she loved this opportunity to smash him into the ground. They may have put their past grievances to bed, but that didn't mean Nadine's competitive spirit was asleep. "What does the winner get?"

"I would be happy with the sweet satisfaction of victory, but we can figure something less refined for you."

She wouldn't let him get to her. "We don't know what we're looking for. What counts as finding something?"

He tapped his knee. "How about we both have to agree it matters."

That was fair, and beating Wes would give her more of an incentive. "I'm in and claim my Miss Marple book discovery as my first point." Already one ahead. She liked this game.

"The room behind your bed is mine."

Damn, but she couldn't think of a reason to say no. "Fine."

They went to the kitchen, where Wes set up tallies on the whiteboard. He put a single line under their names. "It's a tie so far."

They looked at each other for a long moment.

Then they dashed off in two different directions.

# TWENTY-FOUR

hree hours later, they both ended up in the attic. The lamplight in the main house made it too difficult to find little cracks in walls that might indicate secret hidey-holes, and if he was honest, Wes felt a little daunted by the entire endeavor. There were a lot of searchable spots in Dot's house.

He paged through property tax bills in a desultory fashion as he tried to stay awake. He hadn't wanted to break first, vaguely feeling as though he'd be letting Nadine down. She was so involved in the competition they'd made up that he wanted to bring the same energy.

She pinched her shirt between her fingers to fan in some air and looked over quizzically when he made an involuntary sound. "Wes? Are you okay?"

"A little overheated." True enough although not in the way he felt it. That decade-old attraction had kicked up hard the other day when she'd appeared in the attic ready to work, dress swirling around her legs. Despite their constant need to be at each other's throats, he'd been powerless as it grew when she was on her hands and knees taping that ridiculous line on the floor. Tonight in the damp heat, she'd pulled her hair up, and tiny tendrils had escaped to frame her face. The harsh lights lit up Nadine's skin to show the little pattern of freckles across her shoulders, like the sun had peppered her with kisses.

Nadine looked inside the dusty trunk she was about to sort and sighed. Wes sympathized. She sounded like he felt.

"Want a break?" he offered. He'd take one for the team by giving in first. They'd do better if they paced themselves. "I found a curious place earlier."

"*Yes.*" She switched off the light, plunging the attic into a dim twilight. The moon was bright enough for them to find their way through the boxes. "Where is it?"

"Out back."

Nadine looked out the window. "What if there are clues outside the house?"

"Dot could barely walk, and we never saw her outside," Wes pointed out.

She looked relieved. "True. What's this secret place?"

"You'll see." Wes didn't want to tell her the details so he could see the surprise on her face.

They stopped in the kitchen, and Wes opened the fridge to fetch her a can of the fruit beer she preferred.

"Thanks." She handed him a glass of his favorite red. "Where to?"

"This way." They were being so polite, as if exhaustion had sapped the energy to snipe at each other, a habit they still fell into despite their big talk. Wes went straight to the trees they'd assumed had delineated the edge of the property, then ducked into them.

"Is there a path?" asked Nadine as she stepped behind him.

"Yes, but you can barely see it."

They came into the clearing a few seconds later, and Nadine gasped. "No way."

He waved his hand. "Voilà. She wasn't kidding. Dot had a grotto."

It was exquisite. Water fell from a rock formation into a pool that looked like it was hewn from actual stone and was small enough to cross in four or five swim strokes. He couldn't believe it when he found the place. His first thought had been *Nadine is going to love this.*

He was happy to know he was right.

"I checked with Brent, who said it's a legit pool and safe to swim in," said Wes.

Nadine slipped off her shoes as if in a trance. "The water looks perfect."

Her toes shattered the moon trembling on the surface, and Wes joined her, instantly feeling his whole body relax. She was right. He lay back on the inlaid stone surrounding the pool and listened to the water tumble down the surprisingly robust falls at the edge. The warm, dark stillness made him feel as if it was only the two of them left in the world. Not even the ever-present Toronto traffic or sirens broke the peace.

They sat for a few minutes before Wes said, "This is almost like a real vacation."

Nadine laughed without humor. "I needed one. I hate the night shift. Almost as much as Raj hated being obituary editor."

"Your replacement?" He closed his eyes and folded his arms behind his head like a pillow.

Her voice came to him. "It wasn't his thing."

"Did you like it?" He twisted his head to look at her. The moonlight touched her profile, the tip of her nose and chin, and left the rest in shadow. "Obits?"

"Not at first," she said. "Why am I telling you this?"

"Hey, we don't have to be friends to listen."

She sniffed. "I kind of think you do."

"Well, maybe you're about four percent better than I thought."

"High praise."

"Come on, Nadine. Let it out."

"Ugh, only because my therapist is on vacation." She pulled her hair back and let it drop. "You don't do obits over at the *Spear*, right?"

"Nope."

"They call it the dead beat and say it's where reporters go to die. Tom was there for twenty years. I didn't know how he managed it, calling people day in and day out to ask about the lives of those who had passed."

"Didn't or don't?"

She leaned forward to dip her hands in the water. "Past tense. You remember the first time you had to call the family for a crime story?"

He did. "It was hard, going to people reeling from grief and trying to let them talk but at the same time knowing you were on a deadline."

"Yeah." Her shoulders hunched up. "I was only in the obits job for a month, and that wasn't enough time to understand it was different. The people I talked to were sad, but they were happy to talk about the person I was writing about. It was kind of uplifting? Less depressing at least, but I didn't see it at the time because I had a preconceived notion it would be sad." She splashed her feet around. "Enough about me. I'm on vacation. What about you? What's the *Spear* like?"

"I'm on vacation too," he reminded her.

Her laugh rang out, full and happy. Wes liked it. It wasn't like bells chiming or anything like that, but the rich sound of a woman enjoying herself. His home hadn't had much laughter, and he found he craved it like a drug.

"True, but tell me anyway," she said. "We're doing sharesies."

"This isn't the last slice of cake. There's no sharesies here."

"Don't care. You owe me."

He looked at the shadows on her back as she bent forward and how the fabric of the dress showed she wasn't wearing anything under it. Better to talk than think about that. He capitulated. "It is what it is."

"Yowza. That's no vote of confidence." She shifted to face him, causing her dress to dip down low in the front. Wes had to close his eyes. "I have an idea," she announced. "What if we don't use points for our game?"

He cracked an eye open. "What do you have in mind?"

"If I find something, you have to answer one of my questions. On the off chance you do, you can ask me one."

"Why?" he asked. "What do you want to know?"

"If I asked you the question here, it wouldn't make for much of a prize, would it?"

"True, but that doesn't answer why."

Nadine kicked her foot in the water. "We're here for a while," she said. "It doesn't make sense that we stay strangers. We've known each other for years, and we've barely *talked*. It's weird."

He was nodding before she finished. "I like it. Do we start now, since we each have a point?"

"We can." She tilted her head to the sky. He followed her gaze. The city would never get full black thanks to light pollution, but at least there were a few stars visible. She was quiet, and then she pulled her legs in. "Actually, you know what I'm really in the mood for?"

# TWENTY-FIVE

t was a good thing Wes wasn't the kind of guy to have his mind in
the gutter, because he would have been sorely disappointed when
thirty minutes later, they walked into an old-school strip of a diner.

But even if part of him was, the way Nadine's dimple appeared
with her smile as she held the door open went a long way to cheering
him up.

Wes took a seat at one of the red vinyl stools that lined the beige-
and-sand-marble-patterned counter and faced the cooking area. It was
like a time capsule. A woman with dark brown hair in a hairnet flipped
an omelet before tossing some breakfast potatoes next to it. He had
a brief thrill to be out so late without having to deal with his mother
asking where he was going, why, and when he would be back. It was a
relief to do what he wanted without answering to anyone.

"I've never been here," Wes said, sniffing in delight. "I've always
wanted to though."

"Comfort food at its best," said Nadine. "Perfect for one-in-the-
morning munchies."

He knew what Nadine wanted—the fish and chips she'd been talking about on the way over—and read through the items listed on the bright yellow sign that hung on the wall to decide his own order.

"What can I get for you?" The cook came back after serving the only other customers, a few university kids at the giggly level of high.

Although intrigued by the bandeja paisa, Wes went for that diner classic, a club sandwich. Nadine opened her can of Sprite—he noticed she didn't drink caffeine after noon—and watched as the cook tossed the fish into the fryer. "Extra crispy, please," she called.

"You got it."

It didn't take long for the food to arrive, glistening under the bright lights. He bit into the sandwich, the toast abrading the top of his mouth, as Nadine cut into the fish to release a puff of steam. Then she said, "Time for me to claim my point. No surprise, it's the same question you avoided at the grotto. What happened with you at the *Spear*?"

"I'm not doing exactly what I want, but at least I'm working." Not having a choice but to answer made it much easier to talk to Nadine.

"That sucks." Nadine's voice was understanding. "Where do you want to be?"

"The investigative team. I was seconded for six months before they sent me back to Lifestyle." He swallowed down the disappointment that always came when he relived Jason telling him, *Sorry, man, Rebecca insisted she needed you. It's fine. I had my eye on Tyler and convinced him to come on board.*

"I read your stories. You're good, no matter what section you're writing for."

"Yeah?" That made him feel better, because Nadine was not someone to blow sunshine. If she said his work was good, then it was.

"You always were. You used to drive me bananas at school. I called you Mr. Why."

This made him laugh. "Why?"

She grinned. "I prove my case."

"Come on, Nadine."

"You were never happy with the first answer someone gave you," she said. "I noticed it when you were doing a story about the new naming rights for the school athletic center."

"With the donation from the guy rehabilitating his reputation."

"That one. I saw your interview transcript, and you kept asking why. Why did they accept blood money? Why, why, why, until that vice president finally snapped."

"I had a big fight with the faculty advisor," Wes said. That had been one of his scariest days, but he'd been certain of his story. After it resulted in a student protest, Wes had been awestruck with the knowledge that this was what he was meant to do. "I had a name for you too."

"I feel it wasn't flattering."

"It was Nadacity."

She put her fry down to look at him. "What the hell does that mean?"

"Nadine and tenacity." He grimaced at her expression. "I was twenty. Give me a break. It was because you never gave up. You contacted ten people for one of your stories and another five to confirm a point. It was good."

She turned back to her plate. "Thanks. Your name for me is terrible though."

"It's not like yours is winning any originality prizes."

"Fine, I accept that. I haven't used it in years anyway. You said you were seconded? What happened?"

He'd never talked about it, not trusting anyone at work and knowing that Caleb, cheerleader though he was, wouldn't understand. Caleb thought adversity bred opportunity.

"It's not like it's a bad reason," he said. "It's more frustrating. They put me back in Lifestyle because my stories there get good engagement, the best in the company."

Understanding dawned on her face. "Makes sense. I heard the *Spear* was having revenue problems."

"I heard that too, although every staff meeting makes it sound like we've got cash to burn."

"Lifestyle has great stuff," she said. "It's the first section I check."

Wes didn't look up. "Sure, but it's not what I want to do."

"Is that it?" she asked.

He reached for the ketchup to give him some time to decide how to phrase it. "It's not only that they sent me back. It's who they put in my place."

"Who?"

"This guy Tyler Dawlish." The words came out slow. "I found out later that Jason—he's the investigative editor—told my manager Tyler was a better fit for the team anyway." That had stung.

Her eyebrows rose. "Oh?"

"Maybe he is. I'm not aggressive in the same way Tyler is. It's not my thing."

"That's bullshit." Nadine sounded furious, and his heart dropped. He should have known better than to trust her, even within the rules of this game. What was he thinking? "The way you work is incredible, Wes, and you can be forceful without being loud. You listen and observe."

This wasn't what he expected. He didn't know what to say but managed "Thanks?"

Nadine wasn't done. "Let me take some guesses about that team."

He laughed, feeling lighter. "All right."

"One guy talks a lot about shining a light in the dark corners and insists he's completely objective in his reporting. Another got hired because he's friends with one of the editors or an old roommate." She was warming up to her mental template. "One's a legacy. His dad worked there."

"No, her mom worked for the *Herald*, actually."

"I'm also willing to bet the loudest people in the meeting are the ones who carry the day."

Wes looked over. "How do you know?"

"I work for the *Herald*," she said simply.

"It's infuriating," he said.

She reached out to tap his arm. "It is. I'm sorry, Wes. It sucks to feel like that. You shouldn't need to be an extrovert to be a success."

"No, but it helps."

She was silent, unable to argue.

Wes didn't want to talk about himself anymore. He'd answered her question, and it was his turn. "Is that why you left the politics team?" he asked. "Frustration?"

"Is this your question? Are you using your point?"

"I am."

She pushed her plate to the side, then shrugged in a fatalistic way. "I wrote an immigration story that generated a lot of anger, including a death threat from a guy who also came to my apartment."

Wes felt sick. "Nadine."

"He was a subscriber, if you can believe it, and he sent it under his own email. I saw a picture of him before he showed up to my place, so I recognized him."

"What did he look like?"

She thought. "He's one of those men who are the color of teeth."

"Did the *Herald* deal with it?" he asked gently.

"Yes. One of my colleagues had been doxed a couple months before. They'd screwed it up, and she had to move. At least that didn't happen to me." Her hands were balled in her lap.

"It's still frightening. It's good you had support from work." He caught the way her mouth twisted. "Some support?"

"Some. They talk a lot about protecting staff, but there's always a feeling that you can't take the pressure if you complain. My editor was old-school and thinks the best self-care comes from a whiskey bottle and anesthetizing all emotion."

"I know the type," he said. "That's why you moved to obits?"

"Yeah. I'd had enough, you know?"

"I do." He kept his tone soft to encourage her to go on.

"Every time I saw an email from someone I didn't know, I stressed out that it was going to be another hateful message." Her laugh was rough enough to hurt. "I mean, I had that a couple times in obits too, but at least those had attacked my work and not me."

"I get that," he said.

"There's a huge difference between being told I'm a bad journalist because I made a mistake in the date of someone's graduation and being told I'm a bad person because I'm a woman and why didn't I go do something useful like make a sandwich because I'm a waste of space and also ugly."

"That's disgusting." Wes wasn't a violent man, but he wanted to fight on her behalf.

She finished her drink. "I started second-guessing myself, and I couldn't have that. It was getting to the point of moving or quitting. Or worse, getting fired. I needed a break, so I took the obits editor job."

"Did it get better?"

"Clearly not. I fumbled Dot's obit, and they made me night web editor. I feel nauseous every time I have to make a decision because what if I make another mistake? Before, I was always so sure of myself."

"It's okay to make mistakes."

"Is it?" She gave him a wry look. "It's been nice to be at Dot's house. It's important but also secret. I feel comfortable working."

"It sounds like you haven't felt that in a while."

"No," she said. "I'd almost forgotten what it was like not to dread your day."

"It's good that you're finding that again, here at Dot's."

"Thanks." This time, she smiled. "All it took was tracking down a mystery in a mansion with my main competition."

He laughed. "Who knew?"

It was late by the time they finished and drove back to Dot's. Wes was weighed down by the fantastic club sandwich, the knowledge he had to be up in too few hours, and Nadine's story. He knew she didn't want pity, but he wished he could make her feel better. He felt bad he couldn't.

"Good grotto find by the way." She congratulated him as they went back through the gates at Dot's. Her voice was normal, and when he looked over, that dimple was there again. He felt better. Perhaps letting her talk had been enough for the moment.

"God knows what else is back here," said Wes as she parked. "A helipad?"

"An arena."

"A ranch."

"Area 52?"

Trading increasingly wacky suggestions, they locked up and headed to bed. Separately.

Although when Wes watched Nadine's door close, missing Murasaki's tail by a centimeter as she trotted in, he was alarmed but not surprised to find he wished he was going in as well.

# TWENTY-SIX

got one!"

Wes's voice rang through the house, and Nadine backed out from under the bed where she was hunting for clues. She swore as she hit her head and went to go find him, trying to keep her animosity in check and to remember they were on the same team.

They'd split up the house to make sure they checked everywhere, and she found Wes in the hallway of the west wing, holding a copy of *Thirty Pieces of Silver*. Streaks of dust marred his black Cuban shirt, which had a slight V at the collar. There was a freckle near his throat that she couldn't take her eyes off until he waved the book in her face.

"Hold on," she said, refocusing her attention. It took a few seconds. "That's the edition she kept moving around the salon when we were visiting. I recognize the scratch on the cover."

He opened it with a flourish to reveal a newspaper clipping tucked at the beginning of chapter thirteen. "Voilà."

She plucked it out. It was an obituary about a woman named Abigail Spencer, minus the notes or highlights of the other obits Dot had left. Also, no shade to Abigail, but it detailed a fairly uneventful life, without any of the elements Dot usually appreciated. Nadine turned her attention to the book. "Chapter thirteen. Does it have something to do with the text?" she asked. "Judas was thirteenth at the Last Supper."

Wes groaned. "Do you remember doing Machiavelli in Professor Otterly's poli-sci class?"

"That elective nearly killed me." Nadine flipped through the book, looking for other notes. "When we did that chapter of *The Prince*?"

"We thought it was about being Machiavellian."

"Then Otterly was mad because he said it was ultimately about the death of God, and none of us got it." Nadine returned the book, and he reinserted the clipping. "It was like getting to the end of a mystery and finding out some character barely mentioned was the killer."

"That's the first project we worked on together," Wes said.

She shook her head. "That was the narrative journalism class."

"No, it was Otterly. You sat in front of me, and I asked if you had a partner. That's why we ended up doing the narrative project, so we didn't have to juggle a bunch of meetings with different groups."

"Very pragmatic." A sparkling electricity passed through her before she decided she was reading too much into it. Wes's extraordinary memory meant it was normal for him to recall their first project with the same level of detail she had about eating breakfast. "Look at us now."

"I've been on worse jobs," he said. There was a beat of silence where she caught Wes's gaze for a moment too long. He coughed and turned back to the book. "I suggest we find everything and examine them later for connections. We can put them on the table in the library."

She looked at the cabinet. It was third in a row of six, all of them stuffed with enough bric-a-brac to fill the house of a Victorian naturalist. "How did you find it?"

"It was the only book in the whole collection, so it caught my attention." Wes looked regretful. "No pattern or anything we can apply."

"Damn."

"That's one question for me, by the way." He gave her a jaunty wave and headed down the hall. "I'll collect it later."

———————

Wes glanced at Octavia, who had made herself at home in the corner of a cabinet surrounded by vases. "If you break it, you buy it," he warned her.

He must be losing it, talking to Octavia. At least Erma listened, tilting her head to the side whenever he asked her a question. He returned to his examination of the room, which had to be one of his favorites. Winter-nude branches were painted on the pale pink wallpaper and climbed up the ceiling toward a large chandelier with peacock heads for the lights. Small birds sat on the branches, looking so lively it was like the artist caught them midsong. A large daybed covered in dark blue cushions sat on one wall, and matching portraits of a Qing couple in full court dress were displayed above.

He'd looked through and under the bed. Behind the picture frames. Checked inside the vases and under the rosewood chairs. That left one thing, the huge Italian-style bureau that had been lacquered a deep crimson and was a perfect hiding place for a secretive old woman with a perverse sense of humor. The drawers curved out in a smooth belly, each painted with a different scene of junks at a Chinese harbor, and seemed to contain nothing but unused linen place mats.

He couldn't see any clues to Dot's book or her mystery, so he sat in a chair and considered declaring this room done. But he kept looking at that cabinet. "Who does this kind of thing?" he asked Octavia.

Dot Voline did. Had the Agatha Christie story given her the idea in the first place, or was it simply a coincidence? Good old Miss Marple. She would be able to figure out what to do.

Then he slapped himself on the head. She had.

Going back to the cabinet, he emptied out the top drawer again and felt around the back. There it was: a small hole. He grabbed a letter opener shaped like a dagger and used the sharp end to poke carefully until there was a slight click and the bottom of the drawer popped up.

"Nadine," he called, a bunch of newspaper clippings in his hand. "Have you found anything yet, or am I the only one?"

Her scream of fury was gratifying. They might be getting along, but it was still nice to win.

---

Later, Wes watched Nadine walk away after showing off her latest clue.

The woman was addicted to sundresses, and this one had little straps over her shoulders. The skirt reached past her knees but had a disconcerting way of hiking up when she sat or bent over. He refused to let himself linger on this, although he'd looked enough to know she had a birthmark on her right thigh that he could swear was shaped like a rabbit. He wanted to look closer to confirm it. He wanted to sink his fingers into those thighs. He wanted…

Whoa, what the hell. No, he didn't, although Wes hadn't missed her very flattering reaction when she'd seen him shirtless. Her eyes had run up and down his body like a physical touch, making all those hours in the gym suddenly worth it, and he'd had to step behind a box to cover his reaction. He couldn't let that happen again. This was Nadine. Not his enemy anymore, but also not entirely anything else. Their relationship was a shifting liminal zone that wavered between colleagues, irritants, and potential friends. That they worked so well together threw him for a loop. It didn't seem right that they should fit, yet they did.

Regardless, she was definitely off-limits, at least until this investigation was done. He didn't need to muddy already murky waters, especially since he was thinking about Nadine far more than he was about the secrets in Dot's house. Gritting his teeth, he left the room and found a fresh cupboard to turn inside out.

Two days of searching later, Nadine was in the porcelain room trying not to break anything as she put the rug back in place after confirming there was no trapdoor. Last night, Wes had suggested they hold a séance to ask Dot about the secret basement entrance, and although she'd laughed at him, she thought he might be onto something. Finding it was clearly beyond the ability of living beings. At least they were getting along, much to her astonishment. Their work styles meshed well, and despite the frustration of searching hour after hour, they had managed to not take it out on each other. This was unexpected but welcome.

Sighing, she surveyed the room. There were vases and figurines, teapots and plates, and a sewing kit with china needles. Anything that could be made from clay and fired was on display in styles from around the world. It was a collection fit for a museum.

She picked up a photo from a side table, never having seen a porcelain frame before. Forget-me-nots were painted around a black-and-white studio portrait of a smiling woman that might be Dot in the 1970s. When she took the photo out, there was nothing hidden, although a small stamp read "Werner and Knapp, Ottawa." She brought it to the library table in triumph and went to the kitchen to draw a point on her tally.

"Getting there," said Wes as he passed by. "Almost."

He added another one to his side and grinned at her. Nadine should have been annoyed. She was annoyed. She loved winning, and the only thing better than winning was winning against Wes.

But she couldn't help smiling back.

# TWENTY-SEVEN

At one in the morning, Wes flipped his pillow over for the sixth time, looking for the ever-elusive cold side. There was none. Despite the fans beating through the soupy humidity, nothing in the house was cool, let alone cold. Janice the cheetah's crooked eye looked more sunken as the days passed.

He pushed away Erma, who had taken to curling up beside him at night, her fur sticking to his sweaty skin, and sprawled on the bed to consider his options. Sleeping in the library might be more comfortable, and he would feel like a Regency gentleman who had too much punch. If he took a bath, he could soak until he was cold and wrinkled.

Then he sat up. He was thinking like a poor man when he should be thinking like a rich one who had access to his own personal grotto. He didn't have swim trunks, but that didn't matter. It was one of the benefits of living, however briefly, on an estate with no near neighbors. He'd get some beer and go for a swim.

A few minutes later, he was working his way through the mini forest behind the house, and thirty seconds after that, he'd put his clothes on a chair and was floating bare-ass naked in the late Dot Voline's swimming grotto. It was heaven. Pure, unadulterated heaven. He swam to the waterfall and let it hammer down on him, the thunderous roar blocking out the heat, the tension, and everything negative until his mind felt clear.

Time for that drink. He moved into the pool from under the falls, swiping at his face to get rid of the water. The scream came before he had his eyes open, and he lost his footing in shock, causing him to fall back under the waterfall and come up sputtering.

It was Nadine. Topless, by the looks of it, since she had her hands clasped over her chest like the woman on the stripping album. The second they locked eyes, they both dropped down in the pool to their chins. The moonlight covered the water with a white glitter that hid everything under the surface.

"What are you doing creeping around at night, you sneak?" Nadine hissed.

"I could ask you the same thing."

"It was hot. I didn't know you were here."

He pointed at his clothes piled up on a chair. "You missed that?"

She followed his glance and squinted. "I thought it was a pillow." Her eyes bugged out. "Are you wearing any clothes? At all?"

"I am not," he said with as much dignity as he could muster. "Since I thought I would be alone. Are you?"

Nadine dropped farther under the water. "You need to get out of the pool."

He couldn't help but notice she didn't answer the question, leaving him with no doubts. The polite thing would be to leave her to enjoy the water in solitude. Then Wes felt the night breeze on his face and thought about tossing and turning until dawn.

"No," he said.

"That's not fair," she objected. "You've had time to swim alone. I should get the same."

"You snooze, you lose."

"I wasn't snoozing at all," she said, sounding tired. "Not in that steam bath of a house. That's my point."

"Well, you can share this lovely, cool, refreshing grotto, or you can go back inside." He leaned back to look at the sky. "Up to you."

"Then I guess we share." She sounded a bit breathless, which was strange since the pool was shallow enough that they didn't have to tread water.

"If you promise not to peek when I get them, you can have one of the beers I brought," offered Wes, generous in victory.

Nadine laughed. "I brought some as well but we can start with yours." She made a fuss of covering her eyes with her hands before turning around and standing up.

Wes tried not to look, but he wasn't a saint. The water cascaded over her shoulders to where the pool reached her midback. A shadowed line ran down where her spine dipped in, and he couldn't help glancing lower to see if she had those little dimples at the base. He loved those.

Then she shifted enough for him to glimpse... No. He almost threw himself toward the edge of the pool so he could avoid being an asshole. He'd told Nadine not to peek, and it was incumbent on him to show her the same respect. He tried to block his mind from busily filling in the curve that he had been so tantalizingly close to seeing.

He grabbed both cans and left one close to her before retreating to the other side. "Okay," he said.

Nadine looked over her shoulder to see where he was, and Wes did his best not to stare at the shadow of her eyes and line of her cheek. She swam by, and when her body broke the surface of the water, Wes nearly choked on his beer. Nadine turned at the sound of his violent coughing.

"Are you okay?" she asked with concern.

"Fine," he gasped. "Sorry."

She cracked the can open and sat hunched over on the steps so she could stay covered by the water. "I don't know how Dot handled this heat. Either she had ice water in her veins or air-con in her bedroom."

Wes pictured Dot lying happily in a California king with arctic air swirling around her as the rest of the house boiled. "I bet her bedroom is Scandinavian minimalist."

"All light oak and white walls?" Nadine shook her head. "No way. Crimson walls and black satin sheets."

"Paint is for peasants," Wes reminded her. "Dot would have flocked wallpaper."

Nadine laughed. "What wallpaper?"

"The kind that looks like patterned velvet."

"I thought that was so fancy when I was a kid. Yeah, that's Dot for sure."

They drank in the quiet night, Nadine dancing her palm on the water's surface while Wes watched the edges of her wet hair curl on her shoulders.

"I'm going to claim my next question," said Wes to break the silence.

"Choose wisely." Nadine made her voice low and spooky, then bobbed up slightly in the water.

Wes swallowed hard but had his question ready. "Why do you always wear skirts?"

---

"That's your question?" she asked in disbelief.

Wes looked at her with open curiosity, like this was something he truly wanted to know. "I have a few to spend, and I always wondered. I've never seen you in pants."

No one had asked her this before. "You're going to laugh," she warned.

"I promise I won't."

"When I was in grade one, we had to do an activity where everyone sat in a circle to sing a song about clothes. If you had on that article of clothing, you stood in the center while all the kids sang."

"We did that too."

"One day, I was the only one in pants. All the other kids were wearing jeans or skirts or shorts. I stood alone in the middle as everyone sang at me. I started to cry, and when I went home, I cleared out all my pants. Never wore them again." She still remembered the shame of that day and the way her mother had told her there was nothing to be upset about when she'd come home in tears. She'd never cried in front of others after that, or at least not until Dot died.

Wes put his can aside. "That was way darker than I imagined. I thought you just liked them. I'm sorry. Some incidents can be so small and reverberate years later."

Nadine shrugged. "It was a tough day for little Nadine, but now I appreciate how versatile and easy skirts are. I bet not a single kid remembers. My turn. Keeping with sartorial decisions, why do you always dress so well? So unwrinkled?"

He glanced over at his neatly folded clothes. "I never thought about it," he said. "I suppose it makes me feel more confident. Sometimes people tend to overlook me, but they do it less when I'm well put together."

"Overlook you?" Nadine was disbelieving. How could anyone not notice Wes?

"Quiet people tend to be put in the background at most places I've worked."

"That's true." She winced. "That ended up kind of sad too."

"Let's keep with the dark theme then." Wes waited for her nod. "The other day, you were on the phone with your mother. What was bothering you?"

How honest should she be? As she stared at the ripples on the water, she realized she wanted to talk about it. Despite their ups and downs, Wes looked like he might understand.

"My parents want me to move back home. They've been telling me that since the problems I had at work and with that guy, and they don't listen when I say no. They're so certain, I'm starting to worry they're right."

"You don't want to?"

"No." She patted the water. "My parents didn't think journalism was safe either. It's a long-standing complaint about most things I do."

"Do they want you safe or static?" asked Wes.

"It's safe to them and static to me. They don't like risk." She sighed. "It's hard to stand up to parents, even when we know they're wrong."

"Is that you too? Having trouble standing up to your mother?"

"Is that your question?"

"Sure." She'd talked enough.

"Ma is not the most positive person in the world," Wes said, and she heard how carefully he chose his words. "She had a rough life, and my sister says I'm trying to compensate for it."

"How so?" They were inching closer along the edge of the pool.

"I try to make her happy," said Wes. "Usually by being there with her."

"That sounds hard," she said. "Like you have to stay static as well."

"Sometimes. Did you know I got hired by the CBC after that internship?"

That was impressive, but she wasn't surprised and was pleased to find the memory of losing out to him no longer triggered a cortisol response. "I don't remember you working there."

He gave her a little grin. "Keeping track?"

"Whatever." She flicked water at him. "CBC?"

"The job was in Victoria, and I told Ma I was going to accept. She collapsed with a heart problem, and I had to take her to the hospital. My sisters were focused on school, so I couldn't leave them to deal with it."

"That's horrible."

"My sister Amy thinks Ma faked it to keep me home."

"Wes, seriously?"

He dipped down in the water. "Who knows? It's hard to tell what she wants because she always seems disappointed no matter what I do."

He leaned over to get another beer as Nadine tried to figure out the best thing to say. When Wes floated a can in her direction, she picked it out of the water before she spoke. "You're not a disappointment."

He blinked at her, then gave a wry smile. "Thanks," he said. "Enough with questions for tonight, don't you think?"

"Sure." They'd gone to some touchy places. She wasn't sure if she was ready to go deeper with him.

---

Nadine's quick reply made Wes suspect she was feeling as vulnerable as he was. She looked around the grotto as though casting for a new topic. "Is there something behind the waterfall?"

"Like a hidden Hugh Hefner room? I don't know. I didn't go all the way under."

Nadine put her drink down and swam over. "Given the rest of this house, I have high hopes," she said. She passed close enough for him to feel the water swirl around his stomach, then dipped under and disappeared.

He couldn't let her explore alone. What if she found something super interesting? Wes put down his own can and walked through the waterfall, pausing to again appreciate its pressure.

Then he came out and immediately bumped into soft, cool skin. The space beyond the waterfall was tiny and lit by a small line of fairy lights along the edge of the pool. All this was environmental detail that Wes only dimly noted because he was too busy trying to understand that Nadine was in front of him and so close, they were touching. Her back was pressed against the wall. She had nowhere to go, and he should take a huge step back past the waterfall and then get the hell out of this pool.

She blinked, her pretty eyes starry with wet lashes, and he didn't move.

---

Nadine wasn't sure if what she was about to do was a bad idea or a good one.

No, it was a bad idea. Very bad. Anything she did at the moment that was not muttering an excuse and swimming away would result in something she was probably going to regret, if not in the next few hours, then tomorrow morning.

She couldn't bring herself to care.

Who knew being long-term enemies with someone made you think about them endlessly? They might no longer dislike each other, but Nadine wasn't sure where they'd moved to on the relationship spectrum or how she fully felt about it. All she knew was that she'd been thinking about touching Wes—and Wes touching her—more than she liked to admit.

It was almost an out-of-body experience when his hand came up to grip her waist. "Nadine." He only said her name, but it was as if he was asking permission.

In answer, she ran her hand along his arm, feeling the muscles clench as she moved up to his shoulder, down his back, and finally to that snake on his ribs. His wet skin was slick under her fingers. "I've never made out in a pool before," she said.

He threw his head back and laughed. "Me neither."

That broke whatever spell she was under, and Nadine suddenly wanted more of him. All of him. Forget about tomorrow. She stepped closer, and Wes twitched slightly before his eyelids fluttered. He leaned forward, and finally those lips were on hers, fitting as if he'd been made for her. His mouth was warm, and Nadine flattened her hand against his chest, thrilling at the feel of skin and the tight beat of his heart under lean muscle.

Wes made a sound between a sigh and groan that turned her knees to butter, then backed her against the fake stone wall of the grotto. One arm braced by her head to lean in again, but he slowed down to give her a small smile that was far too sweet and way too hot for Nadine to deal with. She pulled him in closer and gasped.

Kissing Wes was to learn him in a new way that instantly ignited every place he touched her. Gone was the buttoned-up Wes, he of the shined shoes and straight collars. This Wes was softer but rougher than she expected, and the mix drove her wild. She couldn't anticipate what he'd do next, but it didn't matter, because he was a mind reader, sensing what she craved almost before she realized what she wanted herself.

She didn't know how long it took before they stopped kissing, but her hair was beginning to dry on top. Wes smoothed it back, then kissed her forehead. They took a minute to catch their breath.

"This is not smart," she whispered.

"Not smart at all." His kiss ghosted along her throat. "I want this. I want you. It's up to you what happens next."

She knew he would stop in an instant if she said the word, almost as certainly as he must know she couldn't bring herself to do it.

"What if we regret it?" she asked. Her fingers were back on that tattoo. She loved it.

Wes's mouth moved up to her ear, and he held her tight enough that her toes lifted off the grotto floor. "I regret lots of things, but I regret the things I didn't do the most. Don't you?"

"Yes." She could barely get the word out.

"We don't want to add to the list, do we?"

"That's not the most persuasive argument."

"How about this?" His hands moved around the small of her back and down as he bent his mouth to her shoulder. Her head fell backward, and her body melted into his.

"That is a more compelling case," she managed to say.

"Thank you." His voice shivered against her skin, and she made the choice. Leave the rest for tomorrow Nadine to worry about.

"Ready to take this on land?" she asked.

Wes lifted his head, closed his eyes as if in prayer, then opened them. "Yes," he said fervently. "Yes."

So they did.

# TWENTY-EIGHT

Wes lay in bed with his arms folded behind his head, Erma purring on his chest, and thought so hard his brain started to disintegrate.

He had slept with Nadine. Or Nadine slept with him. Either way, people had been mutually slept with.

How could he be simultaneously filled with so much regret and lack of regret? Wes lifted his head to stare at the bedroom door, wishing for X-ray vision that could pierce walls so he could see what she was thinking. The thing was, he knew about Nadine's views on everything from the polarization of the political landscape (bad) to the Oxford comma (good), but he didn't know how she felt about casual sex.

Or him.

At the moment, both of those were more important than her thoughts on the need for better media literacy training in schools (vital), because Wes had never been fond of casual sex. He liked to get to know someone before seeing them naked, and he loved the intimacy of the next morning, when sex was more of a confirmation of where the relationship could go rather than a beginning and an end all wrapped up. Sex without those things could be good—often great—in the moment but left him hollow after.

He groaned and Erma leapt off him with an offended trill, digging her claws into his chest to emphasize her disapproval.

Realistically, there was only one adult way to handle this. He texted Caleb the situation and his brilliant solution.

The reply came almost instantly. **You can't seriously think leaving the country is a good idea.**

**The city then,** Wes wrote back.

**People do this all the time. Chill.**

Easy enough for Caleb to say. Until he'd met his now-fiancée, Caleb was the master of the one-night stand. He hadn't seen it as a big deal and chose partners with the same attitude. A bit of fun and no hard feelings.

**Unless you like her,** came Caleb's next message. **Then you got to talk.**

**How do I know?** Wes texted back.

**You know when you know.** With that useless advice, Caleb was gone, leaving Wes to his own thoughts. "You know when you know." What the hell did that mean? He stared at a bubble in the green glass of a bottle that looked as if it might have come from the *Queen Anne's Revenge.* What did he know?

Did he like Nadine? He'd thought he disliked her for so long, it had become an assumption he'd never had to analyze. The sun rose in the east and set in the west, and Nadine would get on his nerves or screw him over.

Except all the things that used to provoke him, he realized with a start, had become almost endearing. He knew he enjoyed working with her, but the pleasure in talking with her about Dot's clues, or anything, was new. The fighting was more out of form than any desire to win. He let his mind trace the edges of what he'd suspected for a few days but hadn't been willing to admit. He didn't like Nadine. He *liked* her. More than that, he might be falling for her. Nadine was smart and industrious, but he'd known that for ages. Witty, he knew that too. Pretty. Correction, incredibly hot, especially the moment when she'd wrapped those full thighs around him and those big eyes had gotten bigger.

He covered his face. This was not the time to relive one of the high points of his life. He had serious contemplating to do.

He'd always thought falling in love would be more of a sledgehammer to the head rather than this slow infiltration. A *fall* rather than a light downward drift. Two months ago, he could barely stand to think of Nadine without animosity. That had changed since they'd been in Dot's house and he'd allowed himself to see her the way she really was. He wanted to be with the woman he saw. He wanted to hold her hand, all that stuff. He wanted more.

This could be hormones speaking. Most likely sex and the resultant oxytocin had worked their magic. He needed to take some time to carefully test where he was on the spectrum of crush, like, or maybe more than like, especially while they had to work together.

He would get dressed and go about his day as if nothing had happened. No, as if what had happened last night was fun but no big deal. That was better.

He gathered his clothes and was about to go wash when he heard Nadine's door open. Cursing himself for not picking a room with an en suite, Wes halted midstep. She couldn't see him with messy hair and unbrushed teeth. He at least needed to be groomed.

Wes waited until her footsteps faded, then ran to the bathroom. It was going to be a hell of a day.

———————

Nadine woke up early and instantly freaked out.

What had she done? What had *they* done?

It was a mistake, obviously. They were a tiny bit tipsy and in a grotto, for God's sake. It was a recipe for friskiness.

Too bad she was having trouble seeing it as a misstep. Last night had felt good, that was for sure, but more than that, it had felt right. She'd kept waiting for it to get weird, and it never had, not even when he'd gotten up to go to his own bed. Nadine had been dozing when he'd given her a kiss on the forehead before he left, and she'd been grateful he'd taken the choice of asking him to stay or go out of her hands. It also gave them time to think, which she needed.

Because she was having feelings about last night. Conflicting feelings. Big feelings.

She didn't like Wes. Or did she? She thought back to their interactions. She'd resented Wes at the same time as she admired his work and his work ethic. She mistrusted him, but that hadn't prevented her from thinking about him for years, although their paths barely crossed.

Did she...like Wes?

Impossible.

Or was it? What if she did? What would that mean? Would it be that bad? She knew Wes, after all. They were—somewhat—getting along. He was, in many ways, the kind of man she hoped to have in her life.

What was the matter with her, picking out kids' names after one night with a guy? It was sex, that was it. They didn't need to talk about it because they were two consenting adults who had known each other for a long time and were in close quarters. And who had developed a mutual desire to get off with each other.

They could pretend this never happened or be honest and talk about it. She'd take her cue from Wes, she decided, then got out of bed with a resolute attitude that didn't match the way her pounding heart prevented her from taking full breaths.

In the kitchen, she boiled water while casting nervous glances at the door, almost queasy with tension. When he finally appeared, she scrutinized him for any changes in attitude. Was he more awkward? Avoiding eye contact? Did he seem like he regretted last night? He looked the same as always, although she couldn't help but see him in a different way now that she knew what was under the ironed cotton shorts.

She couldn't take the pressure. She had to get in front of this.

"We need to talk," she said, summoning her best ice queen self.

"Okay," he said, eyes wide. "Good morning."

The ice melted at his expression and left her instantly exposed. "You start."

He shook his head frantically. "You brought it up. You start."

"That's not how a conversation works. I said words, so you have to respond with more and different words."

He snorted. "If the words are *we need to talk* that rule goes out the window."

"Fine." Nadine held out her fist. "Rock, paper, scissors."

"Seriously?"

She shook her fist at him, and he gave in and held out his own.

"One, two, three, go."

They checked each other's outstretched palms. "Again," she said.

After the fifth matching round, Wes rubbed his bicep. "Jesus, we're going to be here all day. Can I at least get some coffee?"

"I'll allow a break." She peeled a banana and passed him half. "Here. It's our last one."

Wes paused his multistep brewing process. "But you like them."

"So do you." She wasn't going to hoard a banana.

"Oh." He looked at the banana, then gave his head a shake. "Look, fine, I'll start. Last night was…"

He hesitated, and Nadine jumped in, knowing what he was about to say and unable to hear the words out loud. "A mistake," she said. "I agree. It was unprofessional of us."

Wes's face froze. "We should concentrate on work?" he said.

It sounded like more of a question, but Nadine nodded. "That makes sense." She shuffled her feet a bit. "Uh, why don't I leave you to finish the coffee, and I'll get started?"

His eyes were focused on measuring the scoops into the cafetière, which he'd brought from home and Nadine wasn't allowed to touch after he caught her plunging the filter up and down to mix the grounds. "Sounds good."

She hoped he wasn't upset. Surely he had to know it wasn't a rejection of him but the situation. Plus, he'd been the one to say it was a mistake first. Well, not exactly, but that was what he was going to say. This was the best and most workable scenario.

Then why was she disappointed, especially since she brought this on herself?

To her relief, Wes seemed normal by the time he met her in the library with two cups of steaming coffee. This confirmed that she'd done the right thing, although it felt unresolved, like there was more to say but neither of them knew what. They separated to various spots in the house, Nadine's mind half on the search and half on Wes. Or ninety percent on Wes and ten on work if it was a boring drawer, which most of them were.

She was sorting old holiday cards when Wes came in with a matcha latte that she took with gratitude. It must be eleven o'clock. They'd started taking turns to make midmorning drinks and outdo each other with the presentation. Her glass had a green sprinkle on top of the foam that resembled a cat. Yesterday, she'd given him fruit tea decorated with ice she'd frozen petals in.

"Holiday cards?" he asked.

"Nothing useful."

Wes looked stunning, with a pair of black cotton pants and a white T-shirt that was tight enough to show off everything she'd run her hands over last night. He went back out, and her gaze drifted down. On the walls were old group photos made up of individual portraits, and she bet those fine ladies would take one look at Wes and cheer her on. She sighed and went back to the cards.

"Erma!" Her concentration was broken by Wes reprimanding the cat. "Bad cat."

"What did she do?" she called.

"Knocked my notebook down." Wes blew his breath out in frustration so loud she heard it across the hall. "This cat will be the death of me, I swear."

"She likes you," sang out Nadine to cover her jealousy. It was a hit to her ego to be rated second best by the cat.

Wes came in holding Erma so her limbs stuck out and put her where Nadine was working. "Enjoy."

The cat stared at Nadine, hoisted her hind leg, and began grooming.

"Have some respect," Nadine said, nudging the cat with her knee. "Who fed you this morning? Me."

But Erma's memory was short and her conscience pure, because instead of doing anything that could have remotely been interpreted as gratitude, she jumped on a desk and then to one of the mannequins, where she perched on the narrow shoulder of a fancy seafoam dress with lace and black bows.

"Erma!" Nadine scolded.

"She likes you," called Wes in the same voice she'd used on him. "Shit, that's not good. Erma, get down. Not like that! Erma!"

The cat leapt from one mannequin to the next, toppling both over. Wes made a desperate grab to steady them by their tiny nineteenth-century corseted waists, but it was too late. They fell on Nadine in a flurry of very expensive and delicate fabric.

Wes swore from above her. "Stay still," he said.

As he pulled up the mannequins, Nadine saw a small box under the skirts. "Hold on," she said, reaching under the layers of embroidered white silk. She fished out the varnished wooden box as Wes inched the second mannequin back in place.

"I saw that when we were searching for the cat and thought it was part of the base," he said. "Good eye."

Nadine accepted the compliment with a nod and opened the box.

Inside was a single piece of newsprint, and her first instinct was to cry. Another clipping. How many more were in this house?

Then she picked it up to give it a quick scan. *Blackmail attempt by former senator staffer* was the headline. It was written by a *Herald* staff reporter.

A former staffer attempted to blackmail Senator John Wilson, said the senator's office today. Monica Olway threatened to discredit Senator Wilson with allegations of financial and professional misconduct after she was fired with cause from her position last week. Olway told the senator she wanted a new job and compensation or she would release private and, according to the senator's office, falsified information.

Senator John Wilson said he was shocked at Olway's blackmail threat. "As a public figure, my integrity is my shield," he said. "I have nothing to hide. This is part of a targeted harassment campaign, and I will defend myself with vigor."

"She lied on her résumé," said a source in the senator's office. "God knows what else she lies about."

"John Wilson. A politician. A potential *scandal.*" Wes tapped his lip. "Wait. In *Thirty Pieces*, the bad guy was James Walton. *JW.* The initials."

She jumped up, holding the scrap in the air. "We have something!"

"We do." Wes grabbed Nadine by the waist, lifting her and spinning her around. "Incredible find," he breathed as he put her back down. "God, I love you."

Nadine froze. "What?"

---

Nadine's eyes were comically huge, and then as if to underscore the severity of Wes's fuckup in real time, thunder shook the house.

Why?

Why?

Why did he have to go and open his big mouth? Things were going so well between them. Then he had to ruin it.

He didn't realize he was edging away from Nadine until his back bumped against one of the mannequins, forcing him to fumble it straight, which he managed by grabbing the bust with both hands. Just spectacular.

"You what?" she repeated. She didn't sound angry or confused. If anything, she sounded completely emotionless, and Wes couldn't tell if that was better or worse. It only took a second's more reflection to decide it was definitely worse.

If he was lucky, he might be able to get through this with a minimal amount of humiliation, like only five years of shame nightmares instead of a full decade. A psychologist he'd once interviewed told him someone's feelings about him were none of his business, which Wes had found condescending and absurd, although Rebecca loved it. However, it could be reversed. He'd made his feelings Nadine's business, and in the middle of a job. That wasn't cool.

"I'm sorry," he said, the words sticking in his throat. "I didn't mean it. It was a slip of the tongue."

Nadine's expression didn't change. Wes's brain was on its fourth internal chant of *Please say it's okay so I can die in peace*, when she finally blinked. How could any woman's eyes be so clear? They saw right through him, and at the edge of his vision, he saw her rubbing her thumb on her hand. The thin sundress—even in the depths of his disgrace, he could kiss the person who created that style—showed the quick rise and fall of her chest.

Then she said, "Okay."

"Okay?" he repeated.

"Sure." She laughed like it was a great joke. "Don't worry about it. I called Daniel 'Dad' once, and you wouldn't believe the look on his face."

Wes looked at her suspiciously, but she was already rereading the clipping about Monica Olway. Good. She knew he didn't mean anything by it.

Nothing at all.

# TWENTY-NINE

The next day after breakfast, they went to the library for their usual morning debrief. Nadine adjusted the strap of her sundress, which kept falling down. She wouldn't say she'd worn it because it was the cutest dress she'd brought, but it was exhilarating to see how Wes swallowed hard every time it dropped low on her shoulder. He was wearing a very thin black V-necked T-shirt. If he'd chosen it to be as distracting as possible, that was a sly move she wouldn't have expected of him.

Poor Wes. He'd gone almost purple the day before when he'd slipped up with the L-word, and they'd barely talked the rest of the day. However, she'd spent the night alone in bed thinking. If mistakes were on a spectrum, surely having sex with Wes was more on the *oops-I-bought-the-wrong-brand-of-noodles* end rather than the *I-crashed-the-car* end. That meant it was okay to do again, right? If they were both willing.

She looked over to where he sat with his neck bent over a shelf as he checked through the books. She, for one, was definitely willing. They were in this house together without a lot of amusement after all, and they were getting along and clearly attracted to each other. It was logical. It made sense. He ran his hand over his stomach, rucking up his shirt, and she made her decision.

"Wes?" Her voice came out louder than she planned, and Wes jumped.

"What's up?"

She summoned up all her bravery. After all, he'd said they should concentrate on work, not that they should focus entirely on work. There was some room for discussion.

"I have a proposal."

"I preemptively refuse any rules change," he said. "I got first in points fair and square."

She felt there was an argument to be made here but decided to keep on target. "I want to talk about the other night."

Wes turned away slightly. "What's to talk about? You said it was a mistake."

"*You* said it was a mistake," she corrected.

"I actually didn't," said Mr. Eidetic Memory. "You finished my sentence, and I wasn't going to argue with you."

"Okay." She tried to keep her heart rate down when she realized that Wes might not have meant what he'd said in the kitchen, and she'd jumped in with assumptions. "I was wrong."

---

Nadine looked cute like this, thought Wes as she went red after basically declaring she wanted to sleep with him to the library, Octavia, and him. Her hair was down and tucked behind her ears, and the dress she wore made him unable to stop staring, with its flowy skirt and tiny ruffled straps. He remembered how the light had played on her face when she'd stood in front of the kitchen window yesterday.

Right before she'd gutted him when she called their night together a mistake. He didn't want to screw up this opportunity, if opportunity it was. But it was better to be sure.

"I don't want to pressure you," he said carefully.

"Wes. I am literally standing here asking you to have sex with me." She ducked her head down a bit and mumbled the last words. She looked up. "We can be adults about this and continue to work together."

"While indulging ourselves? Friends with benefits." He pretended to think about it, like he wasn't mentally on top of her, smoothing his finger across her hip to see the skin pebble before flattening his hand across the warmth of her stomach. "Say it again."

She stood to her full height. "I, Nadine Barbault, was wrong to say having sex was a mistake. I said it to try to make things not weird between us, not that I had any regrets. I would very much like to do it again, and preferably more than once. We don't have to make a big deal out of it. It can be totally chill."

"Shit, then yes, I agree." Distantly, he recalled his usual stance against casual sex, then decided screw it. He would worry about that later, when Nadine wasn't standing there looking like she'd already undressed him. He put down the book he was holding and came over to her, swearing when he nearly stepped on a cat. "Come here."

---

An hour later, they were dressed again and back at work like the professionals they were. It had been an extremely fun break, and as a reward-oriented individual, Nadine was looking forward to the repeat Wes had promised later that night once they'd finished their daily search goals. This friends-with-benefits thing had been one of her better ideas.

Wes looked at her phone, and she knew what he was thinking, because he'd asked the same thing over and over since they'd found the letter yesterday. Then he said it.

"Has Monica replied yet?" he asked.

She'd sent Monica Olway a message after they'd found her email. They hadn't been able to track down a phone number.

"For the eleventh time, no, and for the twelfth time, yes I am checking."

"I wasn't asking…" He saw her face. "Sorry. I'll lay off. I'm getting antsy. We're running out of time. We only have nine days left in the house."

They separated to search the house as usual. Erma followed Nadine to the game room and hissed at Sidonie-Gabrielle, who woke from her nap on the billiards table before disappearing in a flash. A small patch of matted fur showed it was a favored location for sleepy felines. Nadine absentmindedly picked up the darts to toss at the board as she thought about where Wes might have missed looking in his first pass. They'd decided to search the rooms the other had done to see if a second set of eyes made a difference.

If she was doing Dot's obit today, would she include the darts? The cats? That must be the biggest struggle, to decide what in forty or sixty or a hundred years of living was the core of a person's story.

Feeling empty, she sat on the curved blue couch and pulled out her phone. Her heart dropped to see a message from Lisanne, which was in turn depressing. She didn't want to avoid her friend, but she couldn't bring herself to be normal about this whole work thing. Was she that petty? That self-centered?

Looked like yes, but she would try to be a better person.

I've got something for you, said the message from Lisanne.

Cool, she texted back. What's up?

You know that story I'm working on?

Nadine stuffed the *how can I not* deep, deep down. Of course!

It's bigger than I thought. I could use some help on the political side and Daniel said he'd give you a byline. Thought I'd give you a hand getting back in the game.

Nadine felt her face tighten, then her entire body. She didn't need

Lisanne's pity or help. **Sorry,** she wrote back. **I don't think that will work for me.**

The reply came in seconds. **What? I went on a limb to ask Daniel.**

Nadine flushed. **I never asked you to.**

**No but you need a push. You can't duck out of every opportunity because you're a little anxious. I'm trying to help.**

Lisanne had some nerve. **I don't need your help, thanks.**

**You do because otherwise you'll hide away on the night shift for the rest of your career.**

Nadine didn't answer. She turned off the notifications and put the phone face down as Wes came in.

"Nothing in the upper library," he reported, switching on the fan and angling it toward her. He stopped when he saw her face. "What happened?"

"Work."

He grimaced. "Want to talk about it?"

"No."

"Too bad. I claim question privilege."

She knew if she pushed back, he'd be sensitive enough to let it go, but Wes had shown that he understood her stew of nasty emotions. She told him about the conversation and Lisanne's big chance, keeping it vague because she couldn't leak Lisanne's story to a reporter for the *Spear*, no matter how upset she was.

"I get it," said Wes cheerfully when she finished. "You wish it was you."

Nadine was astounded. "What?"

"Come on, Nadine. You tried to beat me for a decade. Do you expect me to believe your competitiveness shuts off like a tap?"

"Fine." She bit her lip. "Part of me does. I would never say it to Lisanne because it would make her feel bad for being awesome, and I would look like the world's worst person."

"I think it's fairly common, but no one likes to admit it." He gave her a look. "That's not all though."

"Isn't that enough?" she asked morosely. "Plus how do you know?"

"You talked about how you felt about putting yourself out there when we were getting heartburn at the diner."

"Worth it."

"Nadine."

She snorted. "I'm not worried about working on the story if that's what you mean. I just don't want her success rubbed in my face, and I don't want her thinking I need her help."

"*Nadine.*"

"What?"

"Don't lie to yourself. You're scared to take on a story that sounds like it's going to generate a lot of commentary."

Nadine shot to her feet. "You have no idea what you're talking about," she snapped. She stood up and grabbed a dart to throw at the board. How dare he? "It has nothing to do with being scared," she called over her shoulder, throwing another dart.

"Sure."

"What do you mean, 'sure'?"

"I don't believe you." He said it like a fact, not a challenge.

She came around the couch, crossed her arms, and stared at him. "It doesn't matter what you believe because I know. It's not the story for me, okay?"

Murasaki came up, and Wes ran a hand down her back, not saying anything. The cat's contented purr filled the space between them as Nadine glared at the wall, half-acknowledged thoughts tumbling through her head. She didn't want... It was all Lisanne's... It wasn't like she...

Then she threw herself on the uncomfortable couch and kicked out her legs.

"Fine. I was jealous and then I was mad she had the nerve to say I needed her help and under it all I was scared and I took it out on her rather than admit it." Each word came out faster and faster until by the end she was stumbling over them.

"Makes sense," Wes said.

"Does it?"

"Yeah." Wes snatched his hand away as Murasaki tried to bite him. "Like, you're not winning any friendship awards here, and it's not fair to Lisanne, but it's a natural reaction. I get it."

"It's all on me. She's trying to help, and I'm being a jerk about it."

"It's not help if it's unwanted, and you went through a bad situation," said Wes. "She's trying to fix something that's not her thing to fix." He looked as if his own words surprised him.

Nadine sat up. "It sounds like you have experience with this."

Wes shrugged uncomfortably. "What are you going to do?"

Nadine didn't press, not wanting to put him on the spot. "Leave it for now, because we have work to do here."

"You'll have to talk to her sooner or later."

"Later." She didn't want to lose Lisanne's friendship, but she also didn't want to deal with it until she was calmer.

Nadine's phone buzzed before he could reply, and she looked down to see who it was.

---

When Nadine glanced at the screen, her eyes widened, and Wes did his best not to react when he remembered what they were doing the last time she wore that expression. While he appreciated the new shift in their relationship, he had to admit it was a little distracting.

"Monica emailed back with her number," she said.

That wiped the dirty thoughts out of his head. Or mostly until she tugged her sundress back in place. "Let's figure out what we want to ask so we're prepared," he said, eyes on her bare shoulder.

It took them ten minutes to hash out their questions, but when Nadine dialed the number, it was to find that Monica Olway had little patience for a soft approach.

"The man is a worm," she said bluntly after Nadine explained who they were and a bit about what they were looking into. Monica had agreed to be on speaker with Wes but didn't allow them to tape or put anything on the record, claiming she'd been burned before.

"Can you tell us what happened?" Nadine asked. Wes leaned forward, eager to hear Monica's story.

"I was his executive assistant for a year," Monica said. "And yeah, I got the job because I exaggerated on my résumé, but who doesn't? I was good. Ask anyone. Anyway, I was working late one night, and he comes up and he says to me, 'Monica, you know Ian Ali,' and I say yes, because he's in accounting over at procurement, and I knew everyone. Excuse my bragging." She took a breath and kept going. "So he says to me—Senator Wilson, not Ian—he says to me, 'Monica, I want you to follow him and see what he does.' And I say, 'Why?' because that makes no sense, right? And the senator, he says he thinks Ian is stealing and giving the money to someone, and he wants to know who. And I say, 'Ian?' And he says, 'Yeah.'"

"Why did the senator want to know?"

Monica snorted. "Because he's a worm. It's not his business. He could have told Ian's manager to take care of it. He wanted dirt on that poor man, probably to threaten him the same way he did me. I don't know how he found out about my résumé thing."

"What happened next?" asked Nadine.

Wes made the mistake of looking into her eyes and immediately lost his train of thought. He knew the mechanics of a crush. The embarrassed excitement. The increasingly fantastical mental scenarios where you ended up kissing at the top of a volcano or something. He also knew they eventually dulled and were forgotten.

Whatever he was feeling showed no signs of fading, and this morning had not helped. But Monica was talking, and he needed to pay attention.

"He told me if I didn't, he'd have no choice but to let me go without a reference because I exaggerated on my résumé. He knew I needed that job, right? My husband had left a few months before, and it was hard to make ends meet with my kids and all."

"Yes," said Nadine in sympathy.

"I also don't like being bullied, so I told that son of a bitch to go fuck himself. How dare he threaten me. You know what kind of man he is?" She didn't wait for an answer. "I'll tell you what kind of man he is. He'd make me order catering for meetings from Peter and Co., the most expensive racket in town, and then he wouldn't let me put the leftovers in the employee lunchroom. Bastard insisted it all be thrown away. The cookies were even individually wrapped. Individually wrapped! It's like he didn't think we were good enough to eat them."

Wes despised the man on principle because of this.

"What happened after you said no?" asked Nadine to get them back on track.

"He fired me, and my lawyer said I didn't have a chance in hell because I had exaggerated slightly on my résumé *like everyone does*, and I didn't have any proof of his threat. So I say to myself, the hell with that, and I go by the *Herald* to talk to a reporter. Next thing I know, I'm getting smeared in national media and accused of blackmail. I never blackmailed nobody."

"What happened to Ian?" asked Wes.

"I gave him a heads-up, and he quit to work in tech."

"Who was the reporter you talked to at the *Herald*?" asked Nadine.

The answer was prompt. "Irina Skoll. She said without proof, she couldn't do much, but she must have blabbed to someone if Wilson was ready to take me down before I told my story."

"Was there anything else about John Wilson we should know?" asked Nadine.

There was a pause. "A lot of stuff that added up to shadiness. He always had meetings that were off his calendar. Once, I heard a woman crying in his office late at night when I'd forgotten my wallet and had to come back. He took fancy vacations he wouldn't let me book although I booked all his other stuff. Also, like I said, he's a worm."

After she disconnected with Monica, Nadine looked at Wes and counted off on her fingers. "Fancy vacations, blackmail, and off-the-book meetings."

"Don't forget overall worminess." Wes tapped his leg as he thought, taking comfort in the rhythm. "Not looking good for the senator."

"We should go over what we have in detail," Nadine said. "This might help us figure this out."

Wes shivered with nervous anticipation. "We've gone from a rumor that one of Dot's books was based on a politician to the possibility that a senator is potentially blackmailing people." He thought it over. "It could be big, especially given John Wilson's influence over the years. He was considered a rainmaker despite losing that leadership bid that could have made him prime minister."

She nudged him. "Big but good?"

"Yes." He kept the *as long as I'm working with you* to himself.

# THIRTY

Nadine reorganized the table of clues as she waited. There came a point in any investigation where she liked to sift through all the available data, and she was looking forward to doing it with Wes. He was smart, and his memory left her awestruck when she wasn't being envious.

Wes came in, and she admired the clean lines of his body against the light in the doorway. He was just tall enough and broad enough and everything enough to make her want to leap over the table, but she would have to save those impulses until tonight. "Brent called," he said. "No floor plans."

"Damn." That basement door would be the death of her.

He blew his breath out in frustration. "It has to be somewhere. The house isn't that huge. I'm starting to wonder if we suffered a joint hallucination." He walked over to the dumbwaiter and slid the door open. "No, we didn't."

Nadine shared his incredulity that they were being defeated by a door but did her best to put it aside. "Well, we can't find the door, but maybe we can make some headway with the clues we've found so far."

He came over to the table. "Where do you want to start?"

"Here." Nadine pointed to the Abigail Spencer obit he'd found in *Thirty Pieces of Silver*. "This woman doesn't seem to have any connection to Dot, so I put it aside."

"There must be something. Otherwise, why is it there?"

"To mark the chapter, the same way Dot marked 'Strange Jest'? Although I read through chapter thirteen twice, and it's about a visit the main character takes with a friend. I can't figure out the link."

"It might not mean anything," Wes said. "Dot's organizational hierarchy is scattered at best."

"True, although I feel there must be something about Abigail." She shrugged. "I can't figure it out, but maybe it'll come clear later."

They picked through their treasure for items with the most relevance. As well as the first letter they'd found from Allan, there was one from Dot to her husband with an intriguing postscript.

*I promised I'd do it and I will. You know I've never broken a promise to you, love. Except about the cats, which of course I had never planned to keep.*

"There's the promise," said Nadine. "The one she mentioned to Brent, but we don't know what it's about."

They turned to the photo of Dot in the porcelain frame, and a quick search showed that Werner and Knapp had been a popular Ottawa photo studio until it closed twenty years ago, another victim of digital photography. It proved Dot had been in the capital, but that could be for a variety of reasons that had no bearing on their search.

Next were the highlighted obituaries. "What if she left these to taunt me personally?" asked Nadine. That would be so unfair, as she had nothing to do with obits now.

"I wouldn't put it past her, but they might not be entirely targeted to you." Wes held out one about a woman who collected fridge magnets.

"One of Dot's short stories features a similar character." He went to Dot's shelf and pulled out a book, which he passed to Nadine. "There's also a story about a man despised by his entire family." He tapped another obit. "Like Robert Giles here."

"Dot was underlining one when we talked to her in the conservatory, and she told me I needed to look deeper into what made people come alive." Nadine sat down with a thump. "Did she leave them as red herrings?"

"They could be, or she simply collected them for inspiration. I found a bunch with folders grouped in categories. The Computers folder from the 1980s was especially hilarious."

She put the obits to the side. "Let's assume they're not relevant and move on." After the Monica Olway blackmail story, the next set of clips were from the social pages, covering galas and events, which they had found along with news clippings about places ruined by infrastructure projects. "Not really a match to the gala stuff," Nadine said, reading about a bridge that destroyed a small town.

"I noticed that too." Wes looked thoughtful. "Some of them were federal projects, and Wilson was briefly the minister for the public works portfolio. He had access to a lot of information and decisions. Then there's this guy." He pointed at a man in the background of one shot.

The face was familiar. "Matt White?"

"Rumored patriarch of the country's biggest crime organization, who masqueraded as an honest developer through the White Group for decades."

"Damn." She looked through the photos. "Here he is again. It looks like he's in all these clips. These seem like projects he'd be involved in and would make a killing on. Construction. Development."

"They do." Wes pulled forward the last set, about professional and financial misconduct by government officials. "Here are clippings about people who ended up on the wrong side of the integrity commissioner and sometimes the law."

"These articles are all from the *Herald*," she said. "Written by a staff reporter."

"Can you find out who wrote them?" he asked.

Nadine checked the dates and shook her head. "Our online platform would list the writer internally, but these are from before it was implemented."

That started a flurry of research and phone calls until they'd found the common denominator. At one point, all those people had worked for or with John Wilson and been involved in large-scale infrastructure projects. Many of them had died (of natural causes, Nadine was relieved to note), and the rest they couldn't find contact information for.

"That's not enough," said Nadine. "Politics is a small world, and it's natural they'll have worked with him or adjacent to him and those projects. He does seem to find people with flexible views of the law and process who have a bad habit of getting caught though."

"Fall guys?" asked Wes. "Fall people?"

"Maybe."

They debated various theories to no avail.

Nadine was the one who summed it up. "We have a bunch of obits Dot used for research and one, Abigail Spencer, that might be relevant, but we can't find anything unusual. We have a promise from Dot to Allan about a secret that is almost certainly about telling the truth about what inspired *Thirty Pieces of Silver*."

"I think we can confidently say John Wilson is involved, that he's the inspiration for James Walton, the antagonist in *Thirty Pieces*, which fits with what we learned from Monica Olway, who he claims tried to blackmail him, and anecdotally from his ministerial portfolio. We also know organized crime might be involved via Matt White, and extrapolating from that, there might be some shadiness in how contracts were handed out or decisions made, which might also explain those vacations Wilson went on."

"I wish Monica would go on the record." Nadine rolled her

shoulders, feeling the ache in her neck. "We still don't know exactly what happened, by whom, or Dot's involvement, and most of our evidence is a bunch of clips that would mean nothing if they hadn't been collected together."

"At least we know it's Wilson we're building a case against, but we need more," Wes agreed. Then he smiled. "I'm racking up those points."

"Great," said Nadine without enthusiasm.

———

The late afternoon rain continued down in torrents, making it too wet for Wes to go for a brisk outside walk while Nadine cooked dinner. However, he had energy that needed to be burned off after their discussion, so he wandered through the conservatory, deadheading the occasional flower.

It had been a fantastic day. They were *getting* somewhere. It made him want to dance and hug Erma, that terrible animal, who had come out to the conservatory and was looking at the koi pond with a predatory eye.

He checked his phone to see a message from Amy. **All good here, so don't worry.**

Wes took a step back as a thought occurred to him. Although he felt bad about leaving Amy to deal with her, he didn't feel bad about leaving his mother. It was as if Dot's mansion was a Faraday cage shielding him from Ma, because apart from sending a daily text that went unanswered, he'd barely thought about her since he'd arrived. Had the distance given him a perspective he'd been unable to gain living in her house? Or had Nadine's quiet outsider sympathy told him what he knew deep down but had been unable to face—that the relationship with his mother was unsustainable?

Perhaps.

To distract himself, he texted Caleb to see what he was up to.

The reply came quick. **So that wedding therapist.**

Wes had almost forgotten he'd sent the link. Caleb hadn't mentioned it until now. **Did you call her?**

**Not yet. What if it's not the wedding? What if it's us?**

This was big. Eager to escape his own problems, Wes called, and Caleb picked up. "Talk to me," Wes said. "What's going on?"

"It's like, this is supposed to be for the rest of our lives, right?"

"Yes." This was a safe answer.

"But I can't tell the future."

"Are you worried about something in particular?" Spying a rattan armchair, Wes sat down, brushing aside the parlor palm leaves draped over the mossy arm.

"Napkins. Isabel's got three pinks that look freaking identical to me, and I don't care because they're napkins, but when I say that, she gets on my case about emotional labor and mental load or something like that. All I said was to pick one because they all look the same and I don't care! And any time I do care, she says my idea is ridiculous."

"Like what?"

"Like a taco truck for after midnight."

Wes laughed. "That would be amazing."

"Isabel wants some waffle wall thing. Says tacos will wreck the aesthetic. I get she's doing most of the planning, but that's because I'm in Calgary. It's not like I don't want to help."

Feeling as if this was slightly above his pay grade, Wes trod carefully. "What else?"

There was a long silence. "I thought this was supposed to be our day, you know? Together. But she could stuff any dude in a tux and stand him at the altar, and it wouldn't matter as long as the wedding favors are perfect. I don't see the point in those, by the way. That was another fight."

Wes knew this wasn't true because he'd known Isabel for years. However, telling Caleb that wasn't going to calm him down much. "Have you told her?"

"How can I? She's so stressed. She'll cry."

"Isabel would be more upset to know you've been hiding this," said Wes, settling into fixing mode.

"I guess. Goddammit. I should be able to talk to my own fiancée." Caleb blew out his breath so hard that Wes pulled the phone away from his ear. "What if she doesn't listen?"

"Then you have bigger problems than a waffle wall."

"I only want to be with her, man. I don't need all this stuff."

Wes thought. "Does she?"

"What do you mean?"

"Did you assume she wanted a big wedding, or did she assume you wanted one, so she's trying to make you happy?" Caleb loved a party, after all, and Wes never had the sense that Isabel liked being the center of attention.

"Don't all women want a wedding like that?" Caleb sounded puzzled.

"Isabel isn't all women," Wes reminded him.

"I don't know," said Caleb thoughtfully. "I guess we didn't talk about it? Like, I proposed, and we were happy and stuff, but we didn't talk details. We went to Mike's wedding around then, and we were talking about how cool it was, I remember that. It was on a boat, huge blowout."

"Maybe you should talk to her."

"It'll probably pass. I'll deal." He sighed, and Wes could almost see him shake it off. "Enough of me. How's your investigation going? How's Nadine?" He drew the name out like he did when they were teenagers and Caleb was ragging on him about his crushes.

He couldn't help smiling. "She's good. Easy to work with."

"No problems from the other night?"

"We're kind of sleeping together now." When Caleb made a humming noise, Wes went on alert. "What?"

"Be careful, okay, man?"

He stiffened. "Careful how?"

"You don't usually do casual."

LILY CHU

"There's a first time for everything."

"There is, but is this it? How are you going to mesh your need to get in there and be Mr. Fix-It for everyone's lives with letting things just happen? *Casual* means *no feelings.*"

"It's called caring for others, and I can do both."

Caleb laughed as if genuinely amused. "Are you serious? You can't move out from your mom's place because you're worried she'll be upset. There's caring, and there's self-sacrifice."

Wes wanted to argue, but Caleb had known him for years and was only echoing what Amy had also said.

"Wes?" asked Caleb.

"That doesn't have anything to do with Nadine."

"You seriously don't see it? How you put everyone over yourself and how that's not the best way to start a casual thing with a woman you actually might like?"

"I can handle this."

"Sure, bud. How about I think about talking to Isabel and you think about what you're doing with Nadine?"

"Deal."

They disconnected as Nadine's voice came from the conservatory entrance. "Wes? It's dinner."

"Coming."

She waited for him, looking adorable with an apron wrapped around her clothes and her hair a tousled mop. "I made dal," she said. "It's my brother's girlfriend's recipe."

That explained the bright yellow stains on her apron. Turmeric. "Sounds good."

He offered her the bowl of chopped garden cilantro, and she waved it away. "It tastes like soap. I don't like it."

"Then why did you prepare it?"

"In case you wanted it." She handed him the salt and smiled at him. His heart jumped. "Who were you talking to earlier?"

"My friend Caleb."

"The one who's getting married."

He'd mentioned that briefly while they were working in the attic one day. He didn't know why her remembering that felt like a big deal, especially since she was a reporter and was good with names, but it did. He turned the conversation to Dot, who even in death retained main character status. "You're going to talk to Irina tomorrow?" he asked, filling their bowls with salad.

"I'm going to ask her about Monica's story," she said.

"The *Herald* still doesn't know what you're doing here, do they?"

She shook her head. "To them, I'm relaxing on vacation."

"The deal we had with Dot was that we would wait until she's gone," said Wes. "We're free to do what we want with the story now."

"We don't have a story," she reminded him. "We have some suppositions that make a good hypothesis and no proof that's good enough to accuse a senator of being in the pay of organized crime."

"It's a strong hypothesis." To Wes, it was clear as day. "I could talk to one of my editors at this point."

She smiled at him. "We have very different ways of working. No, I want to wait until there's something more solid."

A cat jumping on the table interrupted their conversation, and once Octavia had been shooed off, they started talking about John Wilson, reexamining what they had but finding no new conclusions.

Wes busied himself with the dishes while Nadine took a turn in the conservatory. She was a clean-as-you-go type of cook, and while that wasn't his own inclination, he'd started doing the same to even out the number of dishes they each had. It seemed unfair that on his washing nights, he had half the amount while she was stuck cleaning everything he touched on hers.

Was this fixing things? Or a usual level of care? He cursed Caleb for resurfacing these thoughts.

As he scrubbed, he thought about the next day. It made sense that

Nadine wasn't comfortable talking to her editor until there was something firm, given she was on thin ice thanks to the Dot Voline obituary. She would want to wait until everything was in place.

However, for Wes, it was a good time to loop in an editor. The *Spear's* philosophy was to acknowledge that a digital platform was a benefit. They had been the first in the country to start posting news stories blog-style as updates came. This way, he could give them a heads-up—no editor enjoyed being presented with a fait accompli—and get back on the radar as someone who could handle the big stories.

His goal was to land on the I-team, so it would be best to go straight to Jason. Although Rebecca would be upset to be left out of the loop and furious if she found out he was working on vacation, Wes thought the I-team editor would be more open to a story of a senator's malfeasance. The story had become bigger than Dot. Wes could broaden it out with a deeper look at Wilson's career and questions about corruption in the political system. He could almost see the all-employee email now. *We're pleased to announce Wes Chen will be taking a permanent role with our award-winning investigative team.*

Mind you, he'd make it known this was a joint investigation with the *Herald*. Jason might not like that, but fair was fair. Satisfied, he finished the dishes.

# THIRTY-ONE

adine stretched in bed. She'd decided to go to the *Herald* later in the morning when Irina was sure to be there, and Wes had mentioned leaving early for some errands before checking in at the *Spear*. She had Dot's house to herself.

Correction, to herself and the cats. Wes must have fed them before he left because Octavia was only dozing on her bed instead of meowing as if being cruelly starved. She rolled over to stroke the sleek fur as she tried to process what was happening.

It was a lot.

She thought better when she was moving, so Nadine climbed out of bed. Walking slowly through the house, she greeted Sir Latimer and Cheetah Janice as well as the smaller, more lively, and less taxidermied animals before letting herself outside. She went a bit red as she passed the grotto and hoped Dot didn't have security cameras. Last night's swim had been abruptly stopped and taken to the lounge chairs when she'd seen Wes dripping with water.

After putting out a wicker basket to remind herself to harvest the ripe tomatoes in the garden for the pasta Wes liked making, she took the path past the ornamental herb garden and around to the back. Dot's property was deep rather than wide and depended on cunning design to reveal the space step by step. They thought they'd explored the whole place, but as she walked, Nadine caught sight of another secret path, an intricate and almost lacy design of patio stones with grass poking up through the gaps in a way that looked cultivated and not simply overgrown.

It led to a pagoda. An open-air Chinese pagoda painted in cucumber greens and pale pinks that had been hidden by the trees. Nadine imagined Dot had once covered the wooden benches circling the interior with colorful silk cushions. She took a photo, captioned it **Dot's world of mysteries**, and sent it to Wes, who replied with a series of wide-eyed emojis. She stepped over the tiny moon bridge—the pagoda was surrounded by a miniature moat with water lilies—and went inside, where she lay full length on the bench.

Then she proceeded to ignore the fairy-tale view, including a group of turtles sunning themselves on a log in the moat, and fretted. First up was Wes. They'd had sex, and more than once. That part was incredible. What wasn't was the doubting, fearful part of her that suspected he had some sort of ulterior motive for getting along beyond simply getting laid. Although they'd settled their differences, it was hard to get over knowing they'd been rivals for a decade and worked for competing companies. Worse, a darker part of her wondered if, after all those years of competition, he viewed this as winning in some way, perhaps subconsciously.

This was not a healthy perspective, and it did her no good to dwell on it. Nadine sat up to mentally present the next slide in her worry deck: work.

The conversation with Wes last night had forced her into the actions-have-consequences phase of the Dot Voline project. She didn't have a lot of grace left at the *Herald*, and as Lisanne pointed out, there were always journalists waiting for their chance. Good ones too, brave in the way she used to be, before she got burned. Except this story was much bigger than she anticipated, and Wilson's response to the threat to his reputation and career would be exponentially worse than a reader who was upset she covered a policy he disagreed with.

She left the pagoda and continued on the path, not surprised to find a small Japanese Zen garden at the end, because anything was possible when it came to Dot's house. A few large rocks sat in the middle of clean light gray gravel washed flat from the rain. A bamboo rake leaned against a bench, and Nadine grabbed it. She used to have a miniature desk version and loved it. This would be perfect for not thinking, which was what she needed.

The gravel gave a pleasant crunch under her sandals, and despite the previous day's rain, the garden had drained dry under the bright morning sun. She dragged the rake over to the middle rock and began to trace concentric circles around it, focusing on getting each movement perfect.

The thoughts didn't slow. What did she want from work? Weirdly, it was her old job in the obits beat she thought about more often than the politics side. There was so much she could have done to make the obits more interesting, more reflective of the people they memorialized, in all their humanity. She thought of the collection Dot had hidden, as if to remind her that people were there to explore. But politics was politics. It was important. It was where change happened, where the big stories occurred, like this one. It was what she'd always wanted to do.

Nadine sighed, feeling as if she was on the verge of some break-through but not knowing what, then checked her phone. She could do a couple of hours of searching before she needed to leave. Better to focus on what was in front of her. She crunched back across the garden to return the rake, leaving a line of footprints in the gravel. She'd spent the entire time thinking instead of trying to let her thoughts pass.

Later she would come back and try again. Right now, she was going to find some clues.

---

Rebecca's head shot up when she caught sight of Wes. "You're on vacation," she reminded him, as if he'd forgotten.

"I had to pick up a few things." He'd hoped Rebecca would be working from home so she didn't see him talking to Jason.

"One more day and then I'm off to the cottage," she said. "Think of it, Wes. Two weeks of lazing on the dock with a stack of books and no cell access."

"You forgot the bugs."

She held up her arm. "You'd think the heavy pollutants in my bloodstream would have turned them off, but they do love feasting on my soft, sweet city flesh."

"You could not go," he said.

Rebecca waved that away. "Complaining about bugs is a cottage tradition. I'll bathe in citronella and reconcile myself to itching. Also I bought a mesh hat." She put it on and struck a pose, making him laugh.

He made a fuss of going through his desk until Rebecca left for a meeting. Then with an unhurried pace—nothing to see here, folks!—he walked to the I-team's turf.

Tyler saw him. "Hey, Wes. Where you been hiding?"

Wes might not like Tyler, but he knew the value of maintaining a positive relationship. "Vacation. I've been doing some research."

"What a workaholic. You got to learn to relax." Tyler's bushy eyebrows rose. "Anything interesting?"

Wes knew better than to spill the beans to Tyler. "I think so."

"Mysterious." Tyler yawned as Wes looked around him.

"Is Jason in?"

Tyler shook his head. "JJ took a couple days off. Why? You need to talk about your story?"

Shit, he hadn't thought Jason would be away. He usually took time off in the winter. "I wouldn't mind hearing what he thinks of it."

"What he thinks of it? Doesn't he know?"

"It's something I've been working on," said Wes, doing his best to keep casual.

Tyler shook his head slowly. "I don't know, man. Jason doesn't appreciate the rogue thing—you should know that from when you were here as a temp. He hates not knowing what's going on."

A temp? "It's nothing on the team's radar."

The other man stretched, showing deeper blue patches under the arms of his light blue shirt. "Your funeral. I thought you wanted to join us, but that's no way to go about it. JJ's not going to be happy with you coming in to say you know his section better than him."

"I'm not doing that at all," said Wes in frustration.

"Sure, I know that, but he might not see it that way." Tyler unscrewed his bottle of Coke and drank half of it down, releasing the gas out the side of his mouth. "How about you give me an idea of what it is so I can help you with the pitch?"

"No, that's fine," said Wes immediately. "I'll take my chances."

Tyler laughed. "Listen to this guy. I'm not going to scoop you. I'm working on a hockey coach who bribed students to play on his team. That's why they brought me on, for the broad-appeal stuff."

"That does sound right up your alley," said Wes. "I'll wait to talk to Jason though. It's not urgent."

"Whatever," said Tyler carelessly. "He'll ask if you talked to me anyway."

Wes frowned. "Why?"

"I'm kind of his unofficial deputy during the summer when he's taking vacation." Tyler twirled a pen between his fingers.

Wes glanced at the empty desk in the I-team's zone. He needed to take advantage of every opportunity, and he knew Tyler, for all his loudness and other faults, was trusted by Jason. After all, he was the one who'd been chosen to join the *Spear*'s investigative team.

"I might have something that came out of a tip from Dot Voline," Wes said, lifting his brown leather portfolio. "I think—"

"Isn't she dead?" Tyler looked only politely interested. "There was a mess about her obit, right? If that's what you're working on, I can tell you that's not what JJ is looking for."

Tyler's long-winded interruption as well as his slight mocking tone was enough to get Wes's back up. This was a good story, and he'd prove it to Tyler.

"Apparently, one of her characters is based on a real person active in politics."

"Oh?" Tyler's expression didn't change. "Who?"

"A senator," Wes said. "Who could have been prime minister."

"Seems thin, Wes." Tyler rubbed his chin, fingers digging into his thick beard. "JJ's going to want more than this. Some book character? Where's the immediacy? It's an arts piece. Get Becky to run it." Tyler shrugged. "I wouldn't bother JJ with this one."

"It's not about some book character. It's a significant story, and you'd know if you let me finish." Wes kept his voice calm as Tyler put up his hands in a *whoa, buddy* gesture. "He may have been involved in some unprofessional dealings." No need to go into the details.

"Yeah, that's politics. Everyone knows that." Tyler drank down the rest of the Coke. "Let me give you some advice. You need to think impact. Who cares? Every politician has a few deals in the closet that we all know but won't bother doing a story about because it doesn't hit hard enough. Look at my hockey story. Everyone can relate to hockey. We all watch it, or we've had a coach who we knew was shady. See? There's universality."

"That's not universal at all," Wes said. "And you've misunderstood the importance of what I've found."

"Sounds like that's part of your issue, isn't it? You can't explain it."

Frustrated and feeling beaten, Wes turned away without answering. Tyler didn't seem to care.

Nor did anyone else notice when he went back to his desk and grabbed his bag with his middle fingers conveniently but subtly pointed in the direction of the I-team.

# THIRTY-TWO

Nadine deliberately and immaturely planned her arrival at the *Herald* for when Lisanne had a standing meeting with Hetty. There were a few texts on her phone that she couldn't bring herself to answer. She was still upset after their last exchange about Nadine's byline but also not willing to address it like an adult, making evasion her current MO. She went straight to the Crypt, hoping to find her quarry alone.

She did.

"What do you want?" Irina asked, looking over the rims of her glasses.

"Monica Olway," said Nadine, getting right to it. She put the clipping of the *Herald* story denouncing Monica on the table.

"I don't know her." Irina kept typing.

"I think you do," said Nadine. "I spoke to her yesterday, and she told me about your conversation and that although you weren't able to run her story, this one by a staff writer was published soon after. Was that you?"

Irina looked up and maintained eye contact as she kept her fingers moving on the keyboard. Nadine didn't blink. She was going to find out what Irina knew if it killed her, which Irina's Medusa gaze might.

"Do you know what you're doing?" Irina's question came as a surprise.

"Yes." It might be an exaggeration—Nadine had only the faintest idea what she was doing and more than a few unanswered questions—but those were things to talk over with Wes. Not Irina.

Irina gave her a considering look. "I don't think you do."

"I'm the judge of that." The steel in her voice must have convinced Irina, who finally stopped typing.

"Ten years ago, Monica Olway came into the office yelling that John Wilson was a worm and someone had to do something about it," Irina said, folding her hands in front of her. "I happened to be walking by."

"Then what?"

"She told me John Wilson wanted her to spy on someone and fired her when she refused. There was no corroborating evidence, no proof of any kind, and Olway was driven by a personal vendetta. But I was curious and called Wilson's office for a comment. No reply."

"Did you believe her?" asked Nadine.

"What do you know about John Wilson?"

"Not much besides what I learned online and from Monica. He got into politics because of his father, I believe."

"Yes, a popular cabinet minister who unfortunately died early. John was so mediocre that the party doubted even name recognition would help. However, mediocrity has never been an obstacle to success, and Wilson managed to get more money than expected to fund his leadership campaigns. He lost but had the cash to get the ears of powerful men until he became one himself."

"Do you know why he lost? I thought it was because they didn't think he had the charisma for voters."

Irina snorted. "Are you going to do your own research, or am I expected to do it for you?"

"I am conducting research with an in-person interview. You."

Irina looked unimpressed but she said, "The story was Wilson didn't have the voter touch the way his father had or the brains." She paused to bark "Twenty minutes!" to some poor reporter trying to come into the library. "Yet it seemed he had money to try to buy the power he wanted. A lot of money, more than one would expect, and with no apparent origin."

"He was embezzling?" asked Nadine.

"There's no proof of that. Dot Voline's book *Thirty Pieces of Silver* came out with unerring timing during Wilson's leadership bid. Although there was no way to connect Wilson to the Walton character in the book, some important people who knew Wilson noticed a few similarities. The name, obviously, and the relationship with the father. Wilson always wore his father's old Rolex, Walton his father's signet ring. That's a detail few in the general public would have known."

"The book is also about a lying politician who takes advantage of a woman who loved him," Nadine said. "Was that a similarity as well?"

"Unknown. They were concerned Wilson Junior was covering up something though. Again, that wouldn't have been an issue if he'd come clean with the grand pooh-bahs, but they suspected there were more skeletons in his closet. They didn't care enough to do a thorough check, since it was only a book and written by a woman, but it was enough for them to back another horse."

Nadine's pulse quickened as it always did when she was getting somewhere with a story, tempered with the frustration that Irina hadn't trusted her to tell her this information sooner. Well, she supposed she should be grateful Irina put her on the story at all all those weeks ago. "Do you think Dot Voline was having an affair with Wilson?"

"Do you have any evidence she worked in his office?"

"No."

"Well then."

Nadine took a breath. "I"—better to not raise suspicion with a *we*—"found some evidence that John Wilson might be connected with Matt White."

"Some?"

"Photos in a collection of newspaper clippings. Then more clippings about people who had been caught out for professional misconduct, like Monica. I also found there was a web of people who knew Senator Wilson in some capacity and were involved in getting controversial infrastructure projects through. Ones that benefited the White Group."

Irina gave her a long look. "I sometimes used to get leaks about political staff who had crossed the line. I was told they were from a trustworthy source, though anonymous. Many of those people admitted their wrongdoing, but some I had questions about." Irina moved her hands back to her keyboard. "That led me to wonder why I was getting these convenient tips. After the Monica story broke and I started asking about where that blackmail story came from, the old editor in chief sent me down here."

"Oh." The implication was not one Nadine liked to entertain.

"I ask again if you know what you're doing."

"I do." Nadine thought of something. "Ah, this is currently confidential. If you could not mention it to Daniel, I'd be grateful."

The heavy silence was enough for Nadine to know she'd misstepped. "I'm not in the habit of gossiping about my work with Daniel," said Irina coldly.

Nadine turned to go when Irina spoke again.

"Raj quit," she said.

"I heard."

"They hired a temp for the obituaries."

"I've been reading them," said Nadine, unsure of where Irina was going with this.

"Then you know they're no good." Irina waved her away. "They need a hand like yours. Off you go. I need to work."

A hand like hers. Nadine let herself think of what she could change if she was obits editor before reality took over. She was the night web editor, and no matter what Irina thought, obits wasn't her job.

As she was rushing to get out before Lisanne left her meeting, Jillian Low, an advertising rep and chair of the *Herald*'s diversity committee, grabbed her. "Oh goody, Nadine. I was looking for you."

"I only popped in. I'm on vacation," Nadine said, trying to keep walking. No go. Jillian stood in front of her. Nadine should have known better than to mess with a woman who did sales for a living.

"This will only take a sec." Jillian looked frazzled. "The committee has been tasked with testing the new diversity survey, and I need your opinion."

"Why the committee?" Nadine asked. "Isn't this management's job?"

Jillian smoothed her short black hair behind her ears. "Why do you think? Do you know I'm the third person they asked to run this thing? Gabriela Ramirez told me she spent fifteen hours a week on diversity stuff. Unpaid and over and above her real work. Then they dinged her for not meeting her targets."

Nadine couldn't leave Jillian hanging and felt bad about letting down her colleagues. "Sure, email it to me, and I'll look at it when I'm back."

"Why not now?" said Jillian, handing her a paper. "All you have to do is fill it out so we know the questions are clear. Sorry, but I'm swamped and need this off my plate."

Nadine took it. She might as well get it over with. "Fine." She glanced through, then paused. "This section is about racial diversity."

"It's a diversity survey." Jillian looked up from her phone.

"You don't have anything for mixed."

Jillian pressed her lips. "Management said it would mess up the data."

"Are you kidding?"

"Oh my God, I wish I was. Remember when we said the *Herald*'s problems had to be tackled at the policy and management level, like how we hire and promote?"

Nadine put a finger to her chin and pretended to think. "Let me see. I believe they said it was out of our scope and we should..."

"Hold a diversity potluck to improve employee morale," Jillian joined in. They laughed. Laughing was often their saving grace at work. Jillian took the sheet back. "I'll try again," she said. "Thanks."

Catching sight of Lisanne's hot-pink blazer coming down the stairs, Nadine waved a quick goodbye to Jillian and left, feeling guilty.

By the time she pulled into the driveway at Dot's mansion, Nadine had gone through several cycles of berating herself for not talking to Lisanne before deciding to let it go. She'd text her tomorrow for sure. The more she wallowed in this, the worse it was going to be. Her mood lightened a bit as she pulled into the driveway, excited to tell Wes about her day.

He took the bag of takeout sushi when she came in. "Thanks for picking this up."

"You're not going to believe what I heard," she said.

"Tell me." He took the chopsticks out of the paper wrapper and split them open before handing Nadine a pair.

She stirred her miso and plucked out a tiny cube of soft tofu as she ran through Irina's story.

Wes took some edamame. "That's another thing connecting John Wilson with big crime to get projects passed and threatening people who don't play ball. We're getting close."

She should look at the positives, but they didn't have much time left to find what they needed. "We are."

"Let's have a glass of wine to celebrate."

"Sounds perfect. Can I check something on your laptop since it's out?" she called as he went to the wine fridge, which they'd stocked with a few bottles. "Mine's in my bag."

"Password is amell8." He spelled it out.

"Amell is for your sisters, but what's the eight for?" she asked curiously.

"They make me change the password every ninety days." His voice was muffled from looking in the fridge. "This is the eighth time. Red or white?"

Nadine wasn't listening. She was too busy reading the story Wes had been working on and had left up in the main window. The excitement from her Irina news faded into sick disbelief at what he was typing straight into the *Spear*'s editorial software.

The story about Dot Voline and John Wilson.

Wes's antennae were so attuned to other people's moods he knew something was wrong before he turned to Nadine with the two bottles in his hands. He could feel it, a pressure on his skin that made him prickle with dread.

Nadine sat at the table in front of his laptop. She wasn't looking at him, but her eyes were dancing over the screen and her finger scrolling as she read.

He relaxed when he realized it was only his Dot Voline notes. That was fine. He'd been in the middle of writing up his thoughts to make his pitch to Jason, despite Tyler's indifference. So why did he have this feeling he'd done something wrong?

When she finally raised her face, it was with a look of utter betrayal. "What is this?" she asked.

He put the wine down, unsure of what was going on. It was obvious what she was looking at, so the question had the feeling of a trap. "My notes on what we've found," he said.

"I can see that."

He was more baffled. "Then why are you asking? I went to the *Spear* to pitch the story about Dot and John Wilson."

Nadine's eyes, always big, went as huge as an anime character. She looked as if she couldn't believe her ears. "You absolute asshole. You were going to go behind my back about this? We agreed we wouldn't say anything yet."

"What?" This made no sense. "We talked about it last night."

"At no point did I say, *Yes, green light to talk to editors.* I said the opposite. The *opposite.*"

"That is not what happened at all." Wes was angry now, matching her energy and turbocharging it with a big dose of unfairness. "You knew I was going to talk to the *Spear.*"

"No, you said you *wanted* to tell them, and I said no. The exact word, no. I said we didn't have enough information yet. We didn't have any proof! How could you? You said you were going by the *Spear* to check in." Nadine stood up so violently, the backs of her knees knocked the chair over. She cursed as she snatched it into place.

A little doubt rose in him. Had she said that? He could have sworn they'd agreed they had different approaches but he was good to go. Right? Or had he heard what he wanted to hear? Being unsure led to feeling defensive. "We have enough for me to pitch the story. There's no need for you to be so upset. It's no big deal."

He knew this was a mistake the second he said it.

"No big deal." Nadine's eyes narrowed. "You were trying to get the jump on me. You were trying to scoop me the way you thought I did to you. I should have known you wouldn't be able to get over me getting the best of you all these years."

His defense shifted to offense, because that was untrue, and it was unfair of her to bring up the past. "Is that what you think of me? We talked about that. We resolved it."

"I thought we did, but I guess I was wrong."

"I don't need to scoop you."

She shoved her hair back. "Why, because I'm such a loser at the *Herald* you don't think they'd take the story anyway?"

Wes spread his hands, trying to follow her train of thought. "What the hell, Nadine? I never said that."

"You don't need to." Her fingers on the back of the chair looked like claws, and he saw her chest rise with a deep, deliberate breath.

Wes glared at her. "Stop that," he said.

"Stop what? Breathing?"

"That big I'm-so-patient breath you take when I'm irritating you."

Her arms came up to cross in front of her chest. "Wes, I'm not breathing at you, for God's sake. Quit jumping down my throat!" She stood straighter. "I should have known better than to trust you. You were using me to get the story. I bet you wanted to try to use it to get into the *Herald* since you failed at the *Spear*."

Wes knew it was his job to de-escalate this fight. It was always his job to apologize first, even if he did nothing wrong. But he couldn't. The injustice of her accusation and its sheer meanness made him livid. All the feelings of the day rose up and burst out. All the feelings of his *life*.

"I was using you? You seriously think I want to take your job? You're barely holding on to it, so it wouldn't be hard. If I want to write that damn story and run it in lights along the CN Tower, I can. I worked with you because it was easier. That's it. Jesus, you're being ridiculous."

The words echoed in the kitchen as Nadine stared at him. Between them, a deep silence grew and spread.

"I..." Nadine blinked and dipped her head down, then put up her hand as if she'd had enough. "I need to get some fresh air."

She left him standing in the kitchen alone with the celebration wine, feeling the regret take over. What had he done?

# THIRTY-THREE

N adine was back in the pagoda. She drank the wine, and she felt bad. She hadn't felt bad when she'd left Wes and had gone to her room to pace around, upset and unable to focus. It wasn't until she heard the front door open and close that the doubt snuck in, dragging along its friend regret to the party and eventually leading her to the bottle of wine and lying in a pagoda, hoping spiders didn't drop on her head.

She hugged her knees into her chest. Without the heat of anger, she could map out where things had gone wrong. Wes wanted to talk to his editor. Nadine had said no because she wasn't ready for either of them to escalate the story, and Wes had interpreted it as she wasn't, but he was good to go. That was still weird, but she could at least see how a miscommunication could happen.

Then it had escalated when she saw that story on his laptop. Those doubts about Wes she thought she'd put to rest reared back up. If she hadn't gone on the attack, they could have sorted it out in the moment, but her response had been almost instinctive. She was under no illusions that she could kiss her job goodbye if Daniel found out what she'd been up to, not from her but from the *Spear*. Wes's response had not been reassuring and had added to her fury.

She cringed at how she'd lost control and said those things, even if deep down, she felt they were partially true. If only she could be as clearheaded in the moment as she was after the fact. She probably had to apologize.

However, Wes had been a vindictive asshole, so she wasn't the only one who had to say sorry.

A rustle came from the bushes, and Nadine sat up, listening hard before she grabbed the wine bottle and stood, ready to take on the intruder.

"Nadine?"

Wes stood on the opposite side of the moat. She sagged in a relief that was only momentary because although it wasn't a killer (hooray), she thought she had until morning to figure out a game plan for dealing with Wes. She was going to have to wing it.

He stepped back. "Is this a pagoda?" he asked. "With a moat?"

"There's a bridge on the other side." The small peace offering gave Wes a choice: come in and talk, or leave. For a sickening moment, she wasn't sure what he would do, but then he moved around and came over the bridge.

Nadine watched him approach, heart dancing a cha-cha. She'd covered a lot of corporate apologies for work, but she didn't have a PR person to help her craft a response here. Best not to overthink it.

Once Wes entered the pagoda as a darker shadow against the black of the night, she said, "Misunderstandings were made earlier, and I might have been an ass to you."

"Is that your attempt at an apology?" he asked.

Her desire to be the bigger person withered. She glared at him. "I don't know. Why don't we see after I hear yours?"

"You were the one to jump all over me," he said, hands flat on the bench.

"Right, and when you told me I was ridiculous and you didn't need me?" That had hurt, and she couldn't keep her voice from breaking. "That I was terrible at my job?"

"How about when you said I was a failure at mine?"

They both looked away. It was Nadine who spoke first. "That was wrong of me. I feel awful that I said that to you." She did, too, filled with a sick emptiness that she could have been so nasty.

That reduced the tension between them.

"I shouldn't have said what I did either," said Wes. "I was angry, and it was shitty of me."

"Yes, it was." She looked at the wine and came out with it. "I'm sorry."

Wes sat down. "I'm sorry too." He rubbed the back of his neck. "For what I said and also for going to talk to the *Spear*. I think I might have heard what I wanted when we talked about going to the editor. I should have told you straight out that I was going to talk to Jason and pitch the story to make sure there was no misunderstanding. That's my fault."

"I knew it!" Nadine jumped up, feeling vindicated. "I was right about that conversation. I knew I was. It *was* a big deal."

Wes's face made it clear he was trying his best. "I'm sorry for saying that. I swear I wasn't consciously trying to scoop you."

She raised her eyebrows. "Who did you tell?"

"Jason wasn't in. I talked to Tyler." He told her the conversation, and she sat back down.

"First, what a dick. Second, no one saw the story you were writing?" she confirmed. "You only used Dot's name and not John Wilson? Or mentioned me?"

"No one else's name crossed my lips."

She let her breath out in a slow exhale. "Yeah. Okay. We both made mistakes, but I've long known you're not perfect."

He sat down. "Glad we came to a positive conclusion."

Nadine got the sense he wasn't finished and waited.

"Did you mean what you said?" Wes finally asked in a low voice.

"Which part in particular?" she asked cautiously.

"Not trusting me."

Her hands went cold. Wes was looking over at her, and it didn't take a genius to see however they handled this would be the beginning or the end of what they could be. She was grateful for the night shading her, feeling skittish at the idea of having to talk about her feelings. Maybe that was part of the problem. She put walls up at work to protect herself, but she'd have to build a door that fit him. It was scary that Wes was no longer only part of her professional life. He had become personal, and not only when they started sleeping together. It had started far earlier than that, with the seeds planted before they'd begun work with Dot.

She crossed her legs and pulled the blanket tighter, wanting the comfort even if she didn't need the warmth. "We've known each other a long time," she said slowly. "After we had that talk, we didn't stop competing. What if this is another contest for you? What if you want to win, and then when you have that, you lose interest?"

"In the story?" he asked. "Or us?"

"Us." It was hard to say it.

---

Wes wanted to believe he was the kind of man who could put aside all his anger and negative feelings to think rationally. He was not. He was still mad at Nadine.

No, he wasn't mad. He was hurt. What made it worse was the same mistrustful thoughts had floated through his own mind before he'd dismissed them as being unworthy of her.

Yet she didn't feel the same.

"Do you believe that?"

"You like to win."

"So do you," he pointed out. "This seems more than a little hypocritical."

"It's not the same!" she exclaimed.

"It kind of is." He leaned forward. "I thought we'd sorted this out and agreed to let our past go."

"It's not our past," she said. "That's the problem. It's how we are."

"We like to compete, but it doesn't mean I want to hurt you or I don't respect you. I thought we were having fun. Weren't we?"

His eyes had adjusted to the darker interior of the pagoda, and he saw her duck her head. "We were," she admitted. "It is fun. I love beating you."

"Nadine."

"I like when we compete," she amended, "and I know it's not spiteful. It just fed into everything I was feeling."

"Tonight wasn't great, but we make a good team, competition or not."

She clasped her hands on her lap. "We still don't know each other. Not really."

"I disagree. I think we do know a lot." He moved over to sit near her, careful to keep some space between them. Her head tilted down, but he could tell she was listening, so he kept going. "I know you only use salted butter despite sweet butter's superiority."

Her guarded expression faded a bit. "I know you like to start each morning saying hello to the cats, even though you say you don't like them."

"They're growing on me. I know you like to lie down when you're reading."

"I know you like to sing Britney in the shower."

Wes blanched. "You heard?"

Her smile was huge. "Your rendition of 'Piece of Me' is a classic."

Humiliating.

Then she added, "I like it. When you come out, you smell like that lemony shampoo, and you're smiling. It cheers me up."

He moved so they were almost touching. "As for what we don't know, we can change that. I like to go to farmers markets and buy overpriced bread and cheese to eat sitting on a bench."

She hesitated, then pressed against him. "I like walking around the city for hours watching people."

He grinned. "I do the same thing but on the Queen streetcar. I own two irons and a steamer."

"I bet you have one of those little tools to defuzz sweaters."

"I do!" Amy had bought it for him from the As Seen on TV store.

"I hate the winter."

"I hate being cold," he said. "So I also hate winter."

She turned to face him. "I'm worried about work."

"I'm also worried about work," Wes said, matching her shift.

He could hear the depth of her next breath. "I'm worried this story will bury me if John Wilson decides that's what he wants."

His turn. "When Tyler questioned me earlier, it made me think part of the reason they sent me back to Lifestyle was because he's better at big investigative stories."

"I keep second-guessing myself," she said. "I lost my confidence. I triple-check every fact and then worry that I have it wrong."

Wes reached out his hand and waited for hers to cover his. Her palm was sweaty, and it should have been gross, but Wes held it tightly as they silently sympathized with each other's concerns. There was no need to reassure each other or talk each other out of it. It was enough to hear them out loud.

Nadine said, "I have one more question left. I want to use it."

"Okay." He wasn't sure what it could be, but he steeled himself for anything.

"Do you remember the night when we were at the same house party? Our last year in school. I tripped in the hallway."

"I caught you."

She glanced up and he went on.

"That couple was making out, and she lifted her foot right when you passed. You were wearing a green dress that tied at the side."

"You do remember."

"You know I have a fantastic memory," he said and laughed when she poked him. "Here's what else I remember. I remember you were so beautiful I couldn't take my eyes off you. I remember your hair was parted on the side, and it fell a bit over your face, and I wanted to push it back so I could see your dimple if it came out. I remember holding you and that I'd never had a moment so perfect in my life."

"I remember you were in a black sweater, and you were leaning against the wall," she said. "I remember you smelled like some spicy citrus, and when I went to the store, I sniffed all the testers to figure out what it was. I remember your hands came up behind my back when you pulled me in, and I wondered what would happen if I kissed you the way I wanted."

They were facing each other now. Wes felt his heart hammering. "I have one more question left too," he said.

She nodded, and he took his courage in hand.

"It's more of a comment than a question, to be honest." He could do this. "This friends-with-benefits thing. I thought I could do it, but I don't think I can."

"Oh. You want to keep it as friends."

She looked down, and Wes tightened his grip on her hand. "It's the friends part I'm failing at."

"What?" Nadine raised her face.

"I like you, and more than friends. Much more."

"How much more?" Her voice trembled slightly.

"I don't know. I don't have a scale. Is the exact percentage necessary?"

Her eyes glittered in the night. "Yes, because I think I'm feeling about seventy percent more than friends with you."

His breath caught. "In the spirit of keeping this noncompetitive, I'll also be at seventy percent."

"Finally, we agree on something."

When he wrapped his arms around her, she laughed. He couldn't help but stare. Nadine was lovely all the time, but with her face lit up with joy? She was breathtaking.

He didn't kiss her at first, simply enjoying the moment. She felt right in his arms. Perfect.

"Do you think all those years of hating each other were due to repressed feelings?" he asked to the top of her hair. Her arms were around his waist.

"No, younger you was a dick," she said thoughtfully.

"Hey!"

"Younger me was too," she said.

"Glad older us are so much more mellow." Wes was about to continue his thoughts on the wisdom that comes with age, but she shorted out his entire executive function by snuggling closer.

This time when he kissed Nadine, it was slow and simply for the pleasure of knowing he could. Every sensation of touching her stood out and melted together at the same time. His hand came up to stroke the soft skin behind her ear because he'd never touched her there and he wanted to. He wanted to know every part of her. She gasped, a tight sound that made his heart jump, and pressed her arms tighter around his chest, surprising him with her strength. That was new and intriguing. Another thing to explore.

There would be more talks, he was sure. Like, capital-R relationship, what-are-we talks, but that was all for the future, and he was going to stay in the now.

She smiled at him again, and this time, the kiss was lingering and gentle, with a whisper of things to come and a sense of promise, and all the world melted away.

# THIRTY-FOUR

Nadine slapped her arm over her eyes to block the light. Why did her back hurt? Why was she damp? There were birds chirping. They seemed too close.

"Did we fall asleep out here?" Wes's rough voice came from nearby, and she sat up to see him looking around through puffy eyes. "Stop the sun. It hurts."

Nadine assumed she wasn't looking her best after sleeping out in the pagoda, but the way Wes smiled at her made her feel like she was dressed like a million bucks. She stood up, holding her lower back in both hands as she tried to stretch.

Wes unraveled himself with an unsettling grace her creaky joints resented and reached out to massage her shoulders. "I have a suggestion."

"What?" She leaned back into his hands, happy for his touch that melted the knots out. She knew his hands were magic, but this was next level.

"How about a quick dip in the grotto to wake up?" he asked, digging his thumbs in and making her knees buckle.

"What time is it?" She checked her phone. It was dead, which had to be the number one cause of anxiety for people in the modern age, but here with Wes, it didn't seem to matter as much.

Wes's phone was dead as well, so they had a pleasant debate about the time based on the location of the sun as they went to the grotto.

"Holy shit." Wes shivered, having gone for the all-at-once method of water immersion while Nadine tested a single foot. "This water is colder than I thought."

The surprisingly frigid pool turned what was planned as a refreshing and potentially naughty dip into something that felt disturbingly chaste and healthy. They were back out in minutes to separate for more comfortable showers.

In her ornate bathroom, Nadine stood under the spray, thinking about Wes. They hadn't talked about last night, but at the same time, she was talked out. And she felt comfortable with what they'd discussed, even if there was work to do. That might not be the sexiest thing in the world, but she had a lot going on in her life and only wanted to know that:

1. She and Wes were good.

2. They had a future that was stable and they could work on.

3. Having fantastic sex was still a go.

Drama-free was liberating.

That being said, she thought as she dried off, there was always the chance for things to go seriously off the rails as they so often did.

Luckily, it wasn't at breakfast, where a bowl of fruit sat on the table along with toast cut into little heart shapes. Wes poured the coffee and looked at her as if waiting for her reaction.

"Thank you," she said, taking the coffee. She wanted to give him a kiss and, after a brief hesitation, leaned in and pressed her lips to his. "I love the toast hearts."

His entire body relaxed, and he pulled her in for a much longer kiss than she had risked, making her confidence sing. "I thought you might."

They sat down to eat. As Wes handed Nadine the (salted) butter, he said, "I'm glad we talked last night."

"Me too."

"To confirm, because I want to be sure. Are we in a relationship?" Wes asked.

She grinned, heart pattering. "You want to be?"

"With you?"

She poked him under the table with her foot. "No, Erma."

He glanced at the cat, who was grooming on the counter. "That's a nasty idea on every level. So yes to you, no to Erma."

As if sensing the rejection, the cat jumped down, paws landing with a slight thump, and stalked out of the room with her tail high. "Don't be a sore loser," Nadine called after her.

"Are you competing with a cat?" he asked.

"Looks like I don't need to." It was so easy to be with Wes that she was almost giddy at seeing him across the table.

Wes helped Nadine clear up, stealing small kisses that caused her heartbeat to soar high enough to hit a satellite in geostationary orbit, then pulled her to the couch as they passed through the salon. "We need to talk about the story," he said. "To make sure we understand each other."

Right, because they weren't staying at Dot's house as a sort of happy honeymoon retreat. Nadine ran her hand along the silky tassels. "We only have a week left until Brent needs us out. I don't plan on saying anything to the *Herald* until we're completely finished here."

"I'll do the same at the *Spear*." He shrugged when her eyebrows rose. "What happened is in the past, but I'll refrain from mentioning it again or to anyone else."

"How should we talk to them about a joint investigation?"

They sat thinking, and then Wes said, "We're getting ahead of ourselves. We have time left. Let's decide after we have evidence no one can debate. A slam dunk."

Nadine mimed throwing a basketball, and he laughed, kissing her cheek and making her smile.

---

Six hours later, they had nothing.

Ten hours later, nothing.

The next day, "Nothing," reported Wes as he went to the window for some fresh air. Confident they'd seen everything in the house but that damn basement, they'd decided to power through the rest of the attic boxes.

Nadine fell backward on the floor, a sheaf of papers at her chest. He left the window to lie beside her, appreciating her closeness almost as much as the breeze from the fan. By unspoken agreement, they'd started working as a team. While he'd enjoyed the game of the earlier search, it was nothing on being able to spend time with Nadine talking about everything and nothing, and what they were or were not finding. He was dozing off when Nadine sat up.

"Hey, do you have your notes up here? I want to check something."

"No, they're in my bag." He stood and looked down at her. She must be thirsty. "You want a drink?"

"Yes, please." She bent her smooth neck over another box. He laid a kiss on her bare nape, causing her to shiver in a very interesting way, and then left.

It was when he was staring at his bag that it came to him that he'd left the papers at work. Wes slapped his hand on his forehead, seeing the scene. He'd gone in after their fight, upset and wanting to bury himself in his writing. By the time he was done, he'd been more depressed than angry and was distracted as he was packing up, just as Tyler and a few guys had come in from the bar to grab their things. The printout of the story—he'd never gotten over the habit of printing out a first draft after his computer died when he was under a tight deadline—was in his leather portfolio. At least it was in a pile of papers in an office buried in more paper, so he was confident it was safe and hidden enough no one could stumble across it.

He grabbed two cans of sparkling water out of the fridge and returned to Nadine. Her legs were folded under her skirt, giving her the look of a modest debutante, which was only partly disturbed by her frown as she unfolded a stained newspaper. She looked up as he told her about his notes.

"I'll get them after work when the rush hour dies down and no one's in the office," he said.

"Sure." She sounded distracted.

"Is there something bothering you?" Despite their talk last night, he worried that her mood was directly correlated with him.

In response, she passed over the paper in her hand. It was an old obituary from 2001, a poet whose name Wes remembered from school. He scanned the sheet until he found the poem "Thoughts on Bread." It was about a woman in a bakery examining the day-old sale goods and was a rumination on the role of women in the home. He couldn't make the connection between the poem and whatever Nadine was thinking, and he looked up.

"Did you like the poem?" he asked.

A half smile passed over her face. "Not particularly, but that's not what I was thinking about."

He sat beside her and leaned back against a box. "Deep thoughts about the ephemerality of life?"

"Sort of." She propped herself on her arms behind her, arching her back in a way Wes found absorbing. "When I went to the *Herald*, Irina told me they'd put in a temporary obituary editor after Raj left."

He kept quiet and waited for her to finish.

"My first thought was resentment." She sounded astonished at herself. "That was my job. How dare they give it to someone else?"

"Did you feel that way about Raj?"

"Then, I was too upset about being punished." Nadine went red. "Also I like Raj, and he did a good job. This person doesn't care as much."

"That bothers you?"

"Yeah." She looked thoughtful. "It does. I've been thinking about this since that day with Dot. We live in a world where we can access someone's recordings and audio for eternity after they die, but since that person is gone, it leaves a strange dissonance. An obituary gives closure to someone's time here with us, when they were still alive, and we could interact with them."

She put the empty can aside to shake out her wrists. He took her hand and began to rub along the delicate bones. "You don't have to be on the politics beat," he pointed out.

"You don't need to be on the I-team."

"I know. But I want to. Nothing else calls to me like that, and it's the reason I got into journalism in the first place. I felt alive working on those stories. It sounds like you, on the other hand, might be thinking about opening up your opportunities."

"Do you think so?" Then she gave her head a decisive shake. "No, I want to cover politics. I can make a difference there."

"From what you said before, you can make a difference with obits as well."

"Maybe." She sounded thoughtful. "We should get back to work."

"Or," he said, "we could start in a minute."

She gave him that heart-stopping smile that, for ten years, had always made him feel things. "In a minute," she agreed.

Wes did not in general consider himself a particularly lucky man. He wasn't unlucky—more things had gone his way than hadn't—but he figured that was about average for most people. Sometimes it worked out, sometimes it didn't.

However, with Nadine reaching for him, he was the human equivalent of a horseshoe, four-leaf clover, and maneki-neko all in one. When she straddled him, her hair falling over his face, he couldn't help but shut his eyes to try to separate out the feelings. She tucked in closer and leaned down to kiss him, keeping him in place with her hands on his shoulders. Her mouth tasted like her cherry-mint lip gloss, and Wes knew, deep in his bones, that the scent would come up when remembering the most precious moments of his life. Then Nadine shifted and pulled him down, and he forgot about everything except the soft feel of her thigh under his hand and how that birthmark didn't look like a rabbit at all once he got close.

# THIRTY-FIVE

ole in one," announced Nadine triumphantly as her neon-green golf ball dropped into the hole. Exhausted from a dawn-to-dusk day of searching, they'd decided to leave the house and all Dot Voline mystery talk behind to let their subconsciouses work on the problem over dinner. When they'd passed the mini golf place on the way home, Nadine had insisted they stop.

Wes looked at the scorecard. "How are you so good at this?" She had come in at below par or whatever it was called at each hole.

"My parents liked to go to the same place on vacation every year so they could see the same people, eat at the same restaurants, and play at the same mini golf course." She bent down to retrieve her ball, the stripes of her dress glowing a dull purple.

It was the most calming thing in this entire room. Wes had never played mini golf before and doubted a glow-in-the-dark course was the best introduction. He was lost in an eye-aching neon hellscape, but Nadine was happy, which meant Wes was happy.

He put his own ball down on the most used section of the tee, assuming it must be the best place to putt. "Did you play a lot?"

"So much. My goal was to get a hole in one for every hole." Nadine stopped talking to let him tee off. "Oh, close."

It was close, Wes saw with satisfaction, and all he had to do was tap it in. "Did you do it?"

"All but the hole six windmill. I must have tried it dozens of times. Maybe hundreds."

"You'd think statistically one would have gotten in by chance."

"I know!" she exclaimed. "It's like I beat the system but not in the positive way."

He swung his putter and swore as the ball swooped around the edge of the hole and off to the side.

Nadine laughed and slid her arm around his waist to kiss him on the cheek. "Almost."

There was a difference between a hot sex kiss and the warm, honey-sweet, affectionate one she'd given him. The kiss felt natural and real. He could hear Caleb and Amy telling him to stop overthinking and enjoy it for what it was—a lovely gesture from a woman he loved spending time with and *was in a relationship with.*

However, was a Wes who didn't overthink things even Wes?

He watched as she lined up her next shot, eyes narrowing as she checked the distance, and realized he was having more fun playing this appalling game than anything he could remember. She made it fun. He cheered absently as her ball landed near a set of concentric hi-vis orange circles.

"Wes?" Nadine's teeth glowed when she smiled at him. "You ready?"

"Sorry." He gave the ball a tap, and Nadine threw her hands up, her shout rivaling the kids behind them.

"Hole in one!" She jumped over a garish pink curb and hugged him. "I knew you could do it."

Wes held her and kissed the top of her head, feeling strangely grateful when she smiled up at him. What an odd feeling to have at glow-in-the-dark mini golf. Or any mini golf probably.

Nadine put on the wipers to clear the dust from her windshield when she heard Wes click his tongue. She glanced over. Surely he wasn't upset at being utterly demolished at the game.

No, he was staring at the gas station up ahead. "Can you turn in there?"

"Why? I have enough gas," she said.

"Please, I beg of you." When she saw him holding his hands in a prayer position, she laughed.

"Fine," she said as she pulled in. "Who am I to deny you some gas station snacks."

As she was deciding between the sour cream and onion or BBQ chips—which would leave her with worse breath, and did she care?—Wes came up with a receipt.

"What's that?" she asked, holding the chips.

"Your car is very dirty," he said.

"Oh yeah." She decided on the BBQ. "It gets like that."

"As the loser of tonight's mini golf game, my punishment should be to get it washed."

She was intrigued. "I've never gone through a car wash before."

The receipt jerked in his hand. "You've never washed your car."

"That's what rain is for."

"You can't be serious." He looked faint.

Nadine should have known that a man who ironed his socks would not see this in the same light as she did. She looked out the window and saw the faded "Wash Me" her brother had written with his finger the last time she was home. "All right," she said. "I'll try it."

Wes paid for her snacks, and although he didn't skip back out to the car, it was close.

"What do I do?" she asked.

"Drive over there." He pointed to the entrance. "Then we make sure the windows are up and put it in neutral. That's it."

"No people?" she asked.

"Not at this one."

Nadine pulled up as Wes opened the bag of BBQ chips. "Is this something you do a lot?" she asked. "Go through car washes?"

He picked out the perfect wish chip, its sides folded until they touched, and handed it to her. "It's calming. You'll see."

"You like things tidy," said Nadine. She closed her eyes and made her usual wish, the one that hadn't changed since she was a teenager. The car lurched forward, and a spray of water obscured the windshield.

"I do." He ate a chip. "It makes me feel as if part of my life is under control. I suppose I should have added that to my answer about the ironed clothes when you asked."

Before she could reply, huge rags slapped against the car, and soapy water sluiced over the windshield as Nadine's phone dinged at the same time as Wes's did. "You owe me a beer," she said absently. She hoped the message wasn't another one from Lisanne, although that was gutless, and she should just deal with her friend's success. But she was still too sour about the situation, which she didn't feel good about.

It was her mother checking in, which wasn't much better. **Where are you? We went by your apartment with some food and your downstairs neighbor says you haven't been home.**

She was going to kill Otto when she saw him, the snitch. **He's been in and out so he probably didn't see me,** she lied. It was easier to throw Otto under the bus. One day, she could tell her mother to bug off, but that wasn't today.

**Okay, sweetie! Happy you're safe. Lunch next week? Your dad cleared out your old room.**

That was strange. **Okay, but why?**

**So you can move in! Have you talked to your landlord about your lease?**

Nadine ground her teeth. **Mom, I said I was fine.**

**Sweetie, you know we're right.**

She shut her eyes until she heard Wes put away his phone. He gave her a crooked smile. "My mother."

"No way. Mine too."

They sat in silence as the car shook from blasts of air. Nadine watched the little balls of water slide up the windshield. "You want to talk about yours?" she asked.

"Not really. You?"

"No."

The car jerked, and Wes nodded at the gearshift. "You can put it in drive now. We're done."

Nadine drove away, marveling at how much she could see. Maybe Wes was onto something with this car washing idea. She merged back into traffic.

"The thing is," they said at the same time.

"You go," said Wes.

"You know what we were talking about the other night? About how hard it is to stand up to family?" She waited for him to nod. "I told my mom I don't want to move home, but it's like talking to a wall. How do I make her listen?"

They were through the next intersection before he answered. "I don't know if you can," he said.

"That's not encouraging."

"I know. I was thinking about my own mother. Her worldview is different from mine. In hers, she's constantly battling. Fighting other people, fighting herself. What's at the end of that battle, I have no idea. It's like she needs me and my sisters so she has someone there to be in conflict with."

Nadine touched his hand, and Wes continued.

"I've recently realized I can never win because she refuses to see that she doesn't need to quarrel with anyone. I think fighting is how she feels alive."

"You think my parents' mindset is why they don't listen? Like your mom?"

"It could be. You said they thrive on safety. They may not understand that you don't feel the same way, or they may not be willing to understand."

"Because if I don't feel the same way as they do, they need to question their own assumptions?" This made sense. "Regardless of the motive, it doesn't help me with how to get them off my case."

"I think you're doing it. When they call, you tell them no. You might need to be firmer."

"I thought I had, but maybe I was wrong." Nadine pulled up at Dot's golden gates. "What about you?"

"What about me?"

"Your mom. What are you going to do?"

"There's nothing much I can do at the moment besides keep saving money and hoping for the best." Wes opened the door to get the gate, then got back in the car. "I want to hear more about your mini putt experiences."

She let him change the subject and decided to tell him about the time Noah calculated all the angles for the local mini putt as they entered the house. The story didn't take long, but that was fine. Once they hit the bedroom, they had new ways to distract each other.

# THIRTY-SIX

W es, listen to this." They were drinking iced mango juice on the front steps during their afternoon break. Nadine had found her new favorite obituary, about a mayor who hosted a party for his entire town each July called Summer Winter Holiday for people estranged from their families.

"It was a potluck, and everyone was welcome to bring their favorite food," she finished. "One year, they ended up with all desserts. When he died, they had a final potluck for his funeral and made a cookbook to support the youth home he volunteered at." To her utter shock, her voice hitched as she finished the sentence.

Wes looked over in concern. "Nadine?"

"It says he wanted people to know they had a community, even if they didn't have a family. Oh my God, why am I crying?"

Wes put his arm around her and kissed her temple. "It's okay to be emotional about the passing of a person who brought a lot of warmth to the world."

"It's silly." She wiped the tears away. "I'm not sad."

"Hey. No." He kissed her again. "Dot said she read these because they're life-affirming, remember?"

She scrolled through the obituary. Out of the many she'd read, this was the first one that had touched her with the simple brightness of the subject. He wanted to help people, and he did. It was a beautiful life that deserved to be shared and celebrated. Wes was right. Dot had been right. She bookmarked the page, thinking about the mayor who wanted people to feel like they belonged, if only for a day. This was a story with impact.

"Was it in the *Herald*?" asked Wes.

She sniffed. "Please. All he did was bring people joy. That's not one of the criteria for the *Herald*. I wish it was. Lisanne used to say—" She caught herself.

"Speaking of, have you talked to Lisanne yet?" Wes asked.

"No." She put her phone down. "It's whatever."

"It's bothering you." He drew a star on her thigh with a cold fingertip. "If you don't talk about it, it'll fester."

"Or not," she said hopefully. "We could forget about it and move on." Except they couldn't do that with Nadine ignoring her texts. "Ugh. I know what I have to do."

"Why don't you do it now?"

Nadine pulled out her phone and then put it back in her pocket. "After I'm done with this drink."

Wes kept sending her meaningful glances that she did her best to ignore before finally calling her out. "You've been sipping that juice for twenty minutes. Text her."

"Damn it." He was right, and she hadn't even enjoyed the freaking juice, too much in her head about Lisanne. "Okay."

He plucked the glass out of her hand, and she went to the music carousel room, mind half on naming the instruments—was that a piccolo?—and half on wording a reasonable text. The last message from Lisanne, a basic, **hey, you there**, sat unanswered, the blank space below a declaration of Nadine's inability to be a generous human. Not even. Barely decent and too embarrassed to reply.

She sighed and began to type. **Sorry! Just saw this.**

Lisanne didn't have to be the excellent journalist she was to recognize bull. Nadine deleted it, then went to strum the lute. Possibly it was a mandolin. Lisanne had done nothing wrong. She very reasonably wanted to talk about her work. She saw an opportunity to do Nadine a favor and took it, not to make Nadine feel inferior but because she was a good person. This rupture was all on Nadine.

Her phone buzzed, and she nearly dropped it onto a bongo when she saw the message from Lisanne. **Open the gate, loser.**

Wes came to the door as Nadine looked up from the screen.

"Lisanne is at—" he said.

"I know," said Nadine, waving her phone.

"How does she know you're here?" Wes followed her out. "I thought we were sticking to the original Dot Voline secrecy rules."

"We are. I said I was working with you, but that's it."

"You told her about me?"

"Only for safety, and not that we were here."

"Oh." He looked dejected, then frowned. "It's terrible you had to do that. Also, damn, is she good."

Nadine didn't answer. She went to the front door and pushed the button that would release the gate. Opening the door, she saw the blue Hyundai coming up the drive.

Lisanne pulled in and popped out of the car. "Did I pass swans in the fountain?" she asked.

"They're fake." How on earth had Lisanne found her?

"I figured when they didn't move." Lisanne surveyed Nadine before her eyes widened.

Nadine turned to see Wes behind her, waving a cheery hello.

"What the hell is going on here?" Lisanne sounded almost indignant. "You're having a love tryst? This is your secret story? Investigating what's in Wes's pants?"

"It's not a love tryst!" Nadine tried to shut the door, but Wes simply put his foot out as he watched with interest. "We are working."

Lisanne's face passed through several expressions—disbelief, bemusement, and perhaps some bafflement—before settling on neutral curiosity. "In a Bridle Path mansion?"

"It's Dot Voline's house."

"Of course it is," Lisanne said. "Makes total sense. Wes, we were interns at the *Belleville Recorder* back in the day. Lisanne Eden."

Wes reached out his hand. "I remember. Nice to see you."

They shook, and Nadine stared at the car. "How did you know where I was?"

Lisanne tapped her phone. "We shared locations one time and never turned it off. I've been checking it for the last few days when you didn't answer my texts and realized you hadn't left this spot."

"Nice," said Wes in admiration.

"It indicated you were being held hostage."

"There are other options for staying put that don't include kidnapping," said Nadine.

"Maybe, but on the off chance this was more than you being an avoidant bitch, I thought I should check it out." Lisanne looked Nadine square in the face, then glanced at Wes. "No offense."

"Thanks," said Nadine, oddly touched.

Lisanne looked meaningfully at the door.

"Right," said Nadine. "Do you want to come in?" At least this semi-awkward meeting was putting off the messier and more awkward conversation to come.

"Don't mind if I do!" Lisanne walked in and stopped. "Whoa, is that a Nobel? Obviously, I'd prefer a Pulitzer but respect the flex of letting the world's most prestigious prize hang out in the hall." Before Nadine could answer, Lisanne turned away from Sir Latimer, her attention caught by Janice. "A cheetah? Is this place for real?"

Showing Lisanne the house and introducing the cats took a good thirty minutes. When Wes left them in the study, Nadine knew she could no longer put off the inevitable. At the same time, the forced lightness of conversation with Lisanne hit her hard. She didn't want their friendship to be like that.

Which meant she had to woman up.

Lisanne sat in one of the green leather club chairs in front of the fireplace, an empty decanter on the oak cabinet behind her. Nadine took the other seat.

Luckily, Lisanne was as direct in her personal life as she was in her professional one. "I'm going to leave why you're living in Dot Voline's mansion with Wes for a slightly later but important conversation," she said.

"Okay." Nadine braced herself. "You're here because of the way I've been acting."

Lisanne scowled. "It's obvious it's something I did, and I'm pretty sure it's about my new project, but I don't get why you're being like this."

Obviously, it wasn't on Nadine's to-do list to admit to a friend that she felt envious and threatened. She could lie and say that wasn't true and make up a reason, but if she did, that would be the end of her close friendship with Lisanne. The lie would cause a break that would widen over time, until they were mere acquaintances, then nothing.

"I want to be able to talk to you about my work," continued Lisanne slowly. "I don't want to censor myself because you might be jealous."

Oh, she said it. Named that humiliating emotion right to Nadine's face. Of all the things to accuse a friend of, that was one of the worst. It laid bare Nadine's hopes and dreams and acknowledged that Lisanne had been the one to achieve them. It confirmed Nadine's loser status.

"I am jealous," said Nadine, giving up any pretense to the contrary. If it was this obvious, it would be more embarrassing to deny it.

"Oh my God." Lisanne was on the edge of her chair. "Do you know how many times I had to listen to Daniel praise your work? Watch you collect another award? And you're mad because for once, for *once*, I'm finally getting a chance."

"What?" Nadine stared at her.

Lisanne threw up her hands. "Before you started, Daniel was almost wetting himself with his new star hire. I'd been there a month, and when I started, they didn't bother to send out an email to my team. They didn't have a laptop ready."

"I didn't know that."

"Sorry," muttered Lisanne. "I guess I'd been holding that in for a bit." She let out a huge breath. "I don't get it. The story has nothing to do with your beat at all."

"It wasn't the story," Nadine said, looking at the decanter to avoid Lisanne's gaze. "Things were going so well for you when they were going so badly for me. I had to quit the politics beat. I got demoted from *obits*, for God's sake. Then there was you. Daniel's new favorite and about to embark on the kind of work I wanted to do."

"You *could* have been involved," said Lisanne, her voice rising. "I tried to include you."

"I can't." The words came out high and loud. "I can't. I'll screw it up again."

"That's ridiculous—"

"This is why I don't want to tell you things," snapped Nadine. "You don't get it. It might be ridiculous for you, but it's important to me, okay? It's a problem for me. It matters to *me*."

They stared at each other across the marble-topped coffee table that squatted between the two chairs. Nadine twitched. This was getting intense. She needed to move around.

"Want to go for a walk?" she asked.

"Fuck no," said Lisanne. "I need a drink."

They rose without speaking and went to the kitchen, a trek that took about two minutes and was conducted in silence. Nadine pulled out a bottle of wine and filled two glasses to the brim.

They went out to the garden, and Lisanne was the one to speak first. "It's hard not to read this as you being mad that the attention is off you. It's like you want me to be lesser so you can feel good about yourself."

Nadine's shoulders hiked up higher as Lisanne spoke. "That's the most negative and selfish interpretation you could put on it."

"Then what's the truth?" Lisanne demanded, her voice rising.

"I'm scared, okay?" Nadine yanked on a bean plant. "I'm jealous, but not because you have a great opportunity. It's because if I had it, I'd be scared to do it! Scared that someone is going to come after me again. Scared I'm going to blow it like I did with Dot Voline's obit."

By the end, her voice was ringing around the garden, and Lisanne was standing still, waist-deep in tomato plants, staring at Nadine.

"I didn't know," said Lisanne.

"I know, because you don't get it."

"I get it." Her voice was low. "I just didn't think it was that bad for you. I thought you needed pep talks and you'd snap out of it."

Nadine shook her head. "That's not how it works."

Lisanne absently picked a few grape tomatoes. She handed one to Nadine, who took a bite. It squirted over to hit Lisanne in the arm, causing her to groan.

"Gross." Lisanne flicked the tomato seeds off her arm with a disgusted expression, and that was enough.

It could have been the huge glass of wine she'd guzzled or the stress of this fight and her dread over having to confess that she was a terrible person, but Nadine suddenly felt too drained to keep her feelings hidden.

"I didn't tell you because we were mostly work friends," she said. "You know what the *Herald* is like."

"You were worried I'd use it against you to get ahead." Lisanne sounded flat.

"Not get ahead but lose respect for me at work?" Nadine shook her head. "I don't know."

"I get it." Lisanne sipped her wine, looking thoughtful. "At work, you can like a person, but you're still competing for the same resources. Jobs, assignments. Opportunities. There can be a limit to how much you can trust them."

She understood. Nadine relaxed a bit. "Plus the question of whether you'd be friends if not for work. How many times have you left a job and the people you thought you were tight with never called again?"

"Sometimes they do though, and the friendship continues. I think ours is like this. Who else at the office is doing hostage checks on you?"

Nadine felt the tension lift. "I would do one on you too."

"Good to hear." Lisanne looked at her. "I'm sorry you felt this way."

"I really do want to hear about your work, and I'm sorry for being a bad friend."

"I'll keep my mouth shut about your career. I promise. No nagging, no talking to Daniel about opportunities. I'll listen."

"I could have been more honest," said Nadine.

"I could have been more understanding."

They stared at their wineglasses for a second, then Lisanne said, "Are we good?"

"Yeah."

"Want to be my official work and nonwork friend?"

"Absolutely." Nadine held out her palm.

Lisanne slapped it. "Great, because I've got some gossip for you."

Nadine laughed again, happy to have the conversation successfully concluded. "What?"

"Rumor says Olivia Majors is going to be taking over the *Herald* from her father."

"Huh." Nadine drained her glass. "Interesting. Didn't she work in banking or something?"

"Guess she got bored."

They went back in, swapping stories about Olivia, and refilled their glasses before moving to the front to look at the fountain. The vibe between them wasn't perfect, but it was better. Much better.

"So," said Lisanne, settling on the bench surrounding the fountain. "You want to tell me what the hell's going on?"

Nadine gave her the summary, starting with her conversation with Irina and including all the Wes stuff. Even when glossing over the details of their investigation, there was a lot. Lisanne dangled her hand in the fountain, her eyebrows getting higher as Nadine went on.

When she finished and had answered Lisanne's questions, Lisanne splashed her. "You're with Wes then?" She laughed. "I knew it when you were getting all misty-eyed at the bar."

"Shut up." Nadine cleared her throat. "Tell me about your story."

Lisanne was cautious at first, casting Nadine little glances to check her reaction, but Nadine was on her best behavior, and the shame over her outburst soon faded. This was the reason she was in journalism, and it felt a bit like coming alive again.

"Scummy," she said after Lisanne had leaned in to share one of her latest findings.

"They are." She shook her head. "But we're going to make sure people know."

Nadine toasted her. "You can do it."

Wes came to the door. "I made a cheese platter if you want some," he called.

The two women jumped to their feet. "I've got time until I sober up enough to drive," said Lisanne. "Mind if I hang around?"

"I'd love that."

Lisanne nudged her. "No talking about work though, okay? Wes might be your collaborator, but he's not mine."

"We'll talk about hockey and fancy mustards."

"I can barely name three teams, and I buy the bright yellow squeeze bottles. How about mycology and Mercator maps?"

"Yo-yos and sailing knots?"

They were still laughing when they descended on Wes's cheese tray and then laughed harder when they saw he'd put elegant swirls of several mustards on the plate.

It was good to have Lisanne back.

# THIRTY-SEVEN

When Nadine walked into the kitchen for lunch after a wearisome morning rechecking the house, Wes saw she was in dire need of a break. Her hair was pulled up in a bun that fell half down in the back, and her mouth had a small pout he wanted to kiss away.

So he did.

"We only have two days left." Nadine sagged against him, and he lugged her to the sink to wash her hands.

"I know," he said. "You'll feel better after you eat. I used the last of the Camembert for sandwiches, and the tomatoes in the salad are warm from the garden."

That perked her up the way he knew it would. For a change, he'd set lunch on the island instead of the table near the window. Nadine bit into the sandwich, and a chunk of cheese slid out, off her plate, and onto the floor.

"Erma, get away from that." Nadine hopped down from the stool to fight the cat for the cheese.

When she didn't come up, Wes bent over to see what was happening. "You okay?"

She was running her hand up and down the side of the island. "I feel a draft."

He stretched his hand out. "I feel it too."

Nadine started to get to her feet, and Wes reached over to pull her up. "How do we get in here?" she asked. "There are no cabinet doors."

Wes circled the island as Nadine watched, hands on her hips. Then she followed him, running her fingertips under the edge of the counter. She halted, and Wes looked back, then put his fingers beside hers. There was a thin bulge. "A hinge?" he asked.

They cleared off the island and went to the far end, each taking a corner. At Nadine's nod, they lifted.

The entire marble countertop rose in the air, so suddenly and smoothly that they lost their grip. "What the hell!" yelped Nadine as it dropped. "Did you see that?"

Wes had. Under the counter was an abyss. "Lift it again," he said.

This time, they went slower, and two rods lowered to hold the counter in place. With one hand over their heads in case the heavy slab fell, they peered over the edge.

"Wow," said Nadine. "Wow."

Wes wasn't sure *wow* was adequate for this discovery and stayed staring into the stygian gloom as Nadine ran to fetch the flashlight. She shone it down to reveal a flight of stairs.

"We found the basement door," she announced.

There was no discussion of next steps, because of course they were going down. After a few minutes to lock the curious and protesting Erma in the games room with the other cats, Wes felt around and found a latch that opened the side of the island, then propped the doors in place with the kitchen stools. Nadine texted Lisanne a photo of the gaping counter and a request to send help if she didn't hear back within two hours.

**I don't know how you get into these situations, but give my regards to Dracula**, replied Lisanne.

Safety covered, and after a brief fight over who would go first, Wes took Nadine's hand, and they headed down the stairs to the long-sought basement. "Are you nervous?" he asked.

"No, why?"

"You're using my hand like a stress ball."

She squeezed tighter. "Expectant. Hopeful. A little freaked out."

"All valid." Wes's own astonishment had settled into a spiky excitement that grew with each step. The stairs were surprisingly code-compliant, complete with handrails and anti-slip tape along the edges.

Happily, there were no coffins, corpses, or other spooky scaries.

Nadine's hand clung to his as she swung the flashlight back and forth from their position at the base of the stairs. Wes thought the space would be as big as the attic, but it only seemed to stretch as far as the library. "Doesn't look like there's anything here but those boxes I saw on the video from the dumbwaiter," she said.

"Did you phrase it like that to point out that you saw the boxes first?"

"Yes."

He leaned down to kiss her cheek. "Nice."

She didn't move. "This could be it, you know. Whatever Dot wanted us to learn could be in that corner."

Nadine was right. The entire mystery could be solved in minutes. All they had to do was walk across the concrete floor and open up those boxes. It could be anything. Dot's journal. A handwritten confession. Photographs of John Wilson so compromising that not even the sharkiest lawyer could deny their veracity. Yet they didn't move.

"Hey," said Nadine. Her voice was low under the weight of the basement air. "I want to say there's no one else I'd rather be in a creepy basement with than you."

"Ditto." He didn't say more because his throat had tightened up.

"And that this has been the best three weeks of my life." She looked into his face. "No matter what we find in those boxes."

She kissed him, her mouth slotting into his so naturally it was like they had always belonged to each other. Then she pulled away and whacked him on the ass. "Come on."

They took the last step together, the flashlight holding steady on the boxes ahead.

---

It was in the last box.

They went back upstairs and replaced the counter before they sat down to marvel over their find. "Don't forget Lisanne," said Wes as Nadine washed her hands. Basement grime tinted the suds brown.

"Got it." She shot Lisanne a proof of life photo of her and Wes and got a thumbs-up in reply. "I still don't know how Erma managed to get into the dumbwaiter," she said.

"A mystery we might never solve." Wes spread the piece of paper on the table, and she bent over it, hands feeling shaky.

"It's a staff newsletter from 1977," said Nadine. "From John Wilson's office when he was a member of Parliament." The faded purple mimeographed sheet was like a time capsule, filled with inside jokes about coffee breaks and an open invitation to the upcoming Christmas party. It was only a page, and in the bottom corner was a small caricature of a young woman smiling with her face covered by a pair of huge glasses and holding a pen and folder to her chest. "The irreplaceable Milly Cross," read the caption.

"There was no mention of Milly Cross in any of the obits or the files we found," said Wes.

Nadine knew there was no need to check. Wes's memory was a steel trap.

"Milly Cross." She repeated the name thoughtfully. "That looks a bit like Dot, doesn't?"

"Hold on." Wes jolted up. "Those photos in the dress room."

They released the cats as they went to the west wing.

Wes stood in front of the wall, checking the names. "One was named Cross, I'm sure of it. There. Mildred Cross."

He pointed, and Nadine saw one of the young women in the photos resembled Dot. It was also the image of the woman in the porcelain photo frame taken in an Ottawa studio. "Dot was Milly?" she said aloud as if to test the theory connecting the images of the women. "She could be. We know almost nothing about her early life."

"Everyone floats over it as if being a teacher in small-town Manitoba isn't worthy of investigation, and whenever she spoke about her past, it was always vague," Wes said.

"What if she was hiding her previous life before moving to Manitoba? What if Dot was Milly?" It sounded fantastical as Nadine said it.

"You think Dot Voline was her pen name?" asked Wes. "That was never hinted at in anything I read or by Dot."

"Not only a pen name but a new identity, like Dellia in *Patience*. Dot published it in 2000. It was about a woman who changed her name and started a new life to get away from her husband's affair."

"You think whatever inspired *Thirty Pieces* happened and she changed her name and moved away to start a new life," mused Wes. "How would people from her old Ottawa life have not recognized her?"

"The glasses, maybe, and also they might simply have not expected Milly Cross to be the world-famous author. Kind of the same way you sometimes don't recognize people when they're out of context."

"That makes sense. We need some proof."

Quickly they split up research tasks, and Nadine called Irina at the *Herald*.

"What do you want?" asked Irina when she answered. Would it kill her to say hello?

"I need a birth record," said Nadine, getting right down to it. Irina had access to the best online database for birth, death, and marriage records. "The name is Dot or Dorothy Voline."

"Year of birth?" Irina's voice didn't change.

"It's 1951." That was the number that matched Dot's bio, which said she was born on an isolated farmstead.

There was the sound of what seemed like an unnecessary number of keystrokes for a thirteen-letter name. "None."

"How about a couple years on either side?" If Dot had lied about her past, she might have lied about her age.

More tapping. "None."

"Mildred Cross, same dates?"

"I have one in 1951. Mildred Dorothy Cross, born to Dorothy Cross née Moline and Thomas Cross in Ottawa."

"Ottawa? Not Alberta?" That was where Dot said she'd been born.

"If it was in Alberta, I would not have said Ottawa."

"Right, sorry."

"Anything else?"

"No," Nadine said slowly. Damn. They were one step closer, but they still didn't have what they desperately needed: that critical piece of evidence that screamed *John Wilson is bad and he did bad things.*

"Good." Irina hung up.

Wes came in and tossed his phone on the counter. "Dot Voline appeared in Meadow Lake, Manitoba, in 1979. She said she was from northern Alberta and lost her documents in the move. The town clerk was by all accounts a very nice and trusting man well past retirement age and helped her replace everything."

"How did you find out so fast?" Nadine was impressed but not surprised, given how good Wes was.

"An old friend is from Manitoba, and I lucked out because his mom lives in the neighboring town. Apparently no one doubted her story, although she rarely spoke about her life before Meadow Lake."

"Nice," approved Nadine. Informal connections could yield the best information. She told him about Irina.

Then they stared at each other.

"It's not enough to go up again John Wilson." Nadine put her head in her hands, her excitement dashed. "I give up."

Wes pulled her hands down, and she pressed her face into the curve of his shoulder. He was steady, and his hands held her close.

"Why don't you go for a walk and clear your head while I get lunch back on track?" he said.

She leaned against him for a few beats more, simply letting herself feel small and weak and helpless. She could do that with Wes and trusted him not to shame her about feeling defeated instead of her usual self.

"No." Her voice was muffled in his skin.

---

He held her closer, feeling the concern build. What could he say to make her feel better?

"It's okay, Nadine. We tried." He felt her shake her head and added, "Sometimes trying is all we can do. It's not like this is the end of the road. We might lose access to Dot's house, but we've found plenty that we can continue to investigate when we're done here."

"I know, but it feels like it's not enough. Like once we leave, we'll be stuck."

"We won't be." He kissed her on the head.

"You don't know that." She stepped back, her neck bent. He hated seeing her so defeated.

"I'm sorry," he said, his voice frustrated. "I can't fix this."

"What?" She looked at him in confusion.

"I know I should fix this, but I don't know how."

She tilted her head. "Why do you think you need to fix things that aren't your fault?"

"Because it's my responsibility." He'd never been able to make his mother happy, and now he had to worry about Nadine as well.

"What?"

He thought back to all the times his mother told him he was the man of the house, responsible for everyone under their roof. "I don't know. I like to keep people happy and make sure they're comfortable."

"For your family?"

He nodded. "I tried. I really did. I managed a bit with Ella, but Amy is a mess, and Ma...Ma is herself."

"Oh, Wes." Her face was sad.

"Yeah?"

She leaned over to look him in the eye. "I want to tell you something."

"Okay." He physically braced himself, and Nadine took his hand.

"You are not responsible for making me happy." She said it simply, like it was common knowledge. "That is not your job."

Wes blinked. Amy had said the same thing, but hearing it from Nadine made him reassess the words in a different way. "Yes, it is."

"I don't want this to get too circular, but nope, it's not." She took his other hand. "Obviously, this is not carte blanche to actively be a dick; let me get that clear. You can play a role in making me happy, but ultimately, it's up to me whether I am. Not you."

Wes sat for a few moments, absorbing what she'd said. He felt a little stunned at how matter-of-fact she was, like it really was that simple. Could it be? He could almost feel his mind shifting to accommodate this, and it was a struggle. "It's a lot for me to think about," he said finally.

"Okay," she said. "We'll both take a break."

He kissed her, holding her face in his hands, and then kissed her nose and eyes and cheeks for the pleasure of it. She'd stopped his spiraling, and although he wasn't sure he believed her—it wasn't his job to make her happy?—he was willing to think about it.

Another one of those cables seemed to snap from around his chest, and he breathed freer once more.

# THIRTY-EIGHT

Nadine watched Wes leave, hoping he understood what she was trying to say and aching for his situation. She'd be sure to reassure him until he knew she meant it.

"A break, Nadine." Wes's voice echoed through the room from the kitchen.

"I will." He probably meant a walk in the garden or something, but she followed Erma to the library, where she sat down at Dot's desk for the first time. This was where Dot had written over twenty books. She'd struggled and dreamed and put her thoughts down letter by letter to build worlds for Nadine and millions of others to sink into.

This was the desk where she'd unburdened herself. Unable to publicly accuse her betrayer, she'd sat and written the book out of her soul.

Nadine wasn't sure how long she stared out the window at the trees before Wes came in. "Lunch will be ready in a minute, but I thought you'd like this." He put a cup of tea on the desk. "What are you thinking about?"

"How Dot felt when *Thirty Pieces of Silver* was published. Was she scared? Worried about what Wilson would do? Cold at the idea that her own secret previous life as Mildred might come out before she was ready to reveal it?"

"Or did she feel triumphant?" asked Wes. "Glad to have told her story?"

She'd focused only on the negative, but Wes was right. "I don't know," she said.

"I'll tell you what I think." Wes leaned against the old desk, worn and scratched. "She wrote it, and she was frightened. After all, back then, Wilson had more power. More money. More social capital and people willing to overlook his sleaze for whatever selfish reason they had."

Nadine was listening so hard her ears were buzzing. "Then why did she go ahead with it?"

"Because she needed to call him out, to call out men like him, and this was the way she knew how."

"She named it revenge."

"I prefer to call it justice," he said. "Dot's desire for justice trumped her fear, but she needed a little help to confront him. He's a bad enemy."

"So she's using us."

"She put her faith in us," Wes corrected. "Come to the kitchen when you're ready."

He levered himself up from the table and gave her a little kiss on the forehead, as if understanding she needed to reflect by herself.

The tea was the perfect temperature thanks to the ice cube Wes had dropped in, and she sipped it as she stroked Erma's soft fur. In the sun, the black cat showed lighter, reddish stripes that Nadine hadn't noticed before, and her big eyes were fixed on the wall where Dot's books sat in tidy rows. They were in chronological order, with *Thirty Pieces of Silver* in the third spot, right through to *Nexus Point*. Wait. The last book was *It Is Hellish Gain*. That wasn't part of Dot's standard bibliography, and she'd never heard of it.

Erma rose and curved her back into an arch like a classic Halloween cat as Nadine pulled out the book. The cover was simple, the title in a flowing font and surrounded by flags.

Little golden flags, in the process of unfurling.

There was a clipping tucked in the first page, and she put the book aside to read it. It was a death notice, of a man named Hiro Yamato. He'd been born in the aftermath of the atom bomb that had destroyed his home of Hiroshima, killing most of his family. He'd eventually come to Canada, where he'd suffered the death of a beloved daughter, chronic illness, and the loss of his business. A line from his grandson said, "He was the most resilient person I knew. It's not that he didn't feel the hurt. It's that he knew life was made of pain and happiness, disappointment and hope."

The final line, underlined by Dot, read, "Hiro would say, 'I'm alive, and if I am alive, I have faith.'"

Nadine must have made a noise, because Wes came back in, then dashed over with an exclamation of concern.

"Are you okay?"

In reply, she handed him the book. "The shelves are chronological, and this was last. Not *Nexus Point*."

She saw from his expression that he understood immediately. He opened it. "'October 1977,'" he read. "'Maude Crew knew her love was tainted but insisted on drinking deep from the well. Water from the earth is richer and more satisfying, and to Maude, the slight sulfuric accent made it addictive.'"

"Maude Crew." Nadine blinked. "Milly Cross. Oh my God, is this an unpublished Dot Voline manuscript?"

"It looks like it is." Wes's voice was reverent as he flipped to the last page. "She typed it out, but I don't think it's done."

"I want to read it. This very minute." She made grabby gimme hands.

"Me too, but, Nadine." Wes looked torn. "I can't deal with waiting until you're done. What if we read it aloud to each other?"

"Deal, deal, deal." Nadine was up from the chair and almost hopping with anticipation. "Now, now, now." All the depression of the previous hour had evaporated.

He laughed and started reading.

---

Wes left a message for Brent, who called back to tell them not only had he not known about the unfinished book, but neither had Dot's agent, and she was desperate to get her hands on it. "I told her after you were done though," he added.

"It's all ours," said Nadine when the call finished, her voice greedy.

Wes kept reading, occasionally struggling with run-on sentences and misplaced words. They read about Maude through lunch, as flashbacks told of a poor girl whose parents died and of her job in a politician's office.

"It's nice to see even a Nobel Prize winner has shitty first drafts," Nadine said. He had to agree. However, despite the slow start and meandering story, the book was a testament to the power of Dot's writing. He kept reading, then paused.

"Nice," said Wes. "He starts off seducing her with gifts and helps her move to a better part of town." He appreciated how Dot had captured the breathless exultation of a lonely girl in love who had been overwhelmed to be chosen and how she explained away her doubts.

By midafternoon, Maude was getting uncomfortable with the favors Jean-Pierre Walker, her boss and lover, was asking. "The initials JW again," Wes said, putting the manuscript down to get some water for his parched throat. "Our old senatorial friend John Wilson."

"This is sad," Nadine said. "It started off with keeping some money safe, and now he's talking her into insider trading."

She took over reading, and Wes listened with his eyes shut, in part to absorb the story, in part to enjoy Nadine's voice. She got to the part where, feeling used and scared, Maude finally refused and was shocked by Walker's threats. The next part of the book was more exciting, when Maude did some digging and found out the money was from a shady group bankrolling the Jean-Pierre Walker character's political goals in return for preferential treatment when awarding projects and advance notice of policy changes. "A reference to Matt White," said Nadine.

Wes listened closely as the drama sped up. Maude threatened to go public although she'd also go down thanks to what she'd already done for Walker and was told the group he was working with wouldn't hesitate to keep her quiet.

"No specific mention of organized crime, but we can make an educated guess, especially if we take that to be White," said Wes.

The last chapters were about Maude running away in fear and changing her name to escape Walker. She kept an eye on Walker as he grew in power and saw he'd followed through on a threat against another woman, Anne Spitz.

"AS. Dot likes using initials as clues," said Nadine. "I wonder if this is someone as well."

Wes recalled it immediately. "Abigail Spencer."

"Spencer," she repeated. "I know that name."

"Remember, we found her obit in the copy of *Thirty Pieces of Silver* marking chapter thirteen."

Nadine pulled out the obit, and they read it again. "It wasn't the chapter it marked that was important," said Nadine. "It was the obit itself. Look at her sister's name."

"Sarah Owens, née Cohen." He blinked. "Spencer is her married name."

They soon found a news story about Abigail Cohen. Although the death notice only spoke of her love for animals and charity work, she had been fired for stealing from John Wilson's office in the 1980s, which she denied. The reporters had a field day about the role of women in the workplace, vilifying Spencer and using her as proof they weren't as trustworthy as men.

"Another victim," said Wes. Wilson was a cold man.

"I bet this story triggered Dot's keeping tabs on Wilson," said Nadine. "She saw he hadn't changed." She passed over the manuscript for Wes to continue.

The afternoon turned golden as he read the last page out on the patio, his voice scratchy. "She plans to confront him and that's it," he said. "There's a date scrawled at the end of the page. It's three days before Dot died."

"Then there's probably not a hidden final chapter." Nadine groaned. "I want to know what happened."

"We know what happened, since this is a thinly veiled autobiography." He looked at her. "This is enough for me. I want to go to our editors. Tomorrow."

She moved back into the house without answering. Wes followed her in and saw her put the manuscript down with the rest of their findings before she sat on the couch.

Then he waited for her to speak.

---

Nadine chewed her lip, unsure if she should say what was really bothering her.

"Just say it." Wes ran his thumb along her lip.

"It might start a fight."

"It doesn't need to be a fight, but if we don't talk, it almost certainly will."

"This might be unavoidable, talking or not." She looked up at the ceiling, with the setting sun glinting rainbows through the crystal prisms of the chandelier.

"Say it, Nadine."

"If I bring this to Daniel, I could be out of a job," she said quietly. "He'll tell Majors, who will probably get it spiked. Wilson has been his friend for decades. Knowing I was working with the *Spear* on my own will make him furious as well. I'm already not Daniel's favorite, and Irina was taken off reporting when she asked questions. Not to mention it would have to be tight. Not a single thread untied, and we don't have that."

"We would do that for any story before publication." He pointed at the table. "When you take the entirety of what we have, it's more than enough to get the go-ahead to look into this properly, which we can do after we leave." He took her hand. "I'm going to ask something that might upset you."

"I mean, you don't have to."

"Did you start thinking this once you found out about John Wilson's involvement?"

She tried to jerk her hand back. Wes had called her a coward, basically. "It's reasonable to worry how the *Herald* would react if I came to them with a story that painted John Wilson in an extremely negative light."

"Everyone likes to pretend they're above influence, but journalists are still people."

"The problem is worse when the pressure's internal," she said.

Wes laughed. "When it's not your editor telling you it's a bad idea to investigate your primary advertiser's environmental record but a little voice asking, *Hey, is that the best thing you can do for your career?*"

Nadine brooded over this. "We might not like to think about it that way because we're in it for the journalism, but media is a business, and businesses have owners."

"Not to mention they're usually people the world has treated quite well and who don't necessarily see the need to make changes that would impact that," said Wes. "But it's what we have to work with."

"Well, what about you?" She remained offended that he'd called her out, even if he was a bit right. "Do you want the story out because you want to serve the public good or because you want leverage to get back on the I-team?"

"Both," he said, more calmly than she expected. "I hate the fact that he screwed Dot over and others for personal gain and got away with it. And is likely still doing it. It doesn't matter that she made the experience art. The fact that she wanted the truth known, that she carried it with her for this long, means it was heavy on her mind."

Nadine looked over at the desk. Wes was right, but it was so difficult. She was scared.

"We can't do anything now," she said, wanting some distance to think. "Let's sleep on it and talk about it in the morning."

"Okay." He draped his arm around her shoulders so her head was tucked against him. "In the morning. Do you have anything in mind to pass the time?"

"There's that crokinole board in the game room," she said. "We could play."

Wes lost two games before they moved on to other, more interesting games where neither of them could lose. It helped pass the time even better.

# THIRTY-NINE

Nadine liked to start the morning by glancing through the thirty-plus browser tabs on her favorites bar to make sure all was right but was usually wrong with the world. Celebrity news she scanned religiously but with some shame at her emotional investment in the latest red carpet outfits. Today she spent an ungodly amount of time trying to decide if there were monthly meetings where Hollywood stylists all voted on the color de jour, because every second star was in pine green. Next were her favorite obituary sites. What would Dot have made of the woman who got her first tattoo at the age of ninety, telling her grandkids that she'd always wanted one? Probably cheered her on.

She also made sure to check the *Herald*'s competitor websites, such as the *Spear*, which was why she was the first one to see the story. As Wes slept beside her, face buried in his pillow and Erma curled in the small of his back flicking the occasional ear in Nadine's direction, she stared at the web page, unable to believe her eyes.

*Political scandal unearthed by literary connection,* read the headline. By Tyler Dawlish. In tiny font was *research contributor Wes Chen*.

"Wes. Wes!" She shook his shoulder.

"What?" He sat up bleary-eyed as Erma leapt off with a disgruntled hiss. "Are you okay?"

"No! What the hell is going on?" She passed from shock to fury. "After we talked about this? I said I'd think about it, but you already had plans to run the story? We don't have the details of what happened."

Wes held his hand up. "Am I dreaming?" he asked in a groggy voice. "What happened to the dog riding the shark? Did she win the surf contest?"

"Shark ride this." She shoved her laptop in his face and got up, feeling at a disadvantage to be lying in bed. "How could this happen?"

The color in Wes's face collected into two red spots high in his cheeks. He scrolled to the bottom before lifting his gaze. Immediately she knew he had no more clue than she did.

"This wasn't me," he said. "I don't know why my name is on it."

"I know it's not. Of course it isn't. It's missing information we have. Sorry for losing it. I was surprised." She rested her hand on him for a moment in apology before taking her laptop back. "The question is how Tyler what's-his-face got this and why his name is on it. You said you only gave him a vague outline. You're sure you didn't mention Wilson?"

"No." He frowned. "I only told him it involved Dot and a senator..." He trailed off. "My files."

"The ones you left at work?" Despite the heat in the house, Nadine felt cold. She wrapped her arms around her chest. This was a bad situation.

"I left them on my desk with a printout of my draft." He looked sick. "Tyler must have gone through them. Oh my... Wait here."

He ran out of the room, and Nadine took the opportunity to find some clothes. She was fully dressed by the time Wes came back with his own laptop open and typing with one hand.

"Thank God I didn't mention Matt White by name in that draft," he said. "I might be looking at a pair of concrete shoes. It just says 'criminal elements.' How quaintly 1950s of Tyler."

Nadine closed her eyes. "Surely Tyler wouldn't be so reckless even if Matt's name was in it."

"You'd be surprised," Wes said darkly.

"It says John Wilson didn't answer an email with questions," said Nadine.

"Tyler's method is to give someone about ten minutes to reply. Chances are Wilson didn't see it before the deadline." He sat beside her. "I can't believe that asshole."

"I can because I'm looking at the story." Nadine rubbed her temples.

"At least you're not mentioned," said Wes. "The *Herald* won't connect you to this."

"What about you?" Dread replaced the anger. "Your name is on it."

He shook his head. "I don't know how Tyler did this, but it can't come back on me. I never submitted it, and it wasn't approved. The story wasn't *done*." They sat for a few minutes, looking at the screen as Wes scrolled through again. "How did this get through editing?" he asked. "It was published an hour ago."

"I bet he didn't put it through," said Nadine. She put her arms around Wes and tried to warm his chilled skin. "Why would he do this?"

"That's like asking a snake why it bites. He's an unethical guy who saw a chance for a byline with minimal work. Anyway, his motivation hardly matters. It's out there." Wes put the laptop aside and lay back with his arm over his eyes.

"This probably won't go anywhere," she predicted optimistically. "The media cycle is short."

"Right," said Wes.

"Shit." Nadine was looking at her phone. "It's Lisanne."

**Yikes what a mess,** she'd written. **Daniel is in a rage thanks to that story making it look like the Herald was helping to cover for Wilson. No connections made to other writers though.**

Thank God. She was grateful for Lisanne's deliberately vague wording even in a private text.

**Who are they assigning?** wrote back Nadine. There would obviously be a story in the *Herald*.

There was a minute's pause before Lisanne replied. **Me.**

Nadine stared at the screen as Wes let out a low whistle.

Another message came. **Unfortunately, I had a lengthy and in-depth interview with a source that took me two weeks to set up, so they had to reassign it when I made a fuss.** A winky face ended the message.

**Thanks,** Nadine wrote.

**No problem, but anyone involved in this is going to have a real bad day.**

Wes, reading over her shoulder, sighed. "She's probably right."

Nadine put the phone down. "What are we going to do?"

What were they going to do? First, be grateful he wasn't alone. Nadine believed him. She'd said *we*, not *you*, and that word went far to reassure him.

When she'd woken him up, the cold rage on Nadine's face had convinced him there was no coming back from this, although it wasn't his fault. Or wasn't totally his fault. After all, he'd been the dud who talked to Tyler and left his notes at work. With a single word, she had confirmed they were a team. They hadn't started the job that way, but they would finish as one.

"I need to tell Jason I had nothing to do with this."

"Time for some serious CYA," she agreed.

"Cover your ass," indeed. This was not the story Wes was ready to tell, and its issues made him nauseous. He always knew Tyler was a shitty person, but this was next—and fireable—level. He needed to be careful Tyler didn't bring him down with him.

Why had Wes put the story on the *Spear's* platform? It gave Tyler proof that he was working on it before it was posted.

"Are you going to tell him Tyler is a plagiarizing thief?" asked Nadine.

"Seems redundant as plagiarists are de facto thieves."

"Thanks, Dr. Pedantic. Are you?" she pressed.

Wes looked out the window to the hot-pink Bentley. WWDD? What would Dot do? No doubt make a god-awful fuss, but that wasn't Wes's style. "I'm going to lay out the facts for Jason," he said. "There's no way a reasonable or rational person can look at what happened and think I'm in the wrong."

Nadine gave him a hug and left him to work while she made coffee. It was vital to get to Jason as soon as possible, so Wes called and left a message when he didn't pick up. Then he texted for good measure and sent an email asking to talk and an instant message on the *Spear* platform. He tried calling Rebecca as well before remembering she was out of cell range. Damn. He left a message and then emailed her to call him urgently. He didn't give a summary, not wanting to have anything in writing. She'd be upset he went to Jason to pitch the story but on his side when she heard what he had to say.

Wes debated calling Tyler. In the end, unable to construct a sentence that wasn't filled with profanity, he decided to wait until he cooled down.

He got dressed with one eye on the phone, feeling his tension twist higher. It was still early, but despite leaving the messages, he'd feel better if he went into the office to see if Jason was there or to catch him as he arrived.

As he went to tell Nadine his plan, she came over with coffee. His phone rang with an unknown number, usual for the *Spear*. "This has to be Jason," he said.

Nadine looked at the screen, frowning. "Wait, Wes, I'm not sure..."

Too late, he'd swiped the screen. "Wes Chen."

"Wes, long time."

"Hi?" It was not Rebecca or Jason or that sack of shit Tyler.

"It's Keith Lovel with the *Telegraph*." Keith's voice was warm and friendly.

In his perplexity, Wes answered normally. "Keith. What's up?" He glanced up to see Nadine making dramatic slicing gestures over her throat, and chills hit him when it finally clicked. This wasn't a social call.

"I saw the story in the *Spear*. Tyler's not answering, so I figured I'd give you a ring. It's quite the accusation against John Wilson, and I noticed a few gaps I'd like to ask about."

This was what it was like on the other side of those calls. He tried to think of a good answer. Nadine held up her phone to show her Notes app, where she'd written "LOVE TO TALK BUT GOING IN A MEETING. BYE."

What meeting was she talking about? He could barely think.

"Wes, you there? Did the *Spear* contact Wilson with these allegations?"

His lack of understanding must have been clear, because Nadine made an exaggerated pointing motion to him and mouthed, *You.*

*Oh.* "Keith, I'd love to chat, but you caught me about to go into a meeting. Talk to you soon, okay?" Then he hung up, feeling rude but also incredibly relieved.

Nadine leaned against a box. "Nice save," she congratulated him.

"Thanks to you." He wiped the sweat off his forehead. Was his own approach so nerve-racking? He'd have to monitor that.

She reached over to hold him tight. "I don't want to be a bummer, but I don't think that's going to be the last of it."

He rubbed his temples. "Should I call Amy?" It seemed like overkill, but maybe it was better to be safe.

"Doesn't hurt for her to be on guard," agreed Nadine. "I'll give Brent a heads-up."

His sister picked up on the second ring. "What's wrong?"

"How do you know there's anything wrong?"

"You never call this early."

"It's not a big deal, but there's a story at work I'm attached to that's getting traction." He tried to play down the impact. "Don't answer the phone to anyone you don't know or an unknown number, and can you tell Ma? I'll text Ella."

"What I'm hearing is that I shouldn't tell people you're dead to me after the Havana incident."

That made him laugh for the first time since he woke up. "It's probably best to say you can't speak and hang up, if you answer at all."

"Wes, are you in trouble?" She sounded worried.

"No, no," he reassured her. "It's only a misunderstanding."

"I trust you. Tell me if you need me."

Once off with Amy, he sent a quick message to Ella and turned to Nadine. "I can't believe I had to do that."

"It's weird being part of the story instead of reporting it," she said.

"There's nothing I can do about it, is there?"

"You can only control what's in your control."

"Right." He leaned over and gave her a kiss on the nose to see her wrinkle it. "Which is what exactly?"

She paused. "Making sure the truth gets out?"

He held up his keys. "On my way to the office to make that happen."

"Do you want company?" Nadine asked.

He considered this before shaking his head. "We can't risk you being associated with the story. It's better if you stay here."

She didn't answer at first, too busy looking at her phone. "I can't believe this." Nadine pushed her phone under his nose and leaned over his shoulder. This was an extremely sucky experience, but Wes had to admit having Nadine there made it slightly less so. He'd take the small win because the rest of the morning was a huge loss.

On Nadine's phone was another message from Lisanne, with a link to a story published on the *Herald* home page. It included quotes from

John Wilson, who said he'd called his legal team to defend his honor against libel. Wes read it again because he hadn't been able to make sense of the words the first time.

> **"I'm shocked the *Spear* stooped to gossipmongering and lies in a blatant attempt to increase their readership and negatively impact my important and selfless work on behalf of my fellow Canadians,"** said Senator Wilson. **"This story is absolutely false and a disgusting fabrication. I resent the implications about my character."**

Nadine whistled when they finished. For the first time, they hadn't competed about who could read fastest. "Legal team," she said. "He's coming out swinging."

Wes didn't need to see more. "I'll see you later." He gave her a quick kiss and lingered when she hugged him fiercely, icy hands on his arms.

"Go get 'em."

He hadn't made it halfway down the driveway before his phone beeped again, this time with the message he'd been waiting for. It was from Jason and simply said **Call me** in the subject line. It wasn't sent in reply to any of Wes's **Hey, can we talk?** messages, which gave him the nasty feeling Jason was not going to have his back on this.

He didn't want to take this call in the car. Going back into the house, he met a surprised Nadine coming out of the kitchen. "Wes?"

"Jason wants to talk to me." He faltered. "I don't think it looks good."

Nadine wrapped her arms around him again, and Wes took comfort in the solid pressure of the hold. "I can give you a continuous thumbs-up for moral support from the corner."

Her suggestion, bad as it was, was enough to give him courage. "You can do that when I'm off the call."

She sobered a bit. "Good luck, Wes. You did nothing wrong. Remember that."

He let himself enjoy the feel of her for another minute before untangling himself. "Here I go."

Nadine's eyes were serious, but she smiled at him. "You got this."

# FORTY

'*ve got this*, repeated Wes as he went through the kitchen doors. He wanted to take the call in the salon to channel the indomitable spirit of Dot. *I've got this. I don't need to fix this. This was not my responsibility. I didn't do anything wrong, and I've got this.* He was confident the truth would come out, but it was hard to fight the strain.

Jason picked up on the first ring. "You've got some explaining to do," he said in greeting.

Wes tried to ignore Jason's combative tone and kept his voice steady. "As I said in the email, I came into the office the other day to talk to you about a story I'd been working on. It wasn't Tyler's story, and it was in no way ready to go. I don't know why he did that or why or how it ran." There. His main points were out.

"The story no one had assigned you?"

Wes paused his pacing. Of all the things Jason could pick up on, say for instance Tyler's blatant theft and unethical journalism, why was he talking about that? "It was something I was looking into during my vacation, but I don't think that's the primary issue."

"I know you want back on this team, but this is not the way to do it.

I've talked to Tyler about his lack of judgment here, but I know he's a good guy. What you did was completely out of bounds."

"What *I* did?" Was he in some alternate reality? "I did nothing except mention it to Tyler when I came in to pitch it to you."

"That's not what I hear from Tyler."

Wes's gut dropped. "No?"

"I know it's not Tyler's story. Tyler says you told him it was ready and thoroughly researched and begged him to read it over. He caught the lack of a comment from Wilson and said you asked him to get it because Wilson ignored you. Since Tyler had better credibility, he'd get a reply."

"That's a complete lie." Wes stared at the Group of Seven wall before walking to a statue of a winged goddess holding a dagger, unable to believe Tyler's nerve. "I mentioned it to him and accidentally left my rough draft at my desk. That's it." He decided not to add *where Tyler stole it*. That was obvious.

"Tyler said you asked him to post it through the platform as a favor while you were on vacation, knowing it would help you get some visibility and make your case to get back on the team. He accidentally published it when he meant to send it to me to confirm it was ready to go since he didn't see my sign-off." Jason coughed. "That mistake was on him, and I've talked to him about that. It's a shame his name was attached to the story because of an error."

"It wasn't a mistake." Wes heard his voice echo through the room and fought to control it. "He's lying. None of that happened."

"I've known Tyler since school," Jason said. "I trust him."

*And not you*. Wes heard the unspoken conclusion. "Jason, this is ridiculous. Do you think I'd try to get a story of that magnitude posted before it was thoroughly vetted?"

"Wes, I checked, and you had the story in the editing platform. You put that there. Not Tyler."

"I always write my drafts there," said Wes, moving to the

conservatory door to look at the plants in a futile attempt to get some calm. "That doesn't mean they're ready for publication."

"No, but it shows you were working on it. Desperation can screw with a man's judgment, but this is the kind of underhanded behavior we can't have. My people are fighters, but we know we're a team."

"You can't seriously believe this."

"You think I haven't seen this kind of thing happen before?" snapped Jason. "I'm an excellent judge of people. I know you didn't like getting sent back to Lifestyle, but you took the wrong message from that experience if you think scheming like this will help."

"Fuck you." The words came out before Wes could evaluate the impact, but he didn't take them back. It didn't make him feel better.

"This is what I mean, Wes. You're challenging to work with when you don't get your way." Jason's voice was cool now, as if Wes's outburst had confirmed what he was thinking. "I've talked to management, and unfortunately Rebecca isn't in, but I'm sure she'd agree. Your employment with the *Spear* is terminated as of today."

What? "Tyler ran the story after he stole it, and he's blaming it on me because it's backfiring. Tyler is the one you should fire."

"I understand you're upset, but this is your word against his. Tyler has a lot of goodwill here and has admitted to poor judgment. We've had to give John Wilson an apology and post a retraction on the advice of legal."

Why hadn't he taped their discussion? Wes kicked himself as he put the call on speaker and fumbled for the Record button.

"HR will be in touch about the termination forms," said Jason. "Best of luck in your future endeavors."

Wes hit Record as Jason disconnected. Then he stopped, looking at the flashing 0:03 on the bottom. Three seconds of nothing.

Compared to the years of nothing he had to show for his work at the *Spear*, that was... Well. It was more of nothing.

He tossed the phone down on the settee, ignoring the beep he was sure was the HR email with his official termination. He'd have to get a lawyer, and for one ludicrous moment, he wondered if John Wilson would share his legal team.

Nadine's head poked around the corner. Seeing him off the phone, she inched over as if to give him space to get used to her presence. Erma had no such qualms and raced in to meow at Wes's feet for attention. He picked her up and buried his face in her warm fur, feeling her tiny heart beat against his palm. She wasn't purring, but the weight of her was enough to soothe him.

"They fired me," he said in response to Nadine's questioning look.

"Oh my God." Nadine stopped midstep. "Are you kidding?"

"Do I look like I'm kidding?" Erma rubbed her head against his chin.

"No. I'm sorry." She crossed over to where he stood near the window. "What happened? Do you want to talk about it?"

The strange thing was normally he would say to give him some alone time, but he wanted to talk it over with Nadine. He put the cat on the ground. "Let's go outside, and I'll tell you."

"Okay." She took his hand, looking at him to check that it was all right. Wes tucked her hand under his arm to bring her closer, and they edged through the door together.

He didn't pay much attention to where they were going as they passed the pagoda and then a stone lantern. Nadine handed him a stick. No, not a stick. A rake. "Yard work?" he asked.

"Meditation." She pointed to a Zen garden. Or a version of it, with rocks and gravel that had been raked and trod on. He shook his head. A Japanese rock garden. Dot was something else.

"You?" He pointed at the footprints.

"You can fix them and tell me what happened."

"I'm not a Zen guy," he said.

"Yeah. I'm not a Zen woman, but it worked for me. If it's too annoying, you can sit on this hard wooden bench to talk."

"You make it sound so inviting." This light back-and-forth with Nadine was helping him calm down.

The rake made a pleasant sound as he dragged it through the gravel. He cleared her steps with a single long pull, then traced lines between the rocks. It was a while before he spoke.

"Tyler lied and said I asked him to run the story. That I begged him so I could get another shot at the I-team."

He looked up to check Nadine's reaction. She looked like she was breathing fire. He'd never had someone react like that on his behalf. He liked it.

It didn't take long to recount the conversation, and if she was angry before he started, now she was incandescent. "I will kill him," she said.

Wes paused midrake. "I am trying to achieve my Zen, and your threats of violence are interfering."

"Am I wrong?"

"No." He raked some more. Fantasizing about Tyler and Jason meeting an appropriate comeuppance might not be approved of in the tenets of Zen Buddhism—or maybe it was, he didn't know—but it was certainly gratifying.

"This is so unfair," she said, kicking at the pebbles. "Oh, sorry."

He raked over them. "Again, not helping me achieve Zen, but yeah. It is."

"What a couple of assholes. How does Tyler sleep at night?" She sounded truly flummoxed by how he could find peace. "I think he sabotaged you."

"Me?" He stopped raking to look over at Nadine. "Why?"

"Because if you were on that team, you'd blow him out of the water. I bet that's why he added your name as a contributor. He'd take the credit if it worked out, but you could be the scapegoat if he needed one."

Wes's chest filled when he saw she believed what she said. She thought he was good at his job. It gave him a boost that was instantly extinguished when he remembered the *Spear* didn't agree, and the *Spear* had been the one signing his paychecks.

"I shouldn't have..."

Nadine crunched over to stop him with a hard hug. "No. That won't get us anywhere."

"I can't get over the what-ifs." He buried his face in her neck, rake in hand. "What if I hadn't left my notes there? What if I'd used Word, for God's sake?"

"Wes." Nadine extracted herself to look him straight in the face. "What if this, what if that. I wrecked myself with them too, but what's the point? What if I never ran that obit? What if we never took this job from Brent? What if Tyler wasn't a total piece of shit? Go back far enough, what if John Wilson had been decent and Dot never wrote *Thirty Pieces*?"

"I guess so," said Wes.

"Everything in life is a result of a what-if. Remember what Dot said?"

"She said a lot of things."

"She said the bad stuff in her life eventually opened the way for good stuff." Nadine frowned. "But more eloquently and about flags."

"'Golden threads of possibility knitting into that moment, readying themselves to be unfurled like flags,'" Wes recited.

"That was it." She leaned into him. "I got the gist of it, even without a photographic memory."

"You did." He saw Nadine chewing her lip. "What are you thinking?"

"That we failed Dot," she admitted. "We didn't tell her story. We let the aggressor play the victim."

"No way." Wes thumped the rake on the ground. He had a flush of energy that was almost entirely composed of resentment toward the *Spear*. "We're going back to that hunt right now."

"The story is over. It's out."

"It's not," he said as they left the garden. "Not until we get the truth. We have one more day. Isn't there a saying about never giving up?"

"Yeah, it goes something like 'Don't give up.'" She looked cheered. "We must have missed something."

"I refuse to believe this is the end. I won't let it be."

"We'll do it for Dot," she said, holding her hand in a high five.

He slapped it with his own, feeling a small lift through the heaviness the conversation with Jason had left. "For Dot."

# FORTY-ONE

Despite their eagerness to stick it to John Wilson and peripherally the *Spear*, the rest of the day was spent rechecking the house without success. They were in the dress room, hoping for a breakthrough, when Brent called. Wes put it on speaker.

Nadine took the opportunity to walk around the silver room as Wes went through a quick explanation of what happened with the *Spear*. Brent didn't say anything much beyond "I see" and "They did what?" and "Holy shit, they did *what*?"

"What a mess. I'm sorry that happened to you," Brent said when Wes finished. "Do you think the *Spear* will get sued?"

"If they do, it could be bad news for their financial standing," said Nadine. "Potentially very bad."

"Really?" Brent sounded interested. "Will it be up for sale?"

"No idea," said Wes, looking over to Nadine for help.

Nadine shrugged. She had to budget for a new pair of shoes. It wasn't like she was in the market to buy a media outlet.

When Wes confirmed the story Tyler wrote was based on their actual finds, Brent's intake of breath was audible. "The story is all true?"

"We think so," said Wes. "The problem is we can't prove a more direct connection from John Wilson to Dot, and we don't have proof that he's guilty. Only allegations and a manuscript."

Brent made a disgusted noise. "It really grinds my gears that he's getting away with this, especially if he also screwed over my aunt."

"Us too," said Wes. "We're going to keep looking."

"Well, I have faith in you, and so did Dot."

They hung up. Seeing John Wilson parading around complacently assuring media the "lies and mistruths spread by the *Spear* will soon be put to rest thanks to my legal team" had reaffirmed Nadine's commitment to taking him down. She wouldn't let Dot be forgotten. Not that it was much of a risk, since the woman was one of the country's most beloved authors, but it sounded good in her mind.

She glanced over at Wes, who was doing his best to keep positive and currently stood looking at the Victorian hair art on the wall, seemingly pleased with his lot of searching through a dead woman's belongings. Nadine knew he was putting a good face on it. He occasionally came up to give her a kiss or simply hold her, and she was happy to comfort him. She suspected once he didn't have Dot's mystery to keep him busy, it would be much different. She had already decided to plan some fun dates to keep him occupied. Her online orders should be waiting at her apartment when she got home, and she prayed the packaging was discreet. And double prayed there were no more surprise parental visits.

Perhaps she could take that stripping album from the secret room too.

"Why don't I get lunch and we can eat while we work?" Wes turned around and ran his hand through his hair. They were both sweaty messes. Thank God Wes had seen her during some questionable style choice eras, including the brief period she'd worn dresses over button-down shirts.

"Thanks," she said, raising her face for his kiss. It was incredible how good he felt. She blew him another kiss as he left for the kitchen.

Hours later, they lay in Nadine's fancy canopied bed after working off their frustration at finding nothing in the attic. It would have been gross had Wes not dampened a washcloth in cold water to run over Nadine's sweaty skin. Wes was perfect, she thought as she returned the favor. Make that almost perfect, because when she dropped the washcloth on the side of the bed, promising to put it away later, he sighed, got out of bed, and returned it to the bathroom.

"It'll make the sheets damp," he said as he climbed back beside her. "I'm getting hungry, but I was thinking we work for..." His voice trailed off, and when Nadine looked over, it was to see him staring up.

"Wes?" She followed his gaze. The late afternoon sun had come in at the ideal angle to illuminate a dark outline on top of the bed's pale yellow canopy, as if someone had stored a box or book.

They looked at each other.

It was very like Wes that he pulled on a pair of shorts before grabbing a chair to stand on. Nadine threw on her dress and stood on the bed itself, trying to feel what the rectangle was through the canopy. "It's light," she reported. "Not a book or a box. Maybe a newspaper."

Wes swept his arms across, trying to reach it, but it wasn't until Nadine poked the canopy from below that the object slid close enough for him to grab.

It was also like Wes that he put the chair away before coming to sit on the edge of the bed, treasure in hand. "It's a letter," said Wes. "From Allan to Dot. Undated."

Nadine read it aloud.

*My dear*, it read.

*I've been in Ottawa for a week, and my God, I can't wait to get away. The men here are all blowhards, the kind who think talking is more important than doing, especially him. I wish with all my heart you'd let me do something to wipe that arrogant grin off his face.*

*But I respected your wishes even when I saw him across the room with his arm around a young woman who had a smile that might have been painted on. It got me thinking, though, about what we've spoken of so often.*

*This is the last time I bring it up, I swear. I don't have many weeks left. But I must give one last try, although I know you're stubborn as a mule and prefer to write out your grievances to work through them.*

*You need to let people know what kind of man he is. The back-scratching deal with White and what he did to you and others. All those people, all those lives. I know when you left, you were scared, but we have each other as protection against him and his threats, the ones from before you left and the ones from when your book came out.*

*Deep down, you know I'm right. I'll say no more on this, not even when I'm back in Toronto. But think about what I've said. Wilson doesn't deserve to enjoy his life, and you deserve to be free of his shadow.*

*With love,*
*Allan*

She toppled back on the bed with the letter on her chest, and Wes joined her. "We have it," she said in a faint voice. "What we needed to connect John Wilson with Dot Voline and the White Group. It's here."

"I knew we'd get it." Wes hooked his leg over hers to bring her closer.

Nadine turned to lie on her side, facing Wes. "But it's too late," she said. "After what happened with the *Spear*, Daniel will want much more than a few letters. He'll point out that there are thousands of Wilsons and Whites, and this letter is too vague."

"This would have been enough if we'd been able to act before Tyler did," said Wes. "This won't cause the *Spear* to revisit the story either."

They looked at the letter again. "He really loved her," she said thoughtfully.

"She was lovable."

"She was."

"So that's it."

"Yeah. I think it is."

They lay in bed, holding each other and watching the sun slowly travel across the window. They'd lost, and there was nothing left to say.

Then Nadine sat up. "No."

"No what?"

"You said the other day that Dot put her faith in us. It's not only Dot. Look at all the people Wilson has affected. Dot. Abigail. Monica. Ian, who had to find a new job. Probably Irina. All those people we found clippings about. Those towns who lost out because of his interference."

"That's all true but doesn't change our situation."

"*We* can change our situation. You know what Dot would say if she saw us giving up?" She didn't wait for Wes to reply. "She'd tell us to quit whining and use our heads. You were right. We only have one day here, but Dot's house isn't our only hope, and those clues she collected are just the beginning. She left that manuscript unfinished, and we're going to add the final chapter."

"We can do it," said Wes. "Screw John Wilson."

"Yeah, screw that guy!"

Erma poked her head up to meow her agreement, looking between them. "That's it," said Wes. "Attack cat Erma is on the case. Wilson has no chance."

Somehow, they would get John Wilson. Not today and probably not tomorrow, but someday, thought Nadine. They owed it to Dot.

# FORTY-TWO

t was their last full day. Wes woke early to the sound of Erma purring by his ear. Nadine was on her side with her arm tucked under her head. Wes laid a gentle kiss on the tip of her nose, the only part peeking out from the hair tumbling over her face, before slowly extricating himself to not disturb the woman or the cat. Or the other cat that he'd missed lying by his feet. And the one sleeping in the middle of the floor. Sidonie-Gabrielle, as always, was gone on her mysterious adventures.

He washed up, then made coffee and took it out to the garden to watch the sun rise. Last night had been quiet, as he and Nadine took advantage of their last hours in the house to go over all their clues and the manuscript, hoping to see something they missed or make a connection that eluded them that would force Daniel to accept the story's potential. Not for the first time and he was sure not for the last, Nadine had blown him away with her sheer determination. It had been well after midnight by the time he'd dragged her away from the library table, bleary-eyed and trembling with fatigue and frustration. She'd tossed and turned for an hour in bed before curling up against him and letting him soothe her to sleep.

Wes propped his feet up on the chair and let the sun warm his face. It was going to be another scorcher, but the morning had that slight crispness that hit at the end of August, a reminder that fall was closing in. Would Nadine like to check out the leaves with him on the weekends? Go buy butter tarts at farmers markets and, more important, agree that the ones with nuts were inferior to the plain ones? Then winter would come. They could watch movies under a blanket. Go skating at city hall. All the seasons that he could spend with her lay as stopovers on their road together.

His mother would be furious. The thought came almost clinically and without the tension he usually felt. She never liked the women Wes dated, and he'd learned it made more sense to simply not tell her. He'd have to discuss this with Nadine and see how she wanted to handle it. Later though. It would be easier when he moved, which he promised himself he would as soon as he found another job. He let himself drift off into a fantasy of having his own place. It would look a lot like Amy's, clean and uncluttered. Maybe he'd get a cat, since his mother refused to have one in the house, and he was used to having them around. He heard a muffled meow. Erma's tiny face appeared, and he felt his heart seize when she put a black paw against the glass. Poor kitties. They'd lost Dot, and soon they'd lose their home. Brent would treat them well though.

He'd better.

Erma disappeared, and Nadine came out yawning, her hair a wavy mess and her pajamas, the only pants she ever wore, slipping down to leave a small band of skin around her hips. She shaded her eyes against the new sun. "What are you doing out here?"

"Do you want to meet my mother?" he asked.

She didn't seem to consider this a non sequitur. "If you want, but I'd really like to meet Amy first."

"We can do that." Amy was going to love Nadine.

"Is that what you're doing? Planning dinner dates?"

He pulled her down so she was sitting in his lap with her legs over the arm of the chair. "Thinking about the fall. Do you want to go to a pumpkin patch and take photos in matching cable-knit sweaters?"

She looked at him suspiciously. "Is this a test?"

"Not at all."

"Sure, if we can get hot cider after. I don't have a cable-knit sweater though."

"You can wear one of mine." He liked the thought of her in his clothes and how they'd smell like her smoky rose perfume when she gave them back.

She laid her head on his chest, her fingers resting lightly on his collarbone as he stroked the soft wavy cloud of her hair. Nadine's hair was usually more contained, in buns or ponytails or ruthlessly straightened. He was lucky to be the man she chose to let her guard down with.

"You said you were thinking," she said. "Anything in particular?"

"Not really." He reconsidered and decided to say it out loud. "I want to move out of my mother's house."

"I can see why. Are you nervous about what she'll do?"

"Yeah."

Nadine reached for his hand. "You're going to be around when she truly needs you, but you don't need to be at her beck and call."

"It's hard." There were layers weighing down the two words.

"Amy did it. You can too."

"Maybe." Easier said than done. "I'll think about it. When is Brent coming?"

"Eleven," she said.

He ran a finger down her arm. "We have enough time to get some breakfast and do a tidy of the house."

"Or hear me out," she said. "We don't do those things and go back to bed."

Wes liked a neat house, but sometimes a man had to make sacrifices.

He rose to his feet, managing not to drop Nadine as she squealed and swung her arms around his neck. "We can clean later," he agreed.

———————

Nadine was watching Wes run around with a basket of items he was taking from one spot to put away in other spots when the doorbell rang. She went to let in Brent, unsurprised he would ring before entering what was legally his own house. Small talk about traffic and the weather lasted down the hall to the kitchen, where Wes had come out from his cleaning spree to put on the coffee. They immediately revealed the entrance to the basement, with Nadine giving an animated "Ta-da!"

Brent was floored. "My aunt was something else. I should have known that she'd match a hidden door to the attic to one to the basement. She liked symmetry despite her generalized chaos."

It took more than an hour to walk Brent through all the clues, and at the end of it, he paged through the manuscript for It Is Hellish Gain, shaking his head.

"I don't know if her agent needs to see this," Brent said. "Odette told me Dot never started a story without telling her, and she didn't know about this. I think my aunt meant for this to stay private, particularly given its lack of ending." He put it on the table and sat down on the leather couch, causing the cushion to let out a small whistle. "You said you don't have enough evidence to try to publish?"

Wes answered. "Not after the mess with the Spear. The Herald would be reluctant as well."

Nadine nodded. A gut check with Lisanne had told her what she suspected—Daniel wouldn't touch this with a ten-foot pole unless there was the equivalent of a notarized admission in those clues. There was no way she could put herself out there, even to pitch it. It was too risky.

"Too bad."

"We're going to keep working on it after we leave," promised Wes. "We have some ideas we can follow up on."

"Dot would have appreciated your dedication, and so do I." Brent looked around. "You have any problems with work because of that *Spear* story, Nadine?"

She shook her head. "They don't know I'm involved."

"There's no reason for it," said Wes.

Nadine knew her expression must have turned stubborn because Wes touched her hand.

"We don't both need to lose our jobs over this," he said softly as Brent watched them intently.

"I know you think that," she said.

If Wes heard the ambiguous language, he ignored it. "Good."

Brent sighed. "I'm going to miss this place."

"You're still selling?" Nadine followed his eyes around the lovely room, seeing it as if for the first time. The house was Dot writ large, her personality in architecture. It would be a shame to lose it.

"Yeah, you should see the property tax. Even with the inheritance, I can't justify the cost." He shook his hand above his head to indicate how high it was. It was high. "I wish we could keep it how it is, but that's life."

Nadine didn't have an answer because it's not like she had a few extra millions lying around for real estate investments, and she assumed the same went for Wes. Brent was right. That was indeed life.

"Now for the boring part," said Brent. "The cleaners will be in tomorrow. I know you didn't find exactly what you wanted, but something might come up when we clear the place out."

Nadine was confident there wasn't a page or box or room left unturned. "Tell us if you do. We searched everywhere but Dot's bedroom."

"Why not there?"

Nadine looked at him in confusion. "You said not to. It was off-limits."

"Did I?" Brent shook his head. "Sorry, I don't recall that. I was in a bit of a fog after her death." Erma came in and jumped on the couch next to Brent. He turned his attention to her. "We need to find some new homes for you and your sisters," he said.

Nadine felt Wes stiffen. "You're not taking them?" he asked.

"My partner is allergic." Brent scratched Erma's head. "I'll find them suitable homes."

Wes's eyebrows came down. "They're good cats."

"I know," Brent reassured him. "I'll make sure they're happy. Anyway, want to go check that bedroom? We can do it together before I head out."

Wes and Nadine didn't run down the hall, but they far outpaced Brent.

"Go ahead," he called.

Nadine put her hand on the knob, and Wes placed his hand on top, the same way he had that first day. "Ready?" he asked, smiling down at her. "Still think it's going to be pine and white paint?"

"I thought we agreed on funky wallpaper."

Brent caught up to them and stared at their hands. "Are you going to open that door or what?" he asked.

They twisted the knob and pushed, then stood on the threshold. "This was not what I expected," said Wes. "But somehow also exactly what I expected."

Dot's room was simply beautiful, an elegant and calming space painted pale blue with white accents. It was like living in a Wedgwood cameo. A single piece of art decorated the wall, a portrait of Dot and Allan that had caught them laughing together against a hazy romantic background that would have been the first thing Dot saw when she opened her eyes. A large bed with a reasonable number of pillows was pushed against the wall, with a low blue velvet bench at the foot. A chaise lounge was placed near the gauzy curtains that covered the windows.

They split up the space, and Nadine took the closet, a huge walk-in affair that was a vintage collector's dream. Caftans filled an entire wall, and Nadine first poked through the shoes, which ranged Victorian boots to disco platforms to an entire shelf of orthopedic runners. There were surprisingly few handbags, and all of them were empty apart from some spare change and old gum packages.

"Nothing in the washroom," called Brent.

"All clear on the rest of the room," said Wes.

Nadine heard the men chatting about the house sale and tuned them out. There was the faint smell of amber in the closet, and she reached out to touch a familiar outfit, the psychedelic caftan of their first meeting. It looked almost faded on the hanger, as if it had needed Dot's personality to make it shine.

"Nadine? Brent has a meeting," said Wes. "Did you find anything?"

"Sorry." She came out of the closet. "Not a single thing."

"Disappointing but not surprising." Brent shrugged. "She called her room her oasis and refused to do anything but sleep in bed. She didn't read or work there."

"Goals," said Nadine, and Brent laughed.

They walked Brent to the entrance, going over the details about locking up before they left Dot's house tomorrow. Brent walked down the steps, then paused by his car. "Thank you for everything you've done," he said. "I mean what I said about appreciating your work, regardless of the result."

They waved goodbye and went back in the house. Wes paused as they passed the corridor leading to Dot's room. "That's it," he said. "The last room checked."

"There might be something we missed," she said.

Wes gave her a kiss. "I doubt it," he said. "You're thorough."

"True."

He laughed and went to clear the coffee cups as Nadine walked into the library.

Everything felt gray. Soon she'd be back working the night web shift at the *Herald*. She looked at her phone, where she'd been reworking Dot's obituary since she arrived, taking inspiration from Dot's files and the obits she'd left. She could see how it would look on the page. The story it could tell, if only she had the chance.

And the nerve.

Her mother texted and disturbed her thoughts. **Nadine, we bought some new locks for your apartment doors. Dad will install them on the weekend, and they'll be good until you move home.**

**Thanks, Mom**, she wrote back dutifully. Then Octavia jumped up before she could send and batted the phone right out of her hand. "Octavia! What are you doing?"

She picked it up and settled back in the chair, thinking about her apartment. She was tired of being scared. She wanted to tell her mother she had her life under control and didn't need help. She wanted to push herself. To *trust* herself. Those 3:00 a.m. shadows weren't where she wanted to live. She wanted to be brave again, the way Lisanne was, able to deflect the criticism and, yes, unwarranted hatred. It wasn't right she had to deal with it to do her job, but she wasn't going to change anything by hiding.

Catching sight of Dot's shelves, she realized she was at her own nexus point. She tapped her fingers against the keys of the old aqua-gray typewriter, the letters worn almost to invisibility, and thought about how she felt when she was working. She felt good, as if she was doing what she'd been meant to do.

Yet she'd allowed a nasty, small-minded, hate-filled loser to take it from her, and she'd allowed her parents to pressure her until she doubted that she could manage on her own.

No, she wouldn't blame herself. At the time, she did what she needed to. She took the break she had to.

But she wouldn't let him or her parents steal any more of her life. She was ready to engage with the world again and to take risks.

That decision was like a puzzle piece falling from the sky to land right in the center of her mind, connecting it all together.

She stood up so fast, she made herself dizzy and reached out to the bookshelf in a desperate attempt to keep her balance. Her fingers tugged out one of the books as the black dots cleared in front of her eyes. "Wes!" she called.

"I'm right here." He'd come in without her knowing. "What's up?"

"I'm done being a wuss."

"I hardly think you—"

"Wilson isn't going to win, and we're not going to keep looking for more proof before I bring it to the *Herald*."

"We're not?"

"No," she said. "We have enough here to warrant a larger investigation. More than enough."

Wes raised his eyebrows. "I hate to be unsupportive, but do you think they'll go for it? You were pretty concerned."

"I'm tired of self-censoring. I'm going to fight for this, and I'm going to do it now." This was a good story, and if a powerful man didn't like it? He could suck it. She was going to do her best to get it published instead of waiting and waiting for the perfect moment.

Wes gripped her so tight she gasped. "Are you ready for this?" he asked. "If it goes ahead, there's going to be blowback from Wilson, and you know how people get on the internet."

Nadine hesitated. Was she ready? Then she glanced down at the book in her hand, the one she'd yanked out trying to get her balance. *Thirty Pieces of Silver*. Dot's first attempt to change things.

"Yes," she said. "I'm ready."

"Then you get him," said Wes. "I've got your back, whatever you need."

She grinned, a rush of adrenaline taking over the fear. "Anything?"

He leaned in closer. "Anything."

"Good." She grabbed Octavia away from her phone and handed

the wriggling tabby over. "Take care of her for a second so I can send a text."

Nadine deleted the message to her mother and rewrote it. It was time to make it crystal clear she was fine on her own. **Thanks, but I can take care of my own security. I don't want any more discussion about me moving. I'm staying at my place.**

Then she sent it and felt free, until Wes yelped as Octavia dug in her claws and he dumped the furious cat onto her lap.

It was after midnight by the time they were taking a final farewell swim in the grotto. "Who do you think will buy this house?" asked Wes as he floated near Nadine. The cool water was like a balm. "I hope some hedonistic pop star who has orgies in here."

"It'll probably be some soulless tech bro who will turn it into a cooling chamber for his AI." Nadine paddled her hands against the water.

"This house has some happy memories for me," said Wes, looking up. It was cloudy, tinting the night sky lavender.

"Yeah?" Nadine moved closer. "Like what?"

"Like the time Erma threw up beside my bed," Wes said in a contemplative tone. "Can a man say he's lived until he's stepped in cold cat hair balls?"

"I believe Marcus Aurelius addressed that very topic in his *Meditations.*" Nadine swam nearer. "Is that your only memory?"

"No." He tried to catch his breath. Only Nadine could render him speechless like this.

"Good." Then she kissed him, and soon Wes had a brand-new favorite memory.

# FORTY-THREE

Nadine held the door for Wes as he struggled through with his hands full. After talking earnestly to Erma and the other cats in a low voice, he'd rushed out in the morning to come back with a sour cream glazed doughnut for Nadine and a carful of carriers for the cats.

"They're a posse," he insisted to Brent when he'd called to tell him he was taking all four. "They can't be separated."

Brent had named Wes the cats' official human companion and invited him to take the rest of the organic meals in the fridge as a gift as well as their portrait in the dress room. Wes had accepted the food and regretfully declined the portrait, which Nadine had snapped up.

"Do you know what you're doing?" asked Nadine as he gave them each a treat through the barred windows of their carriers in a futile attempt to stop the cacophony of plaintive meows. It had taken almost an hour to wrangle them all in.

"No." He pointed at Erma. "But how could I leave that face?"

Nadine looked down at his complaining baggage. "They're not going to appreciate their new kibble life," she predicted.

"They're very adaptable animals and know going nonorganic is worth it to be together."

Cats secured in his car, they returned to the front hall for one last look. Nadine could almost see the ghostly figure of Dot in a sequined caftan sweeping by Janice and Sir Latimer. She should be depressed. There was an extremely good chance Daniel would reject her, and they'd fail despite their hard work and best intentions. Instead, she was filled with an intense gratitude to have been able to experience Dot and Wes and everything this magical house had to offer. She looked at the ceiling and gasped. It was patterned with the reflections thrown up from Sir Latimer's armor, and they looked like little flags.

Wes wrapped his arm around her waist as if he would always be there to support her. He whispered, "Thanks, Dot."

Nadine swore she heard that low wheezy laugh and a familiar gravelly voice say, *You got it, handsome.*

Then, they walked out and locked the door to Dot Voline's house for the last time.

# FORTY-FOUR

Wes shifted his gaze from his phone to the clock on the night table beside his childhood bed. In twenty minutes, Nadine had her meeting with Daniel. Her last text had been, **I'm going to throw up.**

He'd sent her back a heart emoji and some gold flags, backed up with the good vibes he'd been aiming in her direction all day. That is, all the ones he could spare, because his mother had not taken his coming home well yesterday and had been especially displeased by the cats. He didn't blame her, but it was another reason he needed to sort out his life.

A text came in from Caleb. **Talk to Pris yet?**

Pris was the employment lawyer he'd recommended and had been as sharp as Caleb promised. She hadn't been sure they could prove Tyler's lies but told him they'd make the *Spear* suffer.

**She's great,** wrote back Wes.

**Remember loyalty is a one-way street for a company. You don't owe them shit.**

Wes had to read this twice. **This isn't your usual defense of capitalism.**

I've been thinking about it a lot. There was a pause. **Talked to Isabel about the wedding.**

Wes sat down, preparing himself for bad news. **And?**

**I was honest about feeling like a fungible asset.**

**Is that how you phrased it?**

**Yeah, why?**

Wes tried not to laugh. Caleb was something. **No reason. What'd she say?**

**Cried, like I said she would, and said she was doing her best, which I know is true. But I asked her why we were doing this. I'm spending my best years away from her and for what?**

**How did it go?**

It took a while for the block of text that was Caleb's reply to arrive.

**Good. She thought I was the one who wanted all this stuff and she'd been doing it to keep me happy, which kind of killed me. You know what the guys at work are like. I hadn't realized how much I'd been doing to keep up with them, and she was worried because she thought she needed to do the same. We've been working sixty-hour weeks for a life neither of us want.**

**Now what?** asked Wes. This was big. Huge, for Caleb.

**First thing is that we've decided to have a small wedding and I'm not taking the contract extension. I want to be with Isabel. She's cutting down her hours too, and then we're going to see.**

**Congratulations.**

**Hey, it's not so small a wedding you can't have a plus-one.**

**Good. Because I think Nadine would love to come.**

**LOL that's my boy.**

Wes put his phone down, and his smile disappeared as Ma's key sounded in the lock. His heart raced. He was astonished to realize it always did when she was home, as his whole body went on alert, trying to anticipate what she would need from him. It had been such a relief to experience not walking on eggshells during the last three weeks that he couldn't believe he'd stood it for all those years. Erma put a paw on his leg, and he gave her a pet.

Well, he didn't have to deal with it much longer. The moment he'd arrived home, he'd known it was time for him to move out, despite his lack of employment. He would give his mother a month to get used to the idea as he searched for a place. He'd sent Ella the money for her Italian internship but still had enough to afford a small, cheap apartment that would be all his own.

The front door closed. Wes thought of raking the Zen garden and walked down the hall to the kitchen to greet his mother.

"Hi, Ma," he said in an even tone calculated not to offend. "How was your day?"

"As if you care," she said, taking the tea canister down and banging it on the maroon laminate counter.

"I wouldn't ask if I didn't care," said Wes.

"If you cared, my tea would have been ready, and you wouldn't have left for three weeks, barely talking to your mother."

"I texted while I was away, and you didn't answer. Amy said she helped out."

"Amy is a good girl," said his mother with satisfaction. "I have one good child." She looked at Erma. "I said I wanted these cats gone."

"No, you said they were my responsibility." Wes gripped the back of the chair. His mother hadn't said a word about getting rid of them. Not one.

"I didn't. I told you to get them out of my house."

A text came in from Nadine. **Meeting pushed up. Going in. Wish me luck.**

He sent back a heart as his mother watched with suspicious eyes. "Who are you talking to?" she asked.

"A friend." Wes wasn't ashamed of Nadine, but he also saw no reason to give his mother more ammunition. He nudged Erma gently with his foot, urging her back to the safety of his room, but she stayed close.

"A friend?" His mother's voice grew high. "I bet it's a woman. You deserted me for a woman. What kind of son are you?" She slapped her hand to her chest as if stunned at his perfidy and started to cry.

Wes watched this anticipated response and waited for the guilt. Instead, he felt new emotions edging in. Was it pity? A bit, and a lot of exasperation. Resentment. He didn't care to look too closely at that one.

"I didn't desert you," he said. "I'm sitting right here in front of you."

"The girls have left me. Your father. Everyone leaves."

"Ma, you're not listening. We're still a family. Amy is only down the street, and when I leave, I'll be close as well." Oh no. He hadn't meant for it to come out like this. He had planned to minimize the impact, although he'd known there would never be a good way to tell her.

"When you what?" Her hands hit the table, and Erma bolted at the sharp sound.

Wes decided to come out with it fully. "I'm going to move out," he said. "Next month, as soon as I find a place."

"Moving out." His mother's laugh had that bitter edge he hated. "This is my repayment. No one to take care of me. All my life, I do nothing but work for you, and I get nothing. Nothing!"

No matter how many times Wes heard a variation on this, it always hurt. He swallowed hard. "Ma, I know it's a change, but it will be good for us to have some space."

"You can't leave," she said loudly. "It's your job to be here, after all the years I took care of you." She clutched at her chest. "My heart. This is your fault. It's your fault my life is like this. You need to fix it."

The guilt and remorse and frustration and all those other feelings were shoved aside in a mighty push as he remembered Nadine's words. "No," said Wes, almost disbelieving it as it came out of his mouth.

His mother stopped crying and stared at him, hand dropping to her side. "What did you say?"

Wes looked straight at her, hoping he could break through and they could finally, for once, talk like adults. "I love you, Ma, and I'll help and support you, but it's not my responsibility to fix everything that went wrong in your life. I'm sorry you had a hard time. I'm grateful for the sacrifices you made for us. But ensuring your happiness is not my job."

Her mouth opened and closed like a fish.

Wes sat down at the table, feeling a confidence that had elements of unreality, like an out-of-body experience. "We need some boundaries until I move."

"Boundaries?" She repeated the word like it was dirty. "I gave birth to you."

"I know, Ma, but this is important to me."

"Enough," she said, her voice getting high. "This is Amy's fault. The new woman. Poisoning you."

"No, it's not. Blaming others won't help."

"Go ahead," she said, crossing her arms over her chest as if daring him. "If I'm such a terrible person, leave. Leave now."

"Ma, please don't be like that. We can work this out if we talk." His mouth was dry with tension, but he didn't want to get a glass of water. Not with his mother standing at the sink, her lips working with outrage.

His calm tone seemed to infuriate her more. "No talking! Go! You're no longer my son. I only hope you treat that woman better than you treat me. Just like your worthless father, you don't care about anyone but yourself. Get out. Out! Out!"

She came at him with hands outstretched as if to shove him out the door, and Wes jumped to his feet, sadness layered with the fear that had always lain like a membrane over their relationship. He didn't trust himself to speak but went to his room, her insults ringing down the hall as he left. It didn't take him long to pack his belongings, and the television in the front room started blaring as he locked the surprisingly docile cats in their carriers. It was as if they understood it was time to go as much as he did.

His mother didn't turn her head from the television as he walked through with his baggage, nor did she move when he finished taking everything to the sidewalk and came back. Despite the ugliness of what she'd said, he couldn't leave without saying something. He stood to her side and looked at her, a small woman with a hard expression who refused to move her eyes from the people laughing on the screen.

"Ma," he said and waited. He spoke again. "I'll be in touch."

When there was no answer, he left.

Wes stepped outside, closing the door carefully behind him before raising his face to the sun. Being outside was like breathing in air after being submerged. He almost gulped it in.

It took a few minutes to maneuver everything into his car, and ten minutes after that, he was at Amy's apartment. He'd always been so hesitant to impose on his sister—he was supposed to be there for her after all, not vice versa—that he'd never thought it was an option, despite Amy's open-door invitation. Nadine had shown him it was fine to ask for what he needed, and he didn't hesitate to ring her bell.

"I thought you were at Ma's," Amy said, opening the door.

"She kicked me out."

"Wes, what?" Her eyes widened. "She did what?"

"We had a fight, and she kicked me out." He was thirty, but the rejection still hurt. To his surprise, no tears came. He felt mostly numb.

"Get in here." Then she saw the carrier in his hand. "What is that? A cat? You have a cat?"

"Not one."

"Wes, how many cats?" She looked around him into the hall. "Oh my God."

"Four." He brought them in as Amy's jaw dropped.

"You don't like cats," she whispered.

"Don't say that around them. They're sensitive." He leaned down to whisper to the cages. "Don't listen to her. You know I love you."

"Oh, you're a cat daddy now." She laughed. "Nice. Well, I was thinking of getting one anyway."

"Four isn't much more trouble than one."

"Sure, Wes."

They released the cats and watched Sidonie-Gabrielle disappear as the rest sniffed around their new environment. "The spare bedroom is yours for as long as you need," said Amy quietly.

A small dart of warmth pierced through the dullness in his mind. "Thanks, Amy."

"I told you, you were welcome anytime." She slung an arm around him. "It gets better when you have time away from her. I swear it does. I'm here to help."

He hugged her, feeling better. "I know."

Amy stepped away. "Welcome home, big brother." She glanced over. "But if your cats scratch that couch, you're dead."

# FORTY-FIVE

Daniel shook his head as Nadine pulled out the letter. "Just no," he said. "Stop."

"What?"

"I don't need to read that," he said. "You were collaborating with a reporter from the *Spear*? Do you know what would happen if it came out we were involved in that travesty of journalism?"

"They lied and ran the story before it was ready. I have more evidence."

Daniel laughed. "Come on, Nadine. That didn't happen. The goal was to embarrass a powerful and influential man, and it backfired because of shoddy work."

"The *Spear*—"

"You know how many people called us with additional information after the *Spear* story? None."

"They might be scared. I'd be scared if it was Wilson threatening my character and the White Group was on his side."

"Nadine." He flipped through her stack of clippings and books. "You say this started with a Dot Voline *book*? Look at what you have.

People's initials in a fiction book. Another unfinished book that is also, may I remind you, fiction. A letter that mentions men named Wilson and White and, for the record, is not addressed to and doesn't mention Dot Voline. It could have been to anyone. You have a bunch of people who admitted to wrongdoing with no direct links to Wilson. Projects that were passed but had some unfortunate side effects for local communities. A bitter woman trying to blackmail a senator but who won't go on the record. None of this adds up to John Wilson's misconduct."

"He's being doing it for years," she said. "He knows how to hide his tracks. You're being deliberately obstructive."

"What did you say?" His voice was icy.

"I have enough to warrant further investigation," she said stubbornly. "I also have a plan for how that can happen."

"No."

"Daniel—"

He kept going. "After what you did to Dot Voline with that shameful obituary, I would suggest it's better for you to stay clear of anything that would call your judgment into doubt. Again."

"What if I limit it to the Dot Voline part of the story?" she persisted. "What he did to her?"

Daniel looked unimpressed. "That was what, forty, fifty years ago?"

"He still didn't answer for it."

"The Herald does not do follow-ups on stories the Spear has already butchered, and even if I thought this deserved attention, I would be concerned your ability to see it through."

"I can do it." She did her best to summon her old ice queen persona, but her voice trembled and tears came into her eyes.

"This is a professional office, Nadine." Daniel's mouth turned down. "Please control yourself."

How could she answer that? She made it to the washroom, but her rage had overtaken her frustration by the time she slammed open the door. Thank God it was empty. She didn't hesitate to text Lisanne, who was there within a minute.

"Who do we need to kill?" she asked when she walked in and saw Nadine's face.

"Daniel."

"That prick."

Nadine laughed despite her tears. "You like him."

"I like what he can do for my career, but I also know the kind of person he is. What happened?"

"He turned down the story I was working on with Wes."

"Shit." Lisanne leaned against the counter. "I'm sorry. What are you going to do?"

What was she going to do? The question troubled Nadine as she went back to her desk later, after Lisanne was sure she was feeling better.

What was she going to do?

Daniel was worried she would embarrass John Wilson. Not that he should be held accountable.

He was concerned about her ability to see it through and her judgment. Forget that she was an experienced reporter with a proven track record.

*Remember Dot Voline's shameful obituary*, he said. Not that this was a chance to fix it.

She stood up and ducked into a phone room, where she called Wes and gave him the rundown of her conversation with Daniel.

"What's your plan?" he asked.

Nadine told him, and he laughed.

"I should have known." He paused. "Are you sure? This won't be easy."

"I need to do it."

"Okay, Barbault," said Wes. "Then do it. I'll be waiting for you."

She hung up and opened her folder to the document she'd been playing with for three weeks. This time, Dot would have had nothing to complain about. The obituary was what Nadine wanted for the *Herald*. Featuring a photo of a very young Dot Voline that Brent had dug up from a family album, it was amusing and engaging yet respectful, briefly covering the significant milestones and impact of Dot's long and illustrious career, particularly her early days as Mildred Cross working in politics before the Wilson travesty.

That was the first part. The second section was the part she put the finishing touches on now, laying out the proof of John Wilson's misdeeds from Dot's clues and the need for further inquiry into his actions. It was strong writing, and a persuasive story.

It was worthy of Dot Voline.

By the time she was three hours into her night shift, Nadine was the only one in the office. She pulled up Dot's story and read it over. Did she have the courage to do what she needed to? She wavered. Perhaps she could try Daniel again. Wes was correct. She'd seen the viciousness with which Wilson reacted to threats. Although she'd been careful to keep the focus on Wilson's treatment of Voline, the story demonstrated there needed to be further inquiry into his actions throughout his career and his alleged connections to organized crime. It was everything the *Spear* story should have been.

"Wait." The voice from behind her made Nadine almost fall off her chair.

"Irina?" Adrenaline caused the name to come out as a gasp.

"Wait. In another hour, it's more likely management will be asleep and won't see it to take it down." Irina's shawl was a deep crimson, and it was wrapped tightly around her body as if she was cold.

"How do you know what I'm doing?" Nadine was flabbergasted.

"Please. Give me some credit."

True, Irina was omniscient.

"Why are you getting involved?"

Irina looked down her long nose. "Why are you?"

"Because it's the right thing to do."

"Then you've answered your question." Irina shrugged, the shawl pulling across her shoulders. "Plus, that asshole is the reason I'm no longer a reporter. He can take what he's owed."

With that, she simply left, leaving Nadine trying to get her breath back under control. Perhaps Irina was right; it would be better to wait. An hour was enough time to give it a final check.

Then it was fifty-nine minutes, and she clicked the Post button before she could second-guess herself.

**By Nadine Barbault**

That byline felt amazing to see again.

It only took a few minutes for Wes to text her. **It's good. Excellent. Way better than Tyler's attempt.**

**Thanks,** she wrote back. **No one has commented yet.**

**Oh,** he replied, **they will.**

It only took a few more seconds for Wes to be proven right.

**Can you believe this?** lakeluver23 commented on the story. **Looks like the Spear was onto something.**

That was the beginning.

An hour after she posted Dot's revised obituary, someone commented, **I knew Milly. It happened.**

Soon, other people were stepping forward with stories of how John Wilson had coerced them, threatened them, or worse. The people who waded in with comments like **Innocent until proven guilty** and **You're ruining the life of a good man and a good Canadian** or worse—usually much worse—were roundly called out and eventually drowned out by people who finally felt safe enough to tell their stories and those supporting them. In death, like in life, Dot was having an impact.

And finally getting her revenge, as Wilson's carefully crafted reputation took hit after hit, especially after OlwayM began to post comments detailing her story. Nadine supposed this took the place of Monica going on the record.

Nadine probably wouldn't see any change while employed at the *Herald* though. She knew posting the obituary would not be the smartest career advancement move, which was confirmed when Lisanne texted her a bunch of exclamation marks and the message **WTF are you doing?**

But strangely, for once, she wasn't scared. She'd been calm after posting, and calm when the calls started coming in from other reporters looking for comments, then from the *Herald*'s own communications manager, reminding her in coded corporate speak that to do any interviews would be the equivalent of digging her own grave deeper.

She ignored it all, confident and at peace, like she was raking that gravel in Dot's garden.

However, it didn't mean she was looking forward to the emergency meeting she'd been summoned to, seven hours after her post went live. The obituary had been taken down, but copies and screenshots were circling the web. In fact, taking it down had added more fuel to the fire, with commentators inflamed by the idea the *Herald* was covering up the story.

"Nadine, Daniel is ready for you in the main boardroom." It was his assistant, Tania, a woman Nadine had always gotten along with, and her face was pinched with concern as she tugged on her micro braids. "He's pretty upset."

"I figured." Nadine tried to smile. Figures her composure would dissipate now that the confrontation was imminent.

Tania looked around. "The story was really good," she whispered. "I always thought that guy was slimy, and Dot Voline was my mom's favorite writer. She named me after one of her characters."

She brought Nadine to the boardroom, making her feel uncomfortably like she was on a perp walk, and left her at the door. Her phone dinged and showed a single gold flag from Wes.

Then a message from Lisanne: a GIF of an octopus punching a fish, with the message, **Be the octopus.**

She waited to see if her heart rate would slow, then decided it was a lost cause and opened the door. Daniel sat at the table to the right of the *Herald*'s owner, Freddy Majors. A woman Nadine recognized as his daughter and rumored successor, Olivia, sat to the left. No one smiled. At least HR wasn't there.

Unless it meant they didn't want witnesses.

Nadine didn't wait to be asked but took a seat near the end of the table across from Majors Senior.

Daniel started. "I am profoundly disappointed in you," he said in the deep voice of a scolding dad. "I said this was not a story the *Herald* was interested in running. You were insubordinate, and you embarrassed yourself as a journalist and the *Herald* as an organization."

Nadine noticed Olivia watching Daniel with a neutral expression. Unlike Freddy, she wasn't nodding in agreement.

"Your article added fire to the baseless claims the *Spear* put forward and that John has been valiantly fighting," said Freddy.

Nadine waited. They waited. Was she supposed to say something? Might as well. It couldn't get any worse.

"I understand the story would be upsetting to Mr. Wilson," she said, grateful her voice remained steady.

"As you should," said Freddy. "I've known him for a long time, and these claims are ridiculous. He's never acted like this around me."

She kept going. "Especially given the replies of many people in the comments who experienced similar behavior from him and who had their own stories of his use of intimidation to advance his career and illegal misconduct."

"Allegations," said Daniel. "Those are *allegations*."

"Nowhere in that story did I state otherwise," said Nadine. "I laid out the proof. If people take it to the logical conclusion, then I suggest again it's a story worthy of another look."

"I told you no," said Daniel. "That should have ended it."

Nadine swallowed down the fear to stand by her actions. "One of Dot Voline's final wishes was to make his behavior known and to take it out of the shadows of fear where it's thrived. She knew the injustice of the situation and wanted the truth public."

Freddy snorted. "Sure. Daniel said she sent you on some wild-goose chase for clues."

Despite herself, Nadine smiled. "That's Dot."

"She could have come forward herself at any time," Freddy said. "Either she was lying or a coward."

"She was neither," said Nadine, louder than she expected.

Daniel spoke up. "I've talked to HR about your inability to handle the politics beat and your mismanagement of the obituary section."

Nadine glared at him. "I handled the beat fine," she snapped. "It was the death threat on top of all the other insulting, hostile, and derogatory messages and emails that Frank expected me to suck up. As for the obit, I accept responsibility for that. I was rushing to make sure we were first online with it. That's on me."

"What do you mean—" Olivia only got out half the sentence before Daniel started talking.

"You are—"

Olivia held up a hand.

Daniel ignored her and kept talking.

Olivia tapped the table. "Daniel, I was speaking." Her voice was firm.

Daniel stopped and looked off to the side, lips in a thin line.

Olivia turned back to Nadine. "What threats?"

Nadine told her about her experience and what the *Herald* had done and how the other reporter had been doxed and had her life turned upside down when the *Herald* refused to take the threat seriously. Olivia said nothing as Nadine told her about the man coming to her door, but her eyes moved to Daniel for a moment before returning to Nadine.

"Well, whatever," said Daniel dismissively. "That's in the past."

"Nor is it the reason we're here," said Freddy Majors.

"It's time to look to the future," Daniel said. "I see no option but termination."

There was silence around the table. Nadine did her best to keep her face impassive. She wouldn't give Daniel the pleasure of knowing how much that hurt to hear, but the moment she opened her mouth, her voice would betray her.

"I disagree," said Olivia. "Nadine has made mistakes, but with coaching and support, that can be fixed."

"What." Daniel didn't phrase it like a question.

"In the brief time the Dot Voline story was on the site, it generated more engagement than any other one this year to date," said Olivia.

"Not from our core readership," said Daniel.

"No. Our future readership. That's the most important metric for me right now. How do we grow the company by bringing in readers from demographics the *Herald* has typically ignored? And *ignored* is being generous."

Freddy looked exasperated. "Olivia, we've discussed this."

She smiled. "I won the debate then too. Data doesn't lie."

Freddy pursed his lips. "I believe John and told him we would take care of this."

"Dad." Olivia looked at him. "We can take that offline, but given our discussions about the future direction of the *Herald*, it's in our best interest to let me make this decision."

There was a pause, then Freddy waved his hand. "Your call, but you explain it to John."

"Absolutely and with great pleasure. Nadine stays." She ignored Daniel's strangled protest as Nadine listened in disbelief. "I hear there's an open spot on the politics beat, and we need someone to follow up on this Wilson story," Olivia continued. "What do you think, Nadine?"

Nadine blinked. This was it. Her chance to resuscitate her dream.

Back to politics where she belonged. She wasn't scared anymore. She could do it.

She thought of Dot and what she'd taught Nadine about making an impact. She thought of Wes and his faith in her. She thought of the mayor and his community potluck and how she felt after she'd finished his story.

She opened her mouth to accept, then found herself saying, "Actually, I have another idea."

# EPILOGUE

N adine checked her email to see another request, this time from a woman whose mother had been one of the first to travel the country by dogsled. *I hope this isn't too morbid, but my mother is dying, and it would be a shame for her to leave this world without anyone knowing her story. She loves your obituaries and says she reads them every day to see who she's outlasted. Despite her little joke, it would be a great honor for her to be in the* Herald. *She would not be averse to chatting with you before she passes.*

Nadine smiled and forwarded it to one of her freelancers to look into. She'd been the obituary editor for two years now, and in that time, she'd made it into the section she wanted. A growing and enthusiastic readership confirmed she'd made the right decisions.

"Hello." Irina came by her desk with a package. "I found this for you."

Nadine unwrapped the tissue with trepidatious fingers to reveal a lovely marble angel with her arms crossed over her chest and one hand raised to her throat. "Irina, this is gorgeous."

"The *Angel of the Resurrection*," said Irina. "The original was sculpted in 1882 by Giulio Monteverde for Francesco Oneto to honor his family's memory."

"Thank you." Nadine's collection had grown to take up half the table and included a model of a Victorian funeral carriage and a skeleton that could be taken apart bone by bone. This was from Raj, who had given it to her over drinks a month after she started back as editor. The hearse remained her favorite and was the paperweight for the collection of obituaries she'd found at Dot's house. Occasionally she read through them for inspiration and as a reminder that every person had a story.

"Hey, you going to the staff meeting tomorrow?" Lisanne popped up when Irina had left, Ying at her side. "Hetty had her meeting with Olivia last week, so we get the updated targets." Hetty had been appointed editor in chief after Olivia had taken charge. Daniel had moved to a paper in Tampa.

Lisanne's story had been such a blockbuster, she was about to go on book leave for six months to do a more in-depth study. Ying, who had turned down a manager position because she loved working with data, would be taking a month to help. They'd moved into their own place in October, and Lisanne had deleted all her dating apps with great fanfare.

"I'll be there." Nadine was distracted by an email coming in from weschen@theapex.com.

The *Apex*, formally the *Spear*, was Brent Tatterly's new venture. He'd rescued the *Spear* from bankruptcy with his inheritance from Dot Voline, saying he'd always wanted to be a media tycoon. As well as a heavy emphasis on the arts—a section run by Wes's old Lifestyle editor Rebecca—the *Apex* had quickly earned a reputation for its investigative journalism. Hetty had tried to poach Wes twice but couldn't compete with the carte blanche Brent gave him. His first story had been about John Wilson, his misdeeds, their impact, and how other powerful men had ignored the whispers and out-and-out complaints over the years. Wilson had been forced to quit politics and lived entirely at his cottage in Muskoka. Nadine had heard there were lawsuits in the works for his financial misdeeds and criminal charges. Other reporters were looking into Matt White and the influence of the White Group. Dot would have liked that, almost as much as Nadine had liked that Tyler had been fired on the first day of Brent's takeover. Jason as well.

The only issue Wes had with his new job was that Brent continued to insist there was a nefarious story behind the use of construction pylons. So far, he hadn't been able to find it.

**Read at end of day,** the subject line said. She checked the time. It was 4:54, so close enough.

> **To the editor of the Herald obituary section. I have an obituary for consideration. Please respond ASAP.**

She scrolled down.

> **Regardless of his actual birth date, Wesley Chen—Wes to his friends—considered his life to have only started in university. Journalism 102, when he met Nadine Barbault, to be exact. She was his rival from the moment he beat her handily on an assignment.**

Here Nadine frowned. She absolutely got the higher mark, and they would have a talk about this revisionist history.

> **A decade of pining and rivalry was alleviated one summer night in a pagoda, when Nadine finally admitted that he wasn't totally awful.**
> **In that moment, Wes became complete.**
> **When Wes was younger, there was a couple—he thought they were ancient, but they were probably only fifty—who he used to watch from his window as they left the house, hand in hand. Sometimes they were laughing. Sometimes, one would pause**

at the bottom to wait while the other locked the door, always twisting the knob to check. How could they be so sure of each other? How could they always trust the other would be there? How could you make your happiness dependent on another?

Meeting Nadine answered all those questions. For the first time in his life, Wes understood how it was possible to love someone so much that home was no longer a where but a who. To have a person to share both your best and worst self. To know you were safely loved even when you felt you didn't deserve it.

During his life, Wes found joy in many things. He loved his work as a journalist and his family. He loved his four gorgeous furry girls: Erma, Octavia, Murasaki, and Sidonie-Gabrielle. He loved going for walks and baking for Nadine, especially after the time she insisted garlic shortbread was made by simply adding minced garlic to a regular shortbread recipe. She was wrong, and for once, she admitted it.

Most of all, he loved Nadine.

They brought each other patience when rushed.

Compassion when troubled.

Inspiration when discouraged.

And acceptance, always.

There was sweetness in every day of his existence, and his wife was the sweetest of all.

Nadine picked up her phone with shaking hands. Wes answered on the first ring.

"Hello," she said, feeling giddy. "This is Nadine Barbault from the *Herald*. I'd like to chat about this obit you sent through."

"Thanks for the quick reply," said Wes. "Is there an issue?"

"A small one I'd like to discuss," she said. "Do you have time to talk?"

"You know, this might be better to discuss in person. Are you available at the moment?" His voice sounded a bit faint.

"I am, yes." She tried to get the smile off her face and keep her voice professional. "Where would you like to meet?"

"I believe there's a small park near your office."

Nadine had never run out of the office faster. She was down the stairs and across the street in less than a minute. Shielding her eyes against the sun, she scanned the parkette until she saw Wes standing under a tree and waving to her. He looked gorgeous as always, with his black shirt tucked into his black pants, the sleeves rolled up, and his hair a little messy.

As if he'd been running his hand through it.

As if he'd been nervous.

"Hello, Nadine."

She stopped right in front of him, smiling so hard she could barely speak. "Hello, Wes."

"So," he said, and she could see the sweat beading his forehead. "You said there was something wrong with the obit?"

"There was. A slight inaccuracy, and the *Herald* prides itself on its quality journalism."

"Oh?" He tried to look surprised, and she saw his pulse flutter in the throat she'd kissed so many times. "What part?"

"The part where it said you had a wife. Can we edit that line to make it correct?" It was like there was a spotlight blotting out everything but him.

"We might not have to." He opened his hand. "Nadine Barbault. My joint and favorite competitor in this game of life. Will you marry me?"

She gazed at the ring sitting in his shaking palm. It was white gold, with an opal and tiny diamonds. Small flags were engraved on the inside. It looked familiar. "Is that Dot's?" she asked.

He went red. "I asked Brent if I could buy it from her estate. You admired it one day, and she told you it was the ring she bought with her first royalty check from *Thirty Pieces*."

"Wes." She could barely speak. "I love it. Thank you."

"So is that a yes?" he asked a bit impatiently. "You're kind of leaving me hanging here."

Tempting though it was to keep teasing him, Nadine threw her arms around his neck and kissed him. "Yes."

He kissed her back, then touched their foreheads together. "Thank God," he said. "Caleb got me worried when he told me this was too morbid for a proposal."

"It's not for everyone," she said.

"That's all right. It only has to be for you." He kissed her again, then covered her face with kisses until she laughed. "I was thinking we could get married at Dot's estate. You know the museum group that bought it from Brent when his buyer fell through?"

"Yes." Sales of Dot's books had skyrocketed in light of Wilson's unmasking, so Brent decided to take the lower offer from the museum, which had kept the house as it was and dedicated it to Dot and her works.

"They're opening up an event space."

"I love it." It had that beautiful symmetry Dot admired. "I love you," she added.

He tucked his head into her neck. "A good thing, because the cats would have been furious if you'd said no."

"Not Erma," said Nadine. "She wants you to herself."

"I am popular with the ladies," he said modestly.

"Ladies?"

He grinned. "Yeah. You and her." He slipped the ring on her finger and kissed her hand. "That's all I need."

Keep reading for a look at Lily Chu's

# THE TAKEDOWN

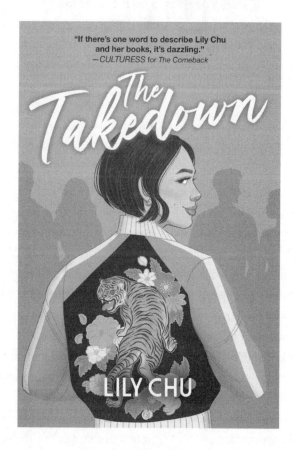

Available now from Sourcebooks Casablanca

**Daily affirmation: I trust the universe to keep my life effortlessly on track.**

According to the many-worlds theory—and possibly an old Gwyneth Paltrow movie—we split our universe with each decision we make. That means I've made a thousand right choices to get to this point, each littering time and space with sadder cast-off versions of me, say with dyed red hair instead of my natural dark brown or living in Tokyo instead of Toronto. Realistically, not even thousands but billions or trillions or whatever illions is beyond that.

I doubt any of those Dee Kwans are as happy as me. Thanks to meticulous vision boarding, wholehearted manifesting, and enough positive thinking to fill the Milky Way with stars, I'm exactly where I'm meant to be, doing exactly what I'm meant to do.

Waking before my alarm, I stretch in bed, warm and content under the thick duvet. The weak December sun streaming through the window lights the soft yellow walls with a golden glow that I admire before grabbing my phone to open my new meditation app. Six deep breaths and two nasal panting cycles later, I get antsy and turn it off. I haven't found the app that best suits me, but honestly, I don't need it. According to Mom, I take after her—happy by nature.

I make my way to the kitchen, where I tie back the retro dotted swiss curtains I installed in place of the old vinyl blinds with their permanently tangled cords, and put in some toast, idly counting the blooming flowers of the de Gournay–style wallpaper above the backsplash until it pops. I'm not lonely but it would be nice to share breakfast with someone. I can see him now, wearing a pair of flannel pajama bottoms as he stands at the white-and-gold marble counter, smiling fondly at me over his shoulder.

"Let me find someone," I say to the old Niagara Falls–themed thermometer I'd left in the window. "A man is not a necessity, but it would be a bonus. Preferably one who can cook. I'll do the dishes."

There, I've sent my aspiration out and trust that the universe, which I assume has nothing urgent that it needs to deal with, will manifest this man for me. I can sit back and wait for him to appear when the time is right.

I dig my toes into the Wedgwood-blue rug that covers the warm wood of the parquet floor and glance at the paper I'd stuck on my bulletin board near the fridge last January. Although "get man" hadn't made the list, it was chock-full of life goals. I read them over as I layer Havarti on my breakfast sandwich.

**No negative vibes!**

I'd written this with little stars to emphasize the positive vibe-ness.

**Meditate ~~daily~~ regularly.**
**Exercise ~~daily~~ regularly.**
**Practice ~~weekly~~ regular self-care for wellness.**
**Be the best Charioteer I can be at work.**
**Remain the Questie queen.**

My eyes linger on the last point. Oh, Questie. I'd discovered the online game last year when I needed a break from painting walls and ripping up carpet, and now spend a few blissful hours each week solving puzzles that lead to clues hidden around the city. Which reminds me, it's time for my daily Questie leaderboard check to confirm that SunnyDay remains numero uno and in the top dog slot.

I grab my phone with one hand and open the app as I bite into my sandwich, tomato spilling onto the thrifted Royal Albert forget-me-not patterned plate. I've been first for the last six months, my position unassailable, although under frequent and unwelcome attack by Teddy9. A faint sense of satisfaction suffuses me as I see that, yes, I am in the lead, a feeling deepened by noting that Teddy9 has dropped to fourth. I click over to the Questie chat and message him privately. We've been sharing good-natured taunts for the last couple months, and this seems like an excellent opportunity to rub in my continued dominance.

Me: May the Fourth be with you. Get it? Because you're in fourth place?

Teddy9: It's December and that joke is so bad I'm not going to dignify it with an answer.

Me: Yet here we are.

Teddy9: It doesn't matter. I have a plan.

Me: Is your devious plan to solve clues faster and with some accuracy, unlike last week's puzzle?

Teddy9: I stand by the fact that clue six was impossible for a normal person.

Me: Sounds like loser talk.

Teddy9: Winning is a state of mind, SunnyDay.

Me: You know, I'm magnanimous in victory. My name's Dee. You can use it.

Teddy9: I'm Teddy.

Me: I suspected.

Teddy: My name could have been 9, you know.

He logs off and I check if any of my friends have contacted me. I don't have many, and lately I've barely seen the ones I do. I'm usually the one to suggest meeting but I've been too busy. I'll reach out today.

I follow my usual getting-ready routine, which means after sunscreen comes my daily affirmation. Over the years, I've chanted everything from "You're good enough" to "The bangs will grow out." If I don't have anything specific, I default to "I delete negativity to live my best life." The important part is that I put my mind on a path to attract good energy and manifest my yes. My older sister, Jade, thinks this is all bull but she can go screw. Thanks to my mindset, life has turned out as I want, and there's no point messing with a good thing.

Since I've been working late all week, I'm going in a bit past my usual time, which has allowed me this unusually leisurely weekday morning. I decide to take the long route through the park near my house. It's quiet this time of day, and a sheet of neon orange with little cuts along the bottom flutters on a lamppost, like someone's advertising for their lost cat. Curious, I move closer.

TAKE WHAT YOU NEED, it says. Instead of phone numbers, the tabs read:

Break from routine

Virtual hug

Moment to yourself

Kindness

Two are missing, and I wonder what other passersby were missing from their lives. Then I shrug and turn away, leaving the tabs for someone else. I have everything I need.

Thirty minutes later, I'm walking up the stairs to Chariot Consulting. The office takes up the third floor of a small heritage building on Spadina Avenue, in easy walking distance of Queen Street's shopping and bars and Chinatown's food glories. When I walk in, it feels like home, which I suppose is natural given the amount of time I spend here.

After I wave to Nadia, the receptionist, I head to my office and stop with a little heart flutter of appreciation that hasn't dissipated since my recent promotion. The card on the door reads Daiyu Kwan because I'm always Daiyu at work. Dee, with its blond-ponytail surfer vibe, is for my personal life.

Then comes the best part of the name plate: Consultant. After doing Chariot's communications for five years, they made me a full-fledged diversity consultant two months ago. It took an entire section of my vision board and endless night classes, but I'm finally in a position to make a difference by helping organizations become places where everyone can thrive. I want a world where people like my loathsome—and estranged—aunt Rebecca don't have the power to stop anyone from achieving their dreams.

I blow the card a kiss as I go in and flip on the light. More cynical people might find it pathetic, and I'm sorry for them, but Chariot gives my life meaning. It's worth every hour I spend at night and on weekends completing extra projects to prove my value. I put down my bag and straighten the copy of my CEO's book, *Diverse Paths, One Goal*, which sits on the shelf behind my desk. I'd ghostwritten it last year, and seeing my name in the alphabetical list of acknowledgments at the back continues to thrill me.

I haven't had time to decorate the space with my favorite motivational posters and soft-light lamps, but I can fix that when I come in on the weekend. The learning curve has been harder than I expected, especially since Chariot hasn't hired for my previous role so I'm currently doing both jobs. They've assured me it won't be much longer.

I look around with a sigh of total contentment and take a of sip of the green tea I brought from home. Everything—*everything*—is going according to plan.

Perfect.

# TWO

'm deep into client survey data when Nadia pokes her head around my door. "Staff meeting," she announces.

I check the time, and to my surprise, it's almost noon. "Sorry?"

"Emergency all-hands meeting," she elaborates. "Right now."

Nadia disappears down the hall before I can ask for details. Concentration broken, I drink my cold tea and stretch, unworried. It's probably a new client announcement. Our CEO, George, likes to summon us to celebrate those together, like a family.

The boardroom is crowded when I arrive, and I hide my disappointment when there's not even a box of Timbits on offer. At least the office Keurig supply was replenished, so I snatch a matcha latte, dropping a toonie into the box.

"I'm taking bets on whether he's retiring or it's a mass layoff," says Nadia as I stand next to her. Her mug says *Don't got time for maybes* in pink cursive and smells like caramel. She looks remarkably unbothered.

Before I can answer, I catch sight of my manager. He's frowning at his feet and muttering something to the IT director, who rubs his beard. In fact, the entire leadership team sports expressions from somber to grave.

"It doesn't look good," I say, heart sinking. Then I rally. "I could be wrong."

"I doubt it." She checks out the crowd over the top of her mug. "I'd say we're screwed."

George strolls in, waving cheerfully, with his tousled gray hair curling over the edge of his collar. He looks tan, as he usually does after one of his Palm Beach breaks. "Good morning, Charioteers!" he booms as he bounds up the makeshift riser at the front. He never needs a mic.

He doesn't wait for the calls of "Hi, George" to finish echoing around the room.

"I have incredible news." George gives us his trademark boyish smile. "I founded Chariot almost thirty years ago when I saw the need for diversity guidance among…"

Having heard our corporate history dozens of times, I tune out George's heartfelt exposition and Nadia's snarky commentary to check the Questie leaderboard, where Teddy9 has moved up a place. He must be completing older puzzles to pull up his score. I message him.

**Me: Sneaky.**
**Teddy: Told you I had a plan.**

I don't like this, but Nadia nudges me as George says, "Diversity and inclusion are changing, and so too must Chariot."

Nadia leans over. "Looks like he might be retiring after all."

"After the fuss he made about wanting to be carried out dead in his chair?" I whisper back.

"I'll be taking on a new role"—George pauses for dramatic effect—"as CEO of my cottage in Muskoka."

He chuckles, but instead of the laughter he clearly expects, the room fills with whispers. Someone calls out, "What?"

"Thank you," says George. "In the immortal words of The Byrds, there is a season."

Nadia snorts. "The Byrds or Ecclesiastes. This is what happens when you don't do his speaking notes."

"Nadia!"

"C'mon, I know you do all his writing." She tilts her mug toward a cluster of blond women standing to the side with neutral expressions. "Like the angels do the rest of his work."

George spends another few minutes extolling the virtues of Chariot and our achievements before saying, "My season, *our* season, here is done. I know you'll keep the Charioteer spirit alive wherever you go."

Understanding filters through the room, and the whispers grow to mutters. The same voice calls, "Wait, are you shutting Chariot down? We're getting laid off?"

"Bingo," crows Nadia in somewhat misplaced triumph. "I knew it."

"Chariot began with me, and I'm saddened and honored it will end with me." George dips his head down as if overcome with emotion and clasps his hands over his chest. Then he looks up. "Your manager will be in touch with details."

I don't pay attention to whatever he says next as I stand there, nauseous from the hammering of my heart. I'd worked so hard to get this job and now it's gone? I didn't even have a chance to show what I could do. I flex my hands to try to physically force my usual positivity back and breathe deep. It's a shock, but this doesn't have to be bad. In fact, it's a good chance to expand my horizons.

We join the escaping crowd after George dismisses us. "You'll need luck," Nadia says.

I steer around two women from finance who have stopped in the middle of the corridor, texting frantically as they shake their heads. "What do you mean?"

She sighs. "You sweet summer child. You've only been a consultant for two months. You think it'll be easy to get a new job? It's back to pension update emails for you."

"I can find a job." I trip on the edge of the carpet. "I have lots to offer."

"You *could* have a chance given what they pay junior consultants."
Nadia looks thoughtful. "The others will be asking for much more."

She leaves me at my office, dragging my confidence behind her like
tissue on a shoe as I wonder if she's right. Chariot is as comfortable as a
pair of worn sneakers, and I don't want to break in new ones. Not when
I was settling in for a marathon here. My throat tightens and I'm grateful
the hallway remains empty so I don't need to talk.

Forcing myself to step into the office that remains mine for the
moment, I sit at my desk and slide my hand up and down the seam of
my notepad while staring at an old nail hole in the wall. I should make
a list. What about my résumé? It's up-to-date, but can I add more?
Finances. My bank account ends each month perilously close to zero.

When the phone rings, I put it on speaker, relieved for a distraction
to stop me ruminating about this setback. No, this *opportunity*, because
I need to start thinking about this in the correct way.

"Hi, Mom."

"Hi, sunshine. Are you taking advantage of the nice weather?" Mom
is a big proponent of taking advantage of whatever the day brings.

"I'm at work." I'll tell her about George's bombshell later, when I've
processed it enough to be in the proper headspace for her pep talk. I
check Questie and see Teddy remains in third place.

"You should go out and get some vitamin D," she says. "It's so good
for improving your mood."

It takes everything in me to not make an immature and hugely inap-
propriate joke. "I'll go for a walk later."

"Make sure you do, sunshine. Well, I have some interesting news."

A chill settles on my skin. I've had a long time to learn my mother's code
words, and *interesting* is as close to *bad* as she gets. "Is it Dad?" I demand.

"Why would you say that? He's out for a walk," she answers breezily.
"Did I tell you I'm making yogurt from scratch? It's wonderful for your
gut ecosystem. Healthy body, healthy mind."

I relax a bit. The yogurt doesn't surprise me. Since her retirement,

Mom has thrown herself into trying all the things she couldn't do while working, like playing tennis, making jam, and finishing a petit point pillow featuring orange tulips that sits on my pretty teal love seat. She'd been working on it sporadically since I was twelve.

"What's going on, Mom?"

There's a brief silence before she clears her throat. "It's nothing to worry about. You know Grandma had a little problem with her hip."

It was a severe fracture that resulted in hospitalization and daily physiotherapy. "Is she okay?"

"The most important part of healing is that she keep her spirits up."

Cheerfulness is not something I associate with my grandmother, who has not smiled in years, at least not at me. I sit straighter. "Mom."

"Your dad and I have been talking, sunshine."

I try to hold on to my pleasant outlook, but dread edges out my self-control. "Tell me what's going on."

"Grandma's not able to live on her own anymore, but you know how she feels about moving into a home."

"Yeah," I say. "I know." She told Mom she'd rather be put out on an iceberg where she could die with some dignity. Exact words.

"I can't do that to her," Mom says. "She can't come live with us up north because it's too far from her medical appointments."

"Okay?"

"You can say no, of course. We won't be angry."

"Say no to what?" I exclaim. "Spit it out."

There's a pause as Mom debates whether to scold me for being rude, but she says, "I'd like to move her to your house."

I say the first thing that pops into my head. "I can't take care of her. I have to work."

"We would do that. Your father and I."

"How are you going to find a place to live?" The housing market in Toronto is so brutal it's one step away from drawing pistols at dawn for a two-bedroom.

"We'd move in with her," Mom says softly. "Back into our house."

Back into their house. Their house, which is supposed to be my house, the home I spent a year and my entire savings getting perfect. When my parents retired and moved up north, they'd generously gifted me the deed with the permission of my sister, Jade, who had no desire to take on what she refers to as the sad urban shoebox. She can take her McMansion Lite north of the city, with its consistent HVAC and enough room for an outdoor pizza oven, because I love my tiny house. Love it with a love that extends past pragma and into agape. Perhaps Eros. It's my castle, where I can pull up the drawbridge and simply be.

On the screen, Teddy moves to second place, but as of four seconds ago, I have bigger issues to contend with than my game rank.

Although it is annoying.

Mom keeps talking. "This is a lovely opportunity for our family to connect."

I don't know why that's necessary, but I'm careful not to voice this particular thought. It took my grandmother until Jade was born to accept that Mom had married a Chinese guy and to start speaking to him directly instead of filtering comments through Mom, at first claiming his accent was too heavy for her to understand. More than thirty years later, the best that can be said for their relationship is that it's not uncivil. We've been getting along fine barely talking for years.

"What about Jade's house?" Halfway through, I shift my whine to a more upbeat tone so the question ends in a squeak.

"She has more room but you know how your sister feels."

I sure do, because if my relationship with Heather Henderson is best described as distant, Jade's is nonexistent. When Jade came out as bi, Grandma refused to believe it. Flat out told Jade she was only confused and would eventually settle down with a nice boy. Things improved slightly after Jade's kids came along, but unlike Dad and despite Mom's incessant pleas, my sister is much less willing to smooth things over for the sake of harmony. She's waiting for an apology that won't ever come, because people like Grandma think they're entitled to behave however they want without consequence.

"Is this the best idea, Mom?"

"That doesn't sound like my Dee," she says in a warning tone.

"No, it's that I wonder if—"

"It will work out fine, sunshine," she interrupts. "You only need a bit of faith and an open mind."

I bang my head against the desk lightly enough so Mom can't hear it over the phone. As if I can say no. It would be monstrous. Unfathomable. Worse, not very nice of me. "Of course," I say in defeat. "It's your house. You're always welcome."

Which is true, but I pictured it more like a weekend visit, not an annexation.

"Dee, it's *your* house. We know this is a change, and we're grateful you're such a good girl."

*You don't have to be good,* says the mean and unhelpful inner voice I've fought to keep buried my whole life. *They gave you the house. It's yours and you don't owe Grandma anything.* I stuff that down guiltily, knowing how disappointed Mom would be with my negative perspective.

She continues to think aloud. "We'll need a place for chili, too."

"Why not the kitchen?"

"I don't like that. Too messy."

I don't have the energy to ask what she could possibly mean by that so I let it slide. "When are you coming?"

"In two weeks. We're putting Grandma's town house up for sale, and she doesn't want to be there for the showings. Does that work?"

"Sure." I'm not sure what my voice sounds like, but it feels like I'm underwater.

"It'll be fine," says Mom cheerfully. "It always is."

We get off the phone, and I drum my fingers on the table. What's done is done, and I'll make the best of it like always. Then my phone beeps and drops down a Questie notification. It's a message.

**Teddy: There we go.**

I scramble to check. Teddy9 is number one on the leaderboard. *Thanks a lot, universe.*

# ACKNOWLEDGMENTS

To admit you like reading obituaries is a strange thing. Some think it's morbid, and I get that. Like Dot, I find it fascinating to read about how people lived their lives and how they were remembered. Whether you fall in the first camp or the second, thank you for reading about Nadine and Wes, Dot and the cats, and I hope you enjoyed their story.

This book almost didn't get written because I thought a rom-com about an obituary editor was too weird to suggest. I should have had more faith in my extraordinary editors, Allison Carroll at Audible and Mary Altman at Sourcebooks, who not only thought it was a fun idea but encouraged me to reach for the wacky. Thank you for loving Dot as much as I do.

To my agent, Carrie Pestritto, thank you for being there as always!

To the Audible and Sourcebooks teams. Each time a book comes out, I'm so grateful for all the work you do to get it into readers' and listeners' hands. Thank you.

To my fantastic beta readers, who are always there to point out problems big and small (mostly big): Allison Temple, Candice Rogers Louazel, and Jackie Lau. Allison gets double thanks for keeping up our weekly writing dates and listening to my whining.

As well as being a beta reader, Dawn Calleja gets massive thanks for her thoughtful insights into the media industry.

And to Trixie and Lola, the inspiration for Dot's cats.

And as always, thank you to my favorite people, Elliott and Nyla, for always being there.

If you'd like to know more about the art and craft of obituary writing, there's a reading list of the resources I used on my website, lilychuauthor.com.

# ABOUT THE AUTHOR

Lily Chu lives in Toronto, Canada, and loves ordering the second-cheapest wine, wearing perfume all the time, and staying up far too late reading a good book. She writes romantic comedies with strong Asian characters.

**Website:** lilychuauthor.com
**Instagram:** @lilychuauthor